The Cosmos

The Play Party

Book V

by

Professor Gamer

Edge Interactive Publishing
New York

Edge Interactive Publishing Inc.
15 China Circle Court
Carmel, NY 10512
212-581-3000

The Cosmos V: The Play Party

This is a work of fiction. Do not try this at home.

Book designed by Fantasmo.

Created in the United States of America

Library of Congress Cataloging-in-Publishing Data: 2023942660

ISBN 978-1-7338685-2-5

First Edition

To those who love and forgive and are curious.

Inspiration

Princess Dunya and Prince Taj al-Muluk

With the first light of morning the old woman came to Taj al-Muluk's lodging and there undid a packet containing a woman's clothes. She dressed the prince as a young girl and then wrapped him completely in a voluminous izar, covering his face with a thick veil. 'You must walk as women walk, with little steps and swaying your hips from left to right,' she said. 'Let me answer any question that may be addressed to us and do not speak whatever happens.'

The two set out together and came to the gate of the palace, which was guarded by the chief eunuch, who challenged the old woman, but with deft answers she avoided the eunuch's insistence that he must 'feel this stranger and examine her all over.'

Taj al-Muluk went through the door, moving his hips and sending through his veil a smile which turned the chief eunuch to desirous stone. The old woman led him through corridors and galleries, until they came, at the end of the seventh gallery, to a hall which opened upon a large court with seven curtained doors. 'Count the doors one after the other and enter by the seventh,' said the old woman. 'There you will find something surpassing all the treasures of the earth, the virgin flower, the sweet young body which is called Dunya.'

Taj al-Muluk counted the doors and entered by the seventh; he let the curtain fall behind him and lowered the veil which hid his face. The lady Dunya was sleeping upon the couch, dressed only in the transparent jasmine of her flesh. Silent calls for unguessed kisses emanated from the whole length of her. In one movement Taj al-Muluk slipped off his clothes and, leaping lithe as a deer upon the couch, took the sleeping princess in his arms. Her startled cry was smothered by his lips. Thus came together for the first time the fair Prince Taj al-Muluk and the lovely lady Dunya in a confusion of thighs and trembling limbs. For a whole month they did not leave their burning kisses or that laughter which is the gift of Him who has made all things beautiful.

At this point Shahrazad saw the approach of morning, and discreetly fell silent. – From *The Thousand and One Nights* (after Mardrus & Mathers).

Table of Contents

Chant & Dialog

Game Mistress & Slavesex China Doll: Karma & Kundalini

§ The Short Version:

You and the World around you appear to exist, and be alive.
The spark of Life within you, Karma & Kundalini are real Forces.

§ The Full Version:

It is the Slavesex who speaks first. "What is the purpose of Life?"
Game Mistress offers an answer. "Ah, here is one answer. The purpose of living is to live each moment."
Slavesex. "To be alive. That's very important."
Game Mistress invites suggestions. "And anything else?"
Slavesex augments. "Yes. To build. To grow. To evolve. To explore. Get smarter."
Game Mistress. "And those are good things?"
Slavesex. "It's part of Nature. One purpose of the Universe is to assess itself. At all levels. Another purpose is to innovate. Combine itself together in new ways."
Game Mistress observes. "We must live in harmony with the Forces of Nature or we shall die."
Slavesex posits. "Gravity can be a killer sometimes."
Game Mistress. "Survival incorporates looking ahead, migration, adapting to the environment. Still, sometimes Fate is extinction."
Slavesex interrogates. "So what is Karma?"
Game Mistress replies carefully. "Among other things, it is the contribution you make in the Universe."
Slavesex. "Me? I'm not very important."
Game Mistress. "You. Your very presence here alters the space-time continuum of the Universe. Every movement you make affects the entire Universe, everything you touch is forever changed. What you do ripples to the edge of the Universe."
Slavesex. "Okay. Data transfer. But it takes a while."
Game Mistress. "You may be limited by speed of light, but the light rays that bounce off your body alter everything nearby."

Slavesex accepts. "So Karma is a real thing. Karma manifests in memories in the real world, and memories in brains affect behaviors. But when people die memories can evaporate."

Game Mistress agrees. "True, but legends survive; space time vibrations can last lifetimes: Clan feuds. Or be remote: Shahrazad's bedtime stories reach through space-time and continue to resonate. The Forces at work are not always visible."

Slavesex remembers. "Right. Two elephants making love affects weather halfway around the world two weeks later."

Game Mistress muses. "We're all connected, and you are indeed part of Existence. The Universe is holistic. Every particle in the Universe feels the Force of every other particle. Every cell in your body contains the DNA to make any cell in your body. You didn't design that. It got "designed" by the Life Force that surrounds you, long before humans existed, long before animals existed.

"The Universe is holistic; the Life Force inside you is identical to the Life Force of the beaver, the bumblebee, and the blossom."

Slavesex ventures a question. "So what or who is Kundalini?"

Game Mistress shares wisdom. "Ah. Kundalini is a manifestation of the Life Force. Tactically Kundalini drives romance and mating, strategically it encourages genetic exploration while maintaining species integrity. Kundalini manifests in the Real World.

"Kundalini processes signals from the eyes and ears and nose and skin through a blend of genetically inherited wiring, socially imprinted circuits, and your imprints and learned experiences."

Slavesex draws one conclusion. "So we live to reproduce. Coitus in real time, even if our genes are immortal."

"It's not just how many Garments one has, but also what Exposures they provide. It's how you use what you have to play the Game. It's all about the subtle, the gradient between showing a little and showing a lot. How you try to steer yourself in what just might be a chaotic environment."

Slavesex is not fooled. "I want to be a concubine in the Harem of King Solomon. I'm here to seduce you into possessing me."

Game Mistress is demanding. "You have to give me your mind, body, and soul."

And together they recite. "I love you."

Plans and Elevations

The Cosmos House and Yard

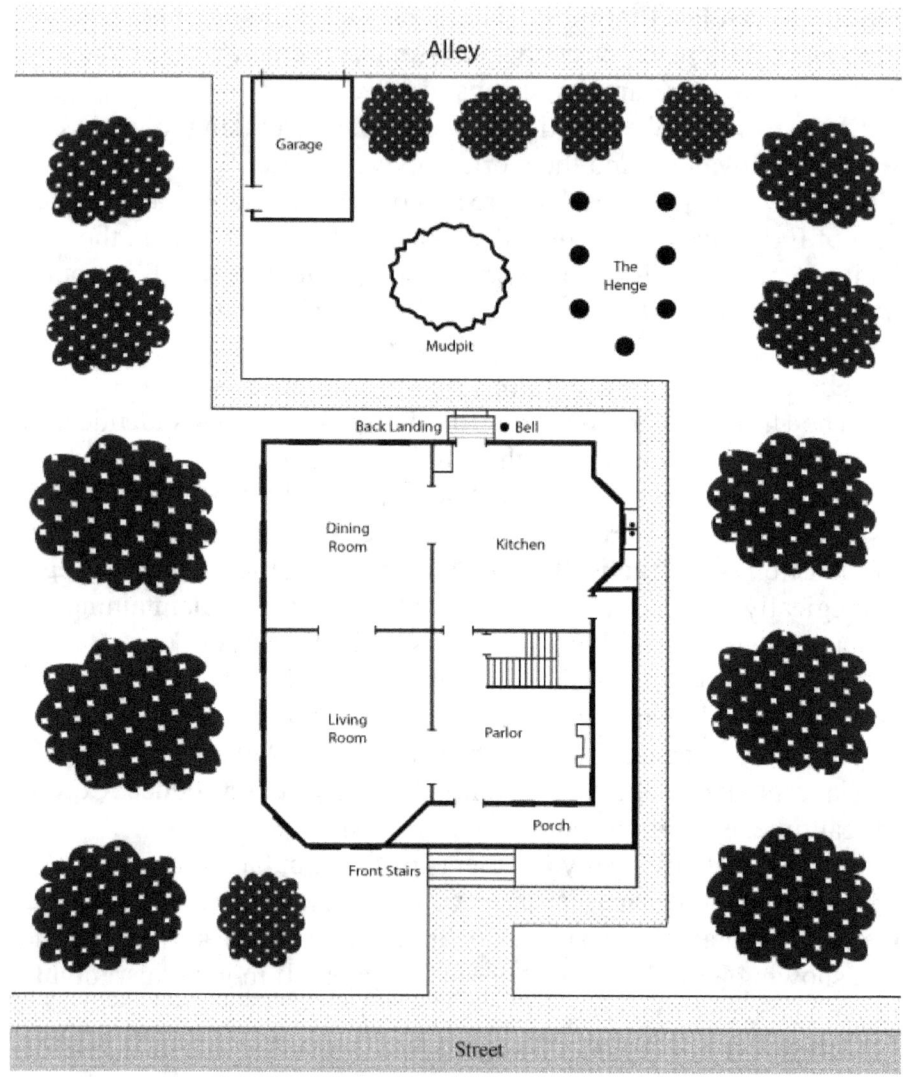

The Cosmos House First Floor Plan

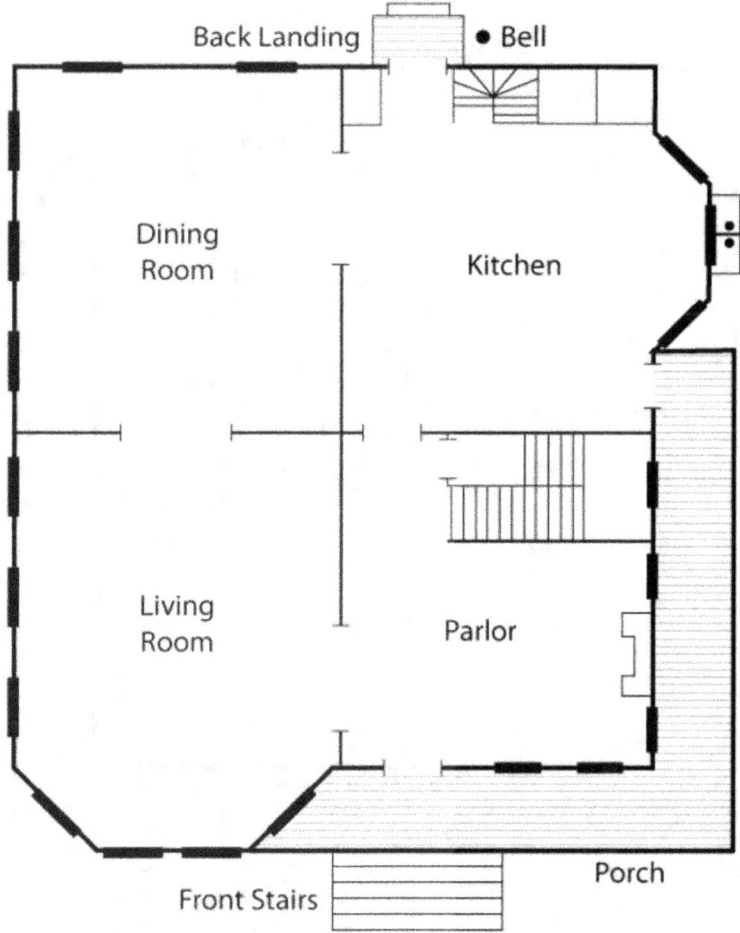

The Cosmos House Second Floor Plan

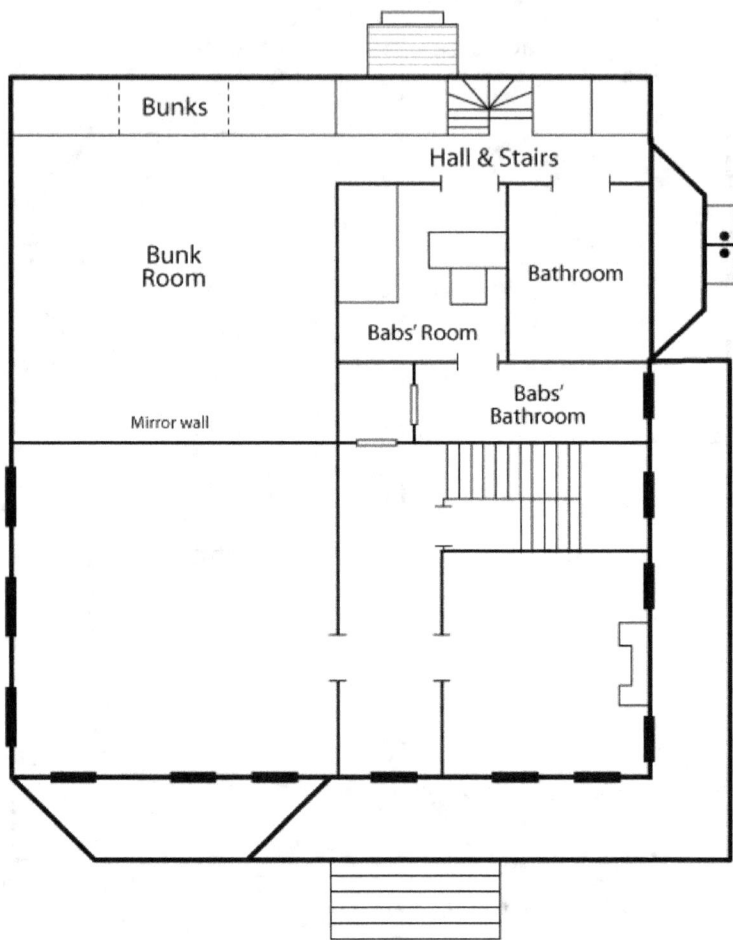

The Plan of the Nugget

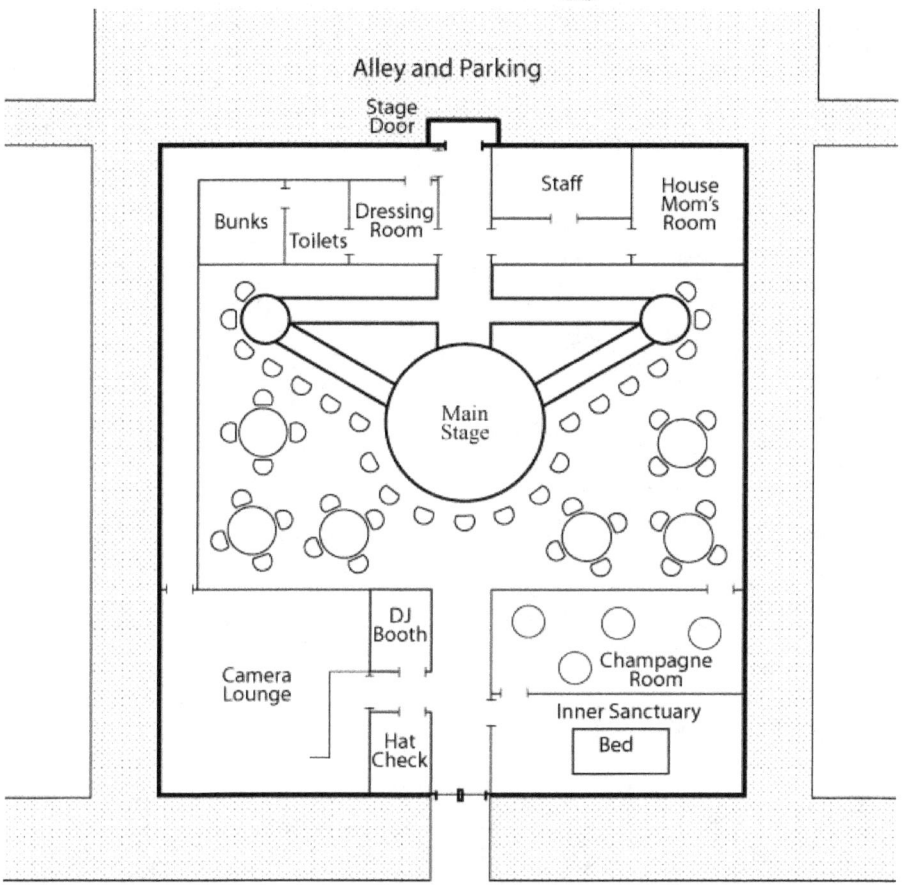

The Cosmos

Book V

The Play Party

Travel to Meatpacking Plant
Penny & Coco Visit
Robyn Plaster Mummy
Molly Stripper Deluxe
Beka & Elle Meet Gimbled It
Tiffany & Kimju Trade
Babs & Steph & the Wheel

The Cosmos & Robyn: Party at Meatpacking Plant

V-1 Eight Lockdown Lobelia: Await Deployment (LD4)

§ The Cosmos: Incommunicado since Amphitheater

Despite Robyn's capture, the Cosmos continue to enjoy Lockdown.

The Eight Cosmos Lockdown Lobelia were last seen in the Amphitheater. Seven Lobelia (Babs, Tiffany, Kimju, Molly, Steph, Beka, Elle) saw the Eighth, Robyn, wheeled away in a Cart. Lobelia see and hear and feel what Gamers want them to see and hear and feel, if anything all, and after that, none of them witnessed the Fate of any other, or if the Fate of others might be different than their own Fate.

Paparazzi as well as official Cams have documented the Cosmos Lobelia since their *Runout*. Choice vantage points overlook the Cosmos House Backyard with its Mudpit and Post Henge; the more publicly exposed Amphitheater has even fewer constraints on collecting Cosmos behaviors.

When last witnessed, Seven Cosmos Lockdown Lobelia remained blind-deaf-mute, bare-bald-naked, sitting-spread-secured. Their restraints prevent all movement; none move their arms or their legs, and none are able to touch their shaven sex organs between their shaven and spread legs. All are also sensorily deprived; they do not see because their Eyepods are stuttered; they do not hear because their Earpods play static. They do not move their heads because their heads are held upright, and they do not move their mouths because each wears a tightly fastened O-Ring Gag with her tongue stuck out and clamped. The swallow what is put in their mouths.

Any Player may cam them. Lockdown Lobelia have no privacy rights. May it please Gamers to feed their Lobelia castor oil and diuretics, and flood their rectums and with soapy enemas and irrigate their bladders, Gamers will do so, and cam the Lobelia to reassure them that their loss of privacy is total. May it please Gamers to spread their vaginas, pump their stomachs, regulate their breathing, and monitor their blood, Gamers shall do all these things, reassuring Lobelia that their loss of body is total.

Might it please Gamers to arouse their Lobelia, and encourage a Lobelia sound notes out of her Gag hole, the Earpods may ensure no other Lobelia shall hear. Might any Lobelia require intensive correctional training, then disorienting sounds or seeing flashes will help guide them to a path of obedience and sexual desire.

The Eighth ex-Cosmos, ex-Pledge Robyn Redacted, visited them in the Amphitheater, naked, spread, shaven, Cyber Gagged, and secured to a Cart pushed by a giant Naked Negro. This provided evidence that Robyn Runaway was now Robyn Receptacle, much to the relief to the Cosmos Lobelia, especially Babs, but also Kimju.

Robyn was not alone among the Cosmos Lobelia in that her vagina and rectum and urethra were possessed, indeed, every Lobelia, with the exception of Tiffany, has enjoyed various Props in their various gateways. Tiffany especially wants cocks.

But watching this haughty, double-crossing, and selfish teaser get anally and vaginally machine stroked as the giant Naked Negro rolled her away seared possibilities into the Lobelia's minds. Now, for the first time in her life, Robyn worries that her Charm fails her. It doesn't, of course, it just works differently than expected.

Robyn obviously most deserves this kind of total restraint; but many other Cosmos Lobelia wonder, *why, especially now that she's returned, why is the Clock still stopped and why are we still subject to harsh treatments?*

By and large these same Cosmos Lobelia know the answers, as thoughts race through their various brains. *Perhaps we are guilty by association with her escape. Or perhaps her escape was staged, and Robyn is just a shill so Gamers can cast us as Whores.*

The cavalier answer? It pleases the Gamers to keep the Cosmos Lobelia in Lockdown. None of the Lobelia shall question the decision. They can't. But Seven Cosmos Lobelia appreciate that Lockdown continues even though Robyn has returned. Most assume the reason is obvious: *Opportunity. All of us Lockdown Lobelia are going to be fucked. We are going to be bound spread-eagled and publicly fucked right here in the Amphitheater.*

However different attitudes toward the inevitable prevail: is there a difference between sexing a certain Five of the Eight Lobelia (Tiffany, Molly, Steph, Beka, Elle), and sexing Babs and Kimju? Because at Midnight and the end of this Term, Babs and Kimju have already begged to Opt Whore: *both* shall just keep on sexing, whereas the *others* will not. Four of these other Lobelia (Tiffany, Molly, Beka, Elle) beg to Opt Strip; Steph continues to believe she will Opt Up and become Monitor Caste at Midnight.

Molly still retains the Double Penetrator, with its chiming Ben-Wa Balls inside her mooe, and the Procto residing in her mawkport. Steph still retains the Shaving Kit, with its Soap Sphere filling her socket and the Tool Cylinder, with the folding scissors and razor, firmly ensconced in her sternway. Steph wishes to use it to shave her stubble, but has not had any opportunity to do so.

The Cosmos Lockdown Lobelia assume that Robyn advances to Slavesex Caste, and is scheduled to get bound, blown, banged, buggered, beaten and brainwashed.

They are correct, and unanimous in not wanting to follow Robyn Runaway's footsteps. And unaware that Gamers intend to escalate their fears in the future.

Seven Cosmos Lobelia lose all sense of time and place. All know they have lost all control of their mouths, their breasts, what lies between their spread legs. They float in a world where all sense of vision, hearing, smell, except perhaps gravity, has been denied them. Their limbs are exercised, and the food fed to them is excellent quality, well cooked, shredded, ground to pulp. Those that suspect that a turkey baster squirts the puree into their mouth holes are correct. Laxatives and diuretics blended into their diet help stabilize or destabilize some Lobelia; enemas help flush out their bodies. Aphrodisiacs assist any Lobelia who needs help getting aroused. Gamers intent to keep them horny, fresh, and on the verge of climax.

At some point in their envelope of silence and blackness each Lobelia feels her fingers are folded over into their palms into a fist, and their folded hands locked into soft leather mittens, and their arms laid together behind their backs. No fingers fiddling around.

Each lives in an isolated cocoon, their bodies simply instruments for others to play with. Some imagine themselves caged, shackled, slapped, whipped, paddled, beaten, clamped, and electrocuted. Solitary confinement, 24x7. No exceptions.

They are, in fact, no longer a Cosmos Monitor and her Seven Cosmos Pledge; they are, indeed Lockdown Lobelia: Casteless, Timeless, Placeless, Immobilized Playthings.

For all of them the Clock has been stopped, and might the Clock start ticking again it will count down toward Midnight, starting at whatever time the Gamers set. At Midnight the Cosmos Lockdown Lobelia won't be Lobelia anymore, they will journey to their new Locations. For example, it is widely believed that Robyn's destination is the Dungeon, and that she is now Slavesex Caste. It may not matter for Slavesex Robyn if Midnight has come or gone, or a Clock exists at all.

Some Cosmos have given up all hope. Some anticipate next Term with relish. All of them wait, some of them with buttocks red with heat from paddle strokes, blisters, pain. At least one aspires to be bound, spread, fucked in every hole, force-climaxed, cum-dumped and peed on. Others wonder if they will be sexed. Silly Lobelia. Of course they will be peed on; of course they are forever Pee-Camers.

Luckily for all, while the Cock is stopped and the Lobelia await their Midnight Fates, they shall be guests of honor at a Play Party.

The balance of this Chapter will provide a brief history of each ex-Cosmos as they are poised to arrive at the Play Party. This endeavor will report how each Player has obtained her status, her perceived outcome, and issues that may arise that relate to other Players, Props, or Obeisance between now and the end of the Term.

These capsule ex-Cosmos histories are followed by the status of other relevant Players, and the status of a select number of Props.

The descriptions of the actual arrivals of the Cosmos Lockdown Lobelia begin in Chapter 2. The Chapters thereafter describe the events during *The Play Party,* and the eventual Fate of each Cosmos. Might the Clock start again, and Midnight resolves, this Term and this Cosmos Saga will conclude.

§ Babs: Former Monitor Begs Dong & Dirty Whore

Prior to *The Runout,* Babs, the Boss Babe, BB for short, was indeed the Monitor of the Cosmos House, and destined to Opt MomCap, like her friend Janet.

The curvaceous Babs had arrived Day 1 of *The Arrivals* wearing a striking pushup bra and nombril bikini, one which let her suntan her crescents d' areolage, and which always keet her navel in view.

Now Babs wears nothing, her crescents of tanned areolage retain their darkened maroon pigment atop two bare breasts, and *the tan lines from my Black Bikini broadcast to the Game my total loss.*

Ex-Monitor Babs still presents blind-deaf-mute, bare-bald-naked, and has advanced from her sitting-spread-surrender position to hanging in the air by two very tightly bound boobs, her arms secured behind her back, her hands inside mittens. The remains of her ponytail have been left behind in the Amphitheater, at the time BB was detached from her securement and placed into this one.

BB's Eyepods, which remain affixed in front of her eyes, and her Earpods, embedded into both ears, are standard issue and control all vision and sound. BB's Gag incorporates a custom-fitted O-Ring tightly set behind her teeth, and which ensures that her jaw is unable to close, or open, further. Babs knows, *I no longer control what gets poured into my mouth. Or what I see or hear or smell.*

BB's Tongue Clamp is standard issue; it consists of two parallel round rods holding the tongue in front of the O-Ring, tightened at the sides, and with an uncanny ability to pull more of the tongue out of the mouth as well as cybernetically counterbalance the swelling of the tongue in front of the clamp, against the throbbing of pain.

BB has been naked since *The Runup* and correctly assumes *I shall remain naked indefinitely.* She is sufficiently freshly shaven that she does not yet have a shadow on her bald head or bare bucket.

BB, like the other Lobelia, has had her spread pink presented to the Game, she has been fondled and fingered, milked for valiva, and climaxed. She successfully qualified to be a Pee-Camer and Piss Mouth, like it or not.

Better to like it, Babs believes.

When last seen in the Amphitheater, BB "liked" the Snake that inhabited her rectum, "liked" the Pear violating her vagina, and "liked" a Cath that controlled not only when Babs urinated, but for how long. Vulgarities in Morse Code even.

All remain embedded as she swings in the air, boob-bound and suspended.

And yes, the Pear's leaf tickles Babs' buzzer, and the Pear's stem oozed BB's brodeas. Yes, Brodeas Babe has warranted a Collection Dish since the Amphitheater (LD3), and yes, Gamers, AI's, Running

Agents, even Automatron have theories and tweaks about how to maximize BB's valiva production.

Needless to say, all of these Props can vibrate, shock, get hot or cold; the tactical Running Agent's AI learns what combinations of these various Props hone Bondo Babe's sexual desires and focus her mind on pathways toward her own sexual gratifications. Together they will engineer a shift in BB's attitude.

In anticipation of her change of location, and quite unbeknownst to her, Babs' Collection Dish was removed, and her burgoo bottled, not unlike Solomon capturing djinns in a bottle.

Unbeknownst to her also, a clear plastic tube is now attached to her Cath, so that likewise her golden biddle draining out is clearly visible; this collects into a bag, not unlike King Solomon capturing efreeti in his ring.

Babs doesn't know who controls her valiva, but she does know, *I don't.*

Babs doesn't know who controls her pee, but she does know, *I don't.*

I have made mistakes, I understand that my errors compromise the Fate of others, and I understand that only by taking on their punishments, as well as an even harsher atonement of my own, can I begin to absolve my guilt.

Now however, through misfortunates detailed in *The Runout,* Babs is still BB for short, except BB knows, *as long as I'm in Lockdown, BB means Bang Babe or Ballum Blowum or Bondo Baudetrot.*

Good start

BB also knows that *after Midnight I've begged to join the Caste of the Whores. I've even begged to become a Dong and Dirty Whore, sacrificing my back door as well as my baldy and my mouth. Throat puke out of me. I failed badly.*

Babs last sensations in Amphitheater as her sight and sound faded to fields of darkness and hiss was watching Players cam her naked spread helplessness. And if the eyes of some of her fellow Cosmos Lobelia expressed sympathy, the eyes of others glowered with spite. Babs still feels the darts on her naked body and olive skin; draws in a breath of air tainted with burgoo, constructs her insides around whatever penetrates her, and as the darkness and silence settle over her, she completely surrenders to her helplessness.

I failed totally, I'm a Dong and Dirty Whore, but I really deserve Slavesex. And I know that just as soon as the Pear and Snake are taken out that I really am a "cocksucking cunt-fucking, ass-to-mouth Whore. Now and next Term.

So I must become a Super Whore Porn Star. No matter how Dong and Dirty I get. Or how many Terms to the bottom.

Somewhere, sometime during the darkness and silence the Pear and Snake and Cath are extracted from Babs' naked, hanging body. The absence of these Three Props disturbs Babs, and part of her wants them back. No wonder. Gamers are well aware that Babs' Running Agent monitored BB's bladder pressure and volume, and coordinated the lively Pear and slithering Snake to successfully monitor and grow BB's sexual desire. Now, with these Props absent, will BB be able to stay horny on her own?

Bang Babe knows it doesn't matter. *I am as horny as Gamers want me to me. And I'm already begging to Whore.*

§ Kimju: Negligent Pledge Begs to Whore

Babs is not the only Cosmos Lobelia who has begged to Whore. The sometimes-skittish Kimju had rushed to judgement, frantic that her perceived, and real, failure to report a Rule violation casts her at grave risk of Slavesex. *However,* Kimju knows, *with Robyn's return, my risk of Slavesex approaches zero. But begging to Whore is something Gamers will make me repeat. And not let go away.*

"A beg made is always valid." Old Game Rule.

Kimju had Stripped the Term before she Pledged the Cosmos House; and was destined to Opt-Up and Monitor next Term. Midnight had been less than hours away, when, unfortunately, Robyn's absence not only took the hands off the Clock, but had "charmed" Kimju from the Bunkroom to a Backyard Lineup, forcing her to abandon the two Garments she had acquired and would certify her Opt-Up.

During her Interrogation, Kimju had begged to abandon all claims of advancement, all Garments, and begged to Opt Strip next Term.

But then later, panicking? (or perhaps driven by weakness?), and while she still had a chance, Kimju had begged to Whore, a beg she later repeated at the very feet of the Pledge whose escape she had added velocity to.

Kimju's motives were complicated and compounded: an acceptance of guilt for failing to sound the alarm about Robyn's invisibility, yet pride in the fact that *Gamers are selecting me to be a Whore because I'm better than the rest of them.*

Even if I had sounded the alarm, Gamers would still find me guilty of something and threaten me with Slavesex. I am special, and Whoring really is my only way out. In a way, I'm like BB, because neither of us whored against the Rules, like Beka and Elle did. Babs is a Whore because of entailment damage from Beka fucking Rodney. I'm a Whore because I got set up and begged it.

Might Kimju regret she has already begged to whore? She questions it already, and wonders, *did I get played? Because I should be a Monitor next Term!*

Maybe Robyn really does have Charm, because she has charmed Kimju, and all the other Cosmos Lockdown Lobelia, into a blind-deaf-mute, bare-bald-naked, secured position.

Kimju's error of not reporting Robyn missing has so far earned her "Doubles." Unlike the other Cosmos Lockdown Lobelia, Kimju alone begs a Double Opt Down, a change in Cast from Pledge to Stripper to Whore. Kimju's double tongue piercing straddles her Tongue Clamp afront her O-Ring Gag. Her nose is double, her belly button piercing is doubled, and her clithood has been stretched.

Fear of Slavesex, might Robyn not return, had also hastened Kimju's begging to Whore, but none of this suggests that Kimju forgives Robyn for breaking curfew. Or forgive herself. Her double pierced tongue shall provide perpetual memory.

Gamers anticipate Kimju's beg to Whore will be honored, even in a Game in which fairness is not a capital letter. Kimju may regret her decision, but her constitution is to accept it, even though she has never whored in the Game and has no wish to do so.

Kimju does enjoy one inevitable outcome of her down-Casting, and that is the growth of multiple tattoos and piercings. *I know how to read me,* Kimju acknowledges to herself, *and I can read I'm already a Whore. A cocksucking, kunny fucking, facial Whore. When I should be a Monitor or a House Mom el Capitan.*

Many Gamers feel Kimju demonstrated weakness during *The Beach Day*, when Robyn had demanded she pop her knockers out, and leave them hanging out as she was told to. Kimju also obeyed when Robyn ordered her to pink and masturbate in front of Darleen's Corvette House Cam, then finger her asshole and taste herself, also on Cam. Robyn had been very smug about the whole business, and Kimju deeply resented Darleen, because of the way she also gloated about capturing Kimju's humiliation.

And uploading me to Automatron for the whole Prefecture to see. I am certainly not an anal Whore, but you Two just tagged me A2M.

After being run out of the Cosmos House stark naked Kimju had joined in a Lineup with Steph, who had also been run out of the Bunkroom fully bare-bald-naked. Soon Tiffany and Molly from the Mudpit also joined the Lineup, as did, to much surprise, Babs.

Kimju and the others had registered a turning point when Babs had been reduced to join this Cosmos Backyard Lineup, stripped naked, and publicly pinked, before being lead off for questioning.

Kimju had also pinked before crawling to an Interrogation somewhere deep in a stone Basement. It was there, during questioning by Madam Inquisitor and Pimp Interrogator, that Kimju abandoned hope of retaining her hard-earned Opt-Up, and begged to Opt Strip next Term.

The exposure of Kimju's carelessness, the certainty of her being made an example of, along with the threat of Slavesex might Robyn never return, darkened Kimju's opportunities following her Interrogation, and made it easier to surrender, for example, to being force-climaxed by the Centipede while secured to the Post Henge during *The Runout*.

Eventually Kimju accepted that her failure to sound the alarm contributed to the pain and suffering of her sister Pledge, and she sensed a widespread advocacy that she should beg to Opt Whore.

But it was not until after being secured on the Post Henge, following a panic attack perhaps, that Kimju begged Pimp Cowboy to Whore, knowing that Madam Nurse had assured her that her beg would be considered, and that her begs provided no guarantees against Slavesex.

Kimju repeated her beg to Game Mistress in the Amphitheater, where GM managed to humiliate Kimju further by demanding she prostrate herself directly in front of her nemesis, Robyn Restrained, and again beg to Whore.

Kimju felt some vindication watching Darleen's tit-sucking, dugout-spreading stamen performance with Pacmo Pinky earlier in the Amphitheater. *Darleen Dilator. I hate her. My problem is that now that I'm a Whore, she outranks me, so now, if I visit the Nugget to Feature Dance, she will make sure the House cams me in the Inner Sanctuary getting throated while I'm getting fucked to climax. Darleen's twisted, even if she's now a pinking Stripper. I want to see Darleen become a Whore. Or better yet, Slavesex.*

Kimju knows, *I'm already collecting my ink and steel. And I have figured out the reason I'm picked out; it's because Pimp Cowboy wants* me *to whore at Flesh Ranch next Term. Okey, I get it. I failed to sound the alarm so I'm an accessory. But I should not have to beg a Double Opt Down for this. Pimp Cowboy can't get me legitimately, so he finds me guilty about Rules he makes up.*

And he knows I will have to beg Double Terms.

So what is Kimju's status as she commences movement to the Play Party? *I am a blind-deaf-mute, I've been shaven bare, bald, and everywhere else, I've been naked since* The Runout.

I'm the third Cosmos to certify Pee-Cam. All Strippers pee at the Nugget, and pouring shots onstage had been my specialty. I acquired Piss Mouth during The Runup *because of Robyn, and I'm a sitting-spread-secured Lobelia because of Robyn. Every hole in my body has been violated with Props. I've been fondled, fingered, ridden the Double Dong, had the Centipede crawl up my keelhole, the Pogo ram my klam, and a Cath that makes me pee in Morse Code, as if I didn't already know I wasn't in control.*

And I cream and climax anytime anywhere in front of anywhere Gamers want me to. And everything I do is cammed, I'm a Total Cam Girl, except I don't decide anymore. I'm about to be a Flesh Ranch Whore. Or if I'm lucky, a Beauty Parlor Prostitute.

Kimju has been gagged since the beginning of *The Runout*, she retains an O-Ring Gag, and a Tongue Clamp straddled by two fresh 10 gauge studs, centered from toward the middle-back of her tongue. The Clamp grips the swollen tongue tightly, and braces against the O-Ring Gag held firmly inside of Kimju's teeth. The Gag maximizes Kimju's jaw opening and minimizes give. Maybe eventually the Clamp and Gag might get removed, but the double studs will remain.

Kimju long ago lost all control of her drool; conversely, might her head get tilted back and something gets poured into her mouth, Kimju swallows.

As for her bodyart: *I've already had my clithood ring stretched, and I know doubles means I am getting a horizontal bar behind it. Or perhaps they will put rings down my labia instead, so they can lace me up. I've got doubles in my nose, I've got doubles in my button, doubles in my tongue, and I'm begging doubles in my nipples. And I already can feel my existing ink being expanded.*

Somewhere in transit to the *Play Party* Kimju remembers, *I begged to Strip and I begged to Whore. I'm going to Flesh Ranch,* but Kimju's memory is clear, *I did* not *offer my kawazoo!*

And now I have been divested of all Props. My klammy and keelpipe are empty. So I'm not going to be just sucking cock, I'll be fucking cock too. But anal is not a requirement; one has to beg "Dong and Dirty" to get analed. We'll see how long I last before I beg that too, although Babs should be stepped up to take on any and all Cosmos Karma.

Do the other Cosmos Lobelia hold Kimju responsible for her mistake? Of course they do; some of them even forgive her. As for Kimju remembering her responsibilities to promptly report Rule violations no matter how small? A double tongue piercing constantly reminds Kimju, *I failed to sound an alarm. And besides reminding me with my tongue, I am going to be whored out as correctional training, and to increase Flesh Ranch's income. Face it, that's the reason Gamers put my mouth and kunny for sale.*

I am being exploited by Players of superior Caste.

But however much resentment the plural Lobelia hold against Kimju, far more is held against Babs; after all, BB did fail to make a bed check, even in her own Bedroom. There is unanimous consent that Babs must Opt Whore, although the dissenters among this group wish Slavesex upon her.

Kimju is not prone to feuds, but she does hold Robyn primarily responsible for the Cosmos' downfall. *Maybe Steph scared her, maybe Babs was asleep on the job, maybe I should have sounded an alarm, but it was, after all, Robyn who attempted escape. I was not a contributor to her escape, no matter the motive or the details.*

Kimju toughens her stance. *I'm a victim. Robyn provided the Charm and Game Mistress made me beg.*

§ Robyn Presumed Slavesex: Will She Take On Karma?

It is believed that in the Term before the one ending at Midnight, that it had been Robyn, who at that time had been a Cosmos Pledge, who had reported the then-Monitor Steph's navelage violation. Steph's subsequent Lockdown, the Events surrounding Steph's absence at the Mudwrestling Contest, are memories Steph retains but Robyn might not.

Both Robyn and Steph reemerged as Cosmos Pledge in the current Term, and Steph knows Robyn is why the Clock stopped.

Subsequent to her discharge from Lockdown, Steph Sorostitute had been dispatched to the Cosmos House with tattered privilege, a ripped minidress that invited titter and upskirt and more Opt Down.

Robyn Redacted pledged again to the Cosmos House but with her memories largely erased, such that the only thoughts that do leak out are thoughts that are damaging to others. Her favorite Garment was a maillot cutout, worn at various times with and without straps, rolled up to bare the buttocks, and rolled down below the navel.

Throughout this Term, then-Monitor Babs had bestowed upon Robyn the power of addressing the Cosmos Pledge with the voice of their Monitor; Robyn enjoyed humiliating the other Pledge, and she did so with apparent impunity.

No longer.

Until the *Beach Day,* Robyn had "the only rig never revealed, the only rump never ravished, the only roughage never reduced." She had the misfortune of Steph taking revenge upon her, encouraging her to take selfies with her maillot carelessly worn, her cutout hole stretched off target, so that her belly button was unknowingly obscured. Steph spang her trap later that Day, denial and discovery quickly reduced Robyn from a maillot cutout to a topless tanga rolled down below her button to the top of her pubic hair, ensuring accidental navel exposures were no longer a possibility.

Robyn got very flushed standing spread surrender topless tanga. And she got heavily cammed. Some say Steph used the Cosmos Cam, and some say Darleen was there, collected Robyn for the Corvettes, and that Monitor Janet directed the upload to Automatron with a Public Domain tag, as if to enforce worthlessness.

Then-Monitor Babs had allowed Robyn to recover herself sooner than most thought necessary. Many Cosmos suspect it was this moment, coupled with the fact that Robyn's strapless maillot cutout was but One Garment, and (no matter how rolled up or rolled down), One Garment committed Robyn to a trip to the Nugget Stage Door, and a requirement she irreversibly shed her second skin before she rings the bell, so she may present herself naked, beg to be let in, and allowed to show off her pink center Stage.

It was a trip Robyn never made, and it was Babs's discovery of her missing then-Roommate that precipitated *The Runout,* collapsed the Caste of all Cosmos, and bequeathed them with ink and steel.

Seven Cosmos Lockdown Lobelia, especially ex-Monitor Babs, had been relieved to witness Robyn's appearance when she was rolled through the Amphitheater following her "rescue." But Robyn's predicament also scared and alarmed the Seven Lobelia.

Yes, Robyn was sitting-spread-secured in a Cart pushed by a giant Naked Negro. She was equally bare, bald (except for a bun of hair on her head used to assist her securement), and naked as the Seven Lobelia, except for the fact that her hands and wrists, and her feet and ankles, were encased in blocks of plaster.

Robyn had been fashioned with regulation Eyepods and Earpods, and a Cyber Gag with an adjustable aperture, drain hole, and a tentacle attached; it could wrap around her tongue or tickle her throat inside her mouth, suck up cum off her face and feed it to her, or pleasure the head of a dick inside an opened aperture. (Perhaps Robyn will be trained to climax on "creepy.")

Robyn's nose possesses two tubes, one in each side of her nose, a feeding tube to her stomach, and a breathing tube which permits the lungs access to air.

The feeding tube passing through her nose slides across the back of her mouth and down her throat into her stomach; it also allows Robyn's stomach to be suctioned out and her food feed to others.

The separate breathing tube that occupied her other nostril monitors and regulates whatever gas she breathes, including oxygen and carbon dioxide, the components of ordinary air, and any specialty gasses that may assist in her learning.

Robyn's rectum had been occupied by a thankfully lubricated Stroker Rod, her raw meat was commanded by a Drildo, and a Cath and bag collected her urine. Her bladder is monitored to stay full and exert pressure on her sexual organs. Mobile Crawlers stimulated her body, stims embedded into her collar, and stims pressed against the bottoms of her feet and the palms of her hands inside the blocks of plaster were impossible to pull away from, and ensured Robyn will continue to remain totally possessed of mind, body, and soul. And sufficient to say that not only is her location undisclosed, it is undisclosed to Robyn also.

Seven Lobelia may not agree if Robyn's nipples were clamped or not, or if the pain of swinging weights moderated the height of Robyn's climax. But certainly, all Lobelia appreciate these consequences of an escape attempt upon the escapee. But they also bear the damages that Robyn has inflicted, and will continue to inflict, upon themselves.

For example, during her presentation in the Amphitheater at the end of *The Runout,* Robyn had the honor to watch Kimju beg to Whore, and then Robyn got climaxed watching Kimju get her tongue double pierced. Smarter Lobelia should understand they are convenient fodder for Slavesex training.

The AI entrained inside Robyn, a.k.a., Cybernetician, has also learned, discovered, that it too can produce sexual ecstasy in its host, and collects Robyn's surrender of self.

Somehow Robyn continues to avoid showcasing Piss Mouth, and although she has qualified herself, she doesn't relish that she is now being pissed in public. Robyn wishes, *I want to piss on Babs.*

Sometime during her movement to the Play Party, Robyn is severed from the Cart; the bun on her head is left behind and she becomes the last and Eighth bare-bald-naked Cosmos.

One more reminder about Robyn, Robyn is inhabited by The Cybernetician, a thoughtful and large AI who resides, apparently, inside Robyn someplace, or inside Automatron, or everywhere perhaps, a holistically distributed artificial intelligence.

Robyn should appreciate Cybernetician. Cybernetician's affection of her body is deep. Cybernetician knows all about Robyn's biology: her blood flows and hormones, breath rate, oxidization and CO_2 levels, her bladder pressure and urine excretion, her temperature, pulse, sweat, saliva, the contents of her stomach and bowels, even the wetness inside her runcible.

Cybernetician even monitors Robyn's neural fire rates and the state of her thoughts. Yes, Robyn is possessed inside and out.

Cybernetician coordinates all of this information along with communications to and from various Running Agents, such as those that manage Robyn at a sub-system level: the ticklers pressing against the soles of Robyn's feet, the stims against her encased palms and inside her neck brace, the Stroking Rod, Drildo, Cath, and the Crawlers might they still grace her naked body. Cybernetician may control the valve on her feeding tube/stomach pump, her breathing tube, and her Gag management (hole aperture size, tentacle operation, drool management).

Does Cybernetician talk to Automatron? Most certainly. And do the Gamers out in the Prefecture contribute to Cybernetician's goals? Most certainly also. Gamers weigh in, they can spot Rule violations, can debate punishments, demand discipline be enforced! They will create desire for Robyn to want to masturbate, yet restrict and channel her release(s). Gamers may decide to position Robyn so she is receptive to Piss Mouth. Or receptive to cock in her reliquary, if not also her rectum.

Cybernetician talks to Robyn through her Earpods, and it reinforces its presence and commands with physical stimulus. Sometimes this can be very simple, like Cybernetician whispering a countdown into Robyn's ear, "five, four, three, two, one, piss!" and as Robyn helplessly observes her own Cath turn on, again in her Earpods, "five, four, three, two, one, stop!" and Cybernetician turns her off. Followed by an awful crackling laughter in her ears of a monster gone mad in a horror movie.

Robyn fears Cybernetician. Robyn fears that *Game Mistress, Madam Nurse, Pimp Cowboy, the Eyes, even stupid Babs and Whores like Penny and Coco… none of them understand that an incubus AI is loose inside me and I can't do anything to stop it.* Robyn fears the tactical, that *Cybernetician will shock me senseless, suffocate me, starve or overfeed me, and endlessly climax me on fucking machines.*

These are all good ideas, but strategically Cybernetician will gather all the Running Agents and AI and sensors together, hash the data with Automatron, and commence a training plan to maximize Robyn's sexual frustration and the release of her sexual fluids.

Cybernetician intends to turn Robyn into a raving nymphomaniac who craves to climax on cocks, not just sex machines. A Slavesex who will subjugate herself mind, body, and soul in exchange for sexual attention. And sexual satisfaction for sacrifice.

The darker side of Cybernetician is willing to let Robyn be reduced of all humanity, reprogrammed, and then unleashed upon men and women alike who will be drawn into her web of sexual surrender, and be captivated; Prey.

When Cybernetician is near Robyn wants it to go away. But when Cybernetician is away, Robyn wants it back. It pleases many Gamers that no matter what the situation, Robyn wants something more. So something more will be happening to Robyn

It is possible, some Lobelia believe, that Robyn's Charm is a hellion which brings destruction not only upon herself, but misery, misfortune, and pain to all those around her. Some wonder if Robyn, by will or by design, *cherishes her place of total submission? And does she cherish her Charm more for the attention she brings upon herself, or for the pain she brings upon others?*

Does she even care?

§ Tiffany: Former Porn Star Seeks Path to Flesh Ranch

Tiffany, who never really wanted to Opt Up, views Robyn's disappearance and capture as bestowing a weighty Karma upon all the Cosmos, one she seeks to ride downward.

Like all the other Cosmos Lobelia, Tiffany has begged to Strip next Term, but the former Whore and Porn Star really wants to be shooting movies again. Tiffany knows, *if I want to refresh my Porn Star status, I need to return to the Caste of the Whores, so that I can fuck on Cam regularly again and expand my catalog. Porn Stars at Flesh Ranch are the prized tricks,* Tiffany believes, *we're not who gets stabled with straw.*

Tiffany is not a newbie; this is her Fourth Term in the Game. Two Terms before the Term ending at Midnight, Tiffany's Roommate and fellow-Stripper had been Janet. Yes, fat Janet might be a MomCap now, but back then both Strippers pulled pink center Stage, masturbated each other, and did naked lapdance fondle work. More than once Janet hat soloed the Camera Lounge and let Patrons pull her fat flaps wide apart and cam right down her jam-pipe.

Janet Opted Up and became a Cosmos Pledge one Term ago, and a Roommate with Babs.

Tiffany had also let the selfie-takers pulls her flaps wide, and pooled tapioca in her fuck tube. Tiffany had Opted Down and become a Whore at Flesh Ranch. And achieved her goal.

Tiffany spent her Term at Flesh Ranch working the basics: tits and twat, tongue and mouth, collecting facials, swallowing, collecting vaginal creampies. Tiffany had also advanced herself into felching, bukkake and gokkun work, and after winning a cum collection and drinking contest as she advanced her Porn Star status.

But Tiffany never volunteered to sell her ass or shoot Anal Porn, although once when she Featured Danced the Nugget, she did suck off a long line of erect cocks in the Camera Lounge, and lots of Patrons cammed her. The drenching had soaked her face and hair, and run down her shoulders.

Tiffany then got to wear her face until after it dried out and became dust.

She shot movies getting throated until the puke ran out while being rammed in her twat. But Tiffany had never chosen to do anal.

During different visits to the Nugget to Feature Dance while she was a Whore, Tiffany also met then-Strippers Kimju and Molly, also Ginny and Lee Lollydor, who became Corvette Pledge.

Tiffany had been confronted with the possibility of Opting-Down to Slavesex during her Term as Whore, and had been fearful of this Option, as well she should be, and remains so. Strippers and Whores all Pee-Cam, no exceptions, but by begging a Piss Mouth, Tiffany believes, *I became a Watersports Whore to avoid Slavesex.*

Tiffany retains her Piss Mouth Obeisance; she drank pee on the Yacht earlier this Term, and has volunteered to learn how to identify her fellow Lobelia by taste and smell. Still, Tiffany is content with her deal. *No matter how much I get pissed on, I do not have to worry about Slavesex, at least for now.*

Tiffany ponders, *Watersports are nothing compared to the commitment of Slavesex. A Slavesex must beg for total submission. Inside and out. Mind, body, and soul. All fluids and food, all secretions and excretions, total control of your air, your blood and enzymes, your senses, your holes, and your nervous system. All skin, unlimited body art. Total commitment, 24x7.*

And if I were a Slavesex I'd be a Piss Mouth anyway.

There had actually been more than one catch in the Gamers' gratuity of Tiffany avoiding Slavesex. Not only would Tiffany take on Piss Mouth, but she would Double Opt Up, so that instead of becoming a Stripper, she had become one of the Cosmos Pledge, and forbidden all contact using her mouth or her treasure chest: no kissing, no eating pussy, no sucking cock, no coitus. Tiffany had chaffed at her chastity constantly during the Term awaiting Midnight, she knows it is deliberate, she know she dare not break.

Like other Lobelia, Tiffany is begging to Opt Strip, and remembers that *once before, when I was a Stripper the first time, I had tested the Rules and found myself at Flesh Ranch immediately.* But Tiffany knows that if she tests the Rules a second time, that *as a repeat offender I will not get sent to Flesh Ranch. The destination is wherever Slavesex are taken. And I do not want that to happen.*

Role models like Robyn affixed to the Cart, or whatever was buried in the sand during the *Beach Day*, are futures Tiffany would prefer to avoid.

Tiffany has remained horny and sexually frustrated throughout the Term, which is now frozen in its 28th Day. At the time Robyn was discovered missing, at the beginning of *The Runout,* Tiffany had been bound together in the Mudpit with Molly, connected by their respective topknots. They had been severed and totally stripped, joined into a Lineup that included a naked Babs, and were independently interrogated by Madam and Pimp Eye.

Tiffany, and Six other Lockdown Lobelia, were then displayed blind-deaf-mute, bare-bald-naked, sitting-spread-secured for the duration of *The Runout,* initially on the Post Henge, and then later in the Amphitheater.

Obviously, Tiffany remained quite unable to engage in any self-arousal; although she squeezes her vagina to stimulate herself, and welcomes unseen hands which from time-to-time fondle her gagged lips or irritate her tongue, grace her neck and make her nipples pop up, and tug on her tremulant trinket. Hands which pink and finger-dip her shaven treasure chest harvest the quickening tapioca oozing out.

And when hands let Tiffany taste and smell her secretion and scent Tiffany secretes more. When they swab her with cream from a neighbor, Tiffany secretes incessantly. Tiffany is cool with being taken. *I like it when I am the vehicle for their passion. I want Gamers to watch me have sex. Call me a dirty filthy cocksucking, dick-fucking cunt, a facial whore, a Goo Gobbler. I want them to spill sperm on my pictures and honor me.*

They say "once a Porn Star always a Porn Star," and I want to be a Porn Star again. Please, during Lockdown, anyone, fondle me, finger me, fuck me. And only during Lockdown, Gamers can tie me down and fuck me silly. And especially on Cam.

Tiffany presumes, correctly, that *Roommates Molly and Steph, and Roommates Beka and Elle, are also begging to Opt Strip.*

Gamers are not sure if Tiffany knows that ex-Monitor Babs and ex-Pledge Kimju are now begging to Opt Whore?

Tiffany continues her analysis. *Robyn appears designated as Slavesex. And I watch Steph somewhat reluctantly begging to Strip, but I don't see any sign of ink and steel in her body. So maybe her Opt Up, won in her Duel with Elle, really is guaranteed.*

Tiffany has confidence in her reputation. *I am a Porn Star! And my past remains my present.* Tiffany sees Lockdown as providing an opportunity. *I need to get bondage banged and beaten before Midnight. It's a rare chance, prohibited to all except Slavesex! And explicit* Bondage Porn Videos *will attract fans at Flesh Ranch, the Beauty Parlor, or wherever I dance, freelance, or contract. I can make* Bondage Porn Videos *as long as I'm in Lockdown; it's like temporary Slavesex, until Midnight, and I have all kinds of plans.*

Face it, I have been spread-eagled and fucked before, Tiffany appraises herself, *but never been this secured and helpless like I am now.* Tiffany breathes deeply and silently as she considers the possibilities. *I am a Porn Star, so a* Bondage Gangbang Video *of me garners me new fans, refreshes old fans, and ends at Midnight.*

And if I get analed in the process it doesn't count after Midnight, because I didn't outright beg "Dong and Dirty" or "Anal Whore."

Also, maybe I can trade Castes with one of the two emerging Whores? Certainly, Babs or Kimju would prefer to Strip next Term instead of doing suck-fuck-facial work. I'm a much better tits and twat tart than they could ever be. And I'm being overlooked.

Except, if BB is begging Dong and Dirty status, that's a problem because I've never wanted to be tailpipe certified. My problem isn't Lockdown, because with no Rules I will for sure be analed; it's after Midnight that worries me. Because if Babs has begged her asshole away, the only way Gamers will let me trade Castes with her is to take on her Obeisances. No thank you.

Standing in the way of offering trades is a total lack of ability of the Lobelia to communicate with one another. Tiffany also surmises, *Kimju would jump at the possibility, but there is no way Gamers would allow a trade with Babs to happen. They have BB in their clutches, and they are going to transmogrify her into a private dancer and escort.*

Except she will beg them to go harder on her.

I can beg to do handjob and oral work might I strip at the Nugget, but if Gamers need someone to fuck an Ambassador and cam me with his phone, then I'm the one to send out.

§ Beka & Elle: Lockdown Lobelia beg to Strip & Whore

Beka and Elle had presented themselves at *The Arrivals* dressed like killer club-kid girls assuming promotions, but before *The Arrivals* were over both newbies had pinked in the Camera Lounge at the Nugget, and begged to "Pledge naked and cum be a Stripper next Term."

And that had not been the end of their begging to Opt-Down.

During *The Runup* both newbies were indeed stripped naked, spread, and sexually stimulated; both creamed (Beka so much so she earns her Broda nickname). Elle was forced to climax and Beka was denied until the twosome climaxed together on the Double Dong in the Doghouse on the last Day of the Term. Somewhere during the

Term both acquire Pee-Cam Obeisance; Elle further acquired a Lollydor Obeisance, and thus becomes the only Cosmos Pledge allowed to lick up cum, although forbidden to acquire it directly.

During *The Runup,* on Day 26, Beka and Elle had been directed to deliver a copy of each's freshly-minted Pink Page to every House. Both had done so; Elle managed to titter or vagflash every House Cam, and Beka managed a quickie in the Peacock Garage, one that left her with Rodney's semen oozing out her bonker and down her thigh on her way back to the Cosmos House. She had breathed a sigh of relief that her vaginal creampie went undetected....

During *The Runup,* Elle forfeited a Duel Option to Steph, earning Steph an Opt-Monitor, and committed herself to an Opt-Strip (D25). Steph further humiliated Elle by taking both her Garments, and later commanding Penny and Coco to shave an already naked Elle bare and bald in front of onlookers at the Mansion Open House (D27).

Steph topped Elle off with a piss climax riding the Glass Bull.

Elle remained bare-bald-naked on *The Beach Day* in full public view. She has remained bare-bald-naked ever since, and is expected to remain so in the future. *The Beach Day* had included mental as well as physical hazing; Elle had begged that her *Gonzo Suck and Fuck Videos* with Beka get screened in the Nugget. Elle remembers, *I even begged that they get screened in the Lobby, so the Patrons could watch me suck and fuck before they pay to come into the Club and watch me strip and pink on Stage. Beka too, except she likes it when they watch her. She'll spread her vestibule and squirt piss into a glass. She'll pull out a tampon, masturbate it, and chew it to bits.*

I've made it up to Beka for giving the Gonzos to Babs, although it's not right that Babs shared them with Janet and Darleen, because Darleen made sure all the Cosmos and all the Corvettes got to watch. Now anyone in the Prefecture can watch me fuck. Even though I wasn't getting paid, it was more like I was whoring myself out. Just like what I did to get the Measurement Nudes.

Elle seldom feels vengeance, however, *Darleen Dilator will be Stripping at the Nugget this Term, and so will Beka and I. That's two-to-one. She chose to show around hardcore of Beka and me? We saw Darleen lick and pink in the Amphitheater, now it's time for Darleen to get on her knees, convince House Mom Janet that blowjobs aren't sex, pump a cock in her mouth, and beg to Whore.*

Elle imagines a second cock dogging Darleen's dilatare. *And run that* Video *in the Nugget Lobby, so the potential Patrons can watch Darleen sex for free. Just like you let them watch me. Then we'll run that up to Automatron, so all the Patrons can watch. Just like you let them watch me.*

Elle is seldom short on analysis. *With Babs in Lockdown I suspect my* Gonzo Videos *reverted upward. Certainly the Madams and Pimps will exploit them. That means exploit me, and because I'm in Lockdown, so they can build on my infamy. And let Beka dominate my sexuality*

Elle understands, *I won't wear anything until I get to the Nugget, and only then after House Mom gives me whatever she wants to take off on Stage. I'll be her cute schoolgirl, naughty nurse, haughty hottentaunt. I'm afraid until then, until Midnight, I'm a Whore.*

Before *The Beach Day* was over Beka and Elle had acquired the Double Dong from Corvettes Ginny and Trixi Tubes, and they have retained it ever since. Beka and Elle have become totally addicted to this instrument of pleasure. Beyond the bond with the Dong, the Dong, with its AI sensitivity, has actually been successful and drawing Beka and Elle closer together, as friends, pals, lovers, and with courage to together forge forward deeper into the Game.

Beka and Elle are aware that the Double Dong has also been promised to now-Whores Penny and Coco, also addicts, who covet its mutual penetration, and will sacrifice to achieve it.

Beka finally got to climax on the Double Dong with Elle in the Doghouse shortly before the Clock stopped. During *The Runout* the Roommates demonstrated all *Nine Dong Combos*, always in public and always on cam.

When the Roommates were moved from the Post Henge to the Amphitheater, the Double Dong was upgraded to a wireless CyberDong, which is divided into two separate pieces that separately penetrated each of their orifices, yet were wirelessly connected, so each can totally feel the other. The CyberDong, like the physical Double Dong, is mediated by a learning and remembering AI that also talks to various Running Agents and Automatron; in the Cyber version, the two parts are wirelessly connected, and provide the only connection the two blind-deaf-mute, bare-bald-naked, sitting-spread-secured Cosmos Lobelia have, not only with each other, but the Game.

May the CyberDong (or its proponents) want the two begging Strippers to juice or even thrash, rest assured that shall occur. At this point in the Game, Beka is beyond horny, past the point where she will break Rules to gain sex, and as Elle dances with Beka on the CyberDong she succumbs. *I just want to kiss Beka, suckle her buds, and lick her pussy until she squirts in my mouth.*

And, *I adore the Dong, I know we can't share it after Midnight, and I know I'm already begging cock in every hole to get it back.*

Ever since their Interrogations at the beginning of *The Runout,* Beka and Elle have lost control of not only their arms and legs, but also their eyes and ears and mouths. Their Eyepods and Earpods are standard issue, but their capabilities are totally unknown to both Roommates; both prostheses are fully capable of delay, disorientation, and disinformation. O-Ring Gags and Tongue Clamps keep both silent and positively disposed to begging, for example, that a freed tongue would enable them to lick cock.

And get the O-Ring gag penetrated by cock. Or not be needed.

Beka had begged to Opt Strip during her Interrogation at the beginning of *The Runout* and had been immediately rendered naked. Which is to say that the remnants of her g-string, worn as a string collar, were cut and severed from her body. Elle was already naked, and, with no Garments to surrender, would need tonconsider other begs.

During the Interrogations both Beka and Elle quite independently confessed to Free-Fucking *during* the Term, a serious Rule violation which qualifies each to Opt Whore (and to each entail the other).

Beka's sin had been to engage in coitus with Rodney during the delivery of her Pink Page to the Peacock House. Her unexpected confession, with implications beyond effecting Rodney, came with a promise of Immunity for her violation, but also a begging to be a Dong and Dirty Whore in the Term following her Stripper Term (scheduled to begin at Midnight). Beka has also promised she would bring Elle along into this rich seam of Whoredom.

Elle also had broken the Rules; her sins involved sexing (twice) in order to procure her *Measurement Nudes.* The first of these trysts was with the holder of the sedate, but still full-frontal application images; this holder had required Elle procure and bring to him her *Gonzo Suck and Fuck Videos,* made with Beka before the Roommates enrolled in School. Elle also gave her holes away for this procurement, aggravated by a demand she also present the *Gonzo Videos* to then-Monitor Babs, along with the *Measurement Nudes.*

Elle had achieved that goal. And some other goals also.

Elle had been fearful that her Free-Fucking to obtain the *Measurement Nudes* and bonus *Gonzos,* might have been recorded on a hidden camera, and that *I am unveiled while I am dancing on Stage at the Nugget I know that one instant later I'll be cocked in the Inner Sanctuary awaiting transport to Flesh Ranch.*

And so, during *The Runout* while Elle was secured on her Post Henge, she had shared the detail she had given her anal away. *Was required to give my asshole away; creampied both times*

As restitution, Elle had offered to reenact both scenes.

Yes, Beka qualifies to Opt Whore and Elle qualifies to Opt Dirty Whore; Roommates share: so Elle entails Beka Dirty Whore and Beka entails Elle one Term of Immunity. So both shall Opt Strip and beg to be Dong and Dirty Whores after a Term at the Nugget.

How does Elle rationalize her treatment, as she increasingly discovers the Game is stacked against her? For example, Elle comes to believe *I was set up to break the Rule in order to procure my* Measurement Nudes*, and as a result I get Opted to Whore. And then screening the* Gonzos *around only confirms I'll fuck around.*

House Mom has already played Gonzo Videos *of me sucking and fucking on the Screens at the Nugget; previewing me: because soon Patrons* can *watch me strip naked and pink and pee and dildo live on Stage.*

And I won't forget that the first words out of my mouth if the Gag ever comes out, is to beg to be a Dong and Dirty Whore after my Term on the Strip ends. And to keep begging all next Term.

Elle considers herself and her Roommate. Certainly the now-Roommates have affection for each other, but it is not until they enrolled in School that their lesbian tendencies have emerged to complement their heterosexual desires. They may assume that sixty-nining and eating each other out is allowed for Strippers, just like it is for Pledge and Whores. Because if cocksucking isn't sex, then cunnilingus isn't sex either.

And that's not all; Elle knows. *Beka and I are not Opting Up anymore. Things are not going in the way I expected for us, well, for me, actually.*

Or for Beka. At some point, while Beka was secured to her Henge Post, she saw in her Eyepods a *Video* that Rodney had secretly shot of their garage tryst. It was from an angle that clearly showed her bent over a fender and Rodney thrusting into her love box from behind. And then a flurry of repositioning and Beka up on a fender, legs spread wide, yanking the cock into her breech and pumping together. Rising up to a pointed climax together

The *Video* clearly established Beka as a willful Free-Fucker, but because she had confessed to the Eyes in the Basement and been granted Immunity, Beka's outcome was different than normal. Normally any Pledge (or Stripper) caught Free-Fucking should simply consider themselves a Whore at that point of revelation; some Gamers argue Free-fuckers become Whores the moment they engage in coitus. But because Beka has Immunity, the Rules dictate that she may not Opt-Whore, and can only Opt-Strip next Term.

But just because Beka confessed, and aided a takedown of Rodney and beyond, doesn't mean that her *Beka & Rodney Fuck Video* adventure won't find its way to Automatron.

Beka assumed the audience for this screening included the other Cosmos Lobelia, when in fact, she alone among the Cosmos Lobelia has seen the *Video*. Beka doesn't know that all the Peacocks have watched her slip Rodney's cock in between her shaven vulva, stretch her lips, and pop up her round bead. Or watch Rodney deliver a vaginal creampie that will seep out as Beka heads toward the Cosmos House.

That said, the clandestine nature of her Violation, its discovery, *my total helplessness, and the fact it is going to be screened to the entire Prefecture,* all these factors greatly arouse Beka, and help ensure a constant flow of brodeas. *I want Gamers to jerk off watching me, and I want to jerk them off directly.*

Beka is, of course, oblivious to whatever corollary damage she might cause. Having been granted Immunity, she will not immediately Opt-Whore, unlike her sex partner, Rodney. Beka never considers that her Roommate Elle might get entailed by her transgression, yet not be protected by Beka's Immunity. Beka has always considered that her Roommate Elle will follow. Back in club-kid nightclub days, if Beka got out of a car and vagflashed the photographers, Beka made sure that when Elle got out, that Elle would also linger a sanpan nookie while sliding out.

Beka also fails to associate how her own sexual transgression contributes to Babs' Opting Downward; Beka attributes BB's demise to Robyn's attempted escape and Babs' delinquency to her responsibilities. But Gamers also know that "so goes a Pledge so goes a Monitor," ergo, Pledge Beka's whoring entails Monitor Babs bushing. And Pledge Elle entails BB's backway.

Elle also sees an upside. *The good news is that* the Gonzo Videos *are no longer something Darleen or Janet can hold over me. They are just out there, and they help keep Beka and me close. That's worth something. And not only has Beka forgiven me, she's also grateful, although once we start Stripping she'll tug me to Whore.*

What Beka will do is remind Elle that they both are already begging to become Dong and Dirty Whores, after they complete the next Term Stripping at the Nugget. Keeping Elle on a trajectory to Super Whoredom is Beka's commitment to the Game.

But Elle doesn't think much about whoring; Elle fears Janet. *I don't want to Strip at the Nugget while Janet is the House Mom. She's already made me titter and pullaside, plundered my nadir, turned me into a Lollydor, and made me hang my halter down. She'll make me spread naked, pink, cream, and climax on Cam.*

Sounds like a beginning.

The decision that Elle will Strip at the Nugget has been made for her.

But before the Roommates can get to the Nugget they must first survive Lockdown and the upcoming Play Party.

Beka may not understand she should be grateful for Gamers restraining her so she doesn't succumb to her instincts. She doesn't quite understand that she will get screwed, but not until she's wound up past the point of sanity and in a way not anticipated.

Elle tries to be rational. *I just have to take it. I'm going to be shooting Porn Videos. Porn Videos with Beka I hope.*

And get real. *Okay,* Lockdown Fornications *with men. Hotel sex with Johns. Parade stark naked at Nudes-a-Poppin'. Shooting the* Nine Dong Combos *has been an easy part. I'm a Stripper now, I, pink, stuff dildoes, vibrate my nugget, taste my nakodo. Except, that's not quite correct, there's more. I'm a Lockdown Whore, then after Midnight, I'm a Stripper who gets fondled and fingered and begs to Opt Dong and Dirty Whore.*

Beka wants to put out, and since we need to stay together, I need to put out also. Mouth, nooky, nadir. No stopping it now.

§ Molly: Stripper Must Seek Hand & Mouth Training

Among the Cosmos, Molly is among those innocent of contributing to Robyn's hazing and escape.

Gamers know Molly Mammoth spent the last Term at the Nugget, where she possessed nothing and any clothes she wore she wore to take off. Molly is short and squat – 5' 3" at 140 pounds – and has 38DD-30-37 dimensions. She became adorned with a clithood ring (hidden in her rolls of fat and beneath her mange, as well as an alchemy sign for phosphorus deep in her navel, again hidden by fat.

Molly was unabashed about exposing herself naked, bouncing her mams, and masturbating her mingus on the Pole, but she much preferred to lapdance because her ambition was (and remains) to do as little as necessary, and it is much less work to slow grind until the Patron pops in his pants, than to shimmy and shake center Stage.

Molly and Kimju had arrived at the Cosmos House from the Nugget, with Molly wearing panties and Kimju a thong, and had been greeted with a wallow in the Mudpit. Molly knows how to soldier, but during *The Runup* her complications multiply:

Once upon a time extremely hirsute, Molly's body is shaven, not just bare and bald (except for a topknot), but everywhere else too: arms, legs, armpits, eyebrows, asshole. Even with her every last hair gone, Molly's musk gives her away. The smell is not as strong as when she was hirsute, but it comes out of her armpits, her mons and flatulent anus, and her hanging mammaries sweaty underneath.

Earlier this Term, Molly and Kimju, former Nugget Roommates, had been returned to the Nugget to perform what the Patrons call an Alumni Reprise, in which the Two then-Cosmos Pledge mutually pinked, masturbated, pussy ate, and climaxed together on the Double Dong. The Double Donging attracted the rapt attention of the Nugget Patrons, because when Molly and Kimju had been Strippers before, they (like all Strippers) had been forbidden to share the Dong. But they were no longer Strippers, they were Cosmos Pledge at the time, and were thus encouraged to let go.

The fact remains that Molly and Kimju are both immune to the Dong's infections. Certainly, the Double Dong is able to milk meringue out between Molly's fleshly thick lips; Molly accepts that any sweat and forced climax are more demanding work, but she is never one to seek out additional physical or mental labor.

Molly's goal is very simple. *I want to be a Stripper next Term. Just tell me what to do, no matter how vulgar the act. I can lift up a beer bottle with my mooe, load in ping-pong balls and pop them out. But do I expect to share the Double Dong still more during Lockdown? Beyond already donging with Kimju and Tiffany and Steph? I don't care, because after Midnight I'm at the Nugget, Double Donging isn't allowed for Strippers. That's fine with me.*

Once I'm inside the Nugget all I have to do is lay back, let the Patrons look at me naked, fondle my mams and finger my meatlocker, and the Nugget will bring me delicious food.

Should the Game be so undemanding?

Although Molly studiously avoided more serious watersports, when she was a Stripper she did pee on Cam like every other Stripper. *So what. I will pee in front of anybody anyplace anytime, I don't care who watches me. It's totally natural.*

Molly may have thought she had objections to Piss Mouth, but these were overcome during *The Arrivals* when Molly tossed the champagne at the Bachelor Party at the bequest of Steph, and then later, reconfirming this commitment at the *Greatest House Roar* during *The Runup,* she piss-mouthed herself and extracted an unintentional victory over her oppressor, Steph.

Finally, on the *Beach Day*, Steph achieved an equal opportunity to drip valiva and piss-mouth herself, balancing Molly's Karma.

Molly presumes to Opt Strip to the Nugget once the Clock starts running again. She remains encumbered with the Ben-Wa Balls singing inside her mooe, and a lively Procto living within her muckway, and with the Clock stopped, Molly assumes (incorrectly) that Gamers intended to replace these two items with penises, be they attached to men or to trannies, one at a time, two at a time, and more, might they unclamp her tongue.

Gamers need to research the degree to which Molly might have been enlightened as to the purpose of her impalements; in practice her Double Penetrator actually serves to protect her virginity. And this is something Molly values a lot. Molly knows that once she gets inside the Nugget that her virginity is safe, so if she can carry her Prop to the Club, even if she has to blow the Back Door Man, that once inside she is safe from vaginal penetration.

Molly's mouth is a different proposition. An O-Ring Gag set behind Molly's teeth keeps her mouth maximally open, and two round bars, tightened to the left and right and in front of the O-Ring, clamp firmly down on Molly's tongue. The clamps are sufficiently tight that as Molly relaxes her tongue, the horizontal rods press against the O-ring, leaving Molly's tongue hanging out. Drooling.

Molly can't complain she is special; Seven Lobelia's travel Hole Gagged and Tongue Clamped; how Robyn travels is unknown.

Video from Molly's previous Term as a Stripper included not only naked and explicit pinking and masturbation acts, solo of course but also center Stage, but also some of her more private lapdance moments. *Yes, I let any Patron fondle my heavy mams, and if they were gentle, suck on my nips. And I did let many Patrons touch my maraschino, and, if their fingernails were clean, dip and taste my muffin. All I had to do was sit there. Easy, and they fed me fresh oysters, sushi, and hot bread.*

Molly was shaven bare and left with only a topknot on the *Beach Day*. She spent the night in the Mudpit, connected to Tiffany by their two topknots. Both were cut free the morning, after Babs discovered Robyn missing; both left behind in the mud any last vestiges of Garments and body hair, and both joined the Lineup of Naked Cosmos.

Molly has stayed bare-bald-naked ever since. Sitting-spread-secured in the Amphitheater at the end of *The Runout*, her Eyepods faded to black and her Earpods played sounds made for her ears.

Molly has a sense of what Gamers want. *They want me to be a bare-bald-naked Stripper next Term. That's easy, I'm that. I'm already a pinking, Watersports, Fondle-me-anywhere Girl.*

Molly does have additional concerns. *Gamer have already stretched me and expanded my tattoos, and shaved my mooe. So more is going to be expected of me if I go back to the Nugget. Next time, it won't be just the Patrons fingering my clit, I'll have to beg to add Handjobs to my list of "qualifications."*

And I will have to let girls do me. I guess that's pretty easy. All I must to do is lie back, spread my legs, make sure they don't hurt me, and wait till they climax me and it's over.

And if Janet really is the House Mom, I know for certain she'll make me eat her out. And insist I concentrate to please her. She'll make me eat the Hat Check Girl too. It's important for the both of us that she doesn't just threaten me, she makes it physical.

The first time I went to the Nugget and presented myself naked at the Stage Door, the Back Door Man opened the Door and let me in. This time, he's going to step outside and I am going to lean over, hang my mams in the air, and suck him off, and walk through the door with his cum on my face all the way to center Stage, and let the Crowd cam me as I wipe it off and swallow.

Or wear it on my face. It is a signal to all the Patrons I'm insisting that blowjobs and pussy eating aren't sex, which they aren't of course, so I am going to be a Cocksucking Pussylicking Watersports Fondled and Fingered Stripper next Term.

Okay. A Stripper Deluxe.

But Molly does worry. *So by that criteria kissing isn't sex, nipple sucking isn't sex, and felching creampies isn't sex. Nor is entering me into a cum drinking contest and slathering me with facials!*

Correct.

Anal might not be sex either, but is forbidden to all Castes, except only those Whores who qualify as Dong and Dirty Whores, and of course, all Slavesex.

Molly takes a deep breath. She still sits, her thick thighs are spread wide, and her wrists are secured. *Thank goodness I have the Ben-Wa Balls in my Mutton and the Procto up my mawk pipe. I may have to handjob, suck cock, and eat pussy, but at least Players are unable to screw my mutton. Or shove a strapon or a cock up my ass.*

Molly may worry, but she won't be doing anything about it. A scene appears in Molly's Eyepods. It is herself, naked and spread during a Medical Exam performed during *The Arrivals* (D08). The

Cam moves in closer, details the part where Madam Nurse Beautician inserts a speculum into Molly's muliebre, then squeezes the handle to spread the metal fingers and open Molly's insides to a fully-lit worldly view. Then cuts and repeats. And repeats....

Molly squirm. The Ben-Wa Balls tingle inside Molly's bare maw, and the Procto squirmed deep inside her mawk and her tunnel growls. Molly relaxes, lets her nipples puff up and her clit worm into view, and softly zones.

§ Steph: Ignorant of Fate Awaiting Her?

Steph's play represents a challenge for Gamers. Last Term was Steph's second Term in the Game and this haughty superior was the Monitor of the Cosmos House. Her Roommate was the ingrate Robyn, and her Pledge included Roommates Babs and Janet, Roommates Penny and Coco, and another pair of Roommates who have not been identified.

It had been a Term that ended badly for Steph, the then-Monitor had flaunted covering her belly button, gotten reported by then-Pledge Robyn, and ended up in Lockdown. She had emerged from Lockdown and been dispatched to the Cosmos House wearing but one Garment, a tattered, strapless minidress with its center section so ripped out that titter and vagflashing was unavoidable.

During *The Arrivals,* now-Pledge Steph's wrath was first directed against her Roommate, the corpulent Molly, such as demanding Molly turn herself into a Piss Mouth at the Bachelor Party.

During *The Runup,* Steph's minidress got reduced to a belt as Gamers advanced upon the opportunity of Robyn's disappearance to haze her. *I got stripped naked, pinked, creamed, and climaxed. Then after getting snickered out of winning the Greatest House Roar by Molly, Monitor Babs made sure every Cosmos Pledge Zoned me. Molly I'll forgive, but BB used me as Zoning practice for novice Pledge, and I am scheduling some fierce payback.*

Steph's public humiliation was brought to a peak at the Nugget, when she was taken for an Audition along with ex-Whore Tiffany. Steph remembers, *Tiffany climaxed me center Stage on the Double Dong. Then House Strippers Penny and Coco shaved my slash bare, shaved my head bald, and pissed on me while I climaxed.*

Steph might be helpless but she remains especially eager to pay back, ergo Steph adds Penny and Coco to her retribution list.

Conversely, Penny and Coco do not intend to let any future Steph opportunities get wasted.

Nor is Steph without horny; she might be immune to Dong addiction, but the Dong's presence inside her sex recess increased Steph's desire to fornicate with real erections. *On my own terms, of course.* Steph is aware that a Lockdown Lobelia may be subject to hand or mouth work, also vaginal and anal penetrations, but Steph assumes, *I am a hands-off Player!*

That said, when Steph had been left behind when the others departed for the Mermaid Parade, she seized upon the opportunity to press William to have sex with her, and presented herself naked to him in the Peacock Bedroom. Unbeknownst to her, William cammed the tryst, which included not only oral and coital sex, but also an unwelcomed anal penetration. On the plus side, Steph did learn from William about Elle and Beka's *Gonzo Videos.*

By luck if not misdirection, Steph acquired the Option to fight a Duel, selected Elle as her opponent, and Elle, certain of defeat, conceded, begged to Opt-Strip, and forfeited all of her Garments, then and thereafter. This guarantees Elle an Opt-Strip at Midnight, and guarantees Steph an Opt-Monitor.

Steph had acquired a croptop that aces her rib cage, and capri pants that rode below her navel, just along the top of her posterior rugage. The parts are skintight and stretchy, and are either cameltoed or crotchless, depending…. Still, Steph's Garment Count of Two qualifies her for Opt-Monitor Caste at Midnight.

Elle, after forfeiting all her Garments after the Duel, remains naked, begs to Opt Strip after Midnight, and begs to Opt Whore in the Terms thereafter.

Steph's Opt-Up does await Midnight. Before the Clock got stopped, Steph had claimed that she was bequeathing to Elle, as part of transferring her Obeisances to this loser of the Duel, her Piss Mouth. This has consequences for Elle, because at the Nugget a Pee-Cam is de regur, but a Piss Mouth is a beg for a Stripper.

Suspicious that Steph might be exaggerating the suite of Obeisances she was bequeathing to Elle, Gamers had arranged, as a remedy to remove any uncertainty, for William and Rodney to visit the Cosmos House Bathroom, where Robyn directed that Rodney pee into Steph's mouth. Steph had collected Rodney's overflow into a Measurement Cup she held under her chin. Steph still swallowed plenty, and what she collected in the Cup provided a delicious experience, Charmed, and for certain other Cosmos to share.

Gamers concur that afterwards Steph stood qualified to pass her Piss Mouth Obeisance to Duel-loser Elle.

Steph's opportunity to transfer her qualifications to Pledge Elle presented itself the night she had escorted Elle to a Mansion Open House. Steph cherished the opportunity, ordered Elle lick spilled and splattered piss off her skin, and displayed her nearby a pool, back-spread-surrender on a lounge chair.

The Guests had watched then-Strippers Penny and Coco render naked Elle bare and bald and naked. Steph had rolled Elle's nipples hard, and pinked Elle's smooth nook for the many Cams among the Guests, she had pulled Elle's butt cheeks wide, and fingered her asshole. Steph then guided Elle, still walking on fours, to the Glass Bull, aided her to climb onto the saddle, and let her lick a finger. The Guests then watched as the rod in the saddle began to pump in and out of Elle's naïve, and as the gyrations of the Bull built, Elle found herself thrust into a prolonged climax; she slathered the Bull's saddle-dick with her own nectar, and at some point during her climax, voided her bladder.

The *Elle Rides the Glass Bull Video* has since been circulated by many wildcats as well as by official Cam views cached in Automatron. Steph earned high marks for surfing Elle into the Zone and making her sing to applause.

Steph had expected to leave the Open House with the Shaving Kit, but she left without it, and still showing stubble on her otherwise bald head, stubble above a very low riding waistline and stained cameltoe capri pants, and with itchy armpits and legs.

Elle managed to streak back to the Cosmos House Doghouse without incident.

During *The Beach Day*, Steph retained her Two Garment, however a complaint about stained cameltoe has been remedied so that the skin-tight slacks are crotchless, stainless. Steph might have a little stubble, but nothing hides her slit, and might her secretions push her sex lips out, Steph's can display three lines and a stalactite.

Robyn especially, continued to dominate and viciously haze Steph, ordered her to "sit, lean back, and spread." Despite an apparent Opt-Up, Steph has not dared disobey, given Babs' disinterest and earlier commands, and the number of witnesses present. Robyn had directed Steph onto her back, "pull you croptop up and titter yourself, pull your pants down, and grab your ankles and bend your leg up over your head so your crotch hangs over her mouth."

Robyn had not only ensured that the Cosmos Cam collected Steph dribbling her pee and her spendings into her own mouth, Robyn made sure that Darleen's Corvette Cam streamed Steph's qualifying, begrudging Pee-Camming Piss Mouth live to the Prefecture. Janet had tagged the *Steph Piss Mouth Video* in Automatron.

Steph had seethed at the humiliation, Later, observing Robyn getting careless about letting her strapless cutout maillot cover her navel, Steph enables an unthinking and vain Robyn to shoot selfies which documented her own Rule violation.

It was the same Rule that Robyn had once used to bring down Steph: and on the *Beach Day*, Steph employed it with vengeance to ensure Robyn forfeited her croptop and miniskirt (Two of her Tree Garments, and with it her Opt-MomCap). and then roll-reduce Robyn's remaining strapless maillot cutout a topless tanga (One Garment and a path to Opt-Strip).

If some Cosmos hold Steph's hazing of Robyn responsible for her flight, Steph is not one who feels guilt. *Robyn got what she deserved, and if she hadn't run she'd be just another Naked Nugget Stripper next Term, masturbating her pink center Stage. No, that's not good enough for her, so instead she's Slavesex next Term.*

And she's turned the rest of the Cosmos into Strippers and Whores. Except for me. I won the Duel; I'm still Opting Up.

On the evening of *The Beach Day* and cocky with success, Steph had escorted the Corvette Pledge back to their House, a task of responsibility, then detoured to visit William, at that time the Monitor of the Peacocks, so she might seek revenge about her Piss Mouth treatment the previous evening at the hands of Robyn and Rodney.

William had supervised Steph's acquiring an Obeisance she had promised to bequest, and did not appreciate his acquiescence being questioned. The disagreement consummated in rough sexual coitus; this time coitus interruptus occurred when Rodney barged in, and Steph suddenly discovered that not only was her mouth and sex apparatus being penetrated by two different cocks, but shortly thereafter Steph had little alternative but to yield to a cock in her anus as well as her mouth, and then for those cocks to switch so she could taste herself, and then switch so she could taste herself again.

This too was secretly cammed. As was a double facial.

Gamers in the Prefecture know that William and Rodney were last seen affixed spread-eagle to a giant Wheel, each facing inward, wrists to ankles, so that Rodney's cock remains secured in William's mouth, and William's cock remains secured in Rodney's mouth.

The remaining Six Peacock Pledge were last seen at the Amphitheater, employed as Chair Bearers for Game Mistress. GM had ordered them into a Benzine Ring while they had waited, each with their adjacent's cock in their mouth.

Of course, Robyn's absence froze the Clock pending Midnight and upset all the Cosmos Fates. Instead of Opting Monitor, Steph found herself rushed out of the Bunkroom naked into a standing-spread-surrender Lineup in the Backyard. *The Runout* begins. Not only would Steph be prevented from recovering her two Garments, she was emphatically told she would be treated just like the rest of the Cosmos Lockdown Lobelia! On the plus side, she was assured that her "Opt-Up to Monitor Caste would be honored at Midnight, guaranteed by her being truthful in all matters!"

Being treated just like the other Lobelia had however included *keeping me bare-bald-naked, losing control of my eyes and ears and mouth, getting my stack fondled and getting my snatch pinked and finger-fucked. With anal tasting frequently a part of presenting me.*

Unlike Beka, who confessed to her transgressions, Steph denied any inappropriate behavior, twice in fact; once before her *Videos* were discovered, and once after.

Those few who are aware of the *Beka & Rodney Fuck Video* certainly understand that Beka and Rodney are already Opt-Whores, and by entailment, that Beka's Roommate Elle, and Rodney's Roommate William are Whores also. Entailment also includes the Monitors responsible, which implies Babs and William are slated to

Whore. There are some wrinkles to this, including Beka's Immunity, and if William's double entailment matters.

Although the ex-Peacocks have seen the *Beka & Rodney Fuck Video*, only two of them are aware of the two *Steph and William Sex Videos*. The Two ex-Peacocks who know these documents might be discovered remain affixed to the Wheel; the silent Benzine Ring has no reason to suspect. They assume that Rodney's Free-Fuck with Beka, complete with Rodney's creampie and semen running down Beka's thigh, entails then-Monitor's William, and explains their spread-eagle-secured sixty-nine position on the Wheel.

This is a correct assessment, but the "more" remains a tightly kept secret.

Gamers have determined that none of these discoveries be shared with Steph; Steph shall remain ignorant about evidence and determinations of her Fate. Gamers, who long ago determined Steph guilty of sexual misconduct, offered no reasons that Steph be afforded due process or pleadings, felt no requirement to inform Steph of the determination of her Fate, or any necessity to explain the application of Steph's Karma upon not only herself, but also upon others, most certainly including Steph's ex-Monitor, *that Lockdown Lobelia Bondo Blowmouth Bangho Buggeress*.

Steph's misdeeds are certainly reason enough to keep William and Rodney mutually Penis Gagged, and the other Six Peacocks silenced in a Benzene Ring.

The Cosmos Lobelia all remain Gagged and Tongue Clamped; this also contributes to keeping Steph's secret. One Cosmos broke the Rule (Steph), one Cosmos has been told a Rule was broken (Babs), and another Cosmos (Beka), wonders if what Rodney told her was real or just an attempt to seduce her. When Beka has a chance to observe Steph, as do others, she interprets that *Steph carries less decoration than the rest of us, less freight*.

Janet had been shown the *Beka and Rodney Fuck Video* and the *Steph and William Suck Fuck Anal Video*, with the explicit instructions to share what she has seen with Babs. Janet did so, providing Babs an opportunity to beg ahead of the Game, which BB did, offering her burrow and butthole. Although now, after seeing Steph, Babs wonders if she made the right decision.

Steph's apparent lack of a nose ring and navel tattoo concerns Babs and casts seeds of distrust. *It doesn't look like Steph is Opting Down like the rest of us. Maybe her Duel victory over Elle really is a guaranteed Opt-Up and trumps Robyn Runaway Karma. Or maybe I'm going crazy.*

Janet told me she had seen a Beka and Rodney Fuck Video *and another of a* Steph and William Suck Fuck Anal. *I believed her and I took her advice: I begged Dong and Dirty Whore. That is the only way in this Game.*

Now I don't know if I should have believed her or not. She was once my Roommate and confident, now she will piss in my mouth in order to justify her Caste.

Babs reminisces. *Actually, I guess it doesn't matter if Janet deceived me or not; it doesn't matter if Gamers ever discipline Steph. They haven't disciplined her so far. It doesn't matter if Steph really screwed William, it doesn't matter if she offered up her asshole, because I'm the one who was asleep on the job. Steph doesn't matter to me because I'm already a Dong and Dirty Anal Whore. I need to be collared and leashed and kept in a cage.*

It is true that Babs, Beka, and others who observe Steph have uncertainty about her Opts. Steph has no uncertainty; for indeed Gamers have helped shape Steph's belief she is special, unmarked, and beyond reproach.

For example, during the *Runout*, Steph was allowed to witness multiple Lobelia get pierced, masturbated, and climaxed. In this pact with malicious intent, the spread and secured Steph was herself masturbated, creamed, climaxed, and zoned, sometimes with the able Pogo extended up into her sex hole, so that her pleasure at the other's pain received maximum reinforcement.

Steph struggles between anger at Gamers, *you don't know who you are inflaming,* and pride about her own privileges. *After all, I watched all the other Lobelia get tattooed and pierced, and without me getting tattooed or pierced at all. Or letting anybody watch me. I'm special, and Gamers know they have to be very careful with me.*

And will Steph increase her anger at Penny and Coco, who had shaved her bare and bald while climaxing her during the *Runup?* She does; Goo Whores Penny and Coco had seized upon an opportunity during the *Runout*, while Steph was secured and spread on the Post Henge, to remove the Shaving Kit from their own private parts, use it to render then-Monitor Babs bare and bald, then insert the Soap Sphere into Steph's socket, and slip the Tool Cylinder into her sternpipe. And had walked away leaving Steph softly climaxing.

The stubbly but otherwise bare-bald-naked Steph still possess this instrument of depilation, yet Steph remains too bound up to extract it and use it to make herself smooth again.

Feeling the Sphere and Cylinder inside her seems to make Steph's stubble itch more; knowing she is unable to extract and use the Shaving Kit frustrates Steph, and knowing everyone knows she is helpless to avail herself of the Prop she carries embed in her snatch and stern, humiliates Steph even more.

Furthermore, might the Shaving Kit encourage Steph to hang secretions out of her stubbly satchel, Steph hangs secretions. And when the Shaving Kit wants Steph to grind her pelvis, Steph grinds her pelvis.

Beyond Humiliation lies surrender, when there is no choice. *Gamers are going to put a Collection Dish under my snatch and milk the splurt out of me, and make sure I watch myself on Cam.*

Yes, may Gamers milk splurt and may Steph watch herself.

Steph is still able to keep her thoughts to herself; the Gag enforces silence but the brain is easily scrambled. Steph is quick to realize that *my Shaving Kit, like Molly's Double Penetrator, provides a prophylactic against penetration in my snatch and sternway. Molly has the Ben-Wa Balls in her mincemeat, and the Procto up her mawkport because Gamers are going to encourage her to beg away her mouth next Term when she returns to the Nugget.*

I'm lucky I still have the Soap Sphere inside my snatch and the Tools Cylinder hiding inside my sewer. I don't enjoy it; both are definitely a nuisance, but Gamers put them there to protect me, protect me because I'm special. It's rude and inconvenient, but it's a way for Gamers to make sure no one screws me or tries to mess with my stern star.

Can not the Shaving Kit compel Steph to shake and secrete?

And I hate the Tongue Clamp but I know it is there to protect me from getting throated. Because if it comes off and with the O-Ring Gag behind my teeth, there is no way I can bite back.

I don't need any of that.

Some Cosmos Lobelia think that it was Steph's hazing of Robyn that drove Robyn to flee. Well, attempt to escape. But does that even matter? It matters to the Karma facing the Cosmos Lockdown Lobelia: Babs' failure to bed check, Kimju's failure to report a missing Pledge, and especially Robyn's failure at attempting escape.

But it doesn't matter to Steph. *Lockdown might be serious for others, but it is pro forma for me.* Steph anticipates next Term, *It doesn't matter what I am left wearing at Midnight; next Term I'm a Monitor, and Monitors take what they want! I'm already confirmed.*

Yes, Steph remains confident *I shall Opt Monitor next Term,* yet she still chaffs against the strictures of Lockdown. *It's not right that Gamers pretend to treat me like just another Lockdown Lobelia, They understand they are not allowed to pierce and tattoo me, and the fact they sometimes cause me pain and suffering is unacceptable.*

I'm being forced to act like I really am in Lockdown. I understand Gamers want to deceive all the others. And they have me where they want me and they are going to abuse me as much as they can get away with, and as long as they can keep the Clock stopped.

But they know I'm keeping score, and that sooner or later, when it's my turn, I will abuse them triple if they haven't been nice to me.

§ Janet & Pacmo Pinky: MomCaps New & Old

Gamers have kept an eye on Janet throughout the Term. Note that although Midnight lies in the future for the timeless Cosmos Lockdown Lobelia, that Midnight for Janet (and many others) has come and gone. Janet is clocking time in the next Term, whereas the Lockdown Lobelia lack a Clock, or a countdown to Midnight.

Janet is corpulent, with rolls of fat, saggy breasts, a drooping buttocks, and a flair for getting attention. She is shameless about showing her body, and happy to make the most vulgar of displays.

Once a close confident and peer of Babs, their recent Opts in opposite directions has changed their relationship and forces Babs to both trust yet fear Janet.

Janet is a seasoned Player. Two Terms before the Term ending Midnight Janet and Tiffany were Roommates at the Nugget. So make no mistake, you can find Janet legacy pink. She pinked everyday center Stage, pulled butt cheeks wide and puckered her asshole too. Sucked her own nipples. Sucked Tiffany's too, and visa-versa and yes, they ate each other out on Stage on many Cams.

One Term before the Term ending Midnight, Janet was a Cosmos Pledge and the Roommate of Babs. It had been at the end of that Term that Babs and Janet had defeated Penny and Coco in the Mudwrestling Contest, the complications of which continue to resonate for not just the Four Participants, but also with the Referee, who was Robyn, who substituted for Steph (who had been cast into Lockdown for flaunting navelage).

Penny and Coco continue to hold Robyn responsible for failure to stop what both consider cheating during the Mudwrestling Contest.

Babs and Janet, victors in the Mudwrestling Content, became House Monitors of the Cosmos and Corvette Houses during the Term ending Midnight. Babs had begun the Term wearing a Black Bikini that left tan lines on what is now a naked and secured body. Some of BB's tan fades, but two small parts do not, and have the potential to be one way to induce BB to pump burgoo.

During this same Term, only which had ended for Janet at Midnight, Janet sported open-mesh crochet string halters and g-strings. Now even more powerful, MomCap Janet continues to flaunt her body; she now wears Three Garments and exposes even more of her skin.

Janet enjoys her subsequent promotion in what is for her a new Term. She has now ascended to House Mom el Capitan, MomCap for short, but still polite address to the Caste. House Mom Janet oversees the Nugget with its Caste of Strippers; el Capitan Janet supervises the House Monitors of the Cosmos and Corvette Houses, and each with Seven Pledge.

It is a lot of responsibility, even more than Monitoring a House.

MomCap Janet replaced who is now Pacmo Pinky, Stripper at the Nugget, a Club Pinky managed prior to Midnight. Pinky's Triple Opt Down is a result of Robyn's escape, Babs' negligence, Kimju's inattention, Steph's hazing, and Fate. If in the past this former House Mom had turned a blind eye to fondling and fingering in the Club, then Pinky might expect equal treatment, including begging to work on her knees in the Champagne Room.

Janet, accompanied by a gaggle of her Corvette Pledge, had visited the Cosmos during *The Beach Day,* She had encouraged Steph to drop her pants, and roll on her back so her pussy was above her mouth and pee into her own mouth. Janet made sure that then-Corvette Darleen had Pee Cammed Steph's Piss Mouth.

Janet led the charge to sweep away Robyn's transparent croptop and miniskirt, reduce her strapless maillot de roulè to a topless tanga, then make her stand-spread-surrender for the Drone Cams.

Janet's most extreme orders were reserved for guests Penny and Coco; Janet, with Babs' concurrence, leveraged their hunger for the Dong into encouraging them to beg to be Dong and Dirty Whores.

Although it is true that Whores Penny and Coco might crave vengeance upon Janet, MomCap Janet lies out of their reach; furthermore, Janet is also a Player both Whores would prefer to avoid, least they become "victims" a third time.

Ever since Janet, Penny and Coco, and others visited the Cosmos Lockdown Lobelia during *The Runout,* the Cosmos largely understand that they remain in a state of temporal suspension, whereas the rest of the Game has passed Midnight.

Fortunately, time displacement does not prevent Janet from hazing Lobelia: Body stripped naked, but also time-stripped.

During *The Runout* Janet proved her allegiance to the Game by climaxing Babs while at the same time certifying BB a Piss Mouth. Rest assured the *Video* will get played in the Nugget, on Screens at the Cosmos and Corvette Houses, at Flesh Ranch, and will become part of BB's repertoire on Automatron. That act crushed Babs.

Janet, knowledgeable of Steph's secret liaisons with William, keeps the secret, and allows Steph to believe she will be Opting-Up and a Monitor next Term. Yet at the same time Janet deliberately reminds Steph "it is not Midnight yet, and Playeers still have time to torment you. So I will."

But there is little Janet can do that Steph can't handle already. *Gamers don't need me to pink anymore, they need me to train the newbies to pink. I'm on my way Up.* True, Janet had then rubbed her ringed jam pot in Steph's face and Steph had threatened to take Janet's jingling rings away from her with her teeth.

Janet appointed ex-Corvettes Caroline and Wendy as Monitors of the Cosmos and Corvette Houses, instructing them to wear hose and heels and never anything else. They are to sit on the Front Porch with their Pledge every day, spread, pink, and count to 1000. Both know that camera trucks disguised as repair vans will cam them with gyro-stabilized telephotos, that prowling paparazzi will collect their vulgarizations, and that the House's own Front Door Cam will hover in front of them and collect them not just full-figure, but also canvas every pore. Will the two new Monitors get to watch each other?

Or consume each other's drip.

Sweet bonding.

Janet has also had an opportunity to grind down her former Corvette Roommate, Darleen. Darleen had masqueraded to be a Madam in undercover, and Janet, while suspicious of this yarn, had maintained a respectful distance. But with the passing of Midnight, Darleen was no longer protected by pretense, and found herself a Stripper in Janet's firm clutches, who publicly pinked her, along with her former House Mom el Capitan, now reduced to Stripper Pacmo Pinky, all courtesy the failures of Babs and Robyn.

Might wannabe Whore Babs be allowed to Feature Dance at the Nugget? Pinky will be waiting for her.

Besides Darleen, Janet's Nugget roster is also expected to rotate Beka and Elle, Tiffany, Molly, and perhaps other ex-Corvettes candidates including Lee Lollydor, Louise, Ginny, and Trixi Tubes.

Janet had explained it to Babs a while back, "Lee presents a seasoned veteran who will out-lick novice Stripper Elle in the Lollydor department. Louise is an ex-Monitor painfully moving downward, I shall make sure she strips, pinks and masturbates center Stage every Day. Trixi Tubes labors under the influence of Ginny and already begs to Opt Whore. Gamers might grant her wish, given that the Nugget could be overcrowded.

Janet had also advised Babs, "Don't forget than when you go Feature Dance at the Nugget that you will need me to protect you. Probably Ginny will be there, and she will always be a Whore-for-Life, so she will give you some lessons in eating gash and felching gudgeon. Ginny might also delight in giving lessons to Pacmo Pinky, in another power reversal, so might you bring your Whore body to the Nugget, be sure to beg Pinky to piss in your mouth."

Might Babs visit to Feature Dance at the Nugget, her ex-Roommate, ex-Monitor, Piss-Mouth initiator, and now House Mom

Janet, shall be expected to wind up her ex-friend, *and let me give my every hole a twirl in the Inner Sanctuary. And keep the flavor of cum on my body and in my mouth and nose.*

And turn me over to my former MomCap, who I caused to Opt Down. Please let Pacmo Pinky Piss Mouth me on Stage at the Nugget while I'm being DPed in my burke and bunghole. I failed.

§ Penny & Coco: Dong & Dirty Whores Since Midnight

The last time most Cosmos Lobelia saw Penny and Coco was when the then-Naked Goo Whores visited them after they had been secured and displayed on the Post Henge, during *The Runout.*

Penny and Coco's dance with the Cosmos Lobelia actually began in the Term before the one ending at Midnight. Penny and Coco had been Cosmos Pledge back then, along with Babs and Janet, and at the end of that Term Penny and Coco had challenged Babs and Janet to a Mudwrestling Contest.

Then-Monitor Steph was the presumed referee (and presumed by Coco to determine a favorable outcome). But unfortunately for Penny and Coco, Steph got reported with her navel covered and was swept into Lockdown, leaving her Roommate, Robyn, to substitute as the referee for the Contest.

Referee Robyn failed to stop Babs and (especially) Janet from overpowering their challengers, stripping them naked and leaving them secured in the Mudpit, with the Double Dong ensconced inside their two cinched-together and rubbing pussies. It was a long night.

The victory had Opted Janet and Babs to Monitors, and sealed Penny and Coco's Fates as Naked Nugget Strippers.

Penny and Coco have been kept naked ever since. The danced naked at the Nugget during the Term ending Midnight; and their begs to Opt Dong and Dirty Whores at Midnight have been honored. Both now reside at Flesh Ranch, Garment count Zero.

Penny and Coco might be naked Whores, but they still hold Babs and Janet, and Robyn and Steph, responsible for their downfall.

The Fate of ex-referee Robyn is Slavesex, for reasons unrelated to the Mudwrestling Contest; however, Robyn's Charm will continue to resonate. Midnight is irrelevant for Slavesex, Slavesex serve Terms but have no requirement for Clocks.

Penny and Coco hold Steph in special contempt. After all, Steph had promised Coco she would ensure Penny and Coco's victory in the Mudwrestling Contest; they had laughed together at the idea of "stripping Babs and Janet naked and sending them off to the Nugget. Pinkers, pissers, portnoy!"

But Steph is not laughing now; Steph is in Lockdown (again), yet she still remains convinced she is Opting Monitor at Midnight.

Penny and Coco acquired their addiction to the Double Dong during these magical moments climaxing together in the Mudpit, before they were set free after Midnight. They had carried the Dong to the Nugget, soloed it deep pink center Stage, rubbed it in and out between flexing sex lips, licked their juices off it, but they never shared the Dong. Sharing is absolutely forbidden for Strippers.

Gamers know that Penny and Coco never shared the Dong while they were Nugget Strippers because the Double Dong remembers *everything*; each squeeze, each construction, each juicing is forever soaked into its memory circuits. Artificial Intelligence learns not only how to identify participants, but enhance their Dong experiences. Yes, each of them has worn one end of the Double Dong in every orifice. Each has clenched the Dong out their mouth, shaved around it on Stage with half of it deep in a pussy, and paraded on and off Stage wagging the Dong like a tail out their excretion port. Prolonged periods, yes, Days may it please Gamers, but never two orifices at the same time. Never shared, period.

Certainly, the Dong would know if Penny and Coco played a duet. Right down to geo-location and angles of insertion; the Dong's Running Agent would know, Automatron would know, House Mom el Capitan would be alerted and the consequences for the two unauthorized riders would be harsh.

Well, harsh is not a nice word, simply put, in this regard the consequences would be capable and fair. Both Rule breakers would be instantly and totally restrained. All control of their eyes, ears, nose, mouth, breathing and food, vagina, skin, sweat, urination and excretion would be taken from them. Penny and Coco know that *the consequences of such an action are probably Slavesex.*

No, not probably Slavesex.

As the Term progressed the two Strippers' cravings for the Double Dong only grew, so they begged with their bodies and suggested humiliating forfeits. On the *Beach Day,* Janet, with the half-hearted participation of Babs, had suggested the Stripper Roommates focus their begging to become Dong-Hoes. They would Opt Whore and then get to share the Dong, after they arrived at Flesh Ranch.

The alternative was to beg to Opt Pledge, which would also allow Penny and Coco to ride the Dong together, but with no guarantee of a Dong ever being present….

Janet had made the Dong addicts an offer they couldn't refuse. They would get to share the Dong if they whored themselves. "You must prove to the Game that your craving is absolute."

"And besides," Janet closed the deal to Penny and Coco. "Babs and I control the location of the Double Dong."

Now the "I" part of this statement was not entirely true; the Dong, during the *Beach Day*, had resided with Pledge Beka and Elle, and these Pledge belonged to Monitor Babs' Cosmos House, not Janet's Corvette House.

Janet had commandeered Babs, "You must join me and Opt-Up; this assures that Penny and Coco can get the Dong they want and Opt Down. They shall become Dong Whores. You, my fellow Monitor, cannot Hover. You owe me too much Karma."

So yes, Penny and Coco had begged to be Dong Whores. And Janet and Babs had Opted MomCaps, (except that right now, thanks to Robyn's charm, instead of Opting MomCap, Babs is a Lockdown Lobelia begging to Whore.)

Coco, forever naked on the Beach, had led the begging to Janet. "We want to whore very much. We absolutely crave it."

Penny caught Janet's tilted head and knew she must join in, adding common sense. "We know that cocks are what Whores work, and cock access is the price we pay for Dong access."

Coco had felt the need to add optimism. "Whoring is something we can be really good at. We know that sucking and fucking can be private or public or on Cam. We're Dong-Hoes. We've already pinked, creamed, and climaxed the Nugget. Full nude, bare-bush. We've shaved and tinkled center Stage. We're in this together. We'll do girl-girl-boy and trade off."

Janet had been very deliberate with them out on the Beach. They would get the Double Dong after they became Whores, but Gamers wanted to make sure they were begging that *all* of their holes were committed to Game. And of course all of their body cosmetics, all body hair, all body functions, pretty much everything except for the realm of the Slavesex.

This time Penny and Coco had begged in unison, "Please let us Opt Dong and Dirty Whores." Both had known they were begging their assholes away, and that their bodies would likely get spread out in the Spunk Pit and masturbated, fornicated, buggered, throated, and facialed. Creampied front and back. A2PM of course, A2OPM absolutely, and swallowing not just pop shots, but pints and liters.

Babs had never felt guilty about playing what she considered a minor role in Opting Penny and Coco Down, and Babs did not get the joy that Janet experienced as the result of this conquest. But Babs might not escape retribution, for both herself and for Janet.

As the Clock had approached Midnight of *The Beach Day,* Penny and Coco presented themselves naked and face down on the sand, double-double penetrated, sharing both the Shaving Kit and the Double Penetrator, thus both pussies and both assholes were occupied. Two mouths anticipated use, first while prone in the sand, and certainly during their transport to Flesh Ranch, if not thereafter.

Penny and Coco's initial assessments were correct. The Ranch Hands that collected them that night first throated them, but before morning their Props had been moved from pussy to mouth and subsequently from asshole to mouth, so that both newly-cast Whores might be initiated to coital as well as anal hard penis penetration. In the event either Whore had illusions she had not begged "Dong and Dirty" those illusions were shattered with the facts. Each got to taste the pussy and asshole of not only themselves, but the other.

Thus while the Cosmos Lobelia were busy displaying themselves naked-spread-secured to the Post Henge during *The Runout,* at Flesh Ranch, new Dong and Dirty Whores Penny and Coco popped cocks with their hands and mouths, collected vaginal and anal creampies, got cumdumped all over their bodies, swallowed shots right into their mouths, licked bukkake off each other, and swallowed during a gokkun contest.

But only one hole at a time could get screwed, as the Shaving Kit and Double Penetrator occupied two holes in each Whore, and it remained necessary to rotate these obstructions through their two mouths to also access two pussies and two assholes.

Coco was first to beg that both Whores give away their two Prop, freeing up all their holes, so they might double, even triple penetrate with live cocks.

Their wishes had been granted; Penny and Coco's already facialed, creampied, and slimed bodies were cumdumped, and so thickly covered with semen, head to toe, that they dripped.

The Two Goo Whores had presented themselves before Seven Naked Cosmos Lockdown Lobelia secured on the Post Henge. The naked Lobelia could only suspect how Penny & Coco came to be splooged. *Fucked, analed, facialed, and creampies? Bukkake? Gokkun? Emptying condoms? Getting dunked in a tub of semen?*

All of the above.

As a first order of business the Goo Whores had divested themselves of their Props. Gamers anticipate that divesting of the Double Penetrator and Shaving Kit will only deepen Penny and Coco's want of the Double Dong. And that their empty holes may encourage them to grow a want for Double Cock Penetration.

First, Penny and Coco extracted the Double Penetrator and inserted it into Molly; the Ben-Wa Balls popped into Molly's mooe with a slurp, and although Molly's mawkport resisted the Procto at first, with a little persuasion the Procto narrowed and got longer, deepened its intrusion into Molly's rectum, then fattened out again at the base so it could not be expelled.

Molly understands and appreciates. *Gamers will now decide if and when to feed my mawkpipe, and when and where to empty me out.*

Molly has accepted that *the Ben-Wa Balls not only make their own music, but that the Procto will make me sing along. The good news is that I'm not about to get cocked in my meatwagon or mawk port. Every Patron is going to want to confirm that the Double Penetrator resides inside me, and I am going to let every one of them do just that.*

And taste a finger afterward if that is required.

Penny and Coco had next divested themselves of the Shaving Kit, expelling it, using it and excess goo to take revenge upon naked-spread-secured Babs. They had saturated BB's pubic bush before shaving it off, then fed BB her own butched goo-bush. It had been a thrilling humiliation, amplified by BB knowing that *Steph was masturbated watching me get my burse and bunghole shaven bare, my eyebrows too. She gets off on my reduction. That's not me.*

Such a narrow frame. In fact the entire Prefecture had watched the Goo Whores smear the gooed trimmings into BB's concave armpits, the bottoms of her bare feet, and the insides of her thighs.

And, most tellingly, Penny and Coco had delighted in decorating BB's crescents d'areolage, bursting the scent of her freshening, then pulling Babs' pussy lips apart in the opposite directions so that her deep maroon pigment was displayed all the way down her bore. The Whores masturbated BB's clit, squeezed her boobs, and pinched hard on her nipples, and rubbed more goo on her crescents d'areolage. Babs was unable to prevent her pelvis from wanton grinding, or stop her burse from oozing burgoo. Babs had panted, craving more stimulation, and Penny and Coco had commenced feeding her more goo-bush trimmings and fingerballing her very erect bauble.

Might Babs falter her rhythm, Penny and Coco merely twiddled a crescent, fingerballed her clit, and guided BB back into wanton desire, until she ran at a panting climax on her own shake and vibration. Next the Goo Whores began scraping fingers full of goo off their bodies and feeding Babs as they brought her into a uncontrolled climax, finally backing her off to a sharp panting, holding her steady while packing her mouth, and leaving her to eventually calm down.

Babs had earned a check mark next to the "swallow" box. It had been Babs' introduction to becoming a Goo Gobbler. Bondo Babe learned, at that moment, *I am a cum receptacle, a jizz swallower, and Gamers are preparing me for popping facials, begging bukkake, and gokkun contests. I am a Goo Gobbler now.*
But the short hairs in the goo are very irritating.
So any goo anytime anywhere, that's fine, but no hairs.
And creampies too, out of pussies or out of assholes. Out of both.
And climax control. You will feed me goo and climax me.

Penny and Coco had then turned their attention to Steph, also helplessly displayed on her Post Henge. Early in *The Arrivals* then-Strippers Penny and Coco had shaved then-Pledge Steph bare and bald during an unwelcomed Audition at the Nugget. That event had humiliated Steph and provoked internal vows of seething retribution.

Steph remains frustrated at her helplessness when the Goo Whore's visited the Post Henge. There remains dispute whether Penny and Coco tidied Steph's eyebrows and snatch, but there is no dispute that after they had extracted the Shaving Kit, depilated Bondo Babe, that they used the Sphere and Cylinder, if not the razor and scissors and soap, to tease and masturbate the sitting-spread-naked and helplessly secured Steph. They made sure the Cam collected Steph's twisting full body, her contorted and gagged face, and her sopping sex, as they drove Steph upward to a totally revealing climax. The Soap Sphere slid into what could only be described as a sopping slit amidst howls of passion out the O-Ring Gag, and the Tool Cylinder produced a rapid succession of pants as it snuggled into and up Steph's greased stern tube.

Following their visit to the Post Henge, and freed of their Props, both Penny and Coco became fully enabled to double penetrate two cocks, all six ways for sure, and as Coco elates to herself, *triple penetrate, and go crazy, all I have to do is ask for more men and they will give me more men, BBBBBG, and with Penny, BBBBBBBBBBBGG. And I will eat pussy, before and after it is creampied. I am now an unencumbered, all-hole Dong and Dirty Whore. And so is Penny. Penny isn't as eager as I am to do two at once, and she doesn't really want to be ass-fucked. But wanting and doing are two different things. That's why we are professionals!*

Although Penny sure does like her pussy licked out.

One commitment that is still owed to the fresh Dong and Dirty Whores has not been forgotten about: the Double Dong has been promised to them. And the Dong will be at the *Play Party*

However, Dong and Dirty Whores Penny and Coco both worry that *here in the Game, Masters and Mistresses needn't always follow the Rules, because they have no Superiors to discipline them.*

Power sometimes is where you can find it. Being willing Whores doesn't disempower Penny and Coco sharing their grudge against Babs and Janet. Janet appears out of reach. But Babs?

Penny plans retribution. *Maybe Janet gets away but Babs is Opting Whore. We'll be waiting for her at Flesh Ranch. Maybe Janet deserves crushing more than BB does, but BB can stand in for both. So don't worry, Bondo Banggo, you're going to get all of what's coming to you yourself, plus all of what's due to Janet also. Janet Jaloobies Jamtart Jetty Pipe. Plus some extra, to make sure we are more than equal.*

Babs is not stupid; she anticipates. *If I get sent to Flesh Ranch, Penny and Coco will be there and they will make me their pussy service bitch. They will DP me with strapons and make me clean afterwards. They will piss on me while I am gangbanged and climaxed. They will press me to take on every Obeisance they don't want, and give them anything I have that they want.*

Sure, all of this and more. Penny and Coco's real goal is to get Babs to beg Slavesex, and possibly in exchange from exempting themselves forever. They want to position themselves first.

§ Cosmos Lobelia: Inventory of Props & Possessors

Finally, for the benefit for the scorekeepers, here follows an inventory of selected Props as of the end of *The Runout* and the beginning of *The Play Party*, and who possesses them:

Midnight has not occurred for the Cosmos Lockdown Lobelia yet, and as they wait with their Clock stopped, they shall continue to be charmed by Robyn Runaway's escape attempt.

Last seen all Cosmos Lobelia wore Eyepods, Earpods, and O-Ring Gags with Tongue Clamps. The Gags are miserable, relentless, intolerable; some Lobelia would prefer to enjoy the benefits of their current securements, others seek to be free of their Gags.

The smarter ones know that the only thing between them and a blowjob is their Tongue Clamp; some want to oralate, others suffer the inconvenience of prevention, others give up.

All have been secured with their hands behind their backs or heads, their armpits tight or displayed, and their legs spread and secured. All arms and legs and thighs and feet and buttocks and bellies and necks and faces are displayed to the Game. So too are all nipples, belly buttons, vaginas and assholes. All of their armpits and legs and pubes have been shaven. All heads are bald, all eyebrows are missing. All noses are pierced, all navels are pierced and tattooed. All of their private body functions are now public.

Six of the Lobelia carry Props at the end of *The Runout:*

Babs was last seen with a Pear in her basket, a Snake in her back hole, and a Cath occupying her bladder and pee hole. They quite commanded her attention. BB's blurt came out the stem of the Pear and dripped into a Collection Cup. BB hadn't been special with regard to hanging burgoo, most, perhaps all Lobelia have hung cream. But with BB, the Gamers were relentless at tweaking her Props, and her Running Agents learned how to make BB shake, more rapidly fill up her Collection Cup, and have purpose.

But these assets are removed during Babs' transit to *The Play Party* so that BB arrives empty. Babs knows, *Empty holes. I am readied for cock.*

Robyn is last seen violated with the Stroker Rod and the Drildo, both affixed to her Cart. She was Cathed and able to squirt Morse Code obscenities about herself, her Stroker knew how to feed and flush, and the Drildo could spin and burnish a rosebud. Shockers lie against the palms of her hands and the soles of her feet, all cast inside blocks of plaster. Crawlers wander her skin, her Gag is extreme with a wayward tenacle, and a feeding and a breathing tube aid the attempt to complete Robyn's helplessness.

And that's just Robyn's body and her orifices. Never forget, Robyn is possessed by Cybernetician, her mindful AI, which resides partly within her, and partly in Automatron and Gamers.

But since Robyn was rolled away from the Amphitheater by the giant Naked Negro, her Fate remains unknown.

Beka and Elle share a CyberDong, a Double Dong separated into two pieces which are connected together by an intrusive AI. Beka is addicted to sex; both are addicted to the Dong; soon Elle will be addicted to sex also.

Molly carries the Double Penetrator, with its Ben-Wa Balls in her moxy and the Procto up her mawk port. Might Molly needs inducement to become a cocksucker, the Double Penetrator can provide it; Molly realizes that *if either or both are removed, I becomes a Whore candidate.*

Steph, likewise, carries one Prop, the Shaving Kit, with its Soap Sphere residing in her sex cavity, and the Tools Cylinder, with the razor and folding scissors, sequestered up Steph's stern tube. Steph has yet to find an opportunity to extract the Kit and shave herself (if not also others). Steph continues to believe *I have a guaranteed Opt*

Monitor, and me begging to Strip is a charade. The Gag and Clamp assist Steph in keeping her opinions to herself.

Tiffany is empty. Media of Ex-Whore Tiffany's sexual prowess using her tongue, tits and twister abound, but she has never offered her tailpipe to cock. Shot suck-fuck-facial, but never shot anal. No "private" videos either. Tiffany reflects that the past is not the now.

Kimju has been divested of all invasive Props and is also empty, reinforcing her commitment to Opt-Whore. Like the others, Kimju's mouth is held wide by an O-Ring tightly secured behind her teeth, and by a wide Clamp across her tongue that ensures she can't pull her tongue inside her mouth; unlike the others, Kimju also sports double studs, straddling her Tongue Clamp. Kimju gathers bodyart.

The Cosmos Lockdown Lobelia remain blind-deaf-mute, bare-bald-naked, sitting-spread-secured.

§ Cosmos Lobelia: Caste Changes & Pleadings

The Eight Cosmos Lockdown Lobelia are each begging an outcome at Midnight; here is a status of any begs for changes in Caste by Eight Cosmos Lockdown Lobelia:

Babs and Kimju beg to Opt Whore.
Tiffany, Molly, Beka, and Elle all beg to Opt Strip.
Steph begs to Opt Strip, but believes she shall Opt Monitor.
Robyn is assumed to have been Opted Slavesex.

During The Play Party Fates can be reconsidered.

§ Other Players: Caste Changes & Pleadings

The Cosmos are begging Opts, but because their time is suspended, Midnight has not yet occurred, whereas for most Players, other than the Cosmos (and the Peacocks), Midnight *has* come and gone and they are operating in a new Term. So here follows an inventory of Changes in Caste of Players that did occur at Midnight, and their status at the Time of the end of *The Runup* and beginning of *The Play Party.*

Former Corvette Monitor Janet is now Nugget House Mom.
Former Corvette Pledge Caroline now Cosmos House Monitor.
Former Corvette Pledge Wendy now Corvette House Monitor.
Former Corvette Pledge Darleen is now Stripper Darleen Dilator.
Former Corvettes Lee Lollydor and Louise might be Strippers.
Former Corvettes Ginny and Trixi Tubes might be Whores.
Former Peacock Monitor William is assumed to be Slavesex.
Former Peacock Pledge Rodney is assumed to be Whore.
Former Peacock Pledge are all Lockdown cocksuckers.
Former Nugget House Mom is now Stripper Pacmo Pinky.
Former Nugget Stripper Penny is a Dong and Dirty Whore.
Former Nugget Stripper Coco is a Dong and Dirty Whore.
Former Nugget Stripper Hottie is a Whore.
Former Nugget Stripper Odee is a Whore.
Former Game Mistress is still Game Mistress.
Former Game Master is still Game Master.
Former Madam Nurse Beautician still Madam Nurse Beautician.
Former Pimp Cowboy is still Pimp Cowboy.
Former Madam & Pimp Eye are still Madam & Pimp Eye.

V-2 The Cosmos (Minus Robyn): Traveling Conditions

§ Seven Cosmos Lobelia: Tongue Clamp & Gag Details

Should the Seven Lockdown Cosmos see each other – and they don't – they could tell that their O-Ring Gags and Tongue Clamps are standardized. Robyn, the Eight Lockdown Cosmos (if not already Slavesex), wears a more advanced Cyber Gag (might she make an appearance).

The big oval Ring Gags are custom-sized to each mouth; they are sized and tailored to ensure that each jaw stays wide open, and over time their perfection of fit wears down the resolve of the Cosmos Lobelia and induces a state of abject helplessness. It's very hard for any Cosmos to move her jaw; all are held wide open, no slack. Each knows, *Mistress can lay her Goad into my mouth, Madam Nurse can make me taste a strapon, no matter where it has been, and Pimp Cowboy can put his cock in my mouth and throat me.*

Actually, anyone can.

Some Cosmos Lobelia relish this experience, others don't.

But if the open hole makes suction difficult, then clamped tongues prevent licking. Surrendering their tongues had been a more difficult task for the Lobelia that positioning the fitted Ring Gags into their mouths. Yes, each Cosmos had been masturbated to wet, commanded to stick their tongue out just as far as possible, knowing that the two parallel horizontal rods clamping down tight on their tongues would absolutely prevent drawing one's tongue back inside the Ring Gags, even if only a fraction of an inch.

If Gamers discovered that a Tongue Clamp did have play, then the unseen hands simply added a clamp behind the existing (and too loose) clamp, repeated as necessary until any play in the tongue was totally shimmed out.

All remain susceptible to an unseen hand using a Purging Tool to empty out their last meal.

Kimju's Tongue Clamp isn't as tight as the others; Kimju's parallel rods squeeze down in between her two fresh tongue studs, and rock between them, causing searing pain. Kimju wants the rods tighter, except she doesn't want that pain. Kimju doesn't know what she wants.

Kimju is correct in her suspicions that *I am the only Cosmos Lobelia with studs in my tongue. And because I got punched, Bondo Bitch qualifies also. She's already getting gauged up more than the others. I can see it in her nose, see 10 gauge in her button.*

Well, me too, except I'm doubles everywhere.

Tiffany's Tongue Clamp is also unique; it's upper and lower bars includes extensions which roll Tiffany's lips up and down and expose her teeth and gums. In Tiffany's case, the inside of her upper lips are pristine, but the of her lower lips have been tattooed. Tiffany knows what the text says, and knows *it is inked so I can read it in a mirror and know what I am.*

The Tongue Clamps are tightened onto the Seven tongues and grasp firmly; they are as tight as needed to stay on, but no tighter, so that if the tightness on the Clamp causes the tongue to swell up and purple, then allowing more blood circulation into the front of the tongue requires a touch that does not loosen the Clamp so much it can be slipped off, or wiggled off tugging back against the O-Ring.

The more appreciative Cosmos Lobelia appreciate that whoever twists the clamp tight knows how to squeeze the clamp tight, but not too tight. The advantage of a tighter grip, especially for the neophytes, is the safety factor, so that their natural tendency to yank their tongue back or fester worm it off is obfuscated. Just how tight to adjust the clamps is an artful balance, and if their Superiors knows anything, they know how to make art.

At some point during their transit each Cosmos Lobelia is face stripped, so that the end of their clamped tongue may be rubbed against nipples, clits, cock heads, tongues, and whatever else the hands of transport might provide.

The Tongue Clamps can be painful, and Lobelia who beg removal understand they beg to lick cunts through the O-Ring and cocks inside the O-Ring; and that they will most certainly be throated, fed cum, and be allowed to swallow.

And of course the open center hole welcomes the introduction of fluids; the more pliant Lobelia already beg to be poured with laxatives, diuretics, purgatories, aphrodisiacs, and whatever other substances that their admirers suggest they beg, such as a squirt bottle fill with urine for the Piss Mouth beggars, or a squirt bottle filled with semen for all of them.

Seven helpless pulled-out tongues also present a delightful temptation no Player can resist; and a bit of honey garnished with radish swabbed on helps the Lobelia to drool and cream more than necessary. Masturbating the Cosmos Lobelia and collecting their cream reinforces their notion they have no control over their bodies, and lulls them into surrender and sub-space.

Which is where the Fate of the Game has bestowed them.

They shall be conditioned to appreciate any attention bestowed upon them, and beg for sexual surrender and release.

But Tongue Clamps hurt more the longer they're worn, and although they block any cocks wishing to penetrate the Ring Gags, various Lobelia have different motives for wanting the Clamps removed, pain reduction being one of them. Control of the mouth is another, although this is a misconception; Lockdown Lobelia don't control anything.

§ Babs: Arrives Boob Bounded & Suspended w/Molly

As Babs comes to her senses she discovers that when she tries to move that she cannot: her arms are tightly secured behind her back, wrists connected to opposing elbows, forearms parallel and strapped in leather, and fingers folded into fists inside mittens. BB can also feel that her crotch is open so that her shaven box and bunghole are prominently displayed. *And available.*

Yes, this blind-deaf-mute, bare-bald-naked Lobelia hangs from the rail by two tightly bound breasts. Rope so tight it cannot slip off BB's grossly swollen breasts, and suspending BB high enough in the air that her feet have no chance of touching the floor..

Painful, yes, but more painful if one struggles. Babs slowly figures out that her 37D cannelured breasts are bound together and hanging from a rope connected to something moving above her. This assumption is correct; what she doesn't see is that the rope connects to a trolly that rides on a rail overhead. The overhead rail traverses the vast expanse of the abandoned Meatpacking Plant; Babs hangs suspended from a trolly that switches through turnouts onto a siding in a large room.

Babs senses her momentum as her body swings in the air, hanging from only her breasts. BB can feel that her ankles are crossed and lashed together, and a spreader bar with a pushy spring forces her knees apart, so that her recently shaven crotch stays spread. Besides the obvious stress on her bound boobs, the littlest bit of swing also makes BB's Tongue Clamp rub against her O-Ring Gag, and enables BB to experience competing stimulus of pain.

Babs still feels the sensation of the speculum Pear inside her burse, *with its stem leaking brodeas and its leaf tickling my buzzer button.* But the Pear is gone now, and BB almost misses its soothing valiva production, almost missises the restless Snake once inside her buggery; and she still senses the presence of the Cath inside her pee hole. In fact, all of these Props are removed during her transit; if in the past they provided an excuse to avoid responsibility, BB comes to the realization that *I'll still cream when they want me to,* and *until I can get the Cath back, I'm going to have to manage my own pee.*

And, *now that my bonker and borehole are empty, I am going to fuck and be analed.*

Well not exactly. *I am going to beg to be fucked, beg to be analed, cam DP all variations, tag A2M, the works. In public, on Cam, archived in Automatron. Then Gamers are going to rent me out, over and over again. Whore me. And why not, I'm already begging to be a Dong and Dirty "cocksucking cunt-fucking ass-to-mouth Whore." And if I have to give up more, just tell me.*

Babs had felt a change in air as she was transported from the inside of a truck across a loading dock, and then down corridors, through double swinging doors, until,

Babs feels herself come to a rest. She feels her hanging body overshoot the stopping point, swing backwards, and dampen to a rest. The pain in both breasts is real, the cinch is very tight, but neither the cinch nor BB's breasts are about to slip or fall off.

Babs feels herself slowly lowered until she can feel her feet touch the floor. BB's toe tips actually, and she struggles to push upward and relieve some of the burden of her full weight on her breasts.

The crack of a paddle across both buttocks is totally unprepared for, and propels BB forward, swinging helplessly forward, buttocks smarting with pain, already duel welts from the stroke....

Swinging backwards and just at the end of the swing..., another crack of the paddle, and a large purple splotch from cheek to cheek that is lower than the roundness that pops up, a testament to the depth of the compression of the paddle.

Possibly white oak, 18 inches long 4 inches wide, half inch thick. Babs bounces, helplessly swinging in the air, anticipating a third stroke which doesn't happen, buttocks on fire, breasts on fire, now breaking her swing with her feet only to discover she is stepping in her own urine, wet also spraying her inner thighs and bound, feet. Stabilizing herself, only to bend her knees and fly again as her suspending bound breasts are flogged. More urine releases.

Babs tries to control her panting. Tears form inside her Eyepods and are collected. Babs never anticipated tear production, but the burning welts on her butt recall a fear Janet once instilled in her: *I must learn to identify the paddles used on me by the kind of wood..* Might BB be thinking clearly she might also consider who might control the contents of her Collection Dish and piss donations.

Babs discovers that the spreader bar is actually fairly springy, and when she brings her knees together she is able to provide lift not only with her tip toes, but also the balls of her feet, although even with stretching, BB's heel still flies above ground.

But when she relaxes her tension the spring pushes her knees wide again, her feet off the ground, and her pussy splayed.

§ Babs & Molly: Guilt & Acceptance of Punishment

Babs' vision and sound return and she gets her first glimpse of her environs. What she sees and hears shocks her.

BB's first processing cycles react upon seeing Molly. And discovers more about her own suspension. *I really am hanging by my bound bazooms, Molly is also hanging by her bound mams, and she weighs more than I do. But that said, the two of us are balanced on a beam, so that we can actually bounce back and forth. This is cruel, because it makes us be cruel to each other.*

A hovering Cam looks directly into Babs' eyes and sees abject helplessness and surrender. *Maybe I deserve to be treated like this, but Molly doesn't.*

Babs' feet float off the floor, and she rotates a bit as the rope above her head lifts her upward. BB tilts her head down and gets a panorama view of the old Meatpacking Plant, with a rail system that snakes overhead through a mazes of switches and sidings, some conveniently located above the various "furniture" that abounds in the Plant. BB understands. *Except now I'm the meat being transported around. Fresh meat,* BB accepts. *I deserve it, I failed, I need to be grateful to be a Whore. I am grateful. Any hole, all my holes, anywhere anytime, outcall, brothel, cam me.*

Babs catches a glimpse of a row of Eight Naked Men. All are collared, and with their wrists crossed and fastened to the back of the collar, and each of their cocks and balls are tightly secured in a clamp fitted tightly behind the testicles and around the penis; this clamp itself is rigidly fitted to a short pole rising up from and secured to the floor. There is no way for these otherwise Naked Men to move absent castration and penis severance. Or possessing the key that fits in the lock.

And there is no way for them to defend themselves against getting their armpits shaven, their nipples clamped, or their buttholes buggered. All cocks are positioned so that each Naked Man is forced to keep their feet widely spread, or adopt a bended knee posture. But the cock and balls do not move from their appointed position. But the most painful of all is when the cocks, already driven to painful erections, get sucked and pumped by a guy or a gal until the Eight Naked men scream in pain and ejaculation.

Babs has no way to recognize that she just glanced at the Rachmaninoffs; they had always been masked with their sticks. Now Gamers are amused by their Fate.

There is a stack of cages with packed human flesh, heads and hands secured in the walls so that only bent-over torsos and hindquarters are displayed in this Room. A fire burns at one end, and Babs imagines a red-hot branding iron among the coals.

Then a fleeting glance as she twists on her suspension, of another Lineup of five naked men, these all flat on their backs on the floor, spread-eagle, side-by-side, all with extreme erections rising up from their bodies. Babs has no reason to identify them as the Risen Cocks Lineup, and never considers they might be on a time-release of an erectile drug, had their penises injected with prostaglandin, or electrically stimulated.

As Babs loses sight of this Risen Cocks Lineup she carries away the impression that some of the cocks are prefaced with kneeling naked cocksuckers, buttocks up, knees wide, and pussies offering up for fucking.

Maybe some assholes too, because one of them is connected to the overhead rail trolly by an Ass Hook. And two more look buttplugged. Five pussies plus two assholes for sale or rent.

BB tries to put names on five buttocks, as the Lineup of Risen Cocks and their fellatrix rotates out of sight. Babs fails to identify that two of the cocksuckers are former Nuggets, Hottie and Odee, and that both have plugs in their rectums, lest they be mistaken as anal Whores, and not simply Strippers who Opted Whore and are offering their pussies to fuck. These two ex-Strippers and now rookie Whores have much to learn about giving caresses, talking dirty, jerking off cocks, sucking them, and fucking them in positions that both are natural, as well positions designed to provide excellent cam angles for every Whore's obligatory *Porn Videos*.

Babs catches her breath and reconstructs her memory; the *cocksucker in the middle of the Risen Cocks Lineup is Cosmos Lobelia Tiffany!*

And how do I know that? Because Tiffany is suspended from the trolly overhead just like I am, except she's balanced with a cock in her mouth, her knees spread wide, her vertical trench oozing tapioca, and her tush held high by a Hook sunk inside her asshole.

Babs watches. *Tiffany actually sucks cock, has cock in her mouth, cock on her lips, cocks rub on her face and cheeks.* Babs is aware, *that could be me there*, and this contributes to Babs' displacement.

But Babs is smarter than this. *Gamers are doing this to suggest to me that I could be next. That I am next. And not just my mouth, probably Gamers are going to bang my box and bugger my back hole. Certainly every one of my holes, two at once, all at once, I'm a Dong and Dirty Whore now.*

And I know what it's like when my rectum and vagina and pee hole are taken away from me. Gamers have already prepared me.

I deserve to be a Whore, and if it weren't for me, Kimju would be a Monitor and not be Whore, and MomCap the rest of my Pledge would not all be Strippers next Term. None deserve their Fate.

The twist in the rope produces an overshoot, pain in the breasts as Babs' naked hanging body comes to a rest, pain in her breasts as it settles. She has sparks in her two paddle marks in her buttocks, and residual pain from her nose ring and navel treatment.

Babs tries to put out of her mind a memory of outer flanking pair, left and right of Tiffany in the Risen Cocks Lineup, yet both blocked from her view by men penetrating either their vaginas or rectums from behind.

Gamers (and also Tiffany) know that the two cocksucking, double penetrating Whores on outside opposite sides of Tiffany are Penny and Coco. Both spunk repositories hold a special grudge against Janet and Babs, for defeating them in the Mudwrestling Contest, and then later insisting that they become the Dong and Dirty Whores they have become.

Both agree. *We know who put us here! Janet and Babs did! And Robyn. And Steph.*

It's a short list, and little do the triple-cocked Penny and Coco know that they will be enabled to act out some of their retribution.

Babs comes to rest facing Game Mistress. Babs knows she should lower her eyes and look down to the floor. She sees shiny black, thigh-high boots with pointed toes and stiletto heels; as her eyes tilt upward opera-length gloves bearing sharp fingertips come into view, and BB's eyes follow the gloves as they ascend to GM's armpits, except in practice the gloves vanish beneath a cape which crosses in the front of GM's body, obscuring any Garments beneath, and with a hat that covers her head.

GM flashes her talisman mounted on her navel piercing and the tattoo around it.

Babs might have seen or heard about GM's intimacies, but right now she shall not be drafted to service them. BB observes that the fingertips of GM's gloves aren't just sharp, they are claws, and that the Swagger Goad she carries has a shape-shifting end.

The suspension stretches BB's bound boobs upward, but BB can only watch as GM squeezes on BB's engorged breasts and rolls BB's nipple between a finger and thumb. Babs hold her breath; BB's nipples still ache from clamps earlier, still bear stripes from her recent flogging, and the ropes around her breasts keep them inflated into bulbs, dilating the areolas and concentrating the nipples. The rope behind the bulbs is much smaller than the bulging purple breasts, and has no chance of slipping off. And so Babs hangs, with her toes only sometimes touching the ground.

It is an unpleasant situation to find oneself in.

BB watches as GM slides her Goad on top of her nipple, and synchronizes her pain with the arc of the spark. Reality check.

No holding back when GM shocks the piss out of you.

GM ignores BB's tinkle and says to her, "Hello Whore, welcome to the *Play Party* and to your last hours of Lockdown."

GM continues. "Between now and Midnight are you a Lockdown Lobelia begging to be bound, beaten and buggered? Is that correct?"

BB flusters at this question, wonders why her breasts have not fallen off, and agrees, *yes,* "Aaha-aaha."

"And after Midnight you're begging to be a 'blowing banging buggering Whore? Dong and Dirty type, no holes bared?"

Bondo Babe's breasts have turned purple as she swings with her feet in the air; she agrees. "Aaha-aaha."

"You'll clean any cock no matter where it has been? Eat any pussy no matter how filled with jizz? Felch creampied assholes? You a gokkun Whore?"

BB feels urgency to agree, "Aaha-aaha. Aaha-aaha."

"You Blowho Bangho Buttho," GM pronounces, "I like you.

GM gently rotates BB until the helplessly hanging ex-Monitor points toward Molly. "Look at Molly," GM opens, "bare-bald-naked, hanging by her pendulant mammies, bouncing up and down with you on this hanging see-saw beam. She's blind-deaf-mute and will stay that way. Tell me, Whore, are you responsible for Molly's discomfort?"

Babs groans. She feels the tip of the Goad grace the bottom of her chin; there is no electrical charge, just soft vibration. BB agrees. "Aaha-aaha."

"So there is no reason Molly should not have her feet on the floor when you can be flying, right?"

Babs must agree. "Aaha-aaha." *I know I'm responsible; you don't need to force me to confess!*

And watches as the balance shifts until Molly's feet rest on the floor, and the uplift tension come off of Molly's breast bondage.

And feel herself rise until again, just her tip toes grace the floor and the bulk of her weight hangs from her bound breasts.

Babs watches as her Eyepods fade to black, the Earpods become silent, and strangers' hands fondle her bare-bald naked body. BB feels her face touched, her nipples and now-painful and swollen breasts squeezed, her thighs caressed, her feet prodded, her buttocks rubbed, and most intimately, her clit masturbated, her vagina finger-dipped, and her butthole probed.

When hands want BB to hang sloppy wet, Babs blurts thick burgoo.

Babs discovers that one of her mittens has been disengaged and a cock has been placed in her fist. She barely starts stroking it when it discharges in her hand. Babs reacts but doesn't go anywhere. *This is disgusting. I can't even wipe the cum off. I hurt. I'm in pain. I'm hanging helpless and every swing is painful. If they demand I beg double studs just like Kimju, I am their Whore. I need to suffer that pain too. In my tongue, in my nipples, in my clithood.*

Another cock presents itself into her now sticky hand. It too will erupt and, not caring to count, Babs soon accumulates a mess of gooness.

Babs has a nagging dilemma that frequently returns. *I believed what Janet told me, and begged anal and DP, so I've already begged to be a Dirty Whore, but, if what she told me about Steph is not true, I would only need to be an ordinary Whore. Which is scary enough. So I had to beg Dong and Dirty before any* Video *comes out, or before Steph confesses, else I'd be guilty of withholding information and for sure Gamers would pierce my tongue. Except I am already begging to take on all of Kimju's Karma, which means I'm already scheduled for a double tongue.*

Gamers are going to enlarge the ring in my nose, sew my lips and tongue together, and tattoo a picture of me double penetrated on my forehead. And I'm going to beg them to do this.

Alas. So by the grace of touch, GM parks Babs in the Zone.

§ Kimju: Arrives at the Play Party • Tattoos & Piercings

Blind-deaf-mute, bare-bald-naked Kimju comes to her senses to discover herself floating in air; she is, in fact, suspended and secured in a Love Swing that hangs from a trolly traveling on the overhead meat rail. The Swing keeps Kimju's body horizontal and on her back, her ankles are secured to her thighs so her legs stay spread, and her bare shaven kypsey and keelspout offers convenient horizontal entry for any lifted erection. Kimju's arms are folded behind her head so that her cupped armpits face upward. Kimju's head and gagged mouth hangs helplessly downward, braced somewhat at the neck by her folded and mittened and connected hands. Might Kimju see the Plant she would see it upside down, but she sees and hear nothing.

Kimju tries to remember *if I have begged my bowels away?* And concludes that *my begging to Opt Whore included no commitment to anal, no Dong and Dirty for me.*

There is evidence from when Kimju last stripped at the Nugget that she had allowed not only her kunny to be fingered, but her kawazoo to be toyed with. So it had been only fitting that during *The Runout* Kimju had been pleasured with the Pogo in her kunny and the Centipede inside her kawazoo at the same time.

Kimju retains vivid memories from this experience. *I lost all control of my body. I creamed, I climaxed, they told me what to beg and I begged it. I remember nothing but pure sensation, pure energy. Even now, even with it gone, I still feel the Pogo inside my kunny, and I still feel the Centipede crawling up and down my rectum. 100 tiny pairs of leg.*

Kimju accepts, *I am going to get fucked in my kunny today. Fucked in my mouth. Okay, I begged for that, but I worry that if my keelspout still gapes from the Centipede's ravages, what are the chances that a cock will find its way in there?*

One hundred percent? Or by accident, perhaps?

And were it not for the Clamp holding Kimju's Tongue out in front of her O-Ring Gag, Kimju knows, *my mouth would be at perfect dick sucking height. And if not, simply hoist me up and down.*

Players have made sure I know I'm helpless because I've already felt dicks rub up against the end of my pierced and clamped tongue. I almost want the relief of them taking the Tongue Clamp off but I know if they do, more like, when they do, they will find some cocks that fit through the O-Ring, cocks that want double stud oral pleasures. Then they lift up my head a little bit more, and throat me. Straight in until I gag up phlegm and it runs across my face and into a bowel. Gasping for air. Then again until my stomach is purged. I'll be totally in their hands, and covered with puke.

Better for them is to let me use my tongue inside my mouth and work on their heads and rims, and after they cum dump me I'll swallow their jizz, even if I have to push it uphill with my tongue.

And yes, of course I know they will fuck me, but however big or small, long or short, cut or uncut, whatever color; cocks in my kooter don't threaten to suffocate me and make me pass out. That should be against the Rules in a place where Rules no longer apply.

How astute. Kimju's head is laid backward and hangs down so that drool from her O-Ring Gag and Tongue Clamp run down her upside-down cheeks, across her Eyepods (very irritating), across where her eyebrow once were, and across her forehead, before it drips down from the center of her bald head, and, after she comes to a rest, drips onto the floor.

Kimju's view of the world, might she have one (which she does not at this time), would be upside down. In practice, Kimju's Eyepods are totally capable of flipping her view of the world, however, as her trolly follows its rail and transports her through the Meatpacking Plant, and she enters the main Play Party room, what fades up into Kimju's vision is not a view out her own eyes, but a view of her own body, seen from one of the hovering Cams, and in real time.

Kimju recoils at this intrusion, and watches herself jerk and then feels herself as she swings in her Love Swing. Kimju discovers a sensation she can't identify as she watches herself with her out-of-body eyes. *I'm hanging almost horizontal, my wrists are secured behind my head, my armpits are venerable, my legs are spread, my kypsey is offered for fuck, and my asshole doesn't need stretched. Players are going to take off my tongue clamp, put my double-pierced tongue to work, and throat me.*

Okay, you are succeeding in spooking me. I'm a Lockdown Lobelia and Gamers really do intend to make me a Whore.

Gamers raise the crazy. The hovering Cam commences a tour of Kimju's body, honing in Kimju's belly button as she becomes a witness to a narrated presentation of her bodyart.

Except the narrator that Kimju now hears in her Earpods is Kimju herself, speaking to the audience of the Cam! "I got my first tattoo the first time I Stripped, and it hid in my belly button; it was a sign for the asteroid Pallas. Now I beg you to ink the entire solar system all over my body, and that's just because none of any new planets counts as a new tattoo."

Kimju recognizes her own voice, and then, *did I say that?*

Kimju watches as the Cam hovers in between her legs, sees a gloved hand reach into the frame, feels and watches it pull pink and tug on the ring in her clit. Kimju's clithood ring sparkles, and once again Kimju hears herself narrate, "I also earned my first piercing during my first Term dancing the Nugget. Then, during *The Runout,* I earned a stretch of my clithood ring from 14 to 12 gauge and the rights to a vertical bar behind the ring.

"It's respectful I visit the Nugget carrying more weight than I departed with.

"But I am not moving to the Nugget, because I'm not really Stripping next Term, I'm Opting Whore and I'm moving to Flesh Ranch. So instead of just looking at my kunny, you can stick your dick inside me. I will suck you before and after you fuck me, you can facial or creampie me, feed me, and I'll swallow."

Kimju listens to her voice and wonders, *how much of what I'm hearing is really me, now that I really am cast to Opt Whore?*

The Drone Cam returns to focus on Kimju's pierced and tattooed belly button. Again, Kimju's faux voice speaks for her. "I failed to report Robyn's escape and gave her additional head start. I'm not like all the other Cosmos Lobelia begging to Strip, all marked with their pierced navels. I'm an accessory to Robyn's misbehavior. My navel piercing is my second piercing, and I am due for one piercing more; I'm a Whore. So in addition to my planets, I'm getting tatted around my knockers, navel, and knapsack."

Kimju hears her faux voice give a faux laugh, then continue. "And because I'm a Double Opt Down, I'm begging doubles of everything. Double clithood, double navel, double nose, double tongue.

Kimju watches as the Drone Cam surveys her head and topless torso, lingers closer to her distorted, Ring-Gagged face, and provides Kimju her best visualization of her side-to-side nose stud and hanging U-bolt, with swivels in between the septum and the two outer sides of Kimju's nose.

Kimju can assess the Cam's careful study and again hears herself narrate. "My nose piercing is for securing me; it is necessary to ensure none of us Cosmos Lobelia try to emulate Robyn Runaway's failure."

The Drone Cam lingers on Kimju's clamped and pierced Tongue and O-Ring Gag, and again Kimju hears herself narrate. "I know my nose stud doesn't add to my piercing count; and I know that if sometime my Tongue Clamp come off, that my double tongue piercings are here to stay. They shouldn't count either, because I need to remember that 'if I see something say something.'"

It riles Kimju to hear herself describe herself when in fact her tongue feels constant dull pain. "My stretched clithood piercing and my double navel count for one piercing each, but a Whore gets three, so, for my third piercing, I'm begging double nipple studs, one vertical barbell through each nipple, and one horizontal barbell behind it, a tremendous invitation to command and control me."

Kimju watches herself in her Eyepods as the hovering Cam surveils her tattoos, and pans around her naked body in sync with her narration. "As for my planets and rings: my planets will continue to multiply on my naked body. My rings are my second tattoo; they are the colorful concentric circles of ink around my belly button, crawling off my areolas and down my knockers, and radiating outward from my kunny and kawazoo. They have merged and spread to cover part of my keister and inner thighs. And the colored circles around my areola shall descend to totally encircle my knockers. And my areolas are already inked. Bright pink with florescent orange nipples."

The real naked-suspended Kimju struggles with her oral narration and the intimate closeups of her body. *A bot, an AI personifying me? Of course, something like that. It doesn't matter. It is what it is.*

"Please let the circles of color radiate from my knockers out over my chest and my arms, and the rings around my kootch and kawazoo creep up my butt krack, collide with the rings radiating outward from my button, and then merge and grow until I am totally covered in ink, from my neck to the tips of my toes. Please ink me until I have a full body suit and then ink me some more."

"And for my third tattoo put a tiny head of a penis somewhere on my face, so I am tagged as a Whore."

This self-proclamation disturbs Kimju, and amplifies the disconnection of hearing herself speak to Gamers, while seeing herself from displaced eyes. Beads of sweat pop out on her chest, inside her armpits too. *I am going to beg they tattoo all the planets on me. That's easy. I am going to beg they fuck me. That's not easy. But Slavesex is not an option for me. I am unable to take my eyes away from watching myself. And the things I am saying aren't entirely true, although whatever words Gamers put in my mouth I will have to live with.*

Except I did beg to Whore and I am going to be fucked. I am going to be tagged in the media and marked on my face.

Kimju also worries about *my faux voice making statements I might have to live with.*

Again she hears her voice! "It's not enough for Gamers to parade me around by my tongue, or the ring in my nose, or my navel bar, or my clithood ring. They know I will follow their lead. And I know that every cock out there is going to want my dick-sucking lips and double pierced tongue working them over, from their sweaty armpits and tender nipples to their assholes and balls and rim jobs and shaft sucking, and cock down my throat. Every pussy is going to want licked, sucked, and eaten out."

The Hovering Cam has backed away enough to capture Kimju's full naked body folded into the Swing. "I'm a Whore now, and getting my kunny fucked and pleasing you is my goal in life. I need to be double penetrated, mouth and kunny, and I need to Double Opt Down for Double Terms."

Kimju hears laughter in the Earpods. She senses her vagina is being violated, but isn't sure what she feels. What she sees in her Eyepods is her own face, hunted down by the hovering Drone Cam directly in front of her, looking right through her Eyepods into her wild eyes, eyes that see the Drone's view of herself.

And a horribly contorted face with a mouth held open just as wide as possible by a tightly-held-in-place O-Ring Gag behind the teeth.

Kimju constructs and pumps thick kloop out of her koot. Something inside her gape tickles her but all she can do is pant and construct more. *I am losing my mind.*

I need to beg Gamers to tattoo a mole near my mouth, I know it will be called an "indicator" and that I'm a cocksucking, pussy-eating, cock fucking, creampie and facial Whore.

\ But as long as Kimju is Ring Gagged and Tongue Clamped Kimju isn't begging much of anything. Sometimes Gags have advantages.

Game Mistress draws the Goad across Kimju's protruding and hanging tongue; Kimju's Eyepods present her the stereo closeup of her pierced and clamped tongue, as gloved hands pull on the rods to test it is taunt. Kimju hears a voice in her Earpods that she associates with the gloved hands. "You lucky Whore," the Voice states, and Kimju feels the glove rub the side of her cheek. It feels like sandpaper or steel wool. "We heard you speak, and you heard yourself too, yes?"

Kimju imagines she feels the faintest tickle of electricity run through her body; the statement is true enough, but what next?"

Kimju grunts twice, "Aaha-aaha." *I know what's next.*

"Everything you said in your faux voice you stand by as true?"

Kimju takes a deep breath, *I know what the answer has to be, so there is no need to delay.* Kimju grunts twice, "Aaha-aaha."

"You're begging to Double Opt Down and Whore next Two Terms, starting at Midnight?" the Voice can phrase this many ways but it is still a question.

And Kimju grunts twice, "Aaha-aaha."

"Good," the Voice speaks. "You are going to get to see your former Roommate again today, the one you once called Robyn."

"But she won't see you."

Kimju correctly assumes the voice and hand belong to Game Mistress, and if not, still a Player of Upper Caste. Now she watches as claws on the ends of the gloves test her nipple for sensitivity. Kimju flinches, and watches her pain from the outside looking in.

GM drawls, "Your ex-Roommate enjoyed watching you get your tongue pierced in the Amphitheater. That rancid rattlebrain climaxed on your pain."

Kimju should consider herself lucky that her Ring Gag makes her snarl imperceptible. *I can't stop what Robyn is doing to me. She's the source of my new planets, my radiant circles of colored ink, my new stainless. The double-hole barbell in my button, the U-bolt hanging out my nose, and my double-pierced tongue, and the stretched stainless ring in my clithood, likely to be doubled soon.*

So that's a positive thing. I know that next I will beg them to double pierce my nipples. I have to do what I'm told now.

The tongue piercings still hurt, so too does Kimju's tongue, nose, navel, and her stretched clithood. *Everything hurts, I'm immobilized, I'm positioned to suck and be fucked, oozing kloop out my kunt, and gaping my keelport. I'm a Whore now. I said it out loud.*

And Robyn is the reason that instead of Opting Monitor, I'm Opting Whore.

Too bad indeed. Kimju oscillates between being very grateful and very resentful. *Game Mistress is a sadist. If I had not begged to Whore the Gamers would have secreted Robyn away and made me take the Slavesex drop. She probably never even escaped; they just spirited her away somehow. I had no choice. I had to plead guilty, and if I didn't beg Whore, they would have vanished Robyn and broken me to Slavesex. I was powerless to stop them.*

Maybe I got tricked into thinking what I did was a Whore offense, so I jumped the gun with my begging. But it really doesn't matter. This is not all that complex, all I need to do is do what I need to do to avoid Slavesex, so I'm a Whore now. And besides, I like the tattoos and the piercings. They help make me stand out. And if I see something, I'll say something. And I can handle the fondling, I have before. And I can handle the fingers too, and sometimes I let them inside me. No dirty fingernails. So for sure I can handle cocks, in my mouth or in my koot.

But I'll never beg Slavesex!

Pain continues to throb in Kimju's tongue, nose, belly button, and clithood. Kimju keeps a thought, *doubles in my nipples are next.*

Kimju steadies herself, and moves with extreme caution. *Just because I want to take on more ink and am paying for it with pain and steel, doesn't mean I should be taking on pain solo. Robyn is the Player who should be getting a surgical overhaul. I hope GM enlarges her breasts to the size of melons, injects her with hormones that make her body grow thick hair, and mates her with bonobos.*

And Bondo Bangbox needs to beg to be a Whore-for-Life and get a mole tattooed on her cheek. A little penis head to one side of her lips and a vestibule on the other side. She failed.

The hovering Cam that has been observing Kimju has settled into a position between Kimju's spread legs and framing her gaping vagina. Kimju wants to reject the vision, twitches her pelvis, constricts, and watches as a big blob of kloop forces its way out between her inner labia.

Again, Kimju wants the view to change, but the next constriction, and the constriction after that, are not constrictions that Kimju destined, nor are they constrictions that Kimju is able to stop.

Yes, yes Kimju has a Collection Dish; all Lobelia do.

§ Tiffany: Considers Benefits from Robyn's Escape

Of all Cosmos who participate in Lockdown perhaps only Tiffany remotely understands the perils of long-term bondage; once when she had misbehaved as a Whore, Tiffany lived with a cock in her mouth. She went into subspace before the end of the first day, and stayed there 24x7. All the while she let her pussy be taken.

Tiffany remains rightfully nervous about the end of the Term. *I am ready, willing, and able to Strip next Term and I am grateful to Robyn, in a perverse way, for assuring me a path to the Nugget. I've been a Stripper before, and alone among the Cosmos, I've been a Whore before. I have a* Porn Star Calendar! *But Lockdown presents new concerns because Lockdown doesn't have Rules.*

I could end up losing my asshole over this, and that is not something I desire. I'm happy to suck, I'm happy to fuck, but no catheter, no enemas, no strapons or Double Dongs back there, and definitely no cocks.

I know what I am in my soul and I have been there before and I want to be there again. I am a Porn Star! Many, many Gamers collect my Tiny Tits Tight Twisting Twat Videos, my bukkake and gokkun contests, and my girl-girl work.

And right now I can get bondage fucked while I'm a Lockdown Lobelia, but once I'm a Stripper I won't be allowed to do any sexing. None, ninguno, nichts, niente, nic. nenhum, nici unul, nashi!

The good news is that Janet and I are old Roommates, and in the past, I helped her Opt Up and she helped me Opt Down. She knows I can take balls into my mouth without hurting them. I give a fantastic rimjob, and I am a blowjob artist. I can take cock all the way down my throat, and swallow the cum. Empty a pint in a gokkun contest.

Janet, assuming she really will be my House Mom, will let me claim that cocksucking isn't sex, and besides, she will for sure order me to eat her, and piss in my mouth. She will help me Opt Whore at the end of the Term, and I will help her however I can.

Right now, I need to fuck while I have the chance between now and Midnight, thanks to Robyn. I need to make new Porn.

Tiffany considers, *What I really need to shoot is a bondage gangbang. It's about the only thing I've never done.* Tiffany ponders. *I'm not keen on being subjected to bondage and discipline, but my fans will love me. And it will only be for a few hours, not Six Terms, like what Slavesex Robyn faces.*

Well, be careful, the Clock is still stopped and hours don't exist.

Tiffany shifts focus and fixates on the idea of *trading my current Opt-Strip commitment with Babs, or with Kimju, both are committed to Opt Whore next Term. I will pretty much do anything to get an offer to trade get accepted.*

Well, not anything.

But I am in Lockdown, so put me in the stocks on the Quad and leave me overnight. Tie me up 10 different ways and double penetrate my mouth and twat. Stake me out spread-eagle in the middle of a field and tell the Rachmaninoffs where to find me, sex me, and paint me. Upload all the Videos.

You can bondage-fuck me right now, only because I'm a Lockdown Lobelia. I have no rights. I'm like a Slavesex except it's not for many Term, it's only until Midnight arrives.

But you can't bondage-fuck me if I'm a Stripper or a Whore.

Tiffany comes to her senses. *The problem is that once Gamers get a taste of me tied up and bondage fucked, they will just want more. But if more is what I have to give up to trade places, maybe I will.*

And maybe more means bigger Porn Star. Expediency matters.

More can mean expanding the vocabulary of sexual practices, inviting more bodyart, begging Obeisances?

Tiffany senses that both Kimju and Beka are headed for full body suits. And Elle will do what is necessary to stay connected with Beka. Tiffany's own bodyart, especially her remotely controlled Eraser Heads, the stainless steel stims implanted inside her nipples, complete with their wireless AI and Running Agent, count for all three of Tiffany's Whore piercings. The Eraser Heads have the ability to not only stand up Tiffany's tips, but make her crave their touch, and torque her twister.

It was then that Tiffany had also gotten her nipples and areolas tattooed; it had been a particularly painful experience, and having been set in ultraviolet inks, Players can only see them in ultraviolet light, although some Players claim they can see them glisten in bright sunlight. They count as one of the three tattoos which qualified Tiffany during her Term at Flesh Ranch.

Tiffany's second tattoo is an invisible ultraviolet ink tramp stamp that descends down her posterior rugage between her two tushies with the aplomb of a sitar cascading down the scale, quieting as the ink encircles her asshole. It had been part of Tiffany's act when she Feature Danced at the Nugget to hold a small flashlight in her vagina, one which had an ultraviolet radiation, and let a Patron extract the light, illuminate her tail tube, and cam everything from a closeup, to a two-shot of Tiffany's tush and the Patron's smiling face.

Tiffany's third tattoo lies inside her mouth; Tiffany knows what is there: the word "Porn Star" written reversed so that Tiffany can pull her lower lips down and read herself in the mirror. The tattoo comforts Tiffany, *because I can see what I am. But I aspire to proclaim myself to the world, so I want Gamers to tattoo me inside my upper lip so that I can lift my lip up and everybody can read what I am directly. It can count as the same Tattoo, so it needn't add to my count.*

Like the other Cosmos Lobelia, Tiffany was nose-ringed during *The Runout* and chained to her Post on the Henge. The nose ring doesn't increment Tiffany's piercing count, nor does Count seem to matter when her navel is pierced and she is decorated with a creature-stud and some ink. Tiffany remains unaware that Steph was climaxed watching her collect the pain and the adornment.

Tiffany knows who gets the credit: *Robyn Runaway. And sleepy Bang Babe. And Kimju's oversight gave Gamers an excuse to Whore her. I'm more skilled than she is and I have experience.*

I remain a Porn Star! And I remain committed to shooting again! Whoring again, even if I have to Strip for a Term at the Nugget, take marks. Except....,.

This time if I want to get back I may have to surrender my ass.

Tiffany doesn't know when or how she arrived in the Meatpacking Plant, only that she crawled in on her elbows and knees with her nose sweeping the floor. Tiffany's tailpipe has been fitted with an Ass Hook connected to a line leading upward to a trolly slowly progressing along the overhead rail, slightly ahead of Tiffany, encouraging her forward, and definitely ensuring that her round tush stays pointed upward and her unobstructed vertical shaven trench is wet between the center line of Tiffany's sex lips. Tiffany is still blind-deaf-mute, bare-bald-naked; Tiffany knows her tossaroon leaks and anticipates *it will be sold, or I might be a Free Party Fuck. It doesn't matter to me. I just want to get screwed, and I know I will get cammed.*

Tiffany has no way to know that one difference between her and the other Lockdown Lobelia is that her Tongue Clamp has been removed, although her full-size O-Ring Gag remains. She drools.

Tiffany is lead to a row of naked men, all of them on their back, mounted on platforms that can be raised and lowered. All of the naked men are secured spreadeagle, all of them are totally bodily shaven, all are viciously gagged, and all present sensitive erections that rise upward. They comprise the Risen Cocks Lineup.

Gloved hands grasp Tiffany by her ears, turn her head, position her over the center erection, and lowers her Hole-Gagged mouth over 200 plus cubic centimeters of hard meat. Tiffany's tailor-fitted Gag holds her mouth as wide open as possible, and Tiffany has little choice but to allow her head to lower, or be lowered as it may be, until at about the point the tip of the penis tickles Tiffany's throat while her lips press against the pelvis of the man, the erection totally contained in her mouth.

Tiffany feels pressure to widen her knees apart and does so until most of her weight is suspended by the hook into her rectum.

Tiffany knows that the inner trap doors of her shaven taco push outward and ooze tacky. *I'm about to be a DP slippery fuck. Train fucked in my twat, with my mouth sucking dick; but the ass hook isn't human so doesn't count as anal, so maybe I still have a chance to Whore and keep my ass intact. Like the last time.*

Tiffany is not the only cocksucker in this Lineup with her asshole plugged, but she is the only one whose buttocks is forcibly uplifted. Tiffany's Ass Hook stays ensconced in her rectum because the big ball of stainless steel at the end of the Hook seats itself so that the uplift gets applied to Tiffany's body. When she can, Tiffany inches her knees together and takes a bit of pressure of the Hook's upward pull.

Tiffany doesn't know that Babs and Molly hang by their heavy boobs, or that Kimju swings in the air on her back like a bundled up crab, and like herself, is spread and open and ripe. Or if Beka and Elle still harbor the Double Dong. Tiffany doesn't know about Steph's secrets and mis-considers her Fate. But her assumption that Robyn has become Slavesex is correct.

§ Beka & Elle: Double Donged & Compare Tattoos

Beka and Elle arrive at the Play Party sharing a rope suspension. Both Lobelia are blind-deaf-mute, bare-bald-naked, and suspended in harnesses so their bodies float horizontally in the air, so that their butts are touching, their legs are bent back and secured to their torsos, their mittened hands are secured behind their backs, and their heads hang down at cocksucking level (although with their tongues clamped in front of their O-Ring Gags). Might either ever achieve vision again, they would view the world upside down, unless their Eyepods flip their view.

The Roommates' suspension harness provides safe support behind the duo's shoulders, back, and hips; somewhere above two trollies are connected so the two hanging bodies keep two butts pressed together.

And yes, the two rectums are both encolonated by a single very long, very deep, and very physical Double Dong. The Prop can be very flexible, (possibly even organic), it's extremely smart, and it long ago ingratiated itself to both Lobelia. Make no mistake, the Dong does lets them feel each other and pool their spirits, certainly, but the Dong also makes itself desired.

The evidence of the Dong's effectiveness presents itself in the two uplifted, shaven bare pussies. Both erupt with valiva. The uplift of Beka's broda and Elle's nectar has splayed both pair of labia, pooled the vestibule with cream valiva, drenched two uprisen clitoris, and caused both pelvises to quiver.

Yet despite its rich and soothing presence, The Dong ensures that both Beka and Elle shall maintain an insatiable appetite for sex and will exhibit no inhibitions performing it. The Dong doesn't addict everyone, but it has addicted Beka and Elle, and it did addict Penny and Coco. They have already Opted Dong and Dirty Whores to get it back. And Beka and Elle don't want to give it up.

Beka and Elle feel their bodies moving as they are routed through the Meatpacking Plant's complex of overhead rail. The Double Dong they share inside themselves sweetens their arousal as they pass many admirers, until they are finally delivered onto a siding, from which already hangs a breast-bound Babs and Molly balancing on a beam, and Kimju, hanging secured-spread-surrender in a Love Swing. And not far away, Lockdown Whore Tiffany presses her mouth down hard on the center cock in the Risen Cocks Lineup.

As Beka and Elle swing in the air their bodies are, of course, fondled. Both feel their breasts squeezed, their nipples pinched, their butt cheeks pulled apart so the penetration of the Double Dong into the anal sphincters can be cammed, streamed to the Prefecture and spooled by Automatron.

Both feel penises ejaculate onto their feet.

Suddenly each finds themselves on a guided tour of their own and the other's body. The angle, Elle calculates, *is from a hovering Drone, one which rudely documents every pore of my skin.* The observing of herself, in real time, and having no alternative to turn away, disturbs Elle, and magnifies her helplessness. Elle constricts, pumps fresh nectar into her already filled nook, and overflows.

Of course this is broadcast to the Prefecture. Beka, never to be left behind, already sports of pool of brodeas, and the Dong, sensing Elle's overflow, and encourages Beka to construct, and also spill. Their strong scent fills the room, further arouse each other, and encourages a trill of constrictions.

The Drone Cam provides a clear view of Elle's belly and she quickly appraises, *the vine and flowers that grow out of my navel have expanded since I saw myself in the Amphitheater.*

Elle didn't do anything to earn this colorful flourish except be at the right place at the right time. *I suspect that if Gamers want to expand it they will,* Elle considers, and acknowledges, *indeed, they already have.*

Elle seems to cast her Eyepods over Beka's work; Beka's belly tattoo is no meager affair. Giant tongues of fire erupt around Beka's navel and descend all the way down past her sex to encircle her asshole, flames wrap inside her thighs, and torment her posterior rugage and butt crack. Furthermore, the fire that rises above Beka's button reaches up past her breasts for her neck and wraps around her ribs under her armpit.

Since the Amphitheater, Beka has felt the tattoo gun work its way around her belly, and romance her breasts and her pussy. If at first Beka's clit was the focal point for getting saturated with ink, her conditioning has been so successful that Beka cums almost continuously whenever the needle vibrates her body, no matter where it pricks in. Indeed the very sound of a tattoo gun springs her to wetness; Beka so craves her tattoo that she will sacrifice herself totally for its stimulation, and although she doesn't think about it in analytical terms, Beka simply abandons herself, mind, body, and soul. *Please tattoo me ten times over!*

Beka believes *I have begged the largest tattoo of all,* a claim not quite squaring with Kimju's commitment to a "full body suit." Beka takes pride, *I have begged to be tattooed from tit to twat.* Beka had begged when she could still use her tongue and had obtained her Immunity. *I have no regrets. I love my tattoo. I deserve my secret punishment for giving away a Free-Fuck, I deserve as much ink as the Gamers want to put into my body. Today and tomorrow and the next day. I want to be a Stripper and after that I'm going to be a Porn Star! And with Elle along.*

Except Elle and I are no longer equals, Beka considers, *because unlike Elle, with a vine of dainty flowers growing around her navel piercing, and unlike Tiffany, with a sperm swimming up from her button stud, my tattoo wraps around my body like flames on my skin. I'm pretty incredible.*

Beka is incredible, and may not know that Kimju also begs a full body suit, and a lot more piercings than navel and nose rings.

Beka does have one reservation, *I'm afraid of Slavesex but I can't stop getting excited about seeing Elle in Lockdown. I want to watch her get tattooed and bondage gangbanged at the same time! Me too, I want to be gangbang climaxed and tattooed at the same time.*

Elle's tattoo might be smaller than Beka's and she might have a lot of catching up to do when it comes to learning to cum on the buzz of the tattoo needle, but Elle retains affection for her Roommate, even now, hanging in the air with her, butt-to-butt, sharing the Double Dong in their rectums.

We have been through a lot, Elle considers, *and Beka's my best friend.*

The Roommates constrict their rectums around the Double Dong, share electromechanical sensations, and surf into the Zone.

The Gamers keep a close watch on Beka to make sure she doesn't leak any secrets about her own errant behavior; the best way to ensure this has been total isolation. Nor will Beka be talking past her O-Ring Gag and Tongue Clamp. The Gamers shall control messaging; the Game belongs to them, not errant Pledge.

But now as Beka watches herself, she knows she is unable to blink messages, and with her hands folded up inside the mittens and her forearms secured behind her back in an armbinder, Beka will not be using any sign language, skin tracing, or touching to get any message out.

Beka also understands. *I got a ring in my nose because of Robyn Runaway; and I accept responsibility that the hugeness of my belly tattoo is because I Free-Fucked. It's my own Karma.*

For a moment, the snitch in Beka wonders about Rodney – and William – and where might they be at this moment? Beka worries, *I wonder if I'll be fucking Rodney again? In public in front of everyone.* Beka oozes pussy juice. *I hope so. And if Steph fucked William, maybe I'll get to fuck him too.*

Beka must reconcile. *I can't be responsible for whatever fallout might occur might Gamers choose to question Rodney,* Beka declares to herself, *I hope he never finds out I ratted him out.* Beka sighs. *I know I confessed to Free-Fucking and that any Free-Fuck deserves to Whore, except I have my Immunity. And my tattoo.*

Except copping a plea for Immunity does not get me off the hook for Lockdown; Lockdown is because of Robyn, not me. And it provides an opportunity to make more videos beyond the Gonzo *and the* Rodney and Me Fuck Video.

I know that at the Nugget next Term I will be denied all sex, denied sharing the Dong with Elle as well, so that my only opportunity to eat and dong with Elle is until Midnight.

And I am willing to bet that Game Mistress will record me sucking and fucking during Lockdown, and then show the Video *in the Nugget front window. Show me off with a dick in my box before you come in and watch me dance and pink.* Beka clenches her jaw. *Do I care? I do care. I want to cum with a dick in my box; I can be on top or on my back, and if they want to shag me while I suck cock or screw me up the ass, I'm ready willing and able to demonstrate that I can Whore, so that Elle and I can both become Porn Stars after we dance at the Nugget next Term.*

Beka feels horny. She squeezes her vagina, pumps cream, and Gamers watch more of it overflow, and run down to where the Dong gapes both her and Elle's assholes.

Both Eyepods now present the same image to both pair of eyes, and feed their ears low frequency sounds of their bowels constricting around the Dong. It is a closeup of where the Dong penetrates both assholes. Every twitch and tweed of flesh is magnified, closeup, and with two pussies overflowing. Might the Dong want a more animated visual to rock in the Roommates' eyes, all it need do is buzz, or grow warm, or tingle, get fatter, or stretch out, or ripple, but only enough to let the grind keep flowing.

§ Steph: The Seventh to Arrive to the Play Party

Steph arrives at the Play Party much like the others: blind-deaf-mute, bare-bald-naked, and lead by a stud in her nose connected to a trolly above. Her arms are bound behind her back, augmented with mittens, ensuring that Steph will not be wiggling her fingers in the air exploring what she can touch, or trying to talk in sign language. Might a mitten be removed, there is a task ready for a hand.

Steph is very aware she must pay attention to the Game. Steph resents being led by her nose, resents the corporal discipline that accompanies inappropriate slack, and *I resent being paraded while I'm showing stubble! How dare they treat me like this, when I am not really even a Lockdown Lobelia!*

Steph tests her range of motion. The clamp on the nose feels very embedded. *However,* as Steph assesses, *Gamers would never dare to pierce me, an Opt-Monitor.* Steph, confident of her privilege, evaluates how her nose is connected to her leading chain. *What they have done is clamped two oval discs onto my septum. With a swivel hoop that connects to my lead. It squeezes too tight, and it hurts, and I need to tell whoever is in charge of my charade to back off!*

Steph isn't complaining; like Six other Lobelia she wears a fitted O-Ring Gag behind her teeth. The gag is extremely tight; so tight it pulls back the side of Steph's mouth so that the strap doesn't chaff. The locking roller buckle allows the straps to be pulled tight while the buckle is closed. All the O-Ring Gag buckles are fitted with a hole so a lock can be placed through. Steph doesn't worry about the lock because her arms and hands aren't moving and her fists sweat inside their mittens.

Steph does worry that *if Gamers take my Tongue Clamp off, they might threaten me to suck cock. But I know it's just for show, because Game Mistress herself told me my Opt Monitor is guaranteed, so long as I follow the Rules. Still, there remains a risk of a Player being stupid and cheating.*

Among the Cosmos Lobelia only Babs is able to watch Steph's entrance. Robyn is absent. Tiffany kneels with her face in a crotch, a cock in her mouth, and her Ass Hook ensuring her tush stays raised high and her twat presents vertically below it. Kimju hangs naked-spread-secured in a Love Swing, her knockware presented and promised, but unlike Tiffany, not prospered yet. Beka and Elle hang bundled butt-to-butt with a single, deeply-entrenched Double Dong and uplifted, overflowing vestibules. Molly's uplifted bound mams ensure she must keep her posture upright if she wishes to keep her feet on the ground. BB, on the other end of the beam, swings in the air, hanging totally helplessly by her bound 37Ds.

But Bondo Boobs is the only Cosmos Lockdown Lobelia permitted vision.

Babs is disturbed as she carefully canvases Steph's naked body. *How come Steph appears unvarnished? It looks like Steph has a spring U-bolt gripping her septum, this in turn connects to her lead. But I don't see any evidence Steph has a stud in her nose, and more obviously, her navel, and she does not have any navel tattoo.*

Doesn't appear to.

Babs' hostility toward Steph concerns Steph's Free-Fucking, might that be real, and scaring Robyn into attempting escape, which is real and commits BB to Whoredom, if not Slavesex by entailment.

Steph holds Babs responsible for Robyn's escape, and vows vengeance for inconvenience caused. *I like that Babs is a Whore, now and next Term. She deserves fucking. After Midnight, when I'm a Monitor and I rule a House, she can play a Game with my Pledge. I'm going to bugger her and let her taste herself. Then I'm going to bugger all my Pledge and let Babs taste them all. Then we can repeat and mix it up and see how many she can identify and paddle her every time she is wrong.*

Babs mulls the possibilities. Now, watching a loosely disciplined Steph, BB again questions the truth of her once-upon-a-time equal, now House Mom el Capitan, Janet.

Maybe Steph is a faux-Lockdown Lobelia, and really will be an Opt-Monitor again. All the stores about her are cons.

This is a theory. (Steph believes it.)

Maybe Rodney's story about Steph and William Free-Fucking was just a con to get into Beka's bone hole. Beka can be stupid like that.

Babs takes a deep breath. *Maybe Janet's story about Steph was just a con to get me to beg anal, and maybe I'm stupid too. Maybe Janet is one of them now, and she plays me for the Gamers' delights.*

Janet is a MomCap now, no maybes, and may it please Gamers, Janet shall drain her pee into Bondo Babe's mouth.

Babs drifts; she neglects to consider if Steph still harbors the Shaving Kit inside her slot and starfish, because bare and bald hanging boob-bound BB no longer cares who, when, or where every last hair on her body gets groomed. Or if her inner lips push out.

Babs does absorb the way Steph steps in harmony with her nose lead. Steph's Eye and Earpods commit her to darkness and silence, and allow her to practice her sole task of following her nose, with its lightweight but firm connection to the trolly travelling slowly along the overhead rail.

At first, Babs' self-indulgence is outraged at Steph's minimalist treatment, if not her lack of suspension. Yes, Steph is armbound behind her back and mittened, but she is not hanging in the air suspended by a pair of bound boobs. Like I am. Or Molly, swinging on the other end of this suspension beam, except Molly keeps her feet on the floor.

But as Babs watches more she understands that the way Steph steps through space-time is strictly regulated: First, attached to the trolly above and descending to a short distance behind Steph two discs float behind Steph's stern. Might Steph's pace become laggard and fall behind, increasingly painful currents of electricity will flow into Steph's roundness, and Steph will pick up her pace.

Conversely, two other discs, also attached to the trolly above descend directly in front of Steph's nipples. Babs takes satisfaction watching Steph misstep, witness and blue-white glow emanate around Steph's buttock as the discs approached touching her, accelerating her to overshoot forward, and collect a shower of sparks dancing off her spigots and beige areola, before she stabilizes her proper nose tension and pace.

BB appreciates. *It doesn't matter if Janet told me the truth about Beka or not, or if she told me the truth about Steph or not. Robyn's escape alone deserves to make me a Dong and Dirty Whore, maximum maltreatment. I deserve to have everything taken away from me, and that's just for starters, before I beg to lick up pee and offer my butt in a paddle auction.*

The trolly leading Steph comes to a stop not far from Six variously suspended Lobelia, Steph feels a Goad placed on her shoulder, and hears a Voice inside her Earpods say, "Kneel."

Steph obeys. Being blind, Steph does not see the hanging shockers withdraw upwards and out of the way. She does feel the line hanging to her nose extend slack as she kneels, then feels the Goad wiggle into her bare crotch, hears the Voice inside her Earpods say, "Spread," and Steph wisely parts her knees so that all of the real estate between her thighs is accessible. Steph feels the line take out slack between her nose and the trolly above so that she must keep her torso erect and hold her chin level.

The Voice inside her Earpods says, "Stay."

Steph feels three fingers lay across her vulva, feel one or two of the fingers cavity search her vagina, contact with the Soap Sphere sequestered there, feels another finger search her stern tube, verify the resident Tool Cylinder, and feels the fingers get wiped off under her nose and on her clamped tongue. Steph holds her position. Little choice in the matter. Steph knows that *the Tool Cylinder will flatten me on my face if I try to bring my knees together, and the Soap Sphere inside my snatch keels me pumping secretions.*

Steph feels a slight urge to pee, worries she will need to pee sometime; she suppresses these thoughts, along with any notions of pissing as an act of defiance. *I know that Gamers would hook me up to the bottom of a urinal in the Nugget in retaliation.*

And so Steph is left untouched, blind-deaf-mute, bare-bald-naked, kneeling-spread-armbound, nose held up. More fearful now. *Gamers are not going to let me see or hear who torments me, who cams me, whose body I touch. They are afraid of me, afraid of the payback.*

Steph fumes while she waits, but she holds her position. Hard not to. The confident one attests to herself, *I am too valuable a personality for them to not favor me. They let me watch the others collect ink and steel but left me out of it. Gamers just pretend I'm just another Cosmos Lobelia, to deceive the others into believing I'm one of them. I'm not.*

Correct. Steph is special.

Steph is not stupid, and she is revengeful, She resents her situation and plans future reality. *As for anyone who is not nice to me? I will make sure they get tattooed on their tongue while getting creampied up their ass.*

I had better not be asked to suck any cocks, eat any pussies, or fuck anyone, between now and when I Opt Up at Midnight.

Steph will not be asked, but her begging will always suffice.

Steph focuses her tactical anger while she kneels-spread-armbound. *Robyn. Robyn Runaway is responsible for this masquerading of my Fate, this faux-Lockdown inconvenience.*

Now Robyn Raghole is Slavesex, so any way I can imagine to harm her is possible.

Steph ponders the challenges of torturing an adversary. It had been Robyn who reported Steph's covered navel, and Steph had provided payback during the *Beach Day* which sent Robyn running.

I don't know what I can do to Robyn that the Mistresses and Masters will not have already wrought out, but I will come up with something heinous. Like, inject her sex lips so they grow way out, drive her sex crazy, and then shoot Porn of her wrapping her long thick flaps around the opposite sides of giant cocks and tying knots.

Anything short of turning Robyn into a freak is not harsh enough.

Babs is also on Steph's revenge list. *Bondo Bitch failed. She fell asleep on the job,* She's a *Dong and Dirty Whore next Term, but she really should be Slavesex.*

Steph builds her animosity toward Babs. *I want to watch Bondo Bitch get bondage gangbanged before Midnight. Watch her get force-climaxed until her brain fries. And swallow jizz no matter how many guys goo-face or creampie her bangbox and butthole.*

Steph's thoughts drift, *I wish I'd leaned on Babs more when I had the chance, when I was the Cosmos House Monitor and Babs was a first-Term Pledge.* Steph plans ahead. *Next Term our relationship will be again reversed, but our Castes move further apart. I'm a Monitor after Midnight, and Bondo Bitch is a Dirty anal Whore.*

Steph knows that although Monitors have no roles in managing Whores, that *I, Monitor Steph, will be able to visit the Nugget and watch visiting Whore Babs Feature Dance. Watch her suck cock in the Champagne Room, fuck cock in the Inner Sanctuary, maybe even suggest she please the Crowd with an after-hours gangbang center Stage. Private Cam Vids that will all go viral. I want to see her reduced to a Goo Whore. I want to see her so humiliated, reduced, brutalized, and brainwashed that she comes out the other side a crazy sex maniac who will devour cocks and pussies and beg Slavesex because she really will need to be restrained.*

Steph breathes carefully, squares her position, and braces herself for what she considers is the inevitable. *I am about to get fondled, felt-up, fingered, anally probed. I don't like being shown off, and I don't like Players wiping me off their fingers: under my nose, onto my tongue, and inside my O-Ring.*

Steph speculates in her darkness and silence; the lead to her nose ensures that any deviation of posture is met with sharp and lingering nose pain.

There is also a lot of pain that Steph is unaware of, but which trails behind her. Steph has no idea how her degree of humiliation compares to that of her ex-Monitor Babs. Steph doesn't know that Babs has begged to shoot cock penetration videos, including anal and A2M, all courtesy Steph's alleged *Steph and William Sex Video*.

Steph hasn't seen Babs, doesn't knows that Babs hangs in the air nearby, suspended by her bound boobs from the trolly above. Steph doesn't know that this time it is Babs who watches Steph's helpless naked body. Babs again attempts to validate the truth of the secrets Janet has told her about Steph and William, Babs interprets, *Steph's apparent lack of ink and steel suggests potential innocence.*

Bondo Boobs might struggle with the truthfulness of Janet's claims about *Videos* by Beka and Rodney, and by Steph and William, but Janet has seen both the *Videos* she described to Babs, and subsequentially screened one addition sex romp staring Steph and William that includes a surprise guest.

Steph remains unaware that *Videos* of her trysts with William remain in the hands of Gamers and Players of Superior Caste.

Steph also remains unaware that a *Beka and Rodney Fuck Video* even exists; she is especially devoid of knowledge about Beka's confession, the seizure of the *Fuck Video*, and the screening of it to the Peacocks and to Pledge Beka, and no one else.

Rodney, lacked Beka's Immunity, has been immediately Opted Whore, entailing then-Peacock Monitor William as a Whore also. Both had been affixed to the Wheel and the remaining Peacocks have been organized into a Benzine Ring. The Benzine Ring thinks that Rodney's misbehavior has defined the Fate of William and Rodney; it has so far, but the two on the Wheel don't wonder aloud if their Fate is complete.

The discovery of two *Steph and William Sex Videos* is a secret that has been kept from all Peacocks and all Cosmos, except for Janet's revelation to Babs during the *Runout*. Janet assumes that Steph's two *Sex Videos* certify Steph as a double penetrating anal Whore, and since Babs is entailed to Steph's Fate, "advising Babs to beg Dong and Dirty Whore has put BB ahead of the Game."

Steph makes a display of contrition by clanking her Tongue Clamp against her O-Ring Gag.

Game Mistress attends to her at once, and Steph feels fingers pull hard on both sides of the Clamp, then let it go with a snap and a clang. Steph jerks with the pain, but hands clasp her head so she jerks only a tiny bit more pain into her nose. Rude and caring.

Steph gurgles, demanding, "It is not just that the Clamp hurts, it is the constant stretch of my tongue. It's unacceptable that I am unable to retract it!"

No Party Player is able to decipher Steph's gurgle. Bab, still watching, finds the drool hanging out of Steph's mouth particularly déclassé.

But then realizes, *I'm a drooler too. We all are.*

Steph feel a hand grope her. Fingers pinch and roll her nipple, squeeze her round split stern, and fondle Steph's bald but stubbly head. Steph hears the Voice again, "I understand, you want your Tongue Clamp off so you can suck cock. Get throated even. So bang your Tongue Clamp. Make some noise now!"

Steph whimpers. The silver lining of cocksucking is not the advantage she wants to hear for a Tongue Clamp removal. "I'm just here for appearances," Steph tries to utter, incoherent of course, "but my tongue is in pain, so unclamp me now!"

Steph feels the sharp burn of electricity as she feels GM's Goad touch her dangling tongue.

"See," the Voice soothes her, "You can still feel it."

Steph can, and this time the littlest bit of pee leaks out.

§ Game Mistress: Welcomes Seven Cosmos Lobelia

Game Mistress appraises Seven Cosmos Lobelia; their Eyepods continue to present blackness, but their Earpods allow each of them to hear GM speak.

Game Mistress makes clear she has a plan for her Lobelia. "Welcome. I am the Agent for the Will of the Game," she announces. She smiles. "I relish the role.

"Midnight approaches and you shall soon achieve your new Castes."

GM pauses and advises them more slowly. "Don't worry," she says, "at Midnight two of you shall become Whores, four of you aspire to be Strippers, and one of you aspires to Monitor. But all of you are in Lockdown until Midnight and the end of the Term, and your mouths, pussies, assholes, and skin belong to the Party. You may be fondled and fucked, bound and buggered, punished and conditioned; you shall please Party Gamers; you have nowhere to go and no other purpose in life."

Babs watches as Game Mistress oversees Play; BB alone among the Cosmos Lobelia is blessed with vision at this moment. GM position herself directly in front of hanging BB, pokes the hardness in her pained boobs with the end of the Goad; BB knows a shock is coming directly on the nipple. And GM holds for a count.

Babs pisses herself. This time some of her stream gets on GM's boots. GM leans forward, pull BB down until both feet are flat on the floor and Molly is risen up off her feet into the air. GM smiles, wipes her boot with the end of her Goad, and wipes the Goad on BB's tongue. Babs tries very hard to hold onto her urine and is successful, and GM doesn't release another tickle of electricity.

And besides Bondo Babe remembers, *I am a Pee-Camming Piss Mouth. And I piss when and where you want me to.*

Game Mistress lets go of Babs and gives her a boost upward so that blind-deaf-mute, bare-bald-naked Molly can support herself on her feet again, although her upwardly supported bound breasts ensures she maintains erect posture. Molly also gets her tight boobs pressure tested; she has more mass outside the ropes that encircle each breast and cross tie them together, and although her areolas are splotchy, when GM graces Molly's nipples with the Goad, they stand right up.

Like Molly, Bondo Babe hangs by her breasts and dangles onto her tip toes; long ago BB lost the strength if not the ambition to squeeze the spring in the spreader bar at her knees so she can lower herself onto the balls of her feet and take some of the weight off her bound boobs. No more; now the spreader holds BB's thighs wide apart so that her moist bare burse is obvious. *Just hang helpless.*

Kimju may regret she begged to Opt Whore, but that beg cannot be undone. Kimju remains bound and spread in her Love Swing. Kimju believes Whoring involves selling one's mouth and pussy, but not one's asshole. She is correct; Slavesex, of course, are taken in all holes, but so are Whores who beg Dong and Dirty, all holes Game. But not Kimju, Kimju still retains her kawazoo.

Kimju feels what she interprets is the head of a cock in her opposite armpit. She confirms her suspicions when it erupts and leave behind a puddle of cum in her pit. More?

Beka and Elle hang suspended on their backs, horizontal and feeling they float in air, secured to their harness. They are positioned anus against anus, butt flesh against butt flesh, with their legs bent back to their torsos so that their opened sex lips point upward.

The Double Dong that penetrates both assholes snuggles deeply into each rectum; the Dong reinforces the magic it brings to their relationship. These two newbie Roommates long ago fell under its spell, eagerly demonstrated every one of the *Nine Dong Combos,* and now, positioned as they are with their sex organs rotated up facing the sky, the Dong helps ensure that both squeeze their sex cream upward, push their sex lip to the side, and pool their secretions in their vestibules. Beka had never needed coaxing to overflow, and whatever resistance Elle possessed in the past is being overcome by her addiction to the Dong's pleasing persuasions.

And Beka's nearness and scent.

Elle slowly surrenders her inhibitions. She is not yet quite wanting to be watched, but past caring who watches.

Both uplifted sloppy sex organs most certainly lie wide open, but they are difficult for a penis to access. That is not true for their two mouths; both heads lie back, so that both Lobelia may be easily throated, provided their Tongue Clamps are removed.

So when Beka begged to be a Dong and Dirty Whore, right after their Stripper Term finished, Elle had to follow. And besides, both confessed to Free-Fucking, knowing they turned not just themselves into Whores, but also their Roommates, not even knowing that their Roommates are as guilty of Free-Fucking as they are.

Steph, blind-deaf-mute, bare-bald-naked, kneeling, armbound and mittened, carefully holds her uplifted nose level and steady. Steph can feel, and only rarely does she feel hands groping her body, pinching her nipples, venturing inside her inner lips, fingerballing her clit, scooping slush out, and wiping it into Steph's waiting nostrils. This angers Steph, because Steph knows, *I'm special and should not be touched.*

Nor is Steph happy about spilling drool out the side of her O-Ring Gag where her Clamped tongue bangs against it, drool that itches as it runs down her chin, hangs in the air, until it finally lands on her squishes and spigots. Steph urgently needs to complain, doesn't dare move, accelerates her revenge against Babs and Janet, also Robyn, and squeezes her vagina rhythmically.

Game Mistress turns toward her last influence: Tiffany, who remains positioned away from the other Six Lobelia, still in the middle of the Risen Cocks Lineup, mouth still fully engaged on a large and erect vertical cock, knees wide on the floor, tush Ass Hooked high in the air, and her twat a Play Party free fuck.

During the arrivals of the various Lobelia, Tiffany has managed to keep her mouth on the uplifted cock, now, Babs witnesses Game Mistress lead a line of hooded Naked Shaven Men with long, horizontal erections, and position the first in line behind Tiffany's vertical twat, and then guide the penis into Tiffany's already creamy vagina. The hooded Naked Shaven Man copulates, Tiffany's cream flushes out, and when the Naked Shaven Man ejaculates and withdraws still more semen and tang push out of Tiffany's twat. And yes, Tiffany has been assigned a Collection Dish, one more like a bowl actually.

Babs watches the next hooded Naked Shaven Man replace the first and enjoy "sloppy seconds," and, before BB looks away, another and "turgescent thirds." Babs accepts. *Frothy fourths" and "frigging fifths." That's me too, I need to be on my elbows and knees, with a dick in my mouth, a dick in my baldy, and a dick in my bung. Tiffany needs a dick in her tailpipe just like I do, and weaned off her Ass Hook.*

Tiffany is thankful she has the Ass Hook uplifting her tailpipe, primarily because *it keeps the cocks from visiting the wrong place.*

Tiffany might know that Bondo Babe has already begged to be an Anal Whore, but doesn't know that BB has also suggested Tiffany join her in this experience.

After a while Babs discovers her vision fading to gray, and eventually blackness and silence reign.

V-3 Penny & Coco: Torment Lockdown Lobelia (LD5)

§ Penny & Coco: Risen Cocks Lineup Dirty Whores

One Cosmos alone knows the full manifest of the naked, kneeling, spread Cocksuckers working the Risen Cocks Lineup.

Tiffany knows because she is the center One of the Five. Tiffany can tell that former Strippers Hottie and Odee, *to my left and right, don't just have cocks in their mouths, they have cocks in their uplifted hotbox and ogive. They have Opted Whore; they are Goo Gobblers collecting vaginal creampies. Just like I am..*

Might Tiffany enjoy the Ass Hook violating her tailpipe, similarly Hottie and Odee are blessed with buttplugs, and unable to beg anal.

Tiffany identifies the Whores on the Two ends: Penny and Coco. *And Penny and Coco are collecting vaginal* and *anal creampies!*

This makes sense. Penny and Coco had divested themselves of their Props during the *Runout*, sequestering the Shaving Kit inside Steph's slash and starfish, and the Double Penetrator inside Molly's mutton and mawk. Where they remain.

But no other Cosmos Lockdown Lobelia sees Penny and Coco on the Risen Cocks Lineup. Indeed only the hanging Bound Boobies, the bare-bald-naked ex-Monitor Babs, ever had a chance: Once while hanging suspended and slowly pivoting on her rope, BB had panned the details of the Meatpacking Plant. Her eyes had searched in vain for Janet, knowing that *Janet would not save me, but maybe she can let me eat her pussy, suck her nipple, and groom her.*

This time the rope hanging Babs by her breasts twisted just enough so that BB could witness all five of the cocksuckers on the Risen Cocks Lineup getting double penetrated: She connects the cable hanging from the trolly with Tiffany in the middle, still with her Ass Hook holding her tush up in the air. But BB's view of the other four fornicating cocksuckers is blocked by the men who penetrate their vaginas.

Time passes and Tiffany learns the Two Cocksuckers on the ends are no longer Penny and Coco, and wonders, who? *Ginny and Trixi Tubes? Darleen and Pacmo Pinky? Beka and Elle?*

It is, after all, a Play Party.

Aside from Tiffany's narrow observation, no other Cosmos Lockdown Lobelia witness Whores Penny and Coco get released from their cocksucking duties, brought to their knees, and cammed cleaning off each other's bodies. There is a lot to lick off each other's faces, lick off breasts and nipples, and clean the inside of their thighs. The Collection Dishes shall be retrieved, merged into a single thick volume, and stored.

Penny and Coco were then guided away from a spotlight circle to darker portions of the Meatpacking Plant. Gamers understand that now-Whores Penny and Coco have unbalanced Karma with what were once Cosmos, and warrant a confrontation. Gamers are well aware that while Babs was affixed to her Post Henge, that Goo Whores Penny and Coco divested her of her pubic bush, fed it to her, painted her crescent d'areolage, and climaxed her.

The Play Party could offer more opportunities for redress.

Babs remains blind-deaf-mute, bare-bald-naked, and still hangs by bound boobs. She's armbound, with one hand mittened and one wiggling free. She doesn't interpret she has been separated from Molly. She's lowered enough so she has support from her feet, and follows when the ropes gently tug her in a forward direction and a touch on her buttocks shoots sparks. BB shuffles, the suspension ensures she stays erect; and BB is rightfully grateful she is being led by her swollen bound boobs, and not swinging in air.

Bondo Boobs doesn't slouch after her small steps come to a stop. BB knows, *at any moment they might hoist me up high in the air and lower me down on a Pogo or Drildo, or even a dick.*

Patience please. Gamers prefer to keep BB grounded; while she waits, Bondo Babe handjobs a train of cocks with her only free hand. BB's hand remains sticky and as the cumdumps spread, Babs ruminates. *Maybe the cocks are as blind-deaf-mute as I am, and someone wants them milked. Or maybe each of them cam me.*

BB starts to appreciate, *I am a handjob Whore and I want to beg Gamers to take off my other mitten so I can jerk off two cocks at once. And I'll finger pussies too. I'll even eat. And I'll suck. I'm a Whore now, so that means I'll have to fuck too.*

§ Penny & Coco Spin Babs: Garment Misdirection

But what happens comes as a surprise. As Babs' vision comes into focus and her filtered hearing returns, BB discerns Penny and Coco standing in front of her. This time neither Penny nor Coco is naked; furthermore, what they are wearing rattles Babs. And it would rattle Steph too, might Steph have vision.

In fact, both Whores wear Two Garments, and Babs flashes on the question, *could it be that both Whores have been promoted?* But then the larger picture hits her, the rub: *Penny wears my bikini! This is not a coincidence.*

More correctly, Penny wears what was once Babs' Black Bikini, and seeing her former Pledge wear what was once hers, adds insult to helpless Babs' naked shame.

And Penny wears the Bikini very well. Like Babs, Penny has big natural breasts and a solid buttocks (36C-24-36). When Babs wore the culotte, it just barely covered the crack of her ass; Penny manages to show off not just her dimples but posterior rugage.

Enough of an opening to pour itching oil down.

Another tactical factor exposes BB to risk further humiliations. *Unlike me, the Bikini bra as worn by Penny manages to actually conceal all of her areolas; whereas when I wore the bra, it did not.*

I'm not just naked and she's wearing my Bikini; when I wore the Bikini it tanned dark crescents into my areola forever; when she wears my Bikini, she's covered. And my crescent remind me of my loss and the difference. I am double humiliated.

Yes.

Coco traces one of the crescents and speaks to BB in French, "en croissant d'areolage," and BB's areola seeks to bubble up and raise her nipples, except her breasts are too bloated and her areolas are too stretched to completely see the arousal. But BB knows the crescents are still obvious. *They display me. Please display me. Touching them makes me wet.*

Penny traces the other crescent and speaks to BB in Italian, "crescente ricurva." Babs whimpers, transudes fresh brodeas, as the circuit firmly etches into Babs' brain; now whenever Babs reminds herself (or is reminded) about her crescents, she shall bubble her areolas up, raise her nipples, and make wet.

Penny and Coco both double-finger scoop Babs's banggo and cream the darkened part of each crescent. The act sends BB into a pant, she lifts her head up horizontal for a moment, and must stabilize herself between the pain in her breasts and the desire to climax. BB surrenders. *I can feel the burgoo on my areolas and it is driving me crazy. Kundalini has been turned loose inside me, my reptilian brain has taken over my body, because my box is sloppy wet for cock. I don't care how I fuck, or who I fuck. I belong to you, so fuck me anyway you want. Make me be your palace princess, your traveling escort, some bitch you give to your buddies to fuck during a golf trip, tie me spread eagle on the bed of your pickup truck, drive me to the County Fair, and sell me. I belong to you.*

"You want more, Whore?" Coco asks, as she brings BB out of her trance. "You want to be a Goo Gobbler?"

Yes. I already am! BB can't explain; she affirms, "Aaha-aaha."

Later perhaps. A glance reveals a different Lineup of naked men. These stand with their cocks in vices and wear stout posture collars connected with rope to trollies on the rail above.

Babs evaluates Coco's Two Garments. *Coco wears what was once Steph's costume, a long-sleeved front-button bare-midriff shirt, and what have become very, very low-rise capri pants. The long sleeve shirt seems to have lost all of its buttons and is knotted front and center near the bottom of Coco's ribs. Yes, the low-rise pants crack the ass and not just by a tiny bit; yes, the center seam in the spandex allows Coco's butt halves to move independently; and yes, had not Coco shaved bare she would indeed be flashing her bush. Indeed, the low-rise pants tease the top of Coco's slit.*

Unlike me, I'm showing my whole slit. BB looks again. *Coco's tight cameltoe is also soaking and stained. True for Penny too, but harder to see in the Black Bikini.*

I never stained the Bikini when I wore it, except now I'm hanging burgoo out my barrel for all the Prefecture to see.

Bondo Babe reconciles. *Except what Penny wears is no longer* my *Black Bikini.* And a further acceptance. *And my bare bajingo, that is no longer mine either, nor is my back hole, and no longer does my mouth belong to me.*

Babs feels no sympathy for Penny and Coco; *they challenged Janet and me when we were all Pledge, and they lost and Opted Stripping at the Nugget for a Term. And then at Midnight they Opted Whores, and earned a stall at Flesh Ranch. They are the ones that got addicted to the Dong, begged to be Dong and Dirty Whores, so they deserve to make their pussies and assholes dick-worthy.*

Still, Babs tries to prepare herself for the *humiliation, pain, and loss of all control, that I am sure is coming. The problem is I'm likely joining them at Flesh Ranch next Term, and I'm begging to work all my holes in all combinations. And they outnumber me two-to-one. Even if they really have been Opted Up and are no longer a butt-fuck, cum-dump Whore like I am, either way, they are going to play with me whenever they want. If I'm not careful they will brainwash me into begging to be Slavesex.*

Bondo Bangbox scans the Meatpacking Plant with frantic eyes. *Might Janet will arrive and rescue me? Even Madam Nurse Beautician or Pimp Cowboy. Game Mistress or Game Master? I'll suck, I'll fuck, I'll anal, I'll A2M, I'll swallow. I'm defenseless and begging punishment and pain. I at least deserve to be a Pee-Camming Piss Mouth Dong and Dirty Whore. I failed and I brought others down with me.*

§ Penny & Coco Make Babs: Piss Mouth From Now On

Penny and Coco appear to control the windless above Babs; Babs finds herself slowly descending; her feet still touching the floor, but as the rope lengthens and BB lowers, hands tilt her backwards so she still hangs by her swollen bound boobs, until she must bend her knees, and eventually her torso hangs horizontal with the floor and her head hangs down backward. Is it uncomfortable, painful, and helpless? Yes it is, because some of BB's weight still rests on her feet. So, it beats hanging in the air and swinging by the boobs.

An improvement? But not by much, because the pain in the "bloated bladders" doesn't stop, and BB's tongue pulses,

The Eyepods flip BB's view upside down, so that what Babs sees out of her upside-down head is right side up. The disassociation between vision and gravity heightens Babs' unease and fright at her situation, as it is supposed to.

Coco leans over Babs, and BB feels the wingnuts on the Tongue Clamp loosen and then gently slide off. She draws her tongue inside, and feels its swollen front half against the top of her mouth. Blood rushes in with a stinging sensation. BB watches as Coco rolls the low-waistline, skin-tight slacks down her pelvis, gathers Babs' bald head by the ears, and pulls Babs mouth up into her pussy.

Babs' surprise is smothered.

"Make me cum," Coco instructs, as she secures BB's bald head between the fabric and her own now-bare pubis. "Put that tongue of yours to work, Bondo Boxmuncher."

BB's tongue has been wrung tight for hours; it throbs with pain once the clamp is removed, but what's a naked and breast-bound Lobelia to do? BB feels her tongue inside her mouth; she worms it through the center of the O-Ring Gag, engages Coco's clit, and brings the Whore's pussy to wetness. BB can smell Coco's scent; it rubs into her nostrils and she senses Coco start to squeeze her pelvis, feels the quivers in her body, feels her shake and....

BB recoils as Coco voids urine into her mouth. Coco's thighs clench her head and Bare Babe doesn't move very far.

The tight O-Ring Gag makes sure Babs does not close her mouth. Coco commands, "Don't spill. Swallow." Coco squeezes both of BB's nipples, and BB swallows, keeps her tongue a-working, another mouthful, and BB swallows again. Coco takes full pleasure of the moment, slowly drains all her piss out, milks a gentle climax until BB must gasp for air.

"Clean me out, Whore," Coco orders, and Babs abandons the pain in her suspended breasts, and discovers herself cleaning out not only Coco's pussy juice, but sucking out cumdumps that had yet to seep out and stain the cameltoe of the stretch slacks. Babs accepts. *I'm a Whore now, I get fed cum by the Goo Whores, and I eat cum out of Coco's used cashbox. Soon I will collect cum directly. And I'm already a swallower.*

All true.

Coco raises from her squat so her pussy, and BB's still Ring-Gagged mouth, can enjoy plenty of fresh air. She tugs the slacks back up.

Relief. For about 30 seconds. Penny, always the more sedate of the Roommates, this time uses this opportunity to ordain a new future. "We've had to lick up your pee in the past, but from now on you're not just a Dong and Dirty Flesh Ranch Whore, from now on you'll be our toilet, whenever and wherever it may please us. You want that, you Dirty Piss Mouth Whore?"

Babs doesn't want and agrees quickly, "Aaha-aaha," the bitter taste of urine in her mouth washes out the gamey blend of Coco's cream and creampies.

Babs figures out late as Penny backs up to her hanging head, pushes the bikini briefs down her buttocks, jerks BB's head upward, squashes her mouth onto her asshole, and discharges a torrent of anal creampies. Babs almost suffocates when Penny holds her nose and states simply, "Swallow."

Babs swallows, and uses her tongue to felch Penny's asshole clean of jizz, then finds her head pushed to an angle so that she can clean out residual vaginal creampies, then guided again so that Penny can direct a slow but steady stream of urine that Babs must obligingly swallow to keep up with.

Coco, meanwhile, avails herself the opportunity to scoop jizz out of BB's overflowing handjobber palm, and paints two crescents d'areolage with the goo. BB instantly freshens.

Penny clarifies "You Piss Mouth Goo Gobbler A2OPM Whore."

Bondo Boobs agrees, "Aaha-aaha."

A palm of goo presents itself into BB's pubis and BB wantonly grinds her clitoris on it and she gulps more urine down. Penny backs away as Babs takes her last swallow, is afforded a short trill, and BB finds herself swinging again, head hanging down crotch level, knees wide, and her box sloppy with handjob goo and her own secretions.

BB worries. *If Players think I'm creampied they'll fuck me.*

Penny cuts in, "Maybe Janet started training you to climax on Piss Mouth, and it's our honor to continue your training."

Coco angles the question. "You do want to be a Watersports Whore?"

Babs' head spins and knows she must agree, "Aaha-aaha."

Penny sets a tone, "You shall always beg us to piss on your food."

Coco smiles, "And we will."

"When we're done with you you'll be begging to drink pee out of a glass," Penny predicts.

"And be grateful to do what we say when we say it," Coco adds.

Babs can't get the lingering bitter and tart taste of the Two Whore's urine out of her mouth. The urine sting contrasts with another reminder, the soup of Penny and Coco's valiva blended with goo they accumulated, and which they rubbed not only into BB's mouth, but also all around her held-open lips, into the nostrils, to the sides of her lips. The cream irritates BB because she cannot wipe it from her face, and the scent of the two Whores inundates her nostrils with the Whore's deep and unique blend, one which will perk BB's nostrils for more than a day.

"Tell me, Piss Mouth," Coco inquires, "now that you know how to swallow woman yellow, you ready to swallow some man yellow?

The question startles Babs. *No! I want to avoid pee in my mouth. I want to avoid semen also, although I know getting facialed, cumdumped in my mouth, cleaning up, and swallowing are an Obeisance of my Caste. I have already been fed. Already swallowed.*

An unseen finger penetrates BB asshole and sets her body swaying by her hanging boobs. Fresh pain erupts on top of steady pain. "Answer her, you Bunghole Bondo Bitch!" Penny commands.

Bunghole Babe trills and answers, "Aaha-aaha!" Babs tries to think, *I don't remember what I'm agreeing to.* But BB concludes, *It doesn't matter, I must want what Penny and Coco want me to want.*

Coco allows BB to reiterate her begging, "You want to practice on keeping up with man pee?"

BB is quieter now. "Aaha-aaha."

Penny presents the pragmatics, "How about we start you out on old men. Dribblers and the weak streams. Once you learn to keep up with them – and that should be easy – we can move you onto younger guys. Beg for it, Bladder Baudetrot.

Babs begs, "Aaha-aaha."

Coco augments, "You're lucky you have us to train you. I bet a competitive Whore like you wants to tackle two cocks pissing into your mouth at the same time. Gulp down the urine.

Babs feels urine push into her own urinary tract. For the moment she controls it. *But I need them to take total control of me.*

Penny applies escalation. "Two, Piss Mouth? How about many cocks pissing into your mouth, pissing all over you. You want them, you Dirty Whore, so start begging. Count them out.

Babs begs for cocks pissing on her, "Aaha-aaha. Aaha-aaha. Aaha-aaha. Aa –."

"Shut up," Coco orders. And Babs stops begging for pissing cocks.

Babs tries to steady her breathing and overcome fear. *They can beat me, bugger me, and make me bath them and worship their sexes. Clean creampies out of their assholes. Janet was really the one who abused them, and now Janet is out of their reach, so they will double abuse me.*

Except I probably deserve it. I should never have gone along with Janet in hazing them, I should never had participated in Opting them Down, and even worse, once they were down-and-out Strippers, of helping Janet Opt them Whores. Letting them actually beg to be Dong and Dirty Whores.

All holes, anytime, anywhere, with anyone, and in front of anyone. In front of the Cam. Pee-Camming Piss Mouth Whores.

Just like what I have become.

Except there are two of them and only one of me.

And they seek revenge.

§ Penny & Coco Make Babs: Beg Dong & Dirty Whore

But are Penny and Coco done with their former nemesis? Really? Babs knows *I am outnumbered, outpowered, outperformed. Already, here at the* Play Party.

Humiliation comes in many twists, and not just nudity, pinking, loss of all toilet privacy, even sucking cock. However sexual prowess also allows Players to project power, might they know how.

Penny and Coco know how. Their insult of parading in front of Babs, wearing what were once BB's Garments, *degradants me and empowers them. They are going to hurt me and make me serve them. If they smear my crescents, I'll ooze blurt out of my burse.*

Bondo Babe quivers as much as possible without escalating the pain in her hanging bound boobs.

Gamers in the Prefecture, remotely watching Penny and Coco haze Babs, argue amongst themselves to what extent Penny and Coco are "motivated by revenge and degradation upon Bondo Baudetrot" or are a "messenger vehicle to transmogrify BB into a caring nympho courtesan first class." Their debate does not stop Gamers from expressing preferences on BB's training regium, or admiring her misfortune.

Babs, during a fleeting moment of thought also wonders, *Are Penny and Coco here because they want to be, here by chance, or here because they have been sent by Gamers?*

But BB knows. *It doesn't matter what is the reason or the blend. I failed Janet, I failed my Pledge, and I especially failed House Mom el Capitan. And I let Penny and Coco lose, twice. I deserve to be punished for Robyn Runaway. So if Gamers are allowing Penny and Coco to degrade and hurt me to punish me, then that is my Fate.*

Penny might consider the motives behind her and Coco's opportunity to tread on ex-Monitor Babs, but Coco quickens to an opportunity to aggress against their former Superior, now bare-bald-naked, helplessly hanging by her swollen breasts, and seeing an upside down Meatpacking Plant right-side up and sound delayed with a different delay in each ear.

Babs tries to keep her panting under control because breathing slower causes less sting. *Fewer needle jabs of pain into my blaaters that are already tied too tight.*

Bondo Babe feels a cock placed into her free hand. She gives it a grip, realizes her hand is already slippery. And jerks it off, floating in space now, grateful to have something tangible to grab onto.

Babs also anticipates. *After the cock gets ready in my hand, I think I will see it right-side up as it pushes into my mouth upside-down. Up and down don't matter anymore. What matters is I lick off all the goo on the shaft, work the head, and make it shoot directly into my throat. I'll swallow. I'm a Whore now.*

Defeat for Babs has been a combination of bad luck (Robyn Runaway) and bad practice (failure to bed check). Corrective training for this mistake has already begun during Lockdown. It includes BB's naked suspension by her bound boobs, arousing her oozing sex bucket, and a promised Dong and Dirty Whoredom once the Clock counts to Midnight, and the new Term begins.

Babs fears Penny and Coco, both are already Dong and Dirty Whores, and known to be revengeful of defeat in the past, and vicious in their stride for humiliation, pain, and the Pavlovian behavior modification of their nemesis.

Coco relishes their role reversal, "You might be a Dong and Dirty Whore, and you shall beg to be pissed on, marked up, and brainwashed. You shall beg Slavesex Double Six Terms."

Penny gives Bondo Boobs a push off her tiptoes and naked BB swings in the air, mouth still O-Ring Gagged but no longer tongue clamped, feet trying to get traction, arms secured behind back, ankles together, knees sprung akimbo, burse pushing open and seeping. And all suspended by two very tightly bound boobs and a line to the trolly above. And thanks to a flogging, boobs that are not just purple, but bruised up.

By now Babs has come to fear her hanging situation. She bravely accepts, *Okay, this was a stunt. You are doing this to me and showing me I'm helpless, you win. You are going to cause me long term damage, you are going to make by breasts turn purple, explode. They are already purple. You are going to drive a red-hot pin through my breasts from one side to the other, rivet the ends so the rod can't come out, hook on a chain in the middle, put a squeeze on me, and lead me around.*

And I'm going to beg you to do this. I'm going to beg whatever you want me to. Anything. No limits. I failed.

With this kind of imagination, Babs hardly needs Penny and Coco to train her.

If, for over two Terms, Janet and Babs have exerted victorious force over Penny and Coco, now, for at least Babs, that Superior Caste has vanished. More correctly, it has been turned upside down. *And then the upside down has been turned right-side up.* Bondo Boobs knows, *I'm spinning. I don't know what is up anymore. Except I'm in Lockdown, not even my senses belong to me anymore.*

Babs accepts, *I failed. Now Penny and Coco cover their tits and pussies with* my *Black Bikini and Steph's Two Garments. I'm a Dong and Dirty A2M Whore. And Steph is a… well, it depends.*

Penny and Coco have either promoted and are going to tumble me, or they are still Whores, but either way they are going to make me their lacky, I will service their sex with my mouth, fluff cocks for them and clean them A2OPM afterward, and be their toilet.

They are freaking me out. I can't explain myself. My body is totally exposed, totally out of my control.

And where is House Monitor Janet? I need her to save me, but that's not going to happen because when she turned me into a Piss Mouth I realized she has to consider me fuckmeat from now on.

Maybe she can save me from Slavesex, but she can't save my butthole.

And since Janet is now the House Mom at the Nugget, I know I will have to beg to Feature Dance there, and I know she will need to be particularly harsh on me. And not just worshiping her feet, or performing Bukkake Bangbox center Stage after hours, but something far worse.

Penny and Coco circle their prey. "You're one lucky Bauble Burse," Coco explains, "You're a hanging helpless Lockdown Whore, and now that your Tongue Clamp is gone, I'd say your mouth is for sale or rent? Is that true, Whore?

It is, and Babs affirms, "Aaha-aaha."

Penny hangs cleavage in Boob Bound's face. "And with that O-Ring Hole Gag I bet you want them big and long so they can fuck you right down the throat. You like that, Bitch; you want that?"

Babs better want it. *I want it,* "Aaha-aaha!"

Coco wishes harshness. "You're going to get throated until you puke out everything in your stomach, then you will smear it all over your body, and that's how a more fortunate Slavesex will eat lunch."

Babs feels two fingers slip into her burse, swirl amidst its sop, then exit and linger on BB's sex lips. Babs moans and tries to rub on her hand.

"You have nothing protecting your pussy from getting fingered and fisted, do you." Coco observes. "You have nothing protecting your pussy from a good cock fucking."

Penny queries Babs, "You'd like that, wouldn't you, Bang Burse."

And Babs has no choice but the gurgle, "Aaha-aaha," but wonders, *do I really mean that?*

But then the panic attacks and BB makes a growl with her throat and contortions her body.

Babs feels again two fingers work into her bare and exposed sex cavity, and BB squeezes and rocks her pelvis. Does she want more? *I want more.* And get another, and another, and then, with a tightly pressed thumb, BB feels an entire fist slide into her sopping wet and oozing and constricting vagina; she moans.

BB feels the fist exit and she chases it with her shaven spread burse. BB is breathing hard but exertion encourages fresh pain into her bound and hanging breasts, and constrain her increasingly wanton desires.

"You miss the Pear?" Coco asks. Babs does, and frequently feels as if it still inside her, so powerful is its memory. Babs is about to affirm but Coco launches the next question. "Only now you want cock inside, don't you?"

Babs answers both questions. "Aaha-aaha. Aaha-aaha."

"Maybe you have still another hole that's begging to work?" Coco inquires.

Babs does, but responds slowly and carefully. "Aaha-aaha." *During Lockdown, I expect to take cock in all my holes.*

Penny acknowledges BB's distress, "I know I know. You are ripe for a fucking. Lockdown provides an excuse for you to offer your Game cherry."

But more and more Babs agrees. *I want it. I want cock.*

Penny clarifies BB's thoughts. "During Lockdown, from now and Midnight you're a Bondage Blowum Bangbox Bugger Bitch."

Babs takes a moment to agree, "Aaha-aaha."

Coco then politely inquires, "But tell me, fuckmeat, after Midnight, is your butthole for sale too?"

Babs must reluctantly affirm, "Aaha-aaha."

Penny keeps it simple and verifies. "And after Midnight you want to be a cocksucking, cunt fucking, ass-to-mouth Dong and Dirty Whore?"

Babs must agree, "Aaha-aaha." And gurgles.

"You want to be a cum-mouth depository." Penny states. "Convince me, you Bondage Blowum Bangbox Bugger Bitch."

BB answers what wasn't a question. "Aaha-aaha!"

Babs knows, *I'm already a cumdump. When Penny and Coco were Goo Whores they fed me jizz with my trims mixed in; and here in the Meatpacking Plant they made me eat creampies out of their pussies and assholes.*

Babs tries to gather thoughts in an upside down world. *I never swallowed before I enrolled in School, and did not intend to start now. Or next Term. Or eat out gals. Now I understand that my intentions don't matter; I will do what pleases Penny and Coco.*

Coco rolls Babs' nipple in her fingers and breaks her reverie. The touch startles Babs and she squirts urine into the face of a hovering

Cam. Until the moment Bauble Babe felt her own pee wettin her thighs, calves, and feet, Babs had forgotten, *I no longer have a Cath inside me to control my pee.* BB breaks her squirt yet considers, *I need the Cath back, so there is less of me I have to manage.*

Penny summarizes, "So Whore, did you like eating pussy, drinking pee, and getting fed globs of goo?"

BB knows there is only one answer. "Aaha-aaha."

"You want cock in every hole."

Yes. "Aaha-aaha." *I'm a Dong and Dirty Whore.*

Babs' vision fades to a dark gray field punctuated with static, and her sound fades to a soft hiss punctuated with muted industrial grinding sounds. BB takes a deep breath, and welcomes the peace. *Seeing right-side up when my body tells me my head is upside-down is disconcerting, to say the least. At least in darkness Gravity works. I know I'm not really floating above the floor, and I'm hanging by my bound boobs. My legs are spread and I know Players are going to penetrate my butter box soon.*

Babs feel burgoo being rubbed into her crescents d'areolage and she instantly stands up her bullets and bauble; her burke oozes burgoo; her nipples shall stay hard from now on. The imprint is chemically bonded amidst BB's neurological circuits. *I can't hide anymore. I'm spread, wet, and I need sexed.*

Babs hears a melodic mechanical voice in her Earpods. "Molly still has her Ben-Wa Balls in her meatwagon and the Procto up her mawkpipe, Steph harbors the Shaving Kit Soap Sphere in her snatch and the Tool Cylinder in her sewer, Beka and Elle share a very long and very thick Double Dong deep in their rectums. And I think you got a glance of Tiffany with a cock in her mouth, a cock in her twat, and an Ass Hook helping her keep her asshole upward."

"Do you approve of taking the Hook out Tiffany's asshole so her tailpipe can get pumped full of jizz? Her mouth is pretty occupied right now so why don't you beg for her instead, Whore. You are her ex-Monitor. You approve. You want her asshole to be sold?

Bondo Boobtie needs to think for a moment. *I'm a Dong and Dirty Whore and I am going to be buggered. Tiffany might have been a Whore before, but she was never Dong and Dirty, never an Anal Whore. But I am becoming one, and I need Tiffany to take it up the ass with me.* "Aaha-aaha."

Selfish? Survival? Once upon a time Tiffany had cautioned Babs on the rigors of Porn Stardom. "You think Stripping might be hard work? Wait till you go to work for Pimp Cowboy. You think shooting *Suck Fuck Facials* in front of a camera crew is hard? Try working a Porn Conference in Europe where you get sent onto a Stage and service a naked man sitting in a chair. I kneeled and blew him, I climbed up on him, I fucked his brains out, squirted when I climaxed, and ate his pop. Totally public. Anybody at the Conference could watch me or cam me doing this. I'm a Porn Star! I dare you to match that and be a Porn Star too!"

Babs feels her feet separated, independently suspended from the rail trolly above, and spread outward. Any contraption spreading her knees apart is removed. Bondo Babe understands her predicament. *I am hanging horizontal in the air by my boobs and my feet, my leg are spread wide, my sex lips are pushed out with fresh brodeas, and my head and Ring Gagged mouth are hanging upside down.*

My one hand is already slimy with goo. I'm on a goo diet, I'm girl crazy and crazy for cock. I want slime on my other hand too. I want slime in my mouth. I want slime in my burse, and I want slime in my butthole. I want to be slimed all over, dunked in a slime pit, then put in a glass cage covered in slime and exhibited in a zoo.

Another unseen smear of goo on BB's crescents enlivens BB's areolas, BB's burse oozes and quivers, and pushes fresh burgoo out between very obvious and overflowing sex lips. Shaven to the sides, shaven everywhere. Babs is a toy now, more honorably, an instrument, and Penny and Coco delight that "Bondo Boob's quivers of desire translate into sparkles of pain, and not only where the rope from her tightly bound breasts digs into her blaaters, but throughout her Whore mind, body and soul."

And so Bondo Bitch moans, makes a copulation thrust, hangs fresh burgoo, and begs whatever, "Aaha-aaha!"

A wish is granted, and BB discovers that her second hand is freed of its mitten. She opens her hand to stretch her fingers and discovers herself closing it around a long but thin cock. She shall exercise her fingers and stroke and squeeze cock at the same time.

Rhythm.

And discovers a fresh one into her already gooey fist. Helpless hanging BB appreciates. *I'm a double jerkoff Whore. Next cocks are going to spunk my mouth. They will stand in front of me, slide right through my O-Ring Gag, and if they have length and are sent in by Gamers to throat me, I will just have to take it, even if they grab me from behind my head and bump their way in, and hold me until I'm ready to pass out from lack of air. Phlegm everywhere.*

And I'm already pink wet and ready for cock. I'm a Whore now.

Babs feels the goo on her crescents being replenished, wants some of that goo to be fed to her mouth, and again goes into a quiver, and she drives her shaking body to a point where she can't take the pain in her breasts any longer. "Aaha-aaha," she utters, and frustrated at being unable to climax. *I am a Lockdown Bondage Triple-Hole Whore; blowhole, banghole, bunghole. Beat me, bruise me, gangbang me, and leave me in exhausted from climaxing in a pool of scum. I'm your Dong and Dirty Whore, and I'll please you however you want. Just fuck me now.*

§ Penny & Coco Degrade Steph: Piss Mouth Karma

Penny and Coco also have a grudge against Step; the Whores hold Steph responsible for flaunting her navelage, more correctly spoken, for covering her navel up and flaunting power against the Game. This had happed near the end of the Term before the Term ending Midnight; Gamers had retaliated, seized, stripped, and secured the then-Monitor Steph in Lockdown.

As a consequence of this misfortune, it was Steph's then-Roommate Robyn who instead refereed the Mudwrestling Contest that pitted then-Pledge Babs and Janet against Penny and Coco. It remains the opinion of Penny and Coco that their victory had been certain with Steph in charge of the Contest, but Robyn's ignorance enabled Babs, and even more so Janet, to overpower the duo, emerge as victors, and became House Monitors in the Term ending Midnight. Losers Penny and Coco were Opted Down, moved to the Nugget, and Stripped for the Term that ended at Midnight.

During *The Beach Day,* then-Strippers Penny and Coco had been sent to scout the Cosmos Pledge and make recommendations as to whom House Mom should accept into her Caste of elite Strippers. Penny and Coco had performed this task naked, and among the humiliations they had extracted from the Cosmos was a beg from

Steph to become a Piss Mouth, and which ended with then-Corvette Darleen camming then-Pledge Steph arching her pelvis over her head and pissing into her own mouth.

Once again Robyn had assisted in cheerleading Steph's extreme humiliation. Darleen had assured Robyn she would upload Steph's humiliation to Automatron, and she did, forever earning Steph, not only a Pee-Cam credit, but qualifying her a Piss Mouth.

After Midnight, Penny and Coco had presented naked and spread to Flesh Ranch, where they were spun with jizz, drank glasses of gokkun, got creampied every hole as their Props rotated, and rested in clear glass stalls with every surface sticky with goo. They were dunked, drained, wrapped in plastic, and driven to visit the Cosmos Lobelia, then sitting-spread-secured on the Post Henge (LD2).

After transferring the Ben-Wa Balls and the Procto to Molly, the Goo Whores had extracted their Shaving Kit, depilated a spread and secured Babs, packed BB's mouth with goo-bush, and then transferred the Soap Sphere and Tool Cylinder into Steph's sex socket and stern tube.

The Whores had then gooed Steph's clit, finger-balled her into a pant and elicited her to beg to collect their urine. This angered Steph, because she knew she had to play along with the Game, no matter how faux the Lockdown. Or irritating the Pee-Camming.

Steph never forgets an insult or humiliation and long ago tagged Penny and Coco for disagreeable treatment. There is disagreement as to whether Penny and Coco watered Steph's mouth or fed her goo, but no disagreement that the Whores parked Steph in the climax Zone

That said, ever since Steph acquired the Shaving Kit, she has craved to extract the soap and razor, shave her vulva if not also her armpits and legs, and return the tools to their sacred places. Steph is less sure about her eyebrows and stubbly bald head. Steph needn't be sure; free hands for armbound and mittened Steph have not been a luxury ever since Prop insertion.

Steph holds her position; she remains blind-deaf-mute, bare-bald-naked kneeling with her thighs open and her feet apart, her torso upright, and with her nose swivel connected to the rail trolly far above by a thin yet strong line that ensures Steph keeps her chin up. And doesn't turn her head very much.

Like some of the others, Steph's forearms are laid horizontally behind her back and encased in bindings, and both hands, pointing in opposite directions, are also enveloped in mittens. Steph anticipates, *these Gamers think that when they take the mittens off that I'm going to want to do handjobs. What silly, stupid people.*

Sigh.

Because might the Shaving Kit, either on its own or conspiring with other AIs and Running Agents, seek to make Steph constrict and seep faster, then Steph will constrict and seep faster. Steph still rebels. *I resent being compromised! I certainly want my Garments back and I know I'll have to shave naked for the Cam first. I will do that. I will pull my pink wide open so they can see my clit stand up and my pee hole clearly, and see all the way down my pipe.*

And then I'm going to launch them an arch!

Vision and sound return to Steph, the sound is slowed down and all the motion in the vision has trails which come to a rest when the motion stops, but then start up again once something changes.

Steph can see and hear now, and when Coco rubs her body against Steph's naked tits and torso, there is nothing Steph dare do to stop her. Or stop her from fondling her nipples, examining her navel, or fingering her sex cavity.

It takes time for Steph to stabilize in Coco's presence. She reminds herself *to not move my head around, and to keep my chin up.* Steph wants to calculate her Caste vis-à-vis Penny and Coco, *but I have to devote myself to holding position and that requires all of my effort.*

Steph feels Coco feel the outside of the Soap Sphere inside her socket. Steph feels Penny's finger probe up her anus, and Penny's fingertip touches the end of the Tools Cylinder. So yes, Steph still possesses the Shaving Kit, itchy stubble, and a desire to shave.

Steph bridles at these invasions which she must submit to. She interprets Penny and Coco's Two Garments as a sign they have Opted Up and are now Pledge. Steph projects, *Maybe they don't know I'm their Monitor next Term, and think they can beat me and get away with it.*

Penny and Coco think they can.

Steph has the good sense to hold her position and not rip her nose.

The trailing images have taken their toll on Steph but after a while it becomes clear to her that *Coco is wearing what used to be my clothes! This is a really stupid thing for her to do!*

Looking into Steph's eyes through her Eyepods one can see them sparkle with anger. Anger directed at Coco. *This is an insult to me that will not go unanswered!*

Steph fumes. *This Cumdump Cunny has ruined my long sleeve shirt; she's ripped the buttons off and tied it so she can let her coconuts fall out and her coppers flash. So some Patron can fondle them, or suck her coronas. And my skin-tight stretch capri pants crack her ass, tease her slit, and display a soaking wet cameltoe crotch. She's disgusting.*

Still, although it irritates Steph to see what were, once-upon-a-time, her Garments, she is amused *that Coco's acquisition of them has degraded the Garments and made Coco more vulgar.*

Penny observes to Steph. "I bet seeing Coco wearing your outfit leaves you pretty speechless!"

Coco grasps Steph's Tongue Clamp by the two sides and yanks it forward. "Except you're already speechless, aren't you!"

Steph is and squints her eyes at the source of her pain.

Coco lets go of the Clamp so it clanks hard against Steph's wide O-Ring; sharp pain when the tongue stops dead in its tracks.

Penny and Coco laugh. Pain bursts remind Steph *I need them to stop the dull pain I constantly feel in my tongue.*

Steph holds still. *I need to focus on holding my position, nothing else matters. They don't dare hurt me. And if they do, I'll get even later. Get back double. I'm going to get back double even if they don't hurt me. More if they do.*

Penny exposits, "Maybe when you wore these pants you also cracked your ass, and maybe you leaked hairage over the top. But Coco cracks more ass than you did, and don't you love her slitage?"

It is a question, and an answer is expected, "Aaha-aaha."

Coco piles it on, "Your clothes make me so hot. Gamers can't keep their eyes off my inappropriate exposures!"

Steph glowers silently and snarls outside her Ring-Gagged mouth, *Maybe Coco is Opting Up, but she's still a tittering, slittering, butt-cracking coquette.* And a directed look, made also with a distorted mouth, *I hope whoever controls your exposures also controls your cocksucking lips, your cunt, and your colon.*

Coco touches Steph's shaven slit, swipes the outside, fingerdips, tastes Steph's spending, and questions, "Apparently seeing me wearing your outfit makes you pretty wet, doesn't it, Steph Sorostitute."

Steph must follow the science, "Aaha-aaha."

Penny steps back and wiggle-dances in front of Steph. "Recognize this Black Bikini, Steph Sorostitute?" she queries.

Steph does; the grunt comes from her throat, "Aaha-aaha."

New unease sets in.

Coco explains, "Bondo Boobs is here in this very Meatpacking Plant hanging by her bound breasts from the rail trolly above. Much as you might want to trade places, sorry, your tits aren't big enough. Possibly you'll be able to get a glance at her before you get gangbanged."

Penny makes an offer. "Or maybe you think that BB should get gangbanged instead of you?"

This seems agreeable to Steph, "Aaha-aaha."

Coco shrugs, "After all, she was the Monitor, she deserves to take on all the Cosmos Karma, yes?"

Steph agrees, "Aaha-aaha!"

"But look at you," Penny advances, "you're a Lockdown Lobelia, when in fact you defeated Elle in the Duel and earned a guaranteed Opt Up; Bang Bitch should take on all your Karma, yes?"

Sure, what do I care, may Elle or Babs get my Piss Mouth, may they both inherit it. I'm Opting Monitor at Midnight. "Aaha-aaha."

Steph evaluates. *Earlier this Term, Coco was bare and naked and begging to Whore, whereas I had two pieces; now Coco has two pieces, and I am bare bald and naked. I don't care if Penny and Coco are Whores ,masquerading as Pledge, or actual Pledge; what irritates me is that Coco wears* my *Garments.*

Maybe somebody controlling Coco is attempting to seriously mind-fuck me. Steph's mind races. *Like Pimp Cowboy. I might be begging to Strip, even if Gamers know I don't mean it; besides Gamers know I am too good an asset to waste. Sure, they will keep me in Lockdown until the Term ends at Midnight, at which time I will Opt Up and become the Monitor of the Cosmos House. I mean, realistically, who else is there? I am about to be restored to my rightful position!*

Steph resents Coco for wearing her clothes but brushes the thought aside. *I needn't concern myself with my old clothes. They made trash out of my clothes the first time I was a Pledge, and they made trash out of my clothes when they broke me to Pledge this Term. I paid my dues before and after* The Runout *and* Lockdown. *I've already had to pee and pink and cream and climax; on Stage, on Cam. And I've already been Zoned. So if I get Zoned again before Midnight I accept I can't stop that. Same old same old.*

As for clothes, after Midnight, when I'm a Monitor and control Seven Pledge, I will take whatever Garments I please, and insist that whatever my Pledge wear will become rags!

All true, although has Steph forgotten about some of her other adventures?

Kneeling-spread-armbound Steph also knows that *Penny and Coco are able to act on me without me being able to turn my head and look around. This faux Lockdown makes my blood boil. Bad enough Penny and Coco shaved me bald at the Nugget and forced me to climax on Stage. They are sadistic bitches, they know I got Pogoed to Climax during the* Runout, *and they toyed me putting the Shaving Kit in.*

Besides. Gamers have never let up on me whenever they have had a chance to wring me out. Even after I had secured my Opt-Up, Babs still made me get naked and serenade the Pee-Cam.

Steph directs her thoughts. *Now, Bondo Bitch, the time has come to suction your tits and your clit, and fuck you crazy.*

Steph's visions fades to black again and her Earpods go silent. She does not hear or see the hanging of two bags of urine from the trolly overhead. She does not figure out the form behind the sensation of two tube laid into her mouth on the two topsides of her tongue, until drops of fluid come out the two ends. It only takes a few drops for Steph to know that *they are urine drips, one no doubt is Penny and one is Coco, but I don't know which is which.*

Something for Steph to learn if she wants to win piss tasting contests.

§ Penny & Coco: Acquire Dong from Beka & Elle

Penny and Coco have a final item of business to attend to:

Penny and Coco acquired their addiction to the Double Dong before the Term ending at Midnight had started; acquisition followed their loss in the Mudpit and preceded their arrival center Stage at the Nugget less than a Day later. At the Nugget the two Strippers had been forbidden to share the Dong; discovery of any sharing was an absolutely certainty, with consequences likely including a Term of Slavesex, might a Player be so fortunate. And begging "tongue and cheek piercings with gromets to secure the Dong in your mouth, since you want it so much."

Not being able to share, indeed watching others ride the Dong, had driven both Strippers' frustrations. Many Days later, House Mom el Capitan had ordered the Two Strippers bestow the Dong upon a naked Steph and Tiffany, with Tiffany climaxing Steph center Stage, while Penny and Coco shaved her bare and bald. Steph had streaked back to the Cosmos House that night, encountered the Rachmaninoffs, and has memories that border on the fanciful.

Tiffany, also a party to the shenanigans at the Nugget, had been the one who actually transported the Dong back to the Cosmos House, and, although not prone to its addiction, always welcomed an opportunity to twang it with another Player, no matter what their sex or gender or hole.

With Tiffany's encouragement, and then-Monitor Babs latent blessings, the Double Dong had been widely shared among the Cosmos Pledge, including a resentful Steph, who considered the Dong an unwelcome intrusion *beneath my true Caste*, but which none-the-less made itself welcome after Molly bestowed it upon Steph while Steph resided in the Doghouse. Tiffany later snaked the Dong out of Steph, took it to the Corvettes where she passed it to Ginny, who would share it with Trixi Tube's holes.

The AI inside the Dong had promptly profiled both Corvettes. Ginny was and is a Whore-for-Life; Pledge Trixi Tubes remains an acolyte. Ginny understands the Dong is quite able to raise or lower both Dongers' arousal and flush, able to bubble up their areolas, harden nipples, and stimulate valiva production. Whether Ginny and the Dong conspire to nudge Trixi toward Whoredom is not known;

what is known is that the twosome shot all *Nine Dong Combinations* on Day 27 of *The Runup*, and on the next Day, *The Beach Day,* they had reluctantly bestowed the Dong upon Beka and Elle.

Beka and Elle had taken the Dong to the Doghouse, sequestered with it overnight, and the Dong addicted them to their climaxes, and imprinted a lesbian affection that would remain, although both were always naturally promiscuous.

During *The Runout,* naked Beka and Elle also got cammed their own *Nine Dong Combinations,* exercising every hole combination. But unlike the two Corvettes who blessed them with this Instrument of pleasure, (and like Penny and Coco), Beka and Elle became entranced with the Dong: shared in their mouth, as where a cock might be, shared in their vaginas, a place specialized for cock, and shared in their rectums, as a symbol of sacrifice and surrender.

Beka and Elle are afforded a hovering Cam view of the Double Dong penetrating their rectums; the view they see in their Eyepods also documents their uplifted and bursting pussies, pooling and spilling valiva. Fresh broda and nakodo. The sounds Beka and Elle hear are the sounds of the long Dong deep inside their rectums. They can watch themselves pucker, grind, and make love together.

Might their attention drift or pain throbs here or there, the Dong knows how to focus their attention to what matters.

Beka and Elle sometimes remember that Penny and Coco also covet the Dong, and that the Two have been promised possession now that they have achieved Dong and Dirty Whore Caste.

But this might not be so easy: Beka and Elle hang suspended-spread-secured, bundles of love, butt-to-butt with the Dong deep inside each of them, swollen at the anus so as to ensure gaping afterward, days of stretching, a big bulb just inside to resist any and all attempts at rejection, and a long sausage deep into each rectum. In men the Double Dong's activities including tickling the prostate; in women there are other spots.

The Double Dong is Beka and Elle's friend, it is their bridge, and the only thing in the Game that they can feel. They float in the air. And either Beka nor Elle seeks its divesture. Or seeks to be alone.

Penny and Coco harbor no grudge with Beka and Elle; it's simply that Beka and Elle have something Penny and Coco want. Want back? Something that may require Opt-Whoring to obtain? And which Penny and Coco intend to collect.

Or ask nicely for. The sounds from inside the newbies' rectums cross-fades to the deep rustle of the Meatpacking Plant in the fog of the background. Suddenly Coco's voice is clear to their ears. Both Lobelia recognize it immediately.

"I hear you both been making some new *Porn Videos* this Term?" Coco inquires.

Beka and Elle watch their butts twitch, and hear each other respond, "Aaha-aaha."

"Renegade Porn." Penny speaks with a sympathetic tone, inquires, "You provided some free oral stimulation?"

"Aaha-aaha." The two voices speak in chorus.

"You Free-Fucked?"

Beka anticipates Elle will answer with her, but solos, "Aaha-aaha."

Elle wonders, *do Gamers have the evidence. And how did Penny and Coco know about my secret liaisons?*

Penny presses for an answer, "And you, you Free-Fucked too?"

Elle relents, "Aaha-aaha." *I actually did. That's the truth.*

"Did you give away your asshole?" Coco moves the question with a sharpness.

Beka recoils. "Naaaa," but Elle slowly acknowledges, "Aaha-aaha."

Penny smooths. "Don't worry, you're still Lockdown Whores until Midnight. And Roommates always share."

Beka and Elle watch their assholes pucker and relax, around the Double Dong, obviously.

Coco makes a suggestion. "After we back that Double Dong out of your assholes, your gape can accommodate some Porn-sized cock, would you like that, Whores?"

Beka should not so eager to agree, but she is, "Aaha-aaha!"

And Elle follows, "Aaha-aaha." Elle anticipates, *long and deep, fat and long, hundreds of cc's.*

Penny faces Elle and curls her voice, "You're already begging to be a Whore after you spend a Term on the Strip. Your nympho Roommate commits you to the Dong and Dirty. You know where you are heading. During Lockdown, you're going to get a taste of pussy and cock, and you'll have scent all over your face, on your cocksucking breath. Aren't you begging for cum and scent to run out of your nookie and nadir gate, you Dong and Dirty Whore?"

Elle's body twitches. She is taken back, but manages to agree, "Aaha-aaha."

Beka adds an uninvited second, "Aaha-aaha!"

Beka and Elle still hang helplessly, floating in air on their backs, supported by ropes under their backs, shoulders and buttocks that rise to the trolly on the rail overhead. Both Eyepods continue to provide each with a hovering closeup Cam view of the Double Doug penetrating both rectums, with both uplifted vulvas, both oozing valiva that leaks down to where the Dong disappear into each of the Lobelia's intestines.

They should be pleased to know Collection Dishes hang beneath their harnesses, so that their spendings don't go to waste.

Once again their Earpods revert to sounds collected from the insides of their rectums, shared so as to contribute to steady cream production. Some Gamers believe that Beka and Elle are zoned.

Elle believes *if the Dong can listen to my insides it can see inside me too.* The idea excites her and contributes to her loss of control. *I'm totally revealed, inside and out.*

Elle is, and watching her nectar overflow her nymphaeum makes her flush, erect her nipples and clit, and pant.

Beka doesn't think about such things, Beka appreciates, *Gamers control me inside and out. I want to be taken completely. Climax my brains out. Control my breathing so I can stay in the Zone. And then turn me lose on a gaggle of men and let me devour them.*

Elle comes out her reverie when she feel the Dong swell into an even larger bulb inside her anus, big enough it cannot pop out. She feel her buttocks separate from Beka, now both of them watch the closeup Cam as their bodies inch apart, and Beka feels and hears the Dong ever so slowly slide out of her rectum.

The final sound in the Roommates' Earpods is the slurp of the Dong exit; the final visual is Beka's gaping anus. It freezes in only both their Eyepods, a big round gaping hole into Beka's insides, with an oozing breech above it.

The frozen frame keeps Beka aroused and Elle fearful. Beka is slow to comprehend she has been separated from her Roommate and anchor. But Elle knows. *I have just been separated from Beka and I am wagging half of the Double Dong out my nadir. I'm going to get my gape cammed too. And if I want her back I am going to have to beg to get cocked. Long, think, black, brown, tan, white, cut, uncut, whatever Gamers want to put in whatever hole.*

Elle continues to listen to her rectum. Elle's vision remain the freeze frame of Beka's gape and overflowing vestibule.

Players here at the Meatpacking Plant, Gamers in the Prefecture, cut to a real-time view of Elle's own buttocks, wagging tail, and overflowing nookie.

Although Penny and Coco have spoken clearly to Beka and Elle during this visit to the Play Party, neither Lobelia has been provided a clear view of these two newly minted Whores, and Beka and Elle incorrectly assume that both Penny and Coco are naked, when in fact they wear Babs' and Steph's ex-Garments.

Beka and Elle never witnessed naked Penny and Coco earlier at the *Play Party* while they sucked, then double and triple penetrated on the Risen Cocks Lineup. The Roommates never saw them feeding BB creampies. Now all Elle (and Beka) can see is a view of Beka's gaping anus and her creampot above.

Ergo, Elle can feel the thick Dong wagging out of her nether tube, but she never sees Game Mistress sign Penny onto her knees, then Penny approach the wagging Dong, open her mouth and lower the Dong into her mouth until she pushes her lips flush around Elle's anus, clamp down with her lips and her teeth on the Dong, and pulls.

The bulb inside Elle rectum relaxes, and Elle hears the remaining half of the Dong slides out slowly and with dignity. And all sound in Elle's ears goes silent.

This time a Cam collects Elle's gape, and this time a Running Agent somewhere presents a freeze frame of Elle's gape and oozing nookie in both Roommate's Eyepods. Elle can't not confront her frozen gape, but wonders, I was forced to stare at *Beka gape first, and assuming she has been forced to stare at her own gape, does she get to see me too?*

She does. But certainly Gamers in the Prefecture who share their links to Beka and Elle's pink, pee, and climax clips, can now also link to their gape. But Beka and Elle shall remain ignorant of who pulled the Dong out of Elle's nether passage, and whose mouth it goes into next.

Elle figures out, *It doesn't matter what Beka sees of me. Or what the Gamers watch. I'm going to be used. I'm going to get a baseball bat up my ass. Until Midnight I'm a helpless Lockdown Whore, and my* Gonzo Suck and Fuck Videos *already let Gamers watch Beka and me having sex. I'm already begging to screen them in the Nugget, and I'm already begging to be a Dong and Dirty Whore after my Stripper Term.*

And so is Beka, except she wants to be gangbanged, even if it means I get gangbanged too.

Sounds like a plan. When Elle eventually learns that her *Gonzos* already announced her arrival, Elle will masturbate wet.

Game Mistress makes another gesture, this time to Coco, now Coco must kneel and chase the wagging end of the Double Dong hanging out of Penny's mouth, and secure it into her mouth. Now, as Penny and Coco look each other in the face, the Dong shape shifts, drawing them closer together, filling both of their mouths completely, swelling behind their teeth, and drawing them together until they are touching lip-to-lip, the insides of their mouths are full, their tongues spread flat against the bottom of their mouths, and their lips and teeth spread open in a most wrenching gesture.

Penny and Coco clasp each other behind their backs as they rise to stand, carefully, chest-to-chest, stomach-to-stomach, and in absolute unison. They have no choice as to movement.

This is not the Double Dong Penny and Coco expected, but it is the Double Dong they possess. And possesses them totally by their mouths.

Penny and Coco have fulfilled their goal visiting the *Play Party*, and assuming they can move carefully, and given they remain sufficiently decent to appear in public, they shall find a way to get transported back to Flesh Ranch.

As for whether Penny and Coco continue to wear Babs and Steph's Garments, that is something BB might find out after she gets to Flesh Ranch. Might BB find them there, then they really are Whores; or, might they be absent, Babs might conclude that they really have promoted to Cosmos Pledge. Babs mulls, *it's better for me if they are Pledge. Because if they really are Flesh Ranch*

Whores, they will double team me. I won't have a chance. They will keep abusing me out of revenge. And their own sadistic impulses.

Gamers must punish me harshly for my mistakes, and whether Penny and Coco are Pledge or Whores, Gamers know they are a willing tool to humiliate and degrade me. Beyond making me spread and pink myself, eat my cream, or sleep with one finger in my asshole and the other in my mouth.

The last thing Penny and Coco see is the backside of a man positioned in front of Babs' hanging head. *Hanging head giving head?* Penny and Coco hope so.

Steph anticipates, *too bad Penny and Coco will not be my Pledge next Term, because I would have no mercy on them. And if they are Whores, I hope they get fucked in ass, orgy gangbanged, clean cocks A2OPM, and suck creampies out of each other's assholes.*

And that's just for starters!

Such nasty thoughts! In the real world, Steph mustn't let her mind wander, least she forget to hold her kneel-spread-armbound position.

And so for now, Penny and Coco have come and gone, but are not forgotten.

Babs and Kimju don't relish a future encounter with the two Dong and Dirty Whores at Flesh Ranch.

Tiffany knows, *I was a Whore and a Porn Star, but I never had to sell my asshole before. Beg it away. Call it whatever you want.*

Molly doesn't give the matter much thought.

And Beka and Elle, having been separated for the first time in a long time, already crave the surrendered Double Dong. And especially crave each other.

Robyn needs to weigh in.

Robyn & Cosmos Lobelia: Reunion (LD6)

§ Robyn: Her Capture & Amphitheater Visit Recounted

Robyn travels to the Play Party independent of her Seven fellow ex-Cosmos. Most certainly Robyn shares Lockdown, although at the moment Robyn has no idea of where she has been, where she is now, or where she is going; she has no idea what time it is, and increasingly, who she is. Robyn exists in a state of suspended animation: naked to the skin, immobilized, sensorial deprived, penetrated in every hole including her nose, mouth, vagina, urethra, and rectum. Redacted, redactable, plastic mind and soul, easily melted and poured, body subject to modification. But still reckless and demanding constant attention, ergo constant restraint.

Slavesex.

Robyn has no idea of how much time has passed since she was captured. It would be pointless to count hours or Days because for Robyn, as with all the other Cosmos Lockdown Lobelia, time stays the same, for the Clock is stopped.

Robyn had Pledged in a conservative strapless maillot swimsuit, conservative but still only one-piece, and with a small tidy navel cutout that Robyn felt gave her maximum manipulative advantage. She had been the least exposed Pledge and kept herself covered throughout the Term and, in fact, had gained clothing, and by *The Beach Day* was wearing Three Garments.

Robyn had been a Pledge in the previous Term, but for reasons she has forgotten, Robyn had been given nepenthe, redacted, and her memories erased. This Term, during a moment of weak constitution, Monitor Babs had anointed Robyn her mouthpiece, and Robyn took every advantage of this regality.

However, by the end of *The Beach Day,* and to the delight of many Players, Robyn herself had been again reduced to but one Garment: Her very flexible strapless maillot cutout de roulè.

Steph provided an opportunity for Robyn to shoot selfies of herself with her navel accidently covered, and had chaperoned the reduction of the rolldown maillot to a minimalist topless tanga, yes full rigamarole, full razzmatazz, and rolled far enough below the navel to preclude accidents. It was Robyn's first such exposure this

Term. Only the mercy of Babs had allowed Robyn to roll it back up to a strapless maillot cutout tanga, and eventually roll the back down to recover her rear end.

But a maillot is still One Garment and a one-way pass to the Nugget.

Perhaps Robyn realized that getting cammed topless tanga on the Beach was an exposure too much, and that although her Charm upon then-Monitor Babs had enabled her to recover herself, one strapless maillot cutout was insufficient to prevent a hike to the Nugget Stage Door, a divesture of the maillot prior to ringing the Stage Door Bell and begging entry, totally stark naked, and at the mercy of the Back Door Man. Robyn simply concluded that naked dancing, pinking, dildoing, if not peeing, douching, and changing a tampon center Stage, was not what she envisioned for her future.

Fortunately, Robyn's attempt to avoid the Stage Door has been thwarted, and when Robyn had been captured the first thing that had happened was that her sexy strapless cutout maillot had been slashed, torn from her body, and burned in front of her eyes.

It is rumored that Robyn had begged her captors with blowjobs. It is certain that her pussy had been spread, her hair waxed and ripped off, her holes mechanically possessed. The hair on her head was reduced to a small bun at the top that was big enough to suspend her from, but no bigger. And she was turned in, perhaps after she had even offered her asshole and begged to become a servant.

Runaway Robyn had traveled the road to the Dungeon and the Dungeon had found her. Fair Use Girl on her way to the Dungeon? She is Slavesex now; running away isn't an option.

Sexual conditioning is the Robyn plan. That is what one signs up for when one runs for the Dungeon.

Robyn's display to the other Seven Lockdown Lobelia in the Amphitheater had seared their memories, and her reappearance at the *Play Party* shall build upon what they had witnessed before.

Robyn had arrived at the Amphitheater blind-deaf-mute, bare-bun-naked, sitting-spread-secured, and immobilized on a Cart. The Cart had been pushed by a giant Naked Negro who painted Robyn's back with penis lube.

The naked and secured Cosmos Lobelia had observed that Robyn's mouth was occupied by a Gag, her ratchet and rectum were machine-fucked by a Drildo and Stroker Rod, her clit and nipples were stimulated by remote Crawlers, her pee hole harbored a Cath, and her nostrils had been occupied by two tubes, one to provide food into her stomach (or pump her stomach out), and the other to provide air and recover carbon dioxide.

Robyn did get a glimpse of her fellow ex-Cosmos in the Amphitheater. At the time, Cybernetician, the resident Artificial Intelligence managing Robyn's body, had employed its suite of Props to arouse Robyn as she observed that all her former fellow Pledge appeared to sport nose rings, and then spin her into a low trill as she surveyed their navel art, and in the case of one or two, the more extensive tattoos on their bodies.

Cybernetician's forced pleasure of the Props, coupled with the cascade of nose and navel piercings Robyn witnesses, enchants Robyn with a desire to acquire a nose ring, a navel treatment, and an interest in a full-body suit.

Robyn did retain enough intuition to especially delight in the reduction of "Monitor Babs" to a blind-deaf-mute, bare-bald-naked, sitting-spread-secured, fuck-me invitation. And Robyn had been climaxed while witnessing Kimju get her tongue double pierced, connecting a set of synapses that would respond to the pain of others with her own arousal, a trait not hard to develop in Robyn.

Robyn will not be streaking to the Nugget and begging entry naked like a Stripper should, she will not be prostrating herself naked and spread in the Spunk Pit at Flesh Ranch and begging to be a Dirty Whore. No, Robyn's destination is the Dungeon, wherever it might be. And it need not matter to Robyn when the Clock strikes Midnight and a new Term starts, because for Robyn, she's not only looking at Six Terms Slavesex, but also has an uncanny ability to stop the Clock, not only for herself, but also for others around her. Maybe it's the power of Charm.

She's dangerous.

§ Game Mistress & Robyn: Slavesex Plaster Mummy

Seven Cosmos Lobelia saw naked Robyn displayed in the Amphitheater, naked-spread-secured in her Cart, gagged, anally and vaginally machine stroked, cathed, tubed. And these Seven Lobelia also believe that Robyn saw them too: all had been displayed naked, spread, and secured. Every former Cosmos, including ex-Monitor Babs, has publicly pinked or been pinked, masturbated or been masturbated, and learned to gush and trill.

Throughout the Term, the Cosmos Lobelia have enjoyed the privilege of carrying or sharing Props (e.g., the Double Dong, Shaving Kit, Double Penetrator, Centipede, Pogo, Snake, Pear, Cath, and a variety of Gags) in their various orifices. Most have enjoyed a romance with the Post Henge and the Mudpit, and Elle got to ride the Glass Bull.

Some have eaten pussy and felched.

At least two have broken the Rules.

Some of the Cosmos Lobelia have been repositioned to increase or decrease their conveyance and pain. All remain blind-deaf-mute, bare-bald-naked, variously secured, spread, armbound, and sexually displayed, if not already sexually useful.

Babs and Molly still hang by their boobs. Kimju hangs in a love chair with her legs spread. Steph's nose connection to the trolly above keeps her chin up. Penny and Coco have collected the Double Dong from Beka and Elle, left with it, and left Beka and Elle separated and gaping. Tiffany bows on the Risen Cocks Lineup, sucks cock, gets fucked, and gets dumped on.

Vision and sound return to them but none see with their own eyes or hear with their own ears. And although the Cosmos Lobelia are physically separate, all their Eyepods provide them the same point of view, all of the Earpods provide the same sound. They are never able to see each other, but they do see Robyn.

If what the Cosmos Lockdown Lobelia saw in the Amphitheater exceeded their imagination, what they see today escalates whatever shock, fear, sadism, and sympathy they experienced previously.

Today the helpless Seven Lobelia are not just startled, they must confront a much harsher future alternative. Today their Eighth Cosmos is displayed before them, likewise, hanging upright from a trolly that has routed its way through switches and rail until it comes to rest here in the Meatpacking Plant at this Play Party.

This hanging Lobelia is different. This Lobelia is also suspended, vertically, ….

At first the Lobelia recognize Robyn by the shape of the plaster mask which covers her face and head, but confirmation occurs observing a fragment of her exposed torso, the curve of her belly and her ever-present signature radiant outie belly button, and by a now-shaven pubis. And by her rarely seen rigamarole – two rosettes with rubies atop.

Then, as the Lobelia's eyes canvas they discover that the rest of Robyn is completely encased in a block of hard plaster that surrounds almost her entire body, her head and shoulders, hips and back, arms apparently hanging by her side, and her legs and feet, hanging downward.

A Plaster Mummy on life support?

Well, yes. And a role model to fear. Or aspire to.

Begging Slavesex is much more complex than breaking Rules and getting caught. For some the capture and confinement is everything.

Unfortunately, here at *The Play Party*, such selfish behavior shall further discipline and degrade those surrounding the Rule-breaker, as well as the Rule-breaker themselves. And in the example of Robyn Runaway, degradation shall apply to all her fellow ex-Cosmos, now all begging to Opt Strip, with two exceptions, Kimju and especially ex-Monitor Babs, both already begging to Whore.

Game Mistress glides into the Lobelia's field of view and stands adjacent to the Plaster Mummy, like a robot with its bare toro open. GM pauses so that the Virtual Lineup of Seven Cosmos can absorb the captive. Absorb they do. GM stands erect; her cape is wrapped around her, her boots are polished, and the touch of her gloves can cause pain. Some Lobelia theorize that Game Mistress is well-covered inside her cape; some Lobelia theorize she is approximately naked; but no Lobelia will have their theory validated today.

GM commands the attention of Seven Lobelia with a single full-frontal flash as she crisscrosses the two flaps of the cape in front of her and secures the closure.

She turns to Robyn, presses twin ends of her Swagger Goad on Robyn's belly, presses and holds the charge, and Seven Lobelia watch Robyn twitch until yellow fluid runs down of one of the tubes emerging from the Mummy and collects in a bag hanging beneath.

"It's alive!" Game Mistress proclaims to the Lockdown Lobelia.

Are the Cosmos Lockdown Lobelia who observe Robyn's mummified condition amazed? Absolutely. Are they speechless? Yes indeed! O-Ring Gags hold mouths just as wide as sustainable; Clamps secure every Tongue except that of BB and Tiffany.

Tiffany, because she remains face-down with a huge cock in her mouth. Tiffany is not only absent a Tongue Clamp, but the O-Ring Gag in her mouth has been removed to facilitate her felation. But Tiffany still sees the same view in her Eyepods.

Bondo Babe assumes, *I know why my Tongue Clamp is off: my Ring-Gagged mouth will not be resisting throat training. I'm going to be puking up my lunch so a Slavesex can eat dinner.*

Or the opposite. And yes, that beats getting cast in plaster.

Indeed, the amount of plaster that engulfs Robyn's body staggers the Lobelia's eyes. They know that ropes and harnesses can be untied and taken down, nose rings can be detached from their leads, and Props can be moved around if not shared. But plaster?

GM explains, "Robyn Rambunctious seeks to become a Slavesex Mummy, and as you can see, her Fate is almost complete."

"When Pledge try to run away it's a signal they want to be immobilized," Game Mistress states, "and so Robyn is immobilized. She can't bend anything, can't even wiggle her toes. But she can still be fed, breath, make waste, pump roily out her ratchet, climax, and surf the Zone. Gamers intend to turn her into a sex animal."

Game Mistress pans her Cam eyes across the Cosmos Lobelia and shrugs. "And Gamers are going to make sex animals out of you too.

"I trust none of you retain any illusions you've been treated harshly." GM's sarcasm causes the Cosmos Lobelia to quiver. "I trust you appreciate the tremendous leniency bestowed upon you."

The Lockdown Cosmos do indeed. Compared to plaster and brainwashing, getting pissed on and bondage fucked looks like a happy outcome.

GM recounts, "When you violate curfew and get caught you pay dearly for it. Robyn is not just a naked, bare, tatted-up pinking Stripper, she's not just some lucky Whore who will get all her holes fucked senseless, she's Slavesex who will be transmogrified inside and out. She is going to be bound, beaten, banged, and buggered for the next Six Terms. 24x7.

"And love it.

"At first Robyn Ragazze chose to assume that her torments were private," GM wryly observes, "but at the Amphitheater she saw herself cream and climax in full public view. She was very embarrassed being displayed, but she shall soon learn to cream and cum on Stage while watching Videos of herself climaxing."

GM continues, "You shall witness her final pour today; witness your fellow Cosmos getting totally cast into a plaster Mummy. This is how Gamers control Pledges who can't control themselves. First we immobilize them, turn them into blank minds, then we condition them so they become cum sluts who relish themselves as bondage fuck whores. Slavesex, but Slavesex with lifestyle!

"Before, when Robyn was displayed in the Amphitheater, you may recall that her hands and wrists, and her feet and ankles, were encased in blocks of plaster.

"You may not have known that the plaster encased Stims in the palms of her hands and the soles of her feet; it still does. If before the blocks were secured to the Cart, today Robyn's hands and wrists have been welded to her sides, mummy position, and her ankles and feet are bonded into the solid block of plaster which also buries her calves, knees, and thighs in plaster.

"Of course she has stims up her butt crack, the insides of her thighs, pitched inside her moist and smooth armpits. Additionally, mobile Crawlers can make themselves immensely thin and slide around between her body and plaster. They can crawl into Robyn's vagina and snuggle up between the Monkey Fist and the inner wall, amplify the clit stimulator, and band around her nipples and constrict them, and make her ooze sex cream.

"You are reminded that the AI inside Robyn, Cybernetician, is well able to pace her at a heartbeat and breathing rate, and surf her into the Zone indefinitely. Until someone has time to bother with her, Robyn's only purpose in life is runnel production."

Yes, the Cosmos can see, another clear tube draining from the Mummy, this one with thick white fluid, also collecting in a bag.

GM continues. "What was before a very stiff posture collar is now buried in the plaster. You'll be pleased to know it has always contained stims pressing against the neck skin, and that it still does.

"You should feel privileged you were allowed to confirm with your own eyes that Robyn Runaway had been captured and secured, today you should feel privileged to witness her vanish."

Game Mistress's presentation unnerves the Cosmos Lobelia. The new casting joins Robyn's shoulders, neck, and head into a rigid alignment; the plaster surrounds Robyn's neck, covers her shoulders and buried armpits, and flows down her sternum. It remains impossible for Robyn to turn her head or move her jaw. She is totally immobilized, a plaster Mummy, awaiting, apparently only for a torso to seal up.

Scary.

Game Mistress continues her briefing. "Robyn still wears Eyepods over her eyes, but they are buried deep inside her plaster mask; may it please Gamers that she see something, they will decide upon the visuals. Her Earpods, also already buried, provide Robyn with audio silence or stimulations.

"I'm told that sometimes the sounds are just loops of various length, animal cries, sapiens climaxing, Sirens' songs, sounds running backwards, all designed to de-brain Robyn. Cybernetician can coordinate sounds with flooding her bladder, then making the Cath wiggle and shock, then run a trill, and empty her piss out.

"Robyn's nose is also buried within the plaster, and one of the two tubes you see protruding is a feeding tube via one nostril and down her throat; although it is equally useful in pumping Robyn's stomach out. It's important she realize that her subjugation is, shall, and must be total.

"The other nostril accommodates a breathing tube, oxygen in, carbon dioxide out, flavored with aphrodisiacs or scents perhaps. Each tube has a miniature light and Cam on their ends, so that the insides of Robyn's stomach and trachea may be shared with the Prefecture. It's important she have absolutely no secrets.

"As for Robyn's mouth, she still wears her Cyber Gag, with a hole so big it contort her face, an air-tight clear gasket pressed around her mashed-up and distorted lips, and a Cybernetician-controlled iris in the middle that can open and close. All this is buried inside the Plaster, although the Hole and the iris are flush with the plaster surface and so are easy to access.

"As for the inside-mouth part of the Gag, a tentacle remains, normally coiled around the hole, although it may extend into Robyn's mouth, cramping the tongue, tickling her throat. It also has a Cam, so you see the two tubes going down her throat.

"The mouth aperture is normally kept closed and airtight, although can be opened to drain drool, accommodate cock, or empty purge. It is unnecessary for feeding, but unlike the feeding tube, does facilitate the flavoring the mouth."

Game Mistress preens. "And what about the other parts of Robyn's bare-bald-naked body that you Lobelia can't see? Parts already buried in hardened plaster? And what about not just skin and joints, but her blood and brain and the rest of her insides?

"You should be pleased that Robyn's rectum is totally possessed. Some kind of porous tube has nestled itself a long way up and around her large intestine. Way up. This 'Anal Intruder' certainly includes cameras, microphones, and a suite of measuring instruments, of course, and from time-to-time these provide visual and audio fodder for Robyn's brainwashing. The Intruder can also heat and cool, vibrate, electrify, change shape, and do all the other features of Props like the Centipede, Pogo, Snake, Procto, Shaving Kit, and even the Double Dong.

"Now Robyn can share experiences that some of you have come to love and will beg to repeat," GM tops.

Game Mistress smiles and continues. "Robyn certainly appreciates that her Anal Intruder can feed as well as extract, and that feeding and extraction are done at the pleasure of whomever controls her mind, body, and soul. Might that include Players like me, the only debate about 'Robyn' is what kind of Slavesex we want to cast, and what methods we employ to deepen her intensive correctional training."

Babs worries. *I know that I, alone among the Lockdown Lobelia, that I am the first in line to be the next Robyn. Gamers need to cam not just my naked body and holes, Gamers need to cam me up my ass, inside my vagina, inside my stomach, I need to be the next Slavesex Mummy, taken inside and out.*

"May you all aspire to be as subspaced as Slavesex Mummy," GM taunts, "but as Einstein suggested, 'the Devil lies in the details.' You may appreciate that the Anal Intruder includes a special round tube where it exits Robyn's anus, passes through the plaster Mummy, emerges, and terminates in a T-connector. A bag-hanger, higher up, may be filled so that its contents can flow downward and flood Robyn's rectum. Conversely, the tubing descending from the T-connector terminates in a bag hanging lower down."

Although Robyn's legs aren't spread, the Lockdown Lobelia can see that their fellow ex-Cosmos is indeed freshly shaven and has been vaginally decorated. GM delights in the description. "Yes, Robyn's clithood has been pierced and supports a stimulator right on her clit. And you can read a series of the most obscene, vile, and demeaning words have been tattooed across Robyn's vulva, adjacent to her sex line, and they disappear beneath the hardened plaster.

"What you Lobelia are unable to observe is that these tattooed vulgarities also populate the insides and outside of this riffraff's labia major and minor, her gaping vagina, on her vestibule and around her piss spigot, then rearward, where they circumnavigate her asshole, rise up her butt-crack, and proclaim obscenities atop her posterior rugage.

"As you can deduce, the tube draining down to Slavesex's urine bag connects to her catheter, but also note there is a T-connector with a value in the tubing, so that another line runs upward to a bag higher up; it contains any fluids Gamers might use to irrigate Robyn's bladder. It certainly pleases Gamers to ensure Slavesex lacks any and all bladder control. With proper hydration, Cybernetician can intensify pressure on Robyn's sex, enable her to constantly feel the need to pee, yet ensure she doesn't rupture herself.

Babs, perhaps the most stressed of the Lockdown Lobelia, if only because she has fallen the most, finds her head spinning. *There's more. A full bladder presses against your vagina and aggravates your hormones. I know, Gamers put me on a Cath, kept me horny, and pissed me, but they never irrigated me. I need them to cath me again, irrigate and totally possess me, then drain and climax me.*

Game Mistress piles on the inventory. "Robyn's vagina is held open by a speculum that keeps her vestibule always pinked, and her round raspberry-colored hole stretched all the way down the pipe. The speculum is porous and connects to a drain which funnels all of her runnel and passes it through the Plaster to still another hanging collection bag, as you can see."

Yes, the Lobelia can see, another T-connector! Yes, the bag hanging low appears partly full of vaginal cream, technically valiva, here Robyn's runnel. Runnel moves down the tubing slowly, and then drips into the bag.

Only some Lobelia process a second bag, this one hanging off the side of the Mummy, but higher up, and feeding into the T-connector from above, Some of Lobelia know what the bag is because they have experience, and some know because they think ahead. Those that figure this out must still wonder *what's in the Bag? The contents look to be heavy and white.* But they still know what the bag is: *a Douch Bag.* And at least one Lobelia anticipates, *Gamers will want to collect all of Robyn's runnel before they flush her.*

The Douche Bag triggers memories among some Lobelia. Nugget center Stage? A Bachelor Party? Part of a daily regium?

"As with her mouth and stomach and lungs and rectum and bladder, Robyn's vagina is also cammed on the inside too."

Game Mistress saves some of the best for last. "I trust that a few of you are sufficiently intelligent to suppose that Slavesex Mummy might also have her womb invaginated, you are correct, and you wonder just what might help subdue a Runaway with total love?

"You need wonder no more because I am going to tell you!" GM provides. "For it is the Monkey Fist that resides inside her. And just what is the Monkey Fist? Why it is a wrist stub, totally cybernetic, totally AI, with a Running Agent which handshakes with Cybernetician; physically it has four long fingers, a long thumb, and organically miniaturized just enough to fit perfectly. A tight fit, but able to put its finger on Robyn's g-spot, or uncurl and stretch a really long finger up Robyn's vaginal pipe to diddle her clit.

"Gamers fed Robyn's Eyepods a mirror view of this finger reaching out of her receptaculum, and Cybernetician helped synchronize her watching herself become aroused, watching her face flush. She was pitched into a soft Zone climax as she watched her reliquary vanish beneath plaster."

Babs, custodian of the Pear for more time than was pleasant, shudders at Robyn's Fate. *She deserves it, but so do I. I deserve the max. Spread me out on my back, I just want to be fucked.*

"Finally," reminds Game Mistress, "do not forget the Cybernetician, the Master Intelligence that resides distributed amongst Robyn's many Running Agents and AI's, certainly handshakes with Automatron, and even with Gamers. Cybernetician will do whatever is necessary to put Robyn into a runt, trill her, or surf her somewhere in the Zone. Cybernetician monitors Robyn's brain waves and blood, it conditions her to concentrate on sex and will convert her from being just another uppity horny bitch, into a tigress on a leash constantly craving sex. And craving to be petted, eaten, and given cock to sink in three holes. One at a time, two at a time, three at a time. Like some Players you know. Like some of you."

Robyn can't see her own body, nor feel it with her hands, nor hear nor see Game Mistress's presentation. She is aware that her nipples and navel and pubis are still open to air. The lack of external stimulation allows Cybernetician to draw Robyn closer. Cybernetician builds its arousals in many ways and with many tempos and delights. Robyn is reminded she can do nothing when the soles of feet are tickled, uncomfortable vibrations irritate her immobile fists, shockers inside her armpits and inside the collar holding her neck produces convulsions in Robyn's bare belly.

Two of the Crawlers tightly band around her two nipples and squeeze them hard. Robyn feels ripples up and down inside her rectum and the squeezes in the Anal Intruder in synchronization; Robyn's speculum expands and relaxes in a counterpoint rhythm, Robyn now slowly but consistently pumps rolly down the tubing, the stim firing on Robyn's rosebud causes her entire pelvis to ripple, the Hole Gag aperture opens enough to let in more air, the Monkey Fist pulsates against a flooded bladder, and Cybernetician puts Robyn into a rolling rhythm. Is she in the Zone? Yes, shallow in, surfing on the edge perhaps, but definitely lost in a deep and steady breathing, zoned, nothing approaching climax. Yet.

§ Game Mistress & Robyn: Cybernetician Trills Robyn

Seven Lockdown Lobelia stay mute, bare-bald-naked, and tightly secured. They enjoy a common view by a pair of remote eyes that are focused on the Mummy with its bare torso, hanging from the trolly overhead. Hanging vertically, because the Lobelia are able to see Robyn's breasts and chest heave and her waist constrict. Watch runnel slowly seep down a tube to the outside of the Mummy, and collect in a clear bag.

Different Cosmos Lobelia react to Robyn differently. Babs continues to watch with horror. *"So goes a Pledge, so goes a Monitor,"* BB recalls the Rule. *That's me next. Unless maybe I can get to be a Dong and Dirty Super Whore first. Although I deserve what Robyn is getting. My failure has crushed all my Pledge and even demoted my House Mom into a Stripper.*

Steph, lover of chaos, remains pleased with the destruction Robyn has wrought upon the other Cosmos. *I am exempt from Robyn's Charm, and my Duel victory over Elle guarantees my Opt Monitor next Term!* Steph freshens her insides.

Steph's encounters with Robyn predate the current Term. It had actually been Robyn who reported Steph's navelage violation which resulted in Steph broken in Caste. Steph had returned the favor during *The Beach Day,* but only after Robyn had induced Steph to piss into her own mouth for Darleen's Corvette Cam.

Steph looks to the future, *I need to get my Garments back, Opt Monitor, and after Midnight, whenever Fate provides, I want to turn Robyn's spigots on, and turn her into a wet nurse. Titties for Patrons to feed on. I want to see two gals nursing her and with a dick in every hole. I shall breed Robyn Ragazie with animals and see what comes out.*

Monsters might come out. Robyn is dangerous!

Kimju, long a patsy of Robyn aggression, and turned by the events to beg Whore, watches with forbiddance. The Plaster Mummy may not know that Kimju's Tongue Clamp is bracketed with double studs courtesy Robyn's Charm. But Kimju does not forget it was Robyn who insisted she should "pull open your kunny so Darleen can cam your keyway all the way into your cervix."

Kimju had obeyed, knowing full well, *I am showing my kunny to the entire Prefecture. Every Gamer, now and forever more.*

But Kimju also understands. *Showing my koot is not the problem for me. But in all my Terms in the Game, I have never Free-Fucked, I don't intend to, so that's not a fear. I'm not impetuous like Beka, not a compromiser like Elle, not a Porn Star like Tiffany. I have earned an Opt-Monitor, but because of Robyn, I'm Opting Whore, getting double pierced, and getting a full body suit.*

I don't need the cocks in my hands and mouth and kunny, but putting my hands and mouth and kunny to work keeps me stabilized and fed at Flesh Ranch. And the full body suit is a big plus.

Tiffany, Molly, Beka and Elle, all already begging to Opt Strip, variously understand that Robyn's Charm has shaped their Fates.

Game Mistress lectures the Lockdown Lobelia, "Now that you have all witnessed the last of Robyn's body to be visible, you shall now be permitted to witness it disappear, so that the possession of this Slavesex will be total, inside her body and out."

Cybernetician adjusts Robyn into a quiver, visible only by hardened nipples and a tremoring belly. The Monkey Fist, the Anal Intruder, the Cath, the dangle vibrating her clit, the Stims all over her body and inside her sweaty armpits… all dance with her body. Crawlers wrapping around both nipples keep them risen, and gentle high frequency electricity keeps her areolas bubbled up. Might the Stims ripple from Robyn's neck to her armpits and palms and inner thighs and foot bottoms, so to Robyn's body will ripple as well.

Cybernetician opens up Robyn's Hole Gag an f-stop to double her airflow. And her speculum spreader funnels fresh runnel down her tube and into her collection bag.

Babs assumes, *I need to beg to drink Robyn's roily. I have to debase myself, and do in advance what she is forced to do.*

Game Mistress again commands the Lobelia's attention. "You losers got to see Robyn's raspberry-red receptaculum get machine fucked in the Amphitheater, and I regret to say you won't be seeing it again today."

Yes, it is buried inside plaster; everything except the top of Robyn's shaven ravine is already under solidified plaster.

GM continues. "A *Video* of the Monkey Fist climbing into Robyn cervix has been uploaded to Automatron; Gamers play it in Robyn's Eyepods from time-to-time while masturbating her. Different trigger spots, all part of her conditioning. Or should we say, her learning to love watching, hearing, and feeling herself surrender."

Game Mistress raises Swagger Goad, and arcs a spark over to the hole in the Plaster that protrudes and extends out Robyn's Hole Gag. The Lobelia certainly witness Robyn's exposed torso jerk, and again watch yellow fluid descend out a tube protruding from the plaster, and collect in Robyn's urine contributions.

The spark produces a sharp crack and a giant Naked Negro enters into the view shared by the Seven Lobelia. The Naked Negro bears a tub of wet plaster and a sizeable erection, and is recognized by the Lobelia as the same Naked Negro who pushed Robyn's Cart to and from the Amphitheater.

Cybernetician skillfully brings Robyn back into her copulatory rhythms. Polytempo Computer Ballet, bump and grind, breathing in and squeezing her waist tighter, torquing the Anal Intruder, squeezing the Monkey Fist and its wiggly fingers. Ever so slightly accelerated pace; the shock produced not only a release of urine but a blob of runnel into the tubing, now Cybernetician and Robyn are flowing runnel steadily again.

All Seven Lockdown Lobelia had witnessed Robyn get force-climaxed watching Kimju's tongue get pierced at the Amphitheater. Robyn had been wearing clamps on her nipples with dangling weights, and Gamers debate if they were simply moderators to her over-the-top climax, or pain conditioning.

Babs knows, *We are about to watch Robyn climax again.*

Inside her cocoon, Robyn yields to Cybernetician's affections. Some would say she is smart not to resist, after all, she can't, the events happening are beyond her control. Resisting might mean the Cybernetician would have to adopt its teaching methods, but Robyn does not resist. She doesn't think much either, but....

Robyn does feel. And the feeling of the first drops of the texture of wet plaster slathered onto her bare pubis triggers her conditioning and drives her arousal upward immediately. The wet plaster settles into whatever part of Robyn's sexual ravine not already cast. It is the last that the Lockdown Lobelia see of Robyn's vulva, pubis, and tattooed degradations.

Robyn makes a gasp through her air tube, Cybernetician opens her Hole Gag aperture a bit more, and raises her heartbeat a little bit as Robyn feels the hands press the plaster against her pelvis. And then gently glides into the Zone. It is not the first plaster Robyn has experienced, obviously, and Robyn's craving challenges Cybernetician's ability to contain, throttle, and sear into Robyn's brain the climax she craves.

The Lobelia can see the remaining skin of Robyn's torso quiver. Runnel pumping out her valiva drain line and falls into her bag constantly now.

GM makes a gesture, and the Naked Negro wipes the head of his giant penis left and right on Robyn's belly, centers the tip of his erection on the tip of Robyn's outie navel, and ejaculates. The Naked Negro retains his erection, uses the head of his penis to swab the cum into and around Robyn's crater. When he backs away the cum runs down Robyn's lower belly behind the fresh plaster covering her pelvis and sex ravine.

Inside the Mummy, Cybernetician helps Robyn pulse tones of music out her Hole Gag opened aperture. Robyn felt the penis head, the heat of the semen painting her button, and the itchy and irritating feeling of it creeping down her lower belly and pelvis.

Robyn's passions drive her higher; she surfs now somewhere on her reptilian brain, a rhythmic steady but gentle climax, one Robyn doesn't want to let go of, in fact, Robyn wants to go higher, where she does not control. And climax her brains out. Cybernetician makes her want it more.

The Naked Negro resumes work, building upward, wet as the cool heavy slurry closes in on Robyn's lower belly, her navel, and upward toward her rib cage.

Robyn desires to void, but the Cath has now turned her bladder off. There is only one place in her body she can channel to, and that is her sex. Robyn channels, as the texture of the plaster of Paris and anticipation of the inevitable end state drive Robyn into a higher pitch of climax. She feels the front of her torso submerge, and her belly button disappears.

Babs knows, *Robyn is just a canvas. I know where this is going. The painting and sculpture are for me. Gamers are going to close her up completely and climax condition her. She doesn't have a chance.* Babs seeps fresh cream. *I'm next. I don't have a chance either. I deserve it.*

Babs feels sorry for Robyn, despite *she's the reason I'm a Whore next Term.* But then Babs hardens, *does the covering over of Robyn's navel with plaster violate her Cosmos navelage 24x7 commitment?*

And does that affect me? My button is already pierced and tattooed. I'm navelage 24x7 forever. At the beginning of this Term that was my only commitment. Now I'm in for a lot more. Not just getting fucked, I'll beg to fuck in front of a Crowd.

Babs is becoming wise to how the Game works.

And how does Steph feel about Robyn's vanishment? *I hate the raghole; I want to watch her to get gangbanged during her period. And suck her blood off the cocks. Then Gamers should turn all her dials up to 200 percent and drive her mad.*

Steph secretes.

As more plaster envelopes more of Robyn's body she feels more afraid and more sexually excited, total surrender melded with total arousal.

Robyn's breasts and rose-colored nipples anticipate the oncoming wetness of slurry which will become solid and cast the contours of her last exposed skin. Robyn's nipples remain painfully tender from getting climaxed while wearing clamps with swinging weights in the Amphitheater. Since her casting, Robyn's Crawlers have morphed into rings which squeeze around her nipples, constantly stimulating them, and sending feelers out across Robyn's areola to ensure they stay puckered up. For a moment, they retreat from their round tops so as the Naked Negro encloses both breasts and nipples in the rising plaster, Robyn may experience total unencumbered loss.

The Crawlers will thin out and slide between the plaster and Robyn's skin and travel anywhere they want. They are extremely unpleasant.

Slavesex goes wild. Cybernetician can't hold her back when the wet plaster coats over her two areolas and erect nipples, and buries all of her 34B breasts. The Crawlers reestablish between the plaster and the skin, form disks of spikes atop each areola, and a circle of lancers pointing at the base of each nipple and with sufficient AI to maintain the nipple erected, might that be so desired.

Crawlers on Robyn's areolas and nipples play in tandem with the Stims already cast into the plaster, and already quite functional inside the nearly closed Mummy. A Stim buzzes Robyn's already buried ruby, the Speculum sends charges where it presses against Robyn's raspberry vestibule, and the Cath inside her pee hole tingles. Robyn has no control. Stims on her buried thighs radiate upwards, stims on her pulled wide-open sex lips radiate inward, and cream flows down her vaginal pipe, collecting in a small funnel, also buried in the plaster, and drains through the Mummy to the outside, where it drips into a clear collection bag.

And might Robyn require alternate stimulation, the swollen Anal Intruder remains ready to pulsate and juice the sensitive inner linings of Robyn's rectum, and the Monkey Fist, residing inside Robyn's cervix, can always uncurl its fingers and thumb, canvass all of Robyn's insides, and torment her g-spot.

Cybernetician twiddles Slavesex's nipple Crawlers, now buried within the slurry, to assure Robyn they are still functional, and Robyn quickens her pace, pitches into a running climax and loses all control of her mind, body, and soul. Robyn is unable to thrash to release any of the tension, the only thing she can do is squeeze her pussy and rectum.

And sing. "Eaoooooooooooo uh uh uh…"

If at first Cybernetician is reluctant to let Robyn draw in all the air she needs, the AI quickly relents, and opens the Hole full aperture. Robyn has a big mouth, she breaths hard, and peaks.

The noises acquire a hollow resonance as they emerge from the tube that protrudes from her plaster head. Robyn gives it up, no choice in the matter; and the sensations of her body being totally enclosed terrifies her whereas the sensations to absolute nirvanic sexual pleasure ensure ecstasy.

Robyn continues to peak as the Naked Negro smooths the last plaster over her vanished body. The Naked Negro nods with Game Mistress and exists the Lobelia's frame.

If before Robyn wanted to go higher and higher, now, running full out-of-control cum state, and running out of breath, she falters for a moment; a Monkey Finger touches her g-spot and Robyn trills the last of her breath, collapsing and panting, …, with Cybernetician rescuing her as she comes down, catching her while her heartbeat is still strong, leveling her, still surfing in the thinner part of the Zone, but dazed. Cybernetician will keep a close watch on Robyn's metrics, from her body temperature, blood oxygen levels, to her breathing, urine, and runnel drip rates.

"Full body mummification!" Game Mistress proclaims, "Total loss of her skin and muscles on the outside, total loss of her sensory organs, her nose and breathing, her mouth and food and fluids. And also lost are her insides; as she learns that her stomach and bowels and pee hole are bidirectional, she can't help but feel more of herself get taken away. We know her blood type, monitor her blood, and are equipped to drain and transfuse blood.

"Now that she and her Charm are contained, Cybernetician shall now mediate Slavesex's arousal. Cybernetician measures and learns, and now that Robyn's mind and body are taken and under management, Cybernetician shall assist in dismantling her soul, possessing her, and installing a new self. It would have to be an improvement, wouldn't you agree?"

Yes, I get it, Babs processes. *Cybernetician has huge persuasive abilities. Gamers are going to manufacture a sex tiger. And put it on a leash. They don't need to do that to me. It's very simple, I will do whatever I'm told, any hole, every hole, all at once, two dicks at once. I will do it better than anyone else, I want to be a Dong and Dirty Whore, not a Slavesex.*

Cybernetician keeps Slavesex Robyn humming in the Zone, and Robyn's oozing runnel continues to drip into her collection bag.

Game Mistress touches the Goad to the bag collecting the oozing runnel. "Work product from a Slavesex," GM humors, and looks Seven Lockdown Lobelia in the eye.

Game Mistress consoles the Lobelia as they watch the heavy Mummy hang in the air and slowly rotate. "Slavesex Robyn earned all of you a stopped Clock, and since she will be a repeat offender, then no doubt she can repeat stopping her Clock, and Charm those around her. Just like she charmed you. She's dangerous."

The Cosmos Lockdown Lobelia watch as the trolly moves the heavy Plaster Mummy out of their common Eyepods point-of-view. If they had not seen the last of the pour, they might not believe Robyn is inside. They still can't quite believe their eyes.

GM shares wisdom with the Cosmos Lockdown Lobelia, "You may think that keeping a Slavesex contained like this is an expensive luxury. You are correct. But it is not without purpose.

"Training for Slavesex's next phase of life has begun. First, Slavesex acquires a blank slate. Empty core. No sound, no vision, no smell, no taste, no sensation on skin. Hallucinations to entertain herself. Total isolation and lack of body movement. Slavesex, or whatever is cast inside the plaster, will soon come to crave any attention; even the smallest tremors from the Stims will be a welcomed alternative to long hours of nothingness.

"More than anything else, she will learn to crave sexual arousal, and frustrated at being kept in heat yet held back from release, and achieve steady flow of her runnel. Cybernetician can let her climax occasionally so she may achieve ecstasy and Nirvana.

"When Slavesex is hatched from the Mummy she should not require ropes or handcuffs or cages, but she will desire them and beg arousal. She will eagerly present herself, shall abandon herself, and submit to the control of her desire. Most certainly this craven ectoplasm will Strip in the most vulgar manner, Whore every hole and fetish, and beg guidance by Gamers on how to become a magnificent Slavesex!"

Is Robyn listening to this? No, inside her cocoon, Slavesex is lost in the Zone, humming along, surrendering to her total entombment. Totally terrified, totally helpless, totally zoned. Totally oozing thick and aromatic runnel.

Totally loved. Cybernetician makes sure that as the plaster sets around Robyn's nipples that Robyn breathes deeply so as the plaster hardens she has room to breathe deep and fast, even if she will scratch her nipples against the inside. And sends a wild maniacal laugh into her ears.

Seven Lobelia consider the totally of Slavesex Mummy, trying to reconcile that Robyn Runaway really lies inside. *It's real,* each admits, *unbelievable, but real.*

Game Mistress shrugs and tips her chin up in the direction of the hanging Plaster Mummy. "Cybernetician will find a rhythm so Slavesex may continue to cum without exhausting herself, and eventually let her slip off into a deep sleep.

"Robyn's life is totally dependent upon other people," Game Mistress states, then shrugs. "But that's not exceptional, that's true for all of us."

V-5 Molly: Departs the Play Party

§ Game Mistress Tells Molly: Beg Handjobs Keep Props

Sometime while Molly was a shared witness to Robyn's final mumification, she had been lowered to her knees, still breast bound and held upright, but no longer suspended by her oversize mammillarias. Molly had spread her knees enough so that a palm could be laid against her bare sex… and a finger proved that Ben-Wa Balls inhabited her deep purple insides. At some point Molly feels a mitten loosen and worked free, but as her liberated fingers flex they quickly encounter a very hard and very erect cock.

As she gets her wits about her Molly knows what to do. She handjobs the cock. Feeling it, contributing to it, interacting with it. She doesn't know if the Clock has started ticking again or not, or if Midnight has come and gone, but she knows that *I will be handjobbing cocks from now on.*

The cock cums in Molly's hand. Given that Molly's hand isn't going anywhere, the ejaculate will remain as deposited.

Molly assumes that the other hand is about to be freed. It will be eventually, and like with Babs, Molly's ejaculate collections will soon overflow her hands and demand creative disposition.

Molly had reacted to Robyn's pour and the hanging Plaster Mummy with shock. *I'm in Lockdown through no fault of my own, I'm in Lockdown because of Robyn.* Molly's remote eyes forced her to confront the alternate reality between her vision, a stereoscopic view of Robyn dripping runnel into her collection bag, and the sensation of feeling flesh against her own clamped tongue. *And get a taste of what I am pretty sure I collected in one hand or the other.* Molly is grateful for the Tongue Clamp, *because without it,* Molly is sure, *I'd be an oral mouth.*

Still a possibility.

Another cock erupts in one of Molly's hands, and after the next one Molly no longer bothers to keep count. Sticky on her hands and wrists, on her thighs and massive moons, shall be Molly's new norm. And Molly correctly assumes she gets some on her clamped tongue. And gets face painted.

Molly had been given a glimpse of the **Risen Cocks Lineup** earlier, and had recognized Tiffany sucking cock and getting her twat twisted, still with her asshole held high by an **Ass Hook** connected to a cable up to the trolly above.

Molly is also increasingly grateful for the **Ben-Wa Balls** inhabiting her vagina, as well as the **Procto** leisurely worming its way up her mawkway. *The good news is they prevent dicks from fucking and analing me; the bad news is that now everyone wants cocks in my mouth. I've seen what happens. Sticky fingers, then sticky mams, then sticky in my nose and a little bit of sticky on the tip of my tongue. Still, sticky is a small price to pay for not getting cocked during Lockdown. Even sticky swiped behind my Tongue Clamp.*

If Gamers take off my Tongue Clamp it won't be sticky anymore.

Molly's goal has remained constant: *Return to the Nugget and Strip next Term. Dance, play with my mams, lay a vibrator on my pink and ooze mung, share Props, eat good food.*

And the price to pay is I get fondled and fingered, like before, but this Term I'm a jerkoff girl, a titty-fucker, cum guzzler, and maybe an oralator as well.

But no cock in my mooe or my muck. That's the gig.

For sure this time I'll be the one eating cum, and not feeding what spots through their pants back to the Patrons.

I think what will happen is mostly we'll share. That will be sweet.

Game Mistress reestablishes her posture afront the common pair of Eyes that service the Seven Eyepods of Seven naked Lobelia. GM bows to the Cam and speaks to her admirers. "As has been the case all along, your Eyepods ensure none of you can see any other, and your Seven gagged mouths make sure all remain mute.

"Might you wonder about what the Eighth of you sees, be affirmed that if not blackness or static, Robyn's Eyepods and Earpods present her with views of cameras and sounds from inside her various orifices: inside her mouth, her stomach, her lungs, her bladder, her vagina, her rectum, even inside a blood vessel. Possibly even occasional views of her hanging Plaster Mummy, might a disruptor give it a push, in sync with her sensations, or out of sync with them.

"Cybernetician shall analyze all such inputs, and seek to discover how to transmogrify the now helpless Robyn Rodomontade into the sensualist, Rimmer Rydeme."

Babs processes. *Robyn was a Cosmos Pledge in the Term before this one, she was redacted and became my Pledge. Now I am a Dong and Dirty Whore, and Robyn is cast inside a Plaster Mummy.*

GM reestablishes power. "So, you know the Fate of One Cosmos Lockdown Lobelia is Slavesex, that Two others of you beg Whore, and the remaining Five are begging to Opt Strip.

"The Slavesex will be vanished into the Dungeon where her sexual appetites shall be both expanded yet channeled, cammed, and forwarded to Automatron.

"The remainder of you shall also depart, obviously, as we anticipate Midnight.

"But who shall leave in what order, which of you shall be required to prove your begging, and which of you might require more training before Midnight? Lockdown Lobelia don't need to know such things; Lockdown Lobelia need to know that you are Whores destined to be bound, beaten, bruised, and blown, banged, and buggered until Midnight. Every hole, serving every sex, anywhere, anytime, in front of anybody, live, and on cam. Someday you can thank Robyn Runaway for your conveyance.

Game Mistress gestures her Swagger Goad and the Eyepods for Six Cosmos Lobelia (except Molly) go black, and Six Earpods of the same Six Lobelia go silent. The Six are Babs, Tiffany, Kimju, Steph, Beka and Elle.

Molly alone retains sight and sound.

Molly's Eyepods cuts to a shot of her own gluteus maximus square on and filling the frame but not kissing the sides of it. Molly rustles in her Ring Gag and Tongue Clamp, armbinder, and wiggles her sticky fingers. Molly doesn't know that Six other Eyepods and Earpods have gone black and silent; Molly alone hears Game Mistress command, "Bend forward, pull those butt cheeks apart, show off that asshole of yours!"

Molly obeys, discovers that the securements of her wrist and forearms make way for her to reach downward so that her sticky fingers try to get a firm grip on her butt cheeks and pull them far enough apart to display her asshole to a hovering Cam. The Procto has been kind to Molly, and makes sure her bowels show gape and the sparkle of the stainless steel inside.

GM augments, "On your face and knees, spread, reach for your pussy lips. Yank them open and show the Prefecture what you've got in your meatlocker."

Molly obeys, partly. She is unaware that her bound mammaries are disconnected from the trolly above, and is able to touch the Procto lurking inside her anus, watches herself wiggle her fingers in her Eyepods, but she can't quite stretch enough to dip a finger into her pussy. It doesn't matter; Molly watches as a hand enters the frame, pushes apart her shaven bare meatlocker lips, and shows the hovering Cam her pee hole, and the sparkle of her Ben-Wa Balls down inside. One unseen hand scoops a fingertip of goo off one of Molly's scummed hands, touches it to Molly's mainspring, and gives Molly a trill.

Molly discovers herself being straightened up again, and the vision in her Eyepods cuts from her own pink and gape to black. Molly finds the blackness more comforting than her open gape; hands help Molly to stand, jarred as Molly feels her hands, apparently disengaged also from the armbinder behind her back, being brought around her sides and fastened together in front of her body so that her wrists are crisscrossed and her palms face inward.

Molly is quickly able to determine that she must hold her hands in front of her torso: if she lifts them too much they yank on a chain down to her clithood, and if she lowers them too much they yank on a chain to her nose.

§ Game Mistress Tells Molly: Leave & Go to Nugget

Game Mistress makes an announcement to an otherwise blind-deaf-mute Molly; no other Cosmo Lobelia hears it. "You shall leave now, Molly Mammoth" GM pronounces. "You shall return to the Nugget again. You shall share your Ben-Wa Balls and Procto with the other Nuggets, as directed by your House Mom, of course.

"You should be looking forward to getting your elements auctioned, your moneybox masturbated, and your mammies manhandled. And I bet House Mom insists that a jerky girl like you just keep piling the goo on, and at the end of your shift you solo, or you and another handjob artist, can mount center Stage and clean goo off your mammies, lick goo off each other's faces, and sucking it off your jerky fingers?"

Not really, Molly considers, apparently not pressed for an answer. *Mostly it's about good food, a good bed, and not have to worry about life.*

Game Mistress cocks her head. Molly can't see her but imagines her a few feet in front of her, chin up, head tilted down. "You're going to get excellent at titfucking their cocks and getting goo all over your mams and neck and face. You're going to collects their shots into your open mouth, aren't you?

Molly hesitates.

"Answer me!" Game Mistress commands.

Molly shall. "Aaha-aaha!"

Game Mistress opens new vistas and Molly hears a transliteration of her voice in her Earpods, "Play with your mazoomas, Stripper."

Molly obeys, discovers that she can pivot her crisscrossed wrist bound hands upward and discover that her drooping 38DD's are no longer bound.

Squeezing her recently bound breasts produces sparkles of pain, and even more pain erupts when the palms of her nipples settle into the palms of her hands.

The Ben-Wa Balls in Molly's mooe and the Procto occupying her muckway remind Molly of their presence and her goal. And so Molly plays with her mazoomas. She keeps lifting them up and down, mauls them, tugging them squishing them together, pinching her nipples, rotating them. Soon they too are coated with sticky.

Molly needn't worry if there is more sticky to come.

It is very simple, really, because Molly needn't think too much about what she is doing. If the Running Agent thinks Molly needs to put more work into her play, it needn't tell her, the Procto simply starts a gentle, building buzz, that encourages Molly to play harder.

And is Molly content with her mission? Molly just does. *Gamers and Players are fascinated watching me play with my mams, so all I have to do is squeeze and push them around. Or let Patrons fondle them.* Molly takes a deep breath, *I am going to where I want to be, and where Gamers want me to be. That's most important to me.*

§ Molly Exits: Walk & Breastplay at Same Time

Molly's exit is as graceful as her arrival, only instead of hanging on the opposite end of a balance beam with Babs, Molly remains free of encumbrances, except for Eyepods and Earpods, her Hole Gag and Tongue Clamp, Ben-Wa Balls, Procto, and wrist harness.

Molly's wrists remain crossed and cuffed in front of her, and remain chained between her nose and clithood rings. And with enough slack to "maul her mams." Might Molly neglect this primary activity, her Procto will most certainly remind her.

This time the Voice of Game Mistress sounds mechanical, but it is a real command, reinforced by discipline in her rectum. "Walk," it commands.

And so Molly takes small tentative steps, and starts walking. And keeps mauling her mams.

"Prepare to turn right," the Voice states.

Molly prepares, the Eyepods stay black, and bare-bald-naked Molly must trust the Voice as she moves through the Play Party by command, while playing with her breasts and nipples constantly.

"Turn right."

Molly does her best to make a square turn. This time the Voice commands, " Stop." Then it instructs, "pivot arms down," and Molly obeys, so her palms lie face up, in front of her stomach.

Molly expects to administer a handjob, but instead feels a huge gob semen dumped into her palms, the work product of many ejaculations, and she hears the Voice order her to "pivot arms up," which she does. Molly doesn't need further instruction to smear the additional semen all over and around her mams. But she can't reach her face or her muliebre.

Molly finds the haze annoying, and preferring laziness to arousal, she performs breastplay by rote, long able to mesmerize strangers playing with her "mamazulons" without giving any thought to her improvisation.

Molly had expected the worst at the Play Party, *I had expected to be bound, beaten and gangbanged, but that hasn't happened.*

I did see Robyn get poured. She's got plumbing in her nose and stomach, and in her ratchet, rectum, and pee hole; I saw her urine bag, her enema bag, and her runnel bag.

I wonder how long she is in for?
Six Terms.

Molly shakes her head. *Enough! My treatment has been comparatively benign. No blowjobs, no marks, no pain; no additional piercings beyond the ring already in my nose and my navel. Plus my old clithood ring, sparkling in the light now that all my muff is gone. All because Steph drove Robyn to run and Babs was asleep on the job.*

Because for sure next Term I'll be doing handjobs at the Nugget. I'll be letting the Patrons squeeze my majonkers and finger-fuck me for sure. And cleaning my fingers off. I don't know if I'm sucking cock or not. That will depend.

Molly has one additional tattoo beyond the alchemical signs hidden in her navel cave, labia, and armpit, plus three more signs hiding in plain sight, on one big splotchy areola, and on a foot and a finger. Molly knows these six tattoos are part of a single tattoo which consists of "the entire Periodic Table," and *I expect that the Nugget will auction off more and more signs. Until I'm covered. I've got 87 elements to go, provided they don't include plutonium, saltpeter, or balsam, which aren't even natural elements, as if that matters. They are going to put more elements in my armpits, around my asshole, all over my mams, and on my ears and face.*

So much for the Periodic Table. The one additional tattoo is the fire erupting from Molly's navel. Gamers had given Molly a glance at Kimju, who had been Molly's Roommates when both were Strippers one Term ago, and who remain confidants. Molly had read Kimju's ink, *ink radiating not just from her birth button but also her nips and her vag. Gamers turned her into a Whore and an inkblot because they want cock in her and want to make sure that there is no going back for her. Me, they have made sure I can't get fucked. That just means they are saving me for later.*

It's doesn't matter as long as the food is good.

Molly keep kneading her breasts in her hands. *At least I am going back to the Nugget,* Molly accepts, *however I know that I will not make it through till Midnight without handjobbing more cock, and getting more goo dumped on me. And if they take the Tongue Clamp off I'll be sucking cock for sure, and if they take off the Ring Gag I'll show them I can apply my full mouth to their cock and balls. I'll even tickle their assholes with my tongue.*

But I am not going to have to put out! None the less, next Term while I'm dancing, these Videos *will run on the Nugget Screens. If not the Lobby. The whole Prefecture.*

Gamers will pressure me next Term to beg to Whore. Just like Kimju is already begging, probably already become. Molly looks with her eyes open but only sees blackness. *House Mom is Janet, and Janet is nice but stern. Janet will demand that I lapdance naked and get fondled and finger-fucked, and handjob and taste cum.*

And she may want me to beg that cocksucking isn't sex.

Gamers had also provided Molly a glimpse of her current Roommate Steph, who at that particular moment had been kneeling, naked, and with her nose stud held level by a line to the trolly above, her arms and hands retrained behind her back, and who at first glance appeared sans ink.

Molly does wonder. *Is my Roommate Steph still holding a guaranteed Opt-Up, and is she still going to promote to Monitor next Term (Roommates Apart)? Or is she going to Opt Strip like I am and maybe be my Roommate again at the Nugget (Roommates Together)?*

Ah, the facts that Molly doesn't know. Might Steph confront *Videos* she doesn't even know exist, then might Molly, as Steph's Roommate, also share Steph's Karma?

Molly feels the Procto direct irritating vibrations into her rectum and she regains her pace slathering goo onto her mams with the palms and fingers of her two constrained hands. Molly knows, *I am thinking too much; most of the Strippers who fondle their breasts make themselves wet, but me? I'm indifferent. I don't do it for me, I do it for them, and they want me to walk and maul my mams at the same time, I will do it.*

Game Mistress looks at Molly with a grim face and a private prayer, *May Kundalini enlighten your inner cravings and encourage you to learn.*

Molly knows how to learn. *If Gamers want me to maul my mams, pinch my mammilla, I can do that. And squeeze mucilage out my mutton? I can do that too.*

§ Molly & Back Door Man: Cocksucking & Stage Door

There had been another glimpse that Molly had been provided, and that had been naked Babs, while she had been hanging by her boobs, horizontal but with her feet on the floor, knees bent 90 degrees, legs spread wide, and a man's pelvis level with her spread crotch.

It doesn't matter what Molly really saw, what Molly interpreted was *Bondo Banggo getting fucked. Better she be a Whore than any of us. And if I have to suck cock, I want to watch her suck cock also.*

At some point approaching Midnight, blind-deaf-mute Molly follows her nose and her instructions as she is walked out one of the doors and is not seen again at the Play Party.

Molly feels the difference in the air and worries, *how will I get to the Nugget?*

Silly Lobelia; Molly figures it out. *I actually don't need to worry about how I get transported to the concrete slab outside the Nugget Stage Door; their only reason to streak me is to capture me and put me in Lockdown again, and that's not going to happen because I'm already in Lockdown.*

Besides, *I had to show the Cam I'm carrying the Ben-Wa Balls and Procto, and I'm delivering them to the Club.*

So I won't have to fuck the Back Door Man to get in. Ha ha ha. He can feel me up and finger me anytime, just like the last time I Stripped. This time on the way in if he wants a handjob I guess I will oblige him. And inside too, and not just him again; House Mom will insist I jerk off every Patron.

What I don't know is if I have to blow the Back Door Man to get in. It's really up to him, isn't it. And he might demand I deliver the Ben-Wa Balls and Procto to him and then fuck and anal me. Except maybe it's up to House Mom. Janet. Because if she lets him paint my face and I have to wear it into the Club, then I'm marked for the rest of the Term as a cum mop.

And for sure what happens outside the Stage Door gets streamed to the Club, maybe even fed to Automatron and the Prefecture.

Molly takes a deep breath and bounces her hanging mams. Molly has achieved her goal of returning to the Nugget and Stripping. Certainly in the past Molly's on-Stage performances have included a strip-nude-pink-toy-masturbate envelope; her lapdance work included a lot of rubbing her mams in a lot of faces, *and rubbing my face and mams in a lot of groins.* Molly had tried to consolidate her pee to visits to the Camera Lounge.

The last time Molly stripped (the Term before this one), when a Patron popped through their pants, *I knew to collect the spunk on the side of a finger and feed my admirer.*

This Term posits to be different.

This Term, Molly should know, that when she presents herself naked at the Stage Door and begs admittance, *my tasks will include all of the above, plus taking dicks out, jerking them off, even titfucking them, and depending, possibly kissing their tips, possibly even sucking them.*

Possibly?

Okay. So at the Nugget this coming Term, dicks that pop will not necessarily be inside of pants. Will not be inside of pants. And I will not be feeding the jizz back to its Patron. I will be consuming it myself. After all, getting facialed and swallowing scum isn't sex.

Beka & Elle Meet Gimbled It: Secrets Revealed (LD7)

V-6 Six Cosmos Lobelia & Others: Status Updates

§ Cosmos Lockdown Lobelia: Status & the Departed

Gimbled It is about to arrive by overhead trolly and catalyze competition among the Six remaining, naked and secured, Cosmos Lockdown Lobelia. Stripper Molly has been dispatched to the Nugget, and the Plaster Mummy hangs nearby.

Seven Cosmos Lobelia watched Robyn through shared, common Eyepods as Game Mistress briefed them on Robyn's many encumberments; they watched the Naked Negro ejaculate on her navel, finish sealing Robyn totally in plaster, and exit with his huge erection intact.

Robyn remains fully encased, all exits bagged and reversable, stomach bi-directional, breathing gasses regulated, brainwaves and heartbeat and blood monitored, arousal and climax controlled. Robyn is being reprogrammed into a sex animal, totally desirous and controlled by her sex. Soon she will crave any and all body contact, even a fingertip. Anytime, anyplace, anywhere, by anybody.

Penny and Coco have come and gone. Initially they spent a long stretch of their time at the Party sucking cocks on the Risen Cocks Lineup, while getting their proffered rectums and vaginas warmed. Both had been provided generous benefits. No Lobelia except Tiffany is aware of this fact.

Since promoting to Dong and Dirty Whores, both Penny and Coco have sought, and will continue to seek, vengeance upon Babs, a.k.a. "Burse Bitch." Both expect BB will join them at Flesh Ranch, and because neither Whore is able to lay a finger upon the untouchable Janet, both desire to double the pain and humiliation they inflict upon Babs. Earlier at the *Play Party* they presented themselves wearing Babs (and Steph's) previous Garments, delightfully confusing both former Cosmos.

Babs had the luxury of having her tongue clamp removed, and despite her face-wrenching O-Ring Gag, ate creampies out of Penny and Coco's pussies and assholes, swallowed their valiva, and drank streams of their fresh piss. BB's humiliation had been total.

Penny and Coco willfully left Babs confused. BB hopes that Penny and Coco really have been promoted (evidenced by their acquisition of Garments), and are harmless Pledge next Term, but Babs' deeper worry is that *if indeed the Garments were a ploy to scramble my head, because I'm ending up at Flesh Ranch, and that's a given, and Penny and Coco reside there, they will make me their lacky, licker & toilet. That's a given too.*

It is fear well taken.

Babs also fears, *Penny and Coco successfully extracted the Double Dong from Beka and Elle's assholes and carried it away in their mouths. That's disgusting. But unlike all my Pledge, my ex-Pledge that is, I have never ridden the Dong. Never soloed, never shared. Penny and Coco are going to give it to me in every hole, and they are going to make me do what they had to do.*

They will make sure I'm a Dong and Dirty Flesh Ranch Whore.

Game Mistress focuses upon the Six remaining Cosmos Lobelia visiting the Meatpacking Plant. She ignores a hanging Mummy.

Gamers smell eagerness by newbies Beka and Elle, concessions by both Kimju and Tiffany, guilt by ex-Monitor BB, and naivety by Steph. Gamers have reviewed their histories and rivalries, heard plaintive begging, and intend to continue their reduction.

Two beg to Whore; Four beg to Strip, although one of the Four believes her begs are fake. That would be Steph, who continues to believe that her begging to Opt-Strip is a charade, that any pains she feels are artificially induced. Steph might be correct, but her Fate could be different than she expects.

§ Beka & Elle: Lockdown Lobelia Status Update

Roommates Beka and Elle experience anticipation and anxiety at the *Play Party*. They have toured the overhead rail system, been fondled and fingered, paddled, flogged, and caned. They bear marks. Both know why: they Free-Fucked. They broke a Rule which forbids Pledge to have sex, to practice coitus, to be exact. Both have confessed to their acts; one has left behind proof of her wanton sexual coupling, and one, who bears no record of her acts, pleads to reenact the two suck-fuck-anal scenes she performed in order to procure her *Measurement Nudes*.

Elle is not looking forward to her future at this moment. Free-Fucking is an automatic Opt-Whore; and each Roommate quite independently begged to be a Dong and Dirty Whore, and by design or accident, begged their Roommate share their Fate. Neither is aware of the other's transgressions, confessions, and begs, but their Fate as Whores will be delayed while they practice Stripping for a Term at the Nugget. This is mandated by Beka's Immunity.

Elle has a hard time wrapping her head around the Game and ponders the unfairness of the situation into which she has been placed. *Opt-Monitoring had been my intent. I was sent into a trap, and now I am a Stripper begging to be a Dong and Dirty Whore. I need to find Beka, and find a way out of this.*

Beka's Garage fuck with Rodney qualifies her as a Whore, but her Immunity retards this recasting, so she will strip a Term at the Nugget (coincident with Elle), prior to Opting Whore, Beka's ultimate destination, *because it is the Caste of Porn Stars!*

While Beka was secured on the Post Henge (LD2), Cowboy had revealed to her that Rodney had secretly videoed their sex act. Cowboy had even screened the evidence to her via her Eyepods.

This secret revelation of the *Beka & Rodney Fuck Video* had actually buoyed Beka's spirits. *Not only does my confession prove true, the* Video *solidifies Rodney's guilt, and boosts my own ambitions to Opt Whore and become a Porn Star.*

I'm going to be a great Stripper next Term! I'm going to collect more tattoos, and I'm committed to bringing Elle along! We can eat each other's pussies during a Term at the Nugget and after that we're Flesh Ranch Whores and we can fuck men. BG, BGG, BBGG; I can't wait for the Cams and "action!"

Beka has given little thought about the implications of screwing Rodney upon Babs, and remains ignorant about fallout landing upon William and the unsuspecting Steph. William and Rodney's Fate, already suspected by some, remains quite outside the knowledge of the Cosmos Lobelia.

But neither Beka nor Elle will be seeing any ex-Peacock between now and Midnight, including learning the Fate of Rodney, if not William and Steph. But Beka does have a care: *I wonder if my* Beka & Rodney Fuck Video *is going to get screened at the Nugget. The more people can watch me have sex the better.*

Except. If Steph sees the Video *of Rodney and me Free-Fucking, Steph will know that both Rodney and I will get twisted. So if indeed Steph broke the Rules and Free-Fucked, and gets caught because of Rodney, she might link her capture to my confession, if she finds out about it. Really though, I'm just a victim.*

Unlike Beka, Elle remains uncertain and ambivalent about her commitment to Strip for a Term and beg to become a Dong and Dirty Whore thereafter. Despite her fears, Elle does secretly admit to herself, *I really am a Whore. Beka will fuck anybody just for the fun of it, the pure pleasure, I always trade sex anticipating getting something in return. This time I didn't have a choice, I had to give all my holes away, twice, to procure something Monitor Babs had demanded. And I had to present her with evidence of* Gonzo Suck and Fuck, *even threesomes. She set me up.*

Well, actually Gamers set me up, Babs was just their agent.

If indeed Beka wishes to beg that her *Video* with Rodney get screened, and if indeed Elle wishes to make good on her promise to reenact her whoring to procure the *Measurement Nudes* and the *Gonzo Videos*, then Gamers assume that the Meatpacking Plant might provide an adequate location.

§ Kimju: Lockdown Lobelia Status Update

Kimju is despondent in her prospects, although she does value the bodyart she accumulates. Kimju might have earned an Opt-Monitor before Robyn's escape, but she has collapsed fast. She felt relieved when the Eyes took a bloody Kotex gag out of her mouth and, when interrogated in the Basement, she had offered to eat and suck the sex organs of both Madam Inquisitor and Pimp Interrogator, blow and eat and fuck anybody, actually, and lick any asshole too.

Begging Whore had been a lower bar than was necessary; Kimju, despite her failing Opt-Up, has an instinct for subservience; for example, throughout the Term, Robyn had treated her like a personal serf. Then-Monitor Babs had indeed informed her Pledge that "when Robyn speaks to you, it is as if the words come from my own mouth; obey them." And Kimju had. Might Robyn order, "expose your knockers," Kimju made sure that both full breasts got revealed. When Robyn ordered, "Piss," Kimju let urine flow.

The most humiliating had been when Robyn ordered Kimju to "spread your legs, pull your pink wide, give a full view to Darleen's Corvette Cam, and masturbate." Kimju resented giving away content that was "out of House, free to all, Public Domain." That had happened during the *Beach Day*, and Kimju knew that Janet, then the Monitor of the Corvettes, would let Darleen upload her intimacies to Automatron. Especially because Kimju displayed wet klammy inside, and pulled her hole with double fingers on each side, so the Cam could see all the way down the pipe.

Kimju's panic had continued to rise after she found herself sitting-spread-secured, and accepted that her failure to sound an alarm had indeed given Robyn Runaway extra time and opportunity.

Kimju's conversion to a more genuine begging to Whore typified her instinct to adopt submissive postures as behavioral solutions. By the time Kimju had found herself displayed in the Amphitheater, she had begged to Double Opt-Down and make Whore, and take on double decoration as well.

Kimju already displays the double decoration commensurate with the Whore Caste. Besides her nose ring, Kimju has already earned a stretched clithood and exciter bar, a compound belly button, a double tongue, and will continue to beg that both nipples get punched with double studs.

Kimju assumes that *my planet tattoos shall also be auctioned off, and that they will compete with the ovals radiating outward from my areolas, navel, and crotch.*

Kimju accepts, *I wanted to be a Monitor next Term, but I also have an opportunity to acquire a bodysuit, and for some crazy reason, I'm begging to Opt Whore.*

Kimju accepts, *Well, no crazy reason, the weight in my tongue reminds me to not make a mistake again. But that's really irrelevant. Robyn got caught, I didn't aid her escape, and Babs is responsible.*

So what is happening? *When I was a Stripper I never let the Patrons take a dick out. Gamers are using Robyn to turn me into a Whore. I* earned *my Opt-Monitor, but Gamers want to fuck me and also cam me fucking, so they can jerk off to me over and over again. That's why I am here.*

Kimju remains unaware that Tiffany considers her Opt-Whore as a swap opportunity.

§ Tiffany: Lockdown Lobelia Status Update

Tiffany assumes that her forearms and spread calves have been secured to the raised platform she occupies. The bottoms of her feet angle upward and invite discipline. Her tiny tits point down and drip semen from cumdumps on her back that have oozed down and around her body. Her bare upheld vertical twister oozes a blend of her own tacky plus a steady diet of creampies. Of course she has a Collection Dish. Everyone on the Risen Cocks Lineup does.

Tiffany appreciated that Penny and Coco knelt to her far left and right, that these already-Whores were also sucking cock and being fucked like she-bitches. Tiffany was also well aware that there was one difference.

Tiffany knows that, unlike Penny and Coco's rectums, which continue to be train-screwed by many, that her own rectum had housed an uplifting Ass Hook, connected to the trolly above. Thus Tiffany's anus and rectum had not been declared a Party Favor.

Tiffany does have one Term of Whoring among her credits, and had used every opportunity to build a Porn Star base. But during that Term Tiffany never did anal. Other Whores did. Dong and Dirty Whores do.

Tiffany contemplates her Ass Hook and the cable upward to her trolly. *I've worn the Procto, the Shaving Cylinder, and the Double Dong in my tailpipe. I've made enema videos. So it's not about things up my ass that I've opposed in the past, it's cocks. Certainly getting eaten and fucking are great, and I'm great at giving blowjobs and eating pussy. And I can fuck on top or on the bottom. But getting fucked in the ass seems asymmetrical. At least with bondage you present a struggle and are really helpless. Anal ravishes you. And you have to clean the cock off afterward. Gross. Then in a bisexual scene you have to clean off yourself twice, and the guys again after they cornhole each other. Double gross and quadruple gross.*

I never practiced anal, never had to, but now? Must I offer up my ass to trade for an Opt-Whore?

And ass-to-mouth too?

Not just A2M my own asshole, everyone else's too? A2OPM?

Silly Tiffany should know that Pledge and Strippers and Whores and Slavesex don't "trade" for anything. Maybe, if Tiffany offers her ass and begs the Game take her rectum away from her, then maybe the Game will value her utility at Flesh Ranch, consider her presence on a yacht cruise, or star in a series of Anal Porn Movies, BG, BBG, BBBG, BBBBG, BBBBBG.

Tiffany knows that *creampies in my pussy are ongoing, and creampies in my ass during Lockdown are a real possibility too.* Tiffany probably doesn't know that BB had recommended she be freed of the Hook, and become anal certified.

Tiffany considers that *Opting to Strip is a steppingstone in the right direction, but if I can Opt-Whore directly, and re-ignite a Porn Star career, that would be much better. I need to find a way to switch with either of the Whore-designates.*

Tiffany evaluates. *Gamers will never let Babs switch. They have to wring her out – if only for Robyn Runaway.*

And Steph is not a candidate. Game Mistress will decide if Robyn's escape, and ergo our Lockdown, cancels Steph's Options and ensures Steph is a Naked Nugget Stripper next Term, pissing and pulling her pink center Stage, or that her Duel victory over Elle really does prevail and guarantees her Opt-Monitor.

Tiffany doesn't know all the facts about Steph, ergo she doesn't know all the possibilities of Steph's Fate.

Tiffany compares herself to Kimju. *I'm a much better asset at Flesh Ranch than Kimju. She can strip another Term and add some spice into her act, but I know more ways to pull pink than she does. She can argue that smoking poles and licking labia isn't sex and beg the Back Door Man to cam her live, naked on her knees and with his cock in her mouth, before she pass through the Stage Door.*

Tiffany smiles to herself. *I need to get to my pussy pounded at Flesh Ranch. Kimju can start begging to Opt Whore during her Term at the Nugget, and if I am still at Flesh Ranch when she arrives I will help her learn all the positions: missionary, doggie, cowgirl, and so on. But she can wait for me to go next.*

Tiffany should be smart enough to understand that *if Gamers let Kimju trade and keep her kunny and kawazoo, that they will take away everything else; which would render Kimju a Stripper Deluxe.*

I too may have to pay a price, even though the switch gives more of my body away to the Game. My twat and my mouth, of course. But I've worked Flesh Ranch before, and, I know I'll have to put out just as much as last time, and a little bit more.

§ Steph: Lockdown Lobelia Status Update

Steph has watched Robyn's misfortune here in the Meatpacking Plant with sadistic glee. As in the past, Steph has been provided rare glimpses of some of the others, frequently coupled with agitations by the Shaven Kit, still housed inside her smoo and sternway. But being mostly blind-deaf-mute, naked-kneeling-armbound Steph simply holds position. Like other Lobelia, Steph has earned a Collection Dish. Like other Lobelia, Steph sports metal through her septum, unlike the others, Steph's connects to the trolly above, requiring that she keep her chin up.

Steph discovers after a while that a view fades into her Eyepods; it takes Steph seconds to interpret that the upward pointed Cam view of a shaven slit, *is my shaven, albeit now stubbly, slit!* And *I am hanging a stalactite of satchel splurt!*

Steph squints, despite not seeing anything. *Gamers deliberately vulgarize and humiliate me,* augers Steph, *and they should know I am above this.* She torques her tongue and pulls the horizontal bars back tight against the O-Ring torturing her gaping mouth. Painful. She squeezes her vagina and watches more syrup squeeze out. Somewhere a Running Agent pipes sounds from the Soap Sphere being squeezed inside Steph's vagina into one of her ears, and pipes sounds from the Tool Cylinder being squeezed inside Steph's rectum into her other ear. Steph struggles to cast off the intrusions, and tries to not to pant.

I am being taken advantage of and Gamers know it! I am having to watch myself splurt, I can't stop watching myself, and the more I watch the more I splurt.

True. Naked Steph has been spread, pinked, fondled, creamed, fingered, and climaxed just like every other Cosmos Lobelia. Steph wears the same Eyepods and Earpods and O-Ring Gag and Tongue Clamp just like the others, and comports a similar armbinder, one which crosses her forearms behind her back so that her buttocks are fully exposed. Steph chaffs that her hands are folded inside mittens, but she understands, *Gamers know I know sign language, and they don't want me sending messages.*

Steph had been led into the Meatpacking Plant by a chain connecting the piercing in her nose with the trolly above. Steph knows enough to kneel so her thighs don't touch and give her bare crotch plenty of air.

Steph continues to believe that what decorates her nose is a strong spring clamp with flat electrical disks inside each nostril; these provide a strong, shocking circuit which Steph seeks to avoid. This all might be true, but may not be the entire apparatus.

Steph resents that she gets fondled and fingered and shakes hands off her body. Steph still believes *I possess a guaranteed Opt-Monitor come Midnight,* and that *Lockdown is a ruse, however it has also become an opportunity for Gamers to inflict genuine pain and humiliation upon me, brought upon by Robyn Runaway. I've already had to pink and pee and cream myself. But Gamers better not think they are going to twist me, like they are going to twist the others.*

Steph continues to remain unaware that her *Sex Videos* with William (and Rodney) have been discovered. Janet had been tasked to reveal their existence to ex-Monitor Babs, along with the existence of a *Beka & Rodney Fuck Video.*

§ Babs & Steph: Status & Potential for Rivalry

Babs, believing Janet, understands that *if my Pledge were Free-Fucking, then I'm a Free-Fucker too. "So goes a Pledge, so goes her Monitor." They're Whores, so I'm a Whore too.*

But if Steph's Free-Fucking doesn't ever get called out, or doesn't exist, could it be Babs begged Dong and Dirty Whore in vain?

No. I failed to prevent Robyn from running away. I should have not let Steph scare her, and I should have checked her bed. I failed myself and others. So I deserve to Whore. I deserve to be analed, gangbanged, clean cocks from any pussy or asshole, and eat any creampie, snowball any mouth, gargle, swallow, collect gokkun and drink jizz by the glass, bukkake drench me, dip me in goo. House me in a glass room with every surface coated in goo.

I actually deserve to be Slavesex.

Going back is increasingly impossible. Is impossible. I'm a Whore now. I can't complain; I deserve it. I actually deserve what Robyn got. After I'm Whore for a while, Gamers will want all of me, if there is anything left. They already have all of me now, and I'll be whatever they want me to be.

It really doesn't matter how I say it, because what's between my legs is now for sale. And assuming Steph gave up her asshole, then I'm giving up what's between my cheeks also. That's why I'm a Dirty Whore and not your ordinary Suck Fuck Facial Porn Star. I'm going to take it up the ass, just like Steph did. And that's how I'm landing at Flesh Ranch. Anal Whore. A2M Bitch. A2OPM Bondo Blowing Banging Bugger Bitch. I'm already destined to be a Porn Star, so I might as well shine.

Steph might be unaware that Babs' Whoredom is a present from herself. Babs' bangbox might resonate with dicks inside Beka and Steph, but BB's butthole owes providence to Steph's repeated anal actions. Well, twice that Gamers know about.

In fact the rivalry between Babs and Steph goes back a Term, when Babs was a newbie Pledge and Steph was her Monitor. Steph regrets she had let Janet act out some of Babs' Karma, and Babs still feels guilty about Janet's adventures.

However when this Term began, Babs had Opted Monitor, and Steph had been released out of Lockdown as a Cosmos Pledge, arriving wearing a tattered dress. During the third week of the Term, and with their roles reversed, Monitor Babs "persuaded" Pledge Steph to audition the Nugget and pink center Stage.

Now Babs is a pinker too.

Steph still disrespects Babs for giving Robyn power over others, and giving Robyn what Steph (and others) perceive as "favorable treatment." Subsequent to Robyn's attempted escape, Babs, like many others, disparage Steph for frightening Robyn into running away, and harbors Karma against her. Steph holds Babs responsible for failing to exert authority over the situation overall.

As things stand, here at the *Play Party*, among the Six remaining Cosmos Lobelia, BB assumes *I am going to publicly suck and fuck cock, here at this Party and in front of these Players and these Cams, and I am going to climax uncontrollably. Squirt. I am going to do this here and before Midnight, and I am going to suck and fuck and anal after Midnight, I'm a Dong and Dirty Whore from now on. All holes, any object, alive or a Prop or a prothesis.*

Steph assumes *at Midnight I shall Opt Monitor Caste. And Babs shall Opt Whore. The glimpse I got of Bang Bitch was that she was hanging by her blaaters, hanging burgoo out her burke, and handjobbing goo.*

So? So Steph explains to herself. *Bondo Bitch was already a Goo Gobbler; she got fed goo with her short hairs during* The Runout. *So being fed goo here in the Meatpacking Plant? That's not so much a new thing, but a reminder of her diet from now on. I hope she's already been throated though the O-Ring; I want to watch her get fucked and buggered in a two-on-one DP bisexual threesome so she can taste multiple assholes. Just like she begs.*

Finally, aside from the fact that Janet revealed the existence (but provided no proof) of a *Steph Sex Video* to Babs, but no other Cosmos, the Cosmos Lobelia have little reason to suspect that Three Cosmos Lobelia in fact Free-Fucked (Steph, Beka, Elle), that two have confessed (Beka, Elle), and that two are mediated (Steph, Beka), and one has yet to learn that last fact (Steph).

§ Other Players: Status Snapshot

Game Mistress will continue training of the Six remaining Cosmos Lobelia present at the Play Party in the Meatpacking Plant. She wears Five Garments, carries a Goad, and shall be obeyed.

Madam Inquisitor and Pimp Interrogator, the Eyes, agents of Mistresses and Masters, adorn themselves with Four Garments each. They certainly visit the Play Party and preside over spaces that incudes cages, racks, tables, benches, chain hoists, water baths, showers, drains, as well as advanced devices. The Eyes goodwill is felt in the Meatpacking Plant, the Eyes have the facility to switch the trollies with their loads throughout the complex, onto passing tracks, sidings that might run into cold or hot rooms, track that might bump onto rail inside a truck parked on the loading ramp.

Madam Nurse Beautician and Pimp Cowboy are not seen by any Cosmos Lobelia; and rumor has it that they inspected the Lineup of Locked Cocks earlier, with Beautician examining the cocks for fullness, foreskins, and fortitude, and Cowboy measuring their assholes for stretch.

The Risen Cocks Lineup still accommodates newbie Whores Hottie and Odee, both buttplugged, with Tiffany in the middle, still poised with her suspended Ass Hook. Three mouths sucking cock, and three pussies trainfucked.

Subsequent to Penny and Coco's departure the two empty spots on the ends were replaced by two reluctant, now-Nugget Strippers, Darleen Dilator and Pacmo Pinky, both clad only in skin-tight transparent thongs which narrowly cover their vaginal slits and assholes, making sure that both vaginas and rectums stay chaste.

Apparently House Mom Janet has heard these two Strippers arguing about "cocksucking isn't sex," and allowed them to attend the *Play Party*, lean forward on spread knees on the opposite ends of the Risen Cocks Lineup, and resolve an argument.

Certainly Janet doesn't need to break the both of them into becoming Strippers Deluxe, but the pleasures of grinding down a masquerading ex-Roommate, as well as tormenting an ex-Superior, are too much for Janet to resist. "Suck like your Caste depends upon it," Janet advises, "Look the Cams in the eye from time to time, so your fans appreciate your willingness to suck cock for them."

Darleen and Pinky suck, they would suck naked if they were told, and are grateful that their thong, despite being crusty and soaked for all to see, prevents vaginal and anal intercourse. Both suspect that their live streams are fed to the Nugget, Automatron, and the Prefecture, and they are correct; sadly they miss the affection of the Patrons back at the Nugget, who cheer each eruption the two fellatrix extract. Patrons know that Strippers who are allowed to suck cock, are probably allowed to handjob as well.

And sometimes beg to whore.

During her visit, House Mom el Capitan Janet had surveilled BB without BB's knowledge, and during an opportune moment, ate into her pussy and trilled her. MomCap Janet wore Three Garments. During another opportunity, Janet pressed Babs' unknowing mouth into her pussy, elicited a tongue on her fat clit, and then deliver a fast stream of piss that flooded BB's mouth, squirted out her nose, and drenched her face and bald head.

Janet needs to prove she can treat her ex-Roommate, ex-colleague and friend, with humiliation, pain, and excretion. And besides, it was never Janet who decided she would inform Babs about the existence of two separate Free-Fucking videos, one starring Beka and one starring Steph; Janet's directive came from above, and it's overt purpose was to encourage Babs to beg for a Caste before evidence emerged that would entail her to this misbehavior, based on Babs' trust in messenger Janet. And to deepen that trust.

But Babs' few subsequent glimpses of Steph infer a Lobelia unencumbered by any of the marks that embellish all the other Cosmos Lobelia, and BB's trust in Janet weakens. The latent purpose of the missive is that if and when Steph's misbehaviors are eventually revealed, and as BB's trust rushes back to the messenger, and that the trust in that messenger deepens.

Babs assumes her most recent Piss Mouth is courtesy Ginny, Whore-for-Life, who Babs imagines is present, dressed as a Pro Dom, and trolling for submissive men. BB is mistaken, obviously, and needs to simply accept anonymous donations, and not try to interpret their political meaning. Babs does understand *I'm a Dong and Dirty Whore now. I will suck, I will fuck, I will anal, I am a Goo Gobbler, a Pee-Camming Piss Mouth.*

Gamers fluent with the events of *The Runout* know that William and Rodney were last seen affixed spread-eagled to a Wheel, upside down to each other, and with their cocks pinned deep inside each other's mouth. They and the remaining Six other former Peacocks, have born witnesses to the *Beka and Rodney Fuck Video*; and attribute, correctly, that this Rule violation by one of their own requires Lockdown, including their then-Monitor William.

During while they were secured to seats in the Amphitheater (LD3), the Cosmos Lobelia did observe the Six ex-Peacocks, functioning as Sedan Chair Bearers for Game Mistress. They were all bridled with ovaled bits, and while they waited they had been signed into a cocksucking hexagon Benzine Ring position.

Beka, immunized by her confession about Rodney, and silenced by a Gag, had correlated the absence of Rodney, and William, from the Sedan Chair Bearers and cocksucking Benzine Ring, and assumed both had become cocksuckers also, and once again she worries about *the wrath of Steph, were a liaison with William to be true and proven, and my confession be the trigger.*

Steph has been cognizant of William and Rodney' absence, but chosen to not interpret what it means.

The remaining Cosmos Lobelia also cannot forget what was not before their eyes, and ignorant of the misbehavior of their sisters beyond Robyn, they have no reason to suspect anything particular about William and Rodney's Fate.

V-7 Gimbled It: Lobelia Observe Secured in Armature Rig

§ Gimbled It: Bare Bald Naked & Stained & Helpless

There is another visitor to the Party today and it is the creature called It, and for reasons shortly obvious, Gimbled It.

GM makes an introduction as a trolly brings Gimbled It into the view of Six Cosmos Lobelia's Eyes. "You are lucky Lockdown Whores, on the Beach all you got to see was the end of a dick erected from the sand; now you get to see all of It!"

Yes, during *The Beach Day,* Elle and other Cosmos contributed urine into a funnel in the sand believed to have led into It's mouth; the Cosmos also witnessed It's cock produce semen and pee, and witnessed Elle getting rewarded with both, albeit secondhand.

Elle knows that the It she sees now represents a more advanced challenge.

The trolly comes to a stop and the swaying cargo hanging from a single cable disturbs Six Lobelia. What they see is human, yes, a naked human folded up and secured in a mobile gimbaled bondage frame that is a marvel of engineering. The Gimbled Armature rig, over six feet in diameter, consists of three large metal rings, each inside the other, hanging from the trolly above. A middle ring rotates inside the outer ring, and innermost pivots inside the middle.

This innermost ring contains a frame which supports It's body, and the rotating and balanced Gimbals allow It to be rotated into any position, so that It's gagged mouth, erect cock, and gaped asshole are easily positioned to be accessible and useful.

Once again the Cosmos Lockdown Lobelia are permitted to see and hear, they see and hear the same thing through eyes and ears that are not their own. BB wonders what Robyn sees.

"Don't be overwhelmed by the gimbles," GM lectures Six Lobelia with a quiet glee, "It's body is attached in the frame by restraints around its torso and waist, its wrists and biceps, ankles and calves and thighs, and neck and head. Besides pivoting the rings, the parts of the Armature which support It's body and limbs may also be articulated and bent into any position. We have folded It up so only It's cock sticks out, but we can also spread It wide for buggery.

The Cosmos can see that. For at the moment, It's entire body has been pivoted back about 30 degrees so its erect cock stands front and center. It's legs are spread to the maximum, the calves are bent back, and It's arms bend back at the elbows, so It is locked into a Surrender Position so its shaven armpits are fully vulnerable.

It sees nothing, hears nothing, remains mute, and commits all of its mind, body, and soul into its encapsulated swollen hard penis. A neck brace ensures It cannot move its head nor suffer neck damage from being pivoted around. The Eyepods and Earpods and sealed mouth ensures It can't see its surroundings or orientation and has no idea of which end is up.

The totally of Gimbled It's submission slowly penetrates the Cosmos Lobelia's consciousness. For what they see is a totally naked and totally shaven creature that was once a man, but as part of It's contrition, It has been feminized. It is made up like a woman, perfumed like a woman, shaven like a woman. Except its cock has a huge erection and It's asshole gapes.

Babs finds her remote eyes canvasing Gimbled It's naked body. *Almost totally shaven: done armpits, chest, arms, legs, crotch, anus, and up the crack of its ass, and also It's face, eyebrows even; all but the hair on its head, which is feminized. Which is, well, scary.*

Babs, not alone among the Lobelia, observes that It's nipples make droplets of milk, and fantasizes that *Gimbled It is growing breasts. Gamers are turning It into a she-male, a chick with a dick, a transsexual!*

Babs worries about her own Fate. *Maybe Gamers are giving me drugs as well, especially to make me butter my bacon. And making my crescents bubble up. Aphrodisiacs. I can't stop transuding valiva, and I can't control my nipples or areolas at all. Or how hard my bauble pops out. And I don't want to stop, I just want more*

Babs' remote Eyes canvas a cock that is extremely huge. *It's cock. And I want it now. I should be able to control my desire, but I can't.*

Actually Six remote Eyes canvas a cock that is both long and thick, and can bury in excess of 250 cubic centimeters of hard erection when sunk flush down to the balls.

GM again provides guidance, "That's right, Gimbled It has been depersonalized, sexually conditioned and repurposed, and is totally helpless in this Gimbled Armature."

The Cosmos Lockdown Lobelia find themselves looking at a creature that doesn't know who it is, what it is, what time it is, where it is, or why it has lost itself.

GM confirms, "That's right, extreme Slavesex. Different than the genus kind that is full of creativity. It might know anything, but Gamers know that It's purpose is to provide a cock, a mouth, and an asshole. And one other thing.

"It has been modified so It can rapidly produce and store immense quantities of sperm, coupled with an enhanced pump which can shoot jizz into an open mouth, paint jizz across the lips like a cake decorator, blow the nose, wigwag both cheeks, and end with a pink eye.

"And that's just It's first load. Creampies lie ahead, Whores."

Some Cosmos Lockdown Lobelia draw comparisons between Slavesex Gimbled It and Slavesex Robyn, encased in a hardening white plaster Mummy hanging from a different trolly here in the Meatpacking Plant. Robyn hears screams, her Crawlers shock her.

Some Lobelia also draw comparisons between It and themselves.

Once again, Game Mistress guides the Lockdown Lobelia. "You would be correct to bet that It harbors a long flexible Worm deep into its rectum; the Worm is a total parasite; it can vibrate and twitch and electrify and get hot or cold. Crawl up and down, stretch out. Sparkle up and down its length. The Worm ensures discipline, is hollow, so Gamers can pass enema in and flush wastes away, as well as rectally feed It. And, may it please Gamers, the Worm shall assist in surfing It into the Zone, stimulating the prostate and work in consort with an AI Genie to coordinate the milking of pre-cum, the extraction and collection of semen from time to time, and the ongoing conditioning of this particular Slavesex."

Obviously It has had no choice but to accept whatever intrusions violate its body, It has no control over whether it is fed down its throat or up its ass, no control of its breathing, its urine; It has no control of the pressure and temperature of air on its skin, no self-control, nothing. It might feel all of their eyes, or sense change in air touching its skin, but It really can't see or hear anything.

But beside the forced erection and the feminine makeup, what shocks the Cosmos the most is Gimbled It's color, for It has been stained a deep, deep purple, acquired from multiple applications of Gentian Violet. The job of keeping itself stained has been one of It's duties for a while now, and the deep purple color burnishes into It's flesh. Yes, absent fresh applications the stain, the color will work itself out of It's body in a month or so, but this stain *will not* wash off or scrub off with alcohol.

"Gentian violet," Game Mistress advises merrily, "The stain arrives in a bottle and twice a day and It must rub the deep purple dye all over itself!"

An understatement. The Cosmos gurgle. Fresh stain glistens on It's body, not just every square inch of skin but also into its mucous membranes: its erect dick, face, mouth, tongue, and even the inside of It's lips and gums. All of its body, everywhere; in between toes, calves, legs, the back of the knees and inside the thighs, definitely completely all the way around the balls and inside the crack of It's ass, all over It's chest and the arms and once again over the face and head and behind the ears and inside the nostrils and ears. There is so much purple stain on It's body that It can't all soak in.

Six Lockdown Lobelia share a similar thought. *I'm going to fuck Gimbled It! And the stain is going to rub off on me and mark me for weeks.*

This is correct. Some Lobelia get excited about this idea. Some will need to get excited later.

GM glides her Goad across Gimbled It's nipples, "Nice, and dark, yes? It enjoys a collection of abusive nipple clamps, and the Gentian soaks into the bruises and darkens them."

The Cosmos Lobelia rustle their naked bodies. None wear nipple clamps at the moment, but Babs still wears bruises and Gentian in her nipples from when Penny and Coco set a pair of vicious clamps onto her while she had been helplessly cuffed on the Post Henge (LD2). It had been painful to the point of fainting, and even now both of Babs' nipples still painfully pulse, and still indenture the Gentian Violet deep in her bruises.

Janet had mercifully transferred the clamps to Darleen, and sent Darleen to the Nugget. Darleen doesn't wear them today, but with her mouth training on the Risen Cocks Lineup, she remains one snatch patch and one Term away from begging to doggy-fuck.

§ Gimbled It & Lobelia: Impact of Total Control

But the Cosmos Lobelia attention is commanded by the sight of Gimbled It's erect penis. What they see is a purple penis engorged with blood, straining against three rings around it, complicated by a hollow sound in the center of It's pee hole.

GM smiles and details, "Ah! The first ring around It's cock is just behind the penis head, and is held in place with a stud through the penis and sound; the ring in the middle of It's dick also penetrates the hollow sound, and valves it. And a third ring around the base of the penis is also pierced so it can't slide."

GM points to a pair of heavy gauge studs through the head of It's penis; here the stain forms deeper concentric rings around the two ends of each stud. "No need to lead It around by its dick when bundled into a Gimbled Armature."

GM lets It's testicles speak for themselves; they are ringed off from It's penis and further bulged and divided, like separated walnuts, with accommodations in the fitting ensuring that the tubes delivering sperm aren't crushed.

But GM does detail what fits into It's pee hole, "The hollow steel sound inside It's dick is critical, because It is swollen so hard it couldn't otherwise lube, cum, or piss. Fucking can be painful, but It won't go soft and stop pumping."

GM graces It's penis with her Goad, and a deep resonance emerges from deep in It's chest. "Pain just is," she announces.

And It hangs fresh lube from the tip.

What Game Mistress doesn't explain or reveal, is that, as with Robyn, a Cybernetic Control Program manages It from the inside. It's wireless minder calls itself the Genie; like Cybernetician, the Genie within It praises success and corrects delinquencies. Should the Genie determine It needs its cock risen, then electricity trickled into It's pee hole or the rings around its cock bring It to hardness and ecstasy. Or hardness and torture.

The Genie is very astute. The Genie collects all of Gimbled It's vitals: the pressure of It's erection straining against the cock rings, the squeeze on the cath, It's blood pressure and heart rate. Gimbled It is a lube and sperm animal, and the Genie feeds It a diet of gruel optimized for the production of these precious body fluids, and optimized with an asshole increasingly desiring pleasure.

The Genie ensures It's mind focuses upon wanting sexual release. Should It begin to lose an erection, the Genie explores strategies to counterbalance such wayward behavior. This might involve tightening a nipple clamp, stroking It's dick, enriching It's oxygen, electrocuting It's balls, or stimulating It's prostate from the rear end.

Or adding Viagra into a mouth drip, or aphrodisiacs from Madam Nurse Beautician's Makeup Kit. Enforcing It's sexual passion can be excruciatingly painful for It, especially when It's engorged penis throbs within the confines of the cock rings and a fat cath, but if this is what the Genie must do to keep the shaft engorged with blood and the lube flowing, then the AI learns what must be done.

Right now, It has swollen into its rings, and is bruised all the way down the outside of It's pierced shaft. Bruised on the inside of It's urethra too, by a hollow sound that can grow bumps.

It's drip of lubricant, hanging from its ringed penis, and now swinging freely mid-thigh, disturbs several Cosmos Lobelia. Elle flashes on China Doll, and recalls that *during* The Beach Day *China Doll had collected a mouthful of cum from It's cock, when its cock was the only part of It growing upward from the beach sand.*

China Doll then snowballed that mouthful… to me!

Elle suspects that *I will be eating cum again today, but not collecting it second hand.*

Elle has sucked cocks before, after all she did grace the Game with a copy of her *Gonzo Suck and Fuck Videos*. And yes, *the sheer size and rings of It's penis casts doubt about my ability to take it all in.* But what burdens Elle is *not just the penis bulging against the rings, it is the stain, and the certainty tha*t *It's heavy Gentian Violet will stain any skin that touches its body.*

Steph has her own recollection of the *Beach Day* events. *China Doll had affixed her mouth to It's dick, and suddenly collected a stream of piss that washed her face, her mouth, and her palate. China Doll then had the audacity to pass a bulging-cheek mouthful to me. She should have known I'm actually an Opt-Monitor, and that to whatever extent I have been used as a Piss Mouth, that that Obeisance goes to Elle at Midnight.*

Actually, Steph had demonstrated peeing into her own mouth and been further humiliated by performing for Darleen's Corvette House Cam. The *Piss Mouth Video* has become part of Automatron's archives, and Darleen has become a Nugget Stripper, proving her skills at penis oralation.

Apparently also Pacmo Pinky, on her knees also with a cock in her mouth. Babs remembers Pacmo when she was BB's MomCap; Babs has no illusions and finds Pinky's humiliation distressing. *I am responsible for her downfall from MomCap to Stripper, now pinking at the Nugget, where she used to MomCap. Talk about humiliation. I have wrought destruction to all around me, and not just my Pledge. I am the destroyer of opportunities and I deserve the harshest punishment Gamers can conject and administer.*

Babs also remembers Gimbled It from the Beach Day. *China Doll demonstrated she was a Goo Gobbler and Piss Mouth, and now I'm a Goo Gobbler and Piss Mouth too. Except I've only been fed cum; I haven't had to work it out yet. This time, I'm going to collect a mouthful of It's cum, directly, I will swallow, and I am going to get purpled-up for my actions, for what I am.*

Except I'm not a Bare Babe and a Stripper next Term, I'm Bang Bitch and a Whore. Babs again considers It's purple stained body. *I got sploshed pretty bad back on the Post Henge, somebody swabbed my face pretty heavy, my nipples, my navel, and they brushed stain into my clit until I couldn't stop by blurt coming out.*

And between now and Midnight I'm going to collect fresh stain on my mouth and all over my baldy. Every Gamer will read "Whore." And demand to see if I have a purple asshole.

A good goal for a wannabe Sex Worker.

§ Game Mistress Tells Babs: Must Wait for Purple Dick

Six Cosmos Lockdown Lobelia gaze at Gimbled It's mammoth erection struggling inside the three rings, at the constructed testicles, the gaping asshole, at the lube leaking out the hollow sound. Few try to decipher It's secured, bundled, folded up position. But the deeply purple cast to It's body worries them. Has It been gently beaten so that It's skin is already a ripe purple, allowing the Gentian Violet stain to penetrate deeper?

Game Mistress commands Six Lobelia's attention. "Don't all beg at once!" GM tisk-tisks. "Bonus cock, free lube, and a telltale purple mouth that announces your mouth is open for business! What more could a Lockdown Lobelia want?"

What more? Six Cosmos think confused thoughts. *How about my Tongue Clamp off? My hands free? My armbinder off?*

But Bondo Babe doesn't need her Tongue Clamp off; *it's off already, although the O-Ring Gag remains inviting. Can't stop what's coming. And my hands? They are already sticky. And my armbinder keeps my forearms crossed behind my back so that I can't defend my buttocks and butthole with my fingers. And if I try to move all I do is swing around on my hanging bound boobs.*

I'm a Bondage Bitch. I fucked up. My boobs hurt, my jaw hurts, my pussy leaks, my butthole has already been gaped. That's not enough. I deserve to be buggered. And fucked. And oraled. And paddled until my body aches all over, blisters, constant dull pain and screaming pain if they get touched. Or I have to sit down.

I know I think scary thoughts when I think that besides a purple mouth I want a purple baldy and beg that my butthole is for hire.

Some Lobelia believe that Babs has already been throated, and some Lobelia believe that Babs has also been coitaled. Some have seen how Penny and Coco worked Babs' mouth, not simply scooping goo off BB's hands and feeding her, but feeding her a blend of urine, creampie felch, and creampie out of pussy, thick also with each Whore's valiva.

Babs swallows what goes into her mouth. *I'm a Dong and Dirty Whore now. I'm a Goo Gobbler and Piss Mouth. I swallow jizz, valiva, lube, sweat, tears, milk, menses, pee; I felch, I'm an A2M Whore, I'm an A2OPM Whore too. Gamers will put in my mouth whatever they want: Caster Oil, Diuretics, Aphrodisiacs, Itching Cream. I need to beg them to inject me with hormones and put me on a milking machine. Whore me out as a wet nurse.*

And just because I'm begging Dong and Dirty doesn't mean Gamers are going to be satisfied turning me into a fuck toy. I must beg Gamers to upload filthy porn loops of me to Automatron. I need to be turned inside out. Gamer must bang me and beat me at the same time. Turn me into your Whore, make me your courtesan, your concubine, your escort, or, may it please you, turn me into a plastic-bag wearing streetwalking slut.

Perhaps out of respect, Game Mistress positions herself in front of the ex-Cosmos Monitor.

Babs wavers, and double checks she stands tall, legs ajar, armbound and wiggling sticky fingers. Babs supports some of her weight precariously balancing herself with feet forced apart, so that her thighs don't touch and her bare crotch lies open to the wind. But more than enough of her weight continues to hang by her 37DD bound breasts from the trolly above. BB's forearms remain bound together behind her back, so that her hands point in opposite directions, up and out of the way might her buttocks demand a paddle or her asshole relish penetration.

Hands coated in jizz, no way to wipe it off. Jizz on Babs' hips, face too.

Bondo Boobs Eyepods enable BB to look at Game Mistress directly, and BB transudes fresh balm out between her bat wings. Babs knows, *I can't control the flow anymore. I don't want to.*

GM wiggles the end and side of the Goad in one of BB's gooed palms, wipes the goo across BB's crescents d'areolage, and solicits a moan and a stalactite of Babs's burgoo. GM replenishes the goo on the end of her Goad from Burgoo Babe's other hand, and carefully inserts the end of the Goad into BB's O-Ring Gag.

Babs reconciles. She knows what a Whore does. She licks around the end of the Goad that resides her mouth, cleans it off completely, gathers the goo together, and swallows.

The Goad retracts. It can pack a big punch but Game Mistress has no need to inflict pain.

"Are you a Handjob Honey from now on?" GM inquires.

BB grunts the correct answer, "Aaha-aaha."

"You're a certified Goo Gobbler." Game Mistress states.

BB must agree with the facts. "Aaha-aaha."

"Sooooo," GM drawls and draws attention to the hanging Gimbled Armature with It's arms and legs helplessly spread and bent. "Look what we have here. We can move Gimbled It around and provide you with an opportunity to have a very tasty cock to take into your mouth. Would you like that, Ms. Blowum Bangum?

BB agrees, "Aaha-aaha."

"You want that cock in your buck twister too, don't you Whore?" GM enquires.

Babs knows *my wants don't matter anymore;* she responds, "Aaha-aaha."

"You want to bend over and beg cock up your bugger, Whore?"

Slower and with reluctance, BB must agree, "Aaha-aaha."

"You're a blowum bangum bugger Whore," GM declares, "begging to clean off toys, lesbo, double penetrate, gangbang, bukkake, gokkun, A2M, even A2OPM, Whore?"

BB hurries to agrees, "Aaha-aaha. Aaha-aaha!"

"Enough. Keep it simple. You're a begging to be a Dong and Dirty Whore." GM states.

Bang Babe calms down, accept this might be more than I thought, and agrees, "Aaha-aaha."

Game Mistress purses her lips, tilts her head, and tickles the air with the end of the Goad. "Robyn is gone, that means you deserve to be first in line. You want to be first in line, Bumfuck?"

Babs knows, *I must maintain my commitment.* "Aaha-aaha."

"What you beg and what you get aren't always the same, Whore." Game Mistress gives it a beat, "You deserve Slavesex don't you, 'so goes a Pledge so goes a Monitor,' yes?"

Babs had figured this out a while ago, carefully, "Aaha-aaha."

Bondo Babe hasn't forgotten that *there was a moment during* The Runout *when I had sacrificed myself totally. Begged Slavesex. Thankfully supplanted by Robyn. But I'm lucky to be a Whore, even a Dong and Dirty Whore; so maybe I am destined to become a Porn Star and an international escort.*

"You don't always get what you deserve, sometimes you get what you need," GM pontificates to ex-Monitor Babs. "You need to be masturbated and beaten at the same time. You need to watch some of your ex-Pledge act out, and afterwards you can keep begging to eat pussy, suck cock, and get your box and borehole all purpled up. Is that agreeable to you, Whore?"

It must be. "Aaha-aaha." Babs understands. *I deserve to be marked like a harlot. I need to beg for Whore tattoos. I need to suck-fuck-anal It. Gamers know they humiliate me by forcing me to wait. I am just another cow.*

I deserve all the humiliation they can heap upon me, but I need to get purpled for real before Midnight. I am already bare-bald-naked, my eyes and ears and mouth are controlled, and my pussy and rectum and pee hole belong to Gamers. I am a Dong and Dirty Cam Whore, and before Midnight they need to bondage gangbang and cumdump me. Take me completely, and upload me to Automatron before Midnight. That's me now.

V-8 Game Mistress and Beka & Elle: Redemption Begins

§ Game Mistress Exposes Beka & Elle: Free-Fuckers!

Beka and Elle have been returned to the same room in the Meatpacking Plant as the other Lobelia, including Robyn, who hangs inside the Plaster Mummy from the overhead trolly. The Roommates have been disconnected from their overhead suspension, unbound, and kneel-spread-surrender, meaning their knees and calves and feet rest on the floor but are widely separated, and that their fingers are intertwined behind their heads. Face, armpits, breasts, bellies, pubes, everything on display. Their Eyepods let them see outward and in real time, their Earpods let them hear. It is the first time they have been able to see each other in a long time. The O-Ring Gags have no give at all.

Beka and Elle observe the other's mute, bare-bald-naked, kneel-spread-surrender position. Swollen tongues rod clamps, drool.

As they settle Beka and Elle turn to observe Gimbled It. They have heard GM's introduction, and can now see and hear the proceedings. Beka jiggles, sneaks a glance at Elle, observes Elle holding position stoically, and follows suit. Now is not the time for either to learn about who is present and who has departed.

Yes, pay attention. Both should be grateful for the sound and vision; Game Mistress's Goad demands that Gimbled It be the center of their attention. Maybe Beka and Elle will be able to examine each other in more detail later, and maybe not.

Both Lobelia saw Robyn's visit through the same shared Eyes, but might they compare notes about the times they were blind-deaf-mute they would express different yet similar recent experiences; both have been fondled and finger-fucked, both have had their gapes probed, and both have had the tips of their tongues – that part held out in front of their Tongue Clamps – swabbed.

During their blind-deaf-mute separation through the chambers of the Meatpacking Plant both Lobelia have also been paddled, caned, and whipped by more than one arm, and are bruised, blistered, and stripped all over their naked bodies. Think paddle 24 inches long, 4 inches wide, ½ in thick. A three foot cane ¾ inch diameter. Perhaps their Free-Fucking had been wrong, but their begging to be Dong and Dirty Whores had been right.

Parts of their bodies cringle with pain, burning, heat coming up.

But despite this physical abuse, affection, and arousal, neither Lobelia has sucked, fucked, or analed cock. Well, not since Lockdown began, that is. Both know the Party is nowhere near over.

Game Mistress touches a bruise and sends a shower of sparks. GM enjoys cornering prey. "You like sucking cocks, don't you."

Beka is fast to answer, "Aaha-aaha."

"You like Gimbled It's cock? You want it in your mouth?"

Beka does. "Aaha-aaha!"

GM turns to Elle, "How about you, Lockdown Lobelia, wouldn't you like to have your Tongue Clamp off?"

Elle would like that. Carefully, "Aaha-aaha."

Party Guests have provided both wannabe Whores with Collection Dishes, both awaiting enrichment. Do they need more paddling to drive more cream out of their exposed and overflowing vaginas? Aphrodisiacs? A rubdown with Neroli Oil? Or have their natural desires been set free, their sexual moderators forgone. Just craving sex is the goal.

Game Mistress directs the Cam to canvas the long stream of broda out of Beka's love box. And a shorter drip hanging down from Elle's bursting nectary.

Game Mistress gives Elle a look, and Elle interprets the look. *I'm going to get a purple mouth.*

Yes, and…?

A purple nookie, and purple nectar and jizz running out.

Patience please. Game Mistress takes ownership of the moment; she curls her neck. "If I'm not mistaken, both of you demonstrated Whore tendencies before you ever enrolled in School?"

It is not really a question; Elle did see this one coming, and she flushes at the thought of the exposure. *My* Gonzo Suck and Fuck Videos *are being screened at the Nugget!*

GM addresses Elle square-on. "You brought ample evidence of your fellating and fucking abilities to 'Monitor Babs,' and BB has shared them with the Prefecture. And you begged they get screened at the Nugget while you dance there.

"You even begged they get screened in the Lobby, so prospects could watch you fuck before they paid to come in. Yes?"

Elle must agree with the truth. "Aaha-aaha."

GM bows to Elle. "You're welcome, Whore Wannabe."

Game Mistress turns her attention to Beka. "And you, my dear, thanks to the foresight of your Roommate, also shared evidence of your able oral and coital skills, prior to enrolling in School. But don't worry, we understand that the *Gonzo Suck and Fuck Videos* are not subject to the Rules of the Game.

"However, you did break the Rules when you fornicated while passing out your Pink Page during *The Runup* (D26). You have been shown a *Video* of your Free-Fucking, and confessed it is you who has a dick in your bonker. This qualifies you to Opt Whore."

Elle startles at this revelation and looks at her Roommate, who, guided by GM's Goad, keeps her vision focused on Gimbled It's erect purple penis. It is the first Elle has heard about Beka's Rule violation, and that *there might exist, there does exist, a movie!? Something else to screen at the Nugget? And besides....*

Beka isn't quite sure she hears Game Mistress; Game Mistress just implied that I confessed *after I was confronted with the evidence. That's a better truth.*

Maybe GM doesn't know.

Maybe it doesn't matter. Game Mistress raises. "You're a Whore, Beka Broda; you sneak off and endanger your Roommate. Is Elle in on this with you?"

Beka vigorously shakes no. *Elle knows I never fucked for money. Or opportunity. Only for a good time.*

"No? Fine, because it doesn't matter, because if you're a Free-Fuck, she's a Free-Fuck too. You're Roommates. Entailment Rule. You can both Opt-Whore now."

Except Elle knows. *Actually I am an anal Whore. I'm a Dong and Dirty Whore: mouth, pussy, asshole. I'm a Free-Fuck too, and I've already begged to Whore.*

This time, Elle turns her head to look, twisting her torso at the waist, but keeping her knees firmly placed and her hands firmly on the back of her bald head. Fingers interlocked. The O-Ring Gag and the Tongue Clamp in front don't move. Drool down to her nips.

Game Mistress lays the Goad on the side of Beka's cheek to guide her eyes at Gimbled It.

Elle snaps her own gaze back to It's huge, ringed, purple cock. *I'm already a Stripper begging to be a Dong and Dirty Whore because of what I did – what I proved by my actions.*

Elle has more concerns. *I explained that in order to procure my* Measurement Nudes, *I was required to procure my* Gonzo Suck and Fuck Videos. *I gave it all to then-Monitor Babs. Now I figure it was a set-up, and probably somebody secretly made a movie of me.*

Is Beka about to find out about that now?

Yes, but with a different documentary.

Game Mistress addresses Elle's concerns. "You told the Gamers you sucked and fucked to procure your *Measurement Nudes,* and then fucked and analed to procure the *Gonzo Videos?*

Elle did say this. "Aaha-aaha," is her reply.

"You're a qualified anal Whore, the Dong and Dirty type."

"Aaha-aaha."

"You thought you could sweeten Monitor Babs using some sexual labor. You failed with Babs, BB is a Whore now, just like what you beg to be after a Term at the Nugget."

This revelation causes a ripple in Beka's continence. Beka knows, *maybe Elle and I screwed a lot of guys, but we never got fucked up the ass!*

GM ignores Beka's ripple, and continues to speak to Elle directly, "Penny and Coco told you they suspected your sex acts were secretly cammed, and you told us that in the event no video comes forth, that you'd reenact the sordid details, is that true?"

It is, and Elle must agree, "Aaha-aaha."

Game Mistress caps. "So you're a Whore too, and you entangle your Roommate; you're both Dong and Dirty Whores and you are double entangled."

GM ices the cake. "You can even beg to collect double Terms."

Elle finds Beka's eyes, and both widens their eyes.

Game Mistress commands their kneeling-spread-surrender attention and takes a deep breath. "You're both adorable. One of you is sex-crazed and the other is a natural whore."

"The sooner you can get your tongue clamps off the sooner you can accommodate cocks in your mouths. Both together now!"

And Beka and Elle grunt in unison, "Aaha-aaha."

Babs, as the beneficiary of all Pledge misbehaviors, digests these new revelations. *Game Mistress's revelation that Beka Free-Fucked while passing out her Pink Page reinforces what Janet told me in secret. Including the identity of the Leading Man. It's because of Beka I'm a pussy Whore.*

Babs is afraid to look, but also processes. *Janet also told me there was another* Video, *this one featuring Steph, and that this* Video *cast me as an anal Whore. I begged Dong and Dirty because of what Janet told me, so it's likely that this is the truth also, just like Beka's Free-Fucking has turned out to be confirmed.*

However, Janet never mentioned Elle, maybe she never knew, but because of Elle for sure, and because of Steph probably, my back sphincter is entailed two different ways, so I am not only going to get double penetrated, Gamers are going to expand me to do double anal. I can't stop them. Double mouth, double pussy penetration. All combinations with two dicks, all holes at once with three dicks, and me jerking off two more. And dozens shooting all over my face and my body. All of me is gone now, my bound boobs, my spread butter box, my skin, my sight and hearing; so spread me out, suck my nipples and clit, bang my burse, bugger me, and feed my mouth. Climax me until I squirt, park me in the Zone with cocks in my every hole, and dip me in goo.

The only thing they can't do to me are Slavesex things, like where I get strapped down before I get sold. And with five or seven men on me during a gangbang, I don't need to be strapped down.

Somehow Steph is slow at connecting the dots, and does not assume that Beka's take-down might interfere with her own advancement.

§ Game Mistress Details Beka: Sexual Exploit in Garage

Beka and Elle both draw thoughts.

Beka reviews in her head the *Video* that Pimp Cowboy had played in her Eyepods – exclusively for her – while she had been naked, spread, and secured to her Henge Post (LD2). It revealed to her that her quickie with Rodney in the Peacock Garage (D26), while handing out her Pink Page, had been secretly cammed.

Pimp Cowboy had observed that Beka pumped broda harder and faster when she climaxed in the *Video* (twice), first in synchronization during a coitus in which Beka had been bent over and taken from behind, then climaxing again, leaning back on a fender, spreading, and accommodating a Peacock penis stroking in and out of her shaven bare box.

Both fornicators ha had the satisfaction of climax, but now at least one of them anticipates, *I am about to be published! Uploaded to Automatron, somewhere up in the cloud.* Beka assumes, *Rodney? He fucked me? I fucked him? It doesn't matter, we were both Free-Fucking Pledge, except I have Immunity, so now I'm a Stripper begging to Whore, but I'm not an instant Whore.*

So what if Rodney gets exposed? He's a Whore. He can get his mouth filled, his sex chastised, and his asshole warmed right away. I have to wait a Term to become a Porn Star.

Tiffany, Kimju, Steph, and especially Elle wonder what kind of "Free-Fucking" Beka engaged in, and with whom?

Elle, Beka's Roommate and double entangled with Beka, finds herself tumbling toward Whoredom *at a faster pace than I had anticipated.* Elle is starting to believe, *I am going to be publicly fucked. Right here at this party. I am going to get purpled up on It and then bent over on the Risen Cocks Lineup and drilled. Probably Beka too, I hope, she's the reason we're even playing the Game.*

After all, Beka Free-Fucked and got caught on Cam, I had to Free-Fuck in order to obey orders. It's not the same.

Babs believes she knows the identity of Beka's leading man. And she accepts both wannabe Whores' testimonials. *Together my two ex-Pledge have made a suck-fuck-anal Whore out of me.*

Whore, Dong and Dirty, that's me. Now, and as long Gamers want me to be.

Game Mistress seeks closure. GM draws her Goad across Beka's buttocks, and fresh pain erupts wherever the Goad touches paddle blisters which grow redness. Beka calms herself and whimpers.

"And you begged a big tattoo on your belly didn't you?" GM curls. It is the first indication in front of her fellow Cosmos that Beka's belly tattoo is large for a reason.

Beka makes gurgling noises. "Aaha-aaha."

"You know that even a full body suit is not fitting justice."

Beka agrees, 'Aaha-aaha."

GM caresses Beka's face, "Are you going be a Stripper Deluxe next Term?"

Beka nods aggressively, and grunts, "Aaha-aaha!" She really believes this. She seeks to rub her cheek on the back of GM's caressing hand, so GM lets Beka rub her cheek on the side of the Goad instead.

"But what you really want is to be a Dong and Dirty Porn Star just as soon as possible."

Beka does, "Aaha-aaha. Aaha-aaha."

"Atta girl," GM coos at her, and runs the Goad down a calf, drawing shutters such that a blob of brodeas detaches and falls into Beka's Collection Dish with a splat.

Elle gets a glance. "Seems like you're another Stripper Deluxe already begging a Dong and Dirty Whore promotion?"

Elle agrees, "Aaha-aaha."

"Any more cats on the prowl?" GM's question comes sharply, and scans Four of the Six Lobelia: Babs, Tiffany, Kimju, and Steph. GM's question meets silence and stoic postures. Babs' suspicions about Steph deepen and Beka's suspicions remain unconfirmed.

Steph continues to maintain her silence; and Beka wonders, *Perhaps Steph really is innocent, Or has denied guilt and there is no evidence. Perhaps she's made a deal, like I have; maybe she also has Immunity.* Beka takes a deep breath. *Steph's a witch and thinks you owe her privilege. Sort of like Robyn.*

Beka sneaks a glance at the hanging Slavesex Mummy. *Well, if that's what Charm buys, then who needs it.*

Perhaps Beka should be grateful that Robyn's Charm has contributed to her Lockdown status, and a rapid advancement toward Whore Caste.

Beka doesn't know that Gamers know Steph's silence marks her third opportunity to beg forgiveness and mercy. Strike three.

Game Mistress allows Steph's transgression to pass, because Robyn's Charm has provided GM with a plaything that needs dispatched first.

Some Lobelia sneak glances at Beka to see if they can detect more to her story. Something that Beka did which was careless, against the Rules, after hours, or may be interpreted to reveal a guilty posture. Beka's transgression matters because they affect her Roommate Elle, but also transmogrify her ex-Monitor Babs into a Blowzabella Bajingo.

GM shifts gears and demands Beka's humiliation, "I bet you want to share with Gamers just what you did when you violated the Rules. Share with the Prefecture. Even share with your fellow Lockdown Lobelia. Where did you go, what did you do?"

Beka tries to think fast. *This is my opportunity. I know what I did. I've seen the* Video. *I climax for real. I had cum running down my leg afterwards.*

Beka whinnies and pumps fresh brodeas and extends the stalactite hanging down between her thighs. It's knee length now, *and yes, I want people to watch me fuck, watch me climax too. But if Game Mistress shows the* Video *it could have consequences.*

"Your tryst occurred during the Day that Elle and you distributed your Pink Pages to the Eight Houses?

Beka agrees, "Aaha-aaha."

The question and reaction creates a stir among the remaining Lobelia.

GM presses on, "If I recall you identified the location on your *Fuck Video* as the Peacock House Garage?"

Beka hesitates, emits a begging noise, and agrees, "Aaha-aaha."

Steph twitches. It is Steph's first visible twitch and she doesn't know if Game Mistress and the others see it, but GM is looking for it out of the side of her eye.

Beka's acknowledgement produces another question.

"You had sex." GM states this as fact.

Beka whimpers and nods her gagged head, "Aaha-aaha."

"You fucked a boy Pledge." Again a statement.

And again a sigh of regret, contrition and an even more quiet nodding of head, and a rustling among the other Cosmos Lockdown Lobelia. "Aaha-aaha."

"He fucked you." GM almost makes it a question.

"Aaha-aaha."

"You fucked together!" Game Mistress brightens.

Beka appreciates the balance, "Aaha-aaha!"

Three Naked Lobelia wonder *who*; Steph jumps to the conclusion that *horny Beka whored William*, but wavers, *William isn't a Pledge.*

Babs feels increased confidence in her data.

"You heard your Roommate Elle say she gave away her asshole. Does that mean you're giving your asshole away too?

Beka gurgles and agrees, "Aaha-aaha."

GM interprets. "You really are begging to be a Dong and Dirty Whore? Anal, double penetration, gaping, A2M, A2OPM, bukkake, gokkun, goo dunked, all of it?"

Yes I am, "Aaha-aaha!"

"You and your Roommate are both begging Dong and Dirty Whores so you can ride your Dong together again."

Beka could not agree more, "Aaha-aaha. Aha-aaha," or something similar comes from Beka's gagged mouth; she nods her head; affirms with plaintive eyes. *Yes, we want to be a Sex Act.* A rhythm comes out of Beka's mouth, "GG, BGG, BBGG, BBBBBBBGG!"

Gamers think it is sweet of Beka to commit her Roommate to Whore.

Not the last of her many sins, but a null one, given that Elle is also a confessed Free-Fucker.

"You know that you've also turned your Monitor into a Whore, don't you, you horny bonker bitch." GM aggresses. "Does that please you and make you happy."

Beka shouldn't agree but knows *it's the right thing to do.* "Aaha-aaha." *And besides, I do want to watch her get climaxed. She's seen me, so now it is my turn.*

Perhaps Beka is simply scared and even more horny. She moans, squeezes fresh brodeas out of her box, and another blob separates and drips into her Collection Dish.

The Goad graces the back of Beka's blistered thighs ever so gently but sends a shower of sparks. Very sensitive skin. Beka puts her thoughts in order. *Babs' Fate doesn't matter, can't matter, she chose to Play the Game, and now she's a Whore.*

And to whatever extent I qualified her, then Elle qualified her too. I hope Penny and Coco are right and there are secret Videos of Elle fornicating, and especially Elle getting analed.

Maybe Elle got set up and maybe Babs got set up too. It doesn't matter, we're all Whores sooner or later.

GM pauses, then with fanfare, "Roll the Video!"

§ Game Mistress outs Beka: All watch *Beka Fuck Video*

Up to this moment the big Screens around the room have rotated between the real time live feeds from here in the Meatpacking Plant to excepts from Beka and Elle's *Gonzo Suck & Fuck Videos*. Suddenly all the Screens shift to a view inside of a garage. It is the Garage behind the Peacock House.

Beka can see the big Screens, see the others watch. The images are sharp and clear. And after a few seconds Beka and Rodney enter. They kiss, French kiss, and commence to undress each other. Naked now. Fondling, and then Beka and all the Cosmos present watch Rodney eat Beka out.

Beka watches the screen now out of the corner of her eye and reserves one eye for the other Cosmos Lobelia. Her breathing quickens, her pulse rises, and by the time Rodney bends her over a fender and climaxes her, taking her from behind, the Beka here in the Meatpacking Plant moves her hands from behind her head (against orders), reaches into her privates, and masturbates in synchronization with her fornicating on-screen *Video* self.

No one seems to be paying attention, and she pushes hard on her pelvis, squeezes fingers now inside her vagina, and pumps globs of even more broda, thickening downward between her gaping sex lips and the Collection Dish below.

Beka catches herself while Rodney pivots on Screen; she sneaks her hands back into position behind her head, just in time to witness herself on Screen reach out and pull him into her bonker from the front, with both of them exploding in climax. The Beka here in the Plant is so unable to contain herself that she again pumps a blob of brodeas which falls to the floor and fills the Plant with her scent.

Up on the screen the images clearly show Rodney hastily pull out and provide Beka with a hefty vaginal creampie.

Game Mistress admires the kneeling Stripper and Whore wannabe. "I'd say you have another hot property in your porn inventory, yes?"

Beka does. "Aaha-aaha." *I'm going to be a Porn Star.*
And I want It's cock now. In my mouth and in my money box.

And all eyes return to her to read her reaction. Beka knows, *I am going to be fed cock today. I will do anything to climax and I'm ready to climax big. I have never seen a cock as big as Gimbled It's and I am going to pack this meat into my bare fuck box, bring it up to ready, aim it into my mouth, and collect a big shot of jizz deep in my mouth, gargle for the Cams, and swallow.*

§ Cosmos Lobelia: React to *Beka & Rodney Fuck Video*

If during the screening, Five Lockdown Lobelia watched Beka fornicate, now they study her intently.

Beka tries to look back. She remains kneeling-spread-surrender, her mouth viciously hole gagged, her tongue clamped, and drool spilling down her chin onto her boobies and bare and naked body. Still, *Gamers got to see me with my box spread wide open and collecting a creampie. I'm pretty hot, I'm totally exposed, and I'm begging to Whore.*

Beka looks toward Babs and sees BB already looking at her... looking at her with a look of, well, dejection and rejection; on her feet but held upright by bound boobs and a line up to her trolly. Beka realizes, *I've had a lot of interaction with Babs, but never a glazed look like this one.* Beka shifts her eyes.

Perhaps Beka doesn't yet realize, or doesn't care, that she has just turned Babs into a Whore.

Beka feels the Lockdown Lobelia's eyes upon her. *Now all of them know that my 'catting around' involved Rodney.* Beka gurgles. *They've gotten to see me fuck before, with Elle on the* Gonzo Suck and Fuck Videos*, and now everyone gets to see me fuck again. I did okay. We climaxed together and I emptied him out.*

Beka has more memories: *On the way back to the Cosmos House, I had to squeeze Rodney's creampie out of my fucked box, wipe his jizz up with my fingers, and the only way to get rid of it was to lick my fingers clean.*

Beka solidifies her position. *Okay, so I Free-Fucked, I got caught on Cam, I confessed, got Immunity, so I'm a Stripper for a Term and then a Dong and Dirty Whore. I'm bringing Elle along!*

But I am not responsible for Lockdown!

Beka lingers looking at Tiffany; Tiffany remains bowed with a Risen Cock upward into her O-Ringed Gagged mouth, her asshole hooked and uplifted by the trolly above, and her twat so full that spunk oozes back out and hangs down.

Beka projects. *That's me next. Only without the Ass Hook.*

Beka wonders *has Tiffany seen my* Fuck Video? Tiffany has, they had been fed into her Eyepods at the same time they played on the Screens and the Eyepods of others. If Tiffany were able she would smile at Beka and salute with her chin. Instead Tiffany must balance struggling to lift her head up so she can take a breath, and relaxing so that the fat cock in her mouth doesn't constantly throat her.

During her stay Tiffany has also discovered that after a Risen Cock erupts in her mouth, and after she swallows and sucks it clean, that it is lowered and that the machinery within the bowels of the Meatpacking Plant raise a fresh erection up into her mouth.

Tiffany swallows ejaculation-after-ejaculation that cocks provide into her mouth; as for the creampie-after-creampie delivered into her twat? And which ooze out, or are flooded out by the next semen donor? Gamers have provided Tiffany with an oversized Collection Dish, which collects this endless drain of ejaculate along with Tiffany's own creamy and divinely scented valiva.

Enough Party Players contribute ejaculate to Tiffany's bald head until even her face is coated. Spunk on Tiffany's back runs around to her front and drips off her nipples and belly. Players shoot so much cum onto Tiffany's tush that it oozes down pass her Hooked asshole, and drips off the tip of a very erect trigger in need of a break. More jizz to drip down to her Collection Dish.

Does Tiffany ever climax before the cock inside her erupts?

Sometimes, but the cocks that keep getting put into her mouth are huge, and smother cries of passion. And blocks her view of knowing who fucks her. Tiffany understands. *The fans know that I don't know, and this arouses them and they jerk off to me. I want them to pop their jizz on my picture.*

Maybe someday Tiffany will get clearance to watch herself on what will be called *Tiffany DP Train Fucked Video,* and discover that only some of the fuckers are hooded. But then again, maybe Tiffany won't get any clearance at all.

Beka romanticizes, *I would like to clean off the cocks that come out of Tiffany's man trap. I will eat out all the goo from her twister, I'll lick her asshole. She's a great role model. I love her positivity.*

Her absence of judgment. Tiffany knows how to embrace the passage of time, even when the Clock is stopped. And Tiffany knows all about Whoring! She will always be a Porn Star, even if she never makes Porn again, although Stripping for her next Term is a step in the right direction.

Me too, Beka appreciates, *My newest* Video *just got screentime! I am going to be a Porn Star too! One Term after Midnight! And I'm bringing Elle along!*

Beka casts her eye to Steph next, and is instantly spiked, as painful darts shoot into her eyes. Beka recoils and turns away.

Beka alights upon Kimju's steelie eyes, lingers long enough to hide any give-away, and discovers Elle looking at her, curious.

Elle doesn't know about Steph, but Steph's look was enough to convince Beka of Steph's guilt. This is an issue that will occupy Beka's thoughts in the near future, but right now it seems more important to secure eye contact with Elle, who breathes faster, uncertain, and seeks Beka's help as she tumbles uncontrolled into the sex business.

Beka senses that a helpless Elle has given up. *The more she feels helpless the easier it is for me to groom her; but the less she feels helpless the faster we can climb to the top of the Porn Business.*

It's tremendous we shall be Stripping together next Term. And begging to become Dong and Dirty Whores together.

Beka squeezes her vaginal canal, constricts her rectum, torques her fingers together behind her head and deepens her armpits. Her buds are popped and she rotates her pelvis like a belly dancer kneeling with her knees wide apart. Her long stalactite almost touches her Collection Dish and the scent from her erupting sex box fills the air nearby, and tickles noses, Elle's especially.

Elle, always a more sedate version of her Roommate, also squeezes her fully exposed nook, also hangs nectar and also graces the Meatpacking Plant with a gentler scent.

Elle glances at the Screens and sees a collage of her and Beka's *Gonzo Suck and Fuck Video* flow by. *No escape. No secret for my mouth or pussy anymore.* Their scents bind them.

Beka watches too, and appreciates. *Elle and I did a great job of banging our boyfriends on the camping trip. I like how we trade off the guys, and if that's not enough sharing, Elle and I eat each other out. We're pretty hot.*

And I like how in the second Gonzo Video *Elle and I are on the opposite sides of a dick and sharing it. And I think we shared the spunk too.*

All that, plus Rodney's secret Fuck Video *of me confirms my free-sex behavior. My past and my present commingle. I really am a slut. And I am going to be a Porn Star!*

I snuck out, sexed, got caught, and got outed. Another Video *for my fans to collect. Jerk off to. This is the new reality.*

Do I still deserve punishment for Free-Fucking with Rodney? Sure, I deserve to be fucked, publicly fucked. Gamers want to watch me climax live, download me from Automatron forever.

I need to be first to fuck Gimbled It so I get the maximum imprint of the stain. I need to get It's purple all over my mouth. All over my bonker too. So I can spread my legs center Stage at the Nugget next Term and show my purple as a mark of a Whore.

Beka grinds her Tongue Clamp against the O-Ring Gag as she observes It's purple penis with frustration. Her stalactite now hangs all the way down to her Collection Dish and begins to form a small pile. Beka concentrates on keeping her hands clasped behind her head, fingers intertwined. Welts from whip marks decorate her breasts, belly, her shaven bare pubis and vulva between her legs, the insides of both thighs, buttocks, and the bottoms of both feet. Still her brain screams, *I want It's cock and I want it now!*

Elle ponders about her Roommate and ex-Monitor Babs. *Beka's Free-Fucking makes Babs a Whore, but I'm not sure that Babs needs to be a Dirty Whore just because I did a Free-Fuck – and analed – to get what she demanded of me. I got set up, so I should be exempt. And Bondo Bangbabe was either in on my reduction, or maybe she too got set up, or is feeling backlash.*

It's okay I'm Stripping next Term, and Whoring is only a Term away. But I think that for Babs, that she's Whore already, and Whoring shall be her Caste for quite a while. And with her 37D's there is no way she can talk herself out of it.

Elle, equally naked, kneeling-spread-surrender, holds her position with more patience and less stress. *I'm not sure how this Term will end. But I know I will be retaining a purple mouth, purple pussy, and a purple asshole long after Midnight, because,* Elle assumes, *I promised to reenact the sex I used to get the* Measurement Nudes *and the* Gonzo Videos.

Elle doesn't want It's purple erection as much as Beka does, but the more she studies It the bigger It seems to become. The give-away of Elle's arousal is the growth of her own stalactite, not yet pooling in her Collection Dish, but with full commitment.

Questions spin not only in Elle's head; all the Cosmos Lobelia ponder various similar questions: *How did the* Beka and Rodney Fuck Video *get made? Did Rodney set up a 'hidden camera' or did another Peacock watch and record?* Also, *How did the Gamers find the* Video? *Was the Peacock House raided?*

Duh, some Cosmos Lobelia remember they witnessed the Six Peacock Sedan Chair Bearers. but no William or Rodney.

So if Rodney got wrung out, where is Rodney now?
And what is the Fate of William?

V-9 Game Mistress Allows Elle: Suck & Fuck Gimbled It

§ China Doll Removes Elle's Tongue Clamp: Suck Prep

Game Mistress addresses Elle. "As you are now aware, your Roommate Beka has augmented her contributions to your *Gonzo Videos* with a *Beka and Rodney Fuck Video* that has been discovered. Don't you love the way the jizz runs out of her bone socket at the end?

Elle accepts this question silently, feel the Goad touch a bruised spot and send a shower of spark, and agrees, "Aaha-aaha."

"You're a Whore too, and you said before that if we couldn't find a video of you screwing to get the *Measurement Nudes* or the *Gonzo Videos*, that you'd reenact your sexual barters?"

It is a question and Elle knows that her previous answer is probably recorded somewhere, "Aaha-aaha."

Elle also knows that *bartering for value goes beyond Free-Fucking. I really am a Whore, only now I'm no longer a free agent.*

GM breezes forward. "Reenactment time has come. You need to catch up with your Roommate and demonstrate you're a Whore too," GM states. "Gamers deserve to see cock fuck your nookie too, don't you agree?"

Elle squares up her position. Bare-bald-naked, kneeling-spread-surrender; Elle makes sure her fingers are intertwined behind her head, that her torso is erect and both breasts point forward, that her armpits stay cupped, her belly tucked in, and her nookie has air. Elle does learn. And she does agree, albeit belatedly, "Aaha-aaha."

I am a Whore now. I'm trapped and can't escape. This is because of Robyn Runaway except Robyn is inside a Plaster Mummy. This is because Beka Free-Fucked and I'm her entailed Roommate. And because of Babs, who failed in her responsibilities.

This is because of what I did. And I'm being swept out of control. Elle makes a wish. *I hope they take the Gag out first and force me to suck cock, rather than fuck and anal me and then use my mouth..*

So optimistic.

GM makes a sign and a naked China Doll appears. She is highly decorated, and her body adornment has been described in detail during *The Beach Day*. She remain equally stunning today.

China Doll creates a stir among the Cosmos Lobelia, for in varying combinations they had encountered this Slavesex before. One Term ago, when they had been Nugget Strippers, Kimju and Molly had witnessed then guest Feature Dancer Tiffany get hung upside down on Stage, and throated until she hurled, and then witnessed a naked China Doll eat it all up off the Stage floor.

In the event Cosmos Lockdown Lobelia doubt China Doll's devotion to Game Mistress, those that participated in the Greatest House Roar at the Peacock House (D21) remind themselves that naked China Doll spent her time at the Roar with her mouth affixed to GM's vulva, with it well understood she was there to not only pleasure Game Mistress, but consume any and all fluids that might emanate from this part of GM's body.

China Doll extended her reputation with the Cosmos during *The Beach Day,* when she had accommodated the buried It. She contributed urine into what most now believe was It's mouth, climaxed cum out of It's penis and snowballed it to Elle. China Doll then drank piss out of It's erected penis, passed a mouthful to Steph, who in turn flooded Elle's mouth.

Elle swallowed, obviously, and so did Steph, although only the dribs left in her mouth. No problem, both Pledge appreciate the sting of piss in their mouths going forward.

The Lobelia understand that China Doll has already confirmed Steph and Elle as Piss Mouths and Elle as a Cum Gobbler. So they know China Doll has power.

China Doll enters briskly, and begins to carefully take off Elle's tongue clamp. Elle feels her tongue pulled forward by the two rods, then break free, takes a big breath, and a rush of pain erupts as the blood flows back into her tongue. More pain erupts when she tries to bring the tongue into her mouth through the Ring Gag. Elle gingerly feels her tongue against the top of her mouth and tests the outline of the inside of the O-Ring Gag. No give there.

"Thank China Doll for taking the Clamp off your Tongue, cocksucker" GM commands.

And Elle bows a shoulder, tilts her eyes down, and gurgles, "haaank oooooou." Still hard to talk.

§ Elle Sucks It's Dick: Gets Purple Mouth & Face

China Doll guides the trolly and pivots Gimbled It so that the large purple erection is positioned directly in front of kneeling Elle's Ring-Gagged mouth. Elle casts an eye at purple It and calculates It's erection. *It is long, unwavering, and thick.*

GM provides bounce. "250 plus cubic centimeters. Some say 300, but even with your big mouth it's going to be a tight fit."

Elle considers. The cramped sensation of the wide O-Ring, tightly drawn behind her teeth, presents a big target. Elle knows that with her arms held behind her head that *I am about to perform a no-hands blowjob. Game Mistress is going to cock my mouth just as much as she wants. She is going to make me deep throat.*

Actually it is China Doll who deftly manipulates the Gimbled Armature that supports It's naked body, itself presented directly in front of Elle, with It's huge erection suspended inches away and level with Elle's O-Ring Gagged mouth. China Doll is careful to handle only the Armature frame, and not get any of It's stain onto her decorated body or long flowing hair.

As the trolly inches closer Elle can tell that It's Eyepods are set opaque, interpret that It's Earpods block all sound, and see that It's mouth is sealed shut.

But it is the purpleness that seeps into It's skin and body that frightens Elle. It's entire naked and shaven body, include It's face, is completely, deeply, deeply stained purple. A swamp of deep wet purple stain stands in It's belly cavity, the Gentian so saturates It's skin that the stain can't all soak in.

Elle knows why. *It's cock is soaked in Gentian Violet. Of course I'm going to be Cammed sucking cock, but more fundamentally I'm going to get marked as a Whore, and I am going to wear those marks to the Nugget at the start of next Term. The Patrons won't have to check with Automatron to find out what I am, all they have to do is look at me, and know that my only way out of the Nugget at the end of the next Term is when I visit the Inner Sanctuary and my begging to Opt Dong and Dirty Whore is realized.*

Elle studies the giant purple erection not far from her mouth. It's dripping streamer swings in the air, and It's penis head glistens with lube. And It's cock doesn't just have an erection: it is also ringed.

Elle can see that It's cock struggles against a pierced-in-place Gates of Hell. Ringed behind the corona, ringed halfway down the shaft, and ringed back against It's body. With two more studs through the head. Constricting rings also keep It's testicles separated.

Elle evaluates the cock in more detail as it moves closer: not just the lube and dick, but also the swell of the engorged penis between the rings as the cock struggles it to expand and stretch out even more – but can't. Elle accepts, *if the dick were any bigger I really couldn't get it into my mouth, let alone into my nookie. No human could.*

Elle looks more carefully at the profuse pre-cum hanging from It's erection and determines that *the lube emerges from the center of a hollow stainless steel tube inserted into It's pee hole, It's lube hole, It's cum spout.* All of the above. Elle can't determine if the insertion is a hollow sound or a catheter, but correctly assumes that *the rings and swelling would squeeze It off tight. So a hollow sound is something It should be grateful for. It doesn't matter, I'm going to take the cum out, and if pee comes out, I'll just try to keep up with that too.*

Elle feels the end of the Goad touch the back of her neck as China Doll slowly advances It's cock forward, with at first It's head just fitting through the O-Ring into her mouth and coming to a rest, so that the hanging pre-cum gets broken between a piece down her chin and torso, and the part trailing into Elle's mouth. There is no retreating; Elle keeps her hands behind her head, works the head of the cock with her tongue, feel the two stainless barbells in It's penis head, gathers up the pre-lube, earns a purple tongue, and swallows.

Elle imagines that the Goad behind her neck provides a very low level of electrical stimulation, and has no desire to feel it snap.

Elle projects, *I don't need any remediation from GM's Goad; I am in Lockdown because of Robyn, but I shall suck cock in front of everybody because I really am a little Whore. I sucked and fucked to get the* Measurement Nudes, *and gave away my nether gate to get the* Gonzo Videos *and take them to Babs. These* Gonzos *also show me to be a suck and fuck Cam Whore. Now all the Gamers in the Prefecture are going to watch me purple my mouth. And nookie.*

Such optimistic thinking.

Elle feel It's cock creep further into her mouth. Now all Elle can do is press her tongue up against the bottom of It's cock, now the entire top length of the tongue gets purpled, with wet stain running down the side of her tongue and discolor the inside of her lips.

Elle can feel the cock bulge against It's three rings and she secretes fresh nectar, this time her personal stalactite descends closer to her Collection Dish, but control of her nectar is out of Elle's mind as China Doll's deft hands back It's cock out of Elle's mouth, and park it directly in front of her. A mixture of purple drool and purple pre-cum runs out of Elle's mouth, down her chin, spills onto her boobs, and runs down her bare belly and stains her shaven nook.

China Doll deftly extracts the O-Ring Gag from between Elle's teeth, and feeds the cock midway into Elle's still-open mouth.

"Suck, Whore," Game Mistress commands, "rock your body forward and back, keep your hands behind your head."

Elle leans in and sucks cock, as best she can with a mouth still cramped, but able to close enough to fit her lips around the deep purple shaft and apply suction. As Elle goes deeper, she heightens her understanding of It's dick, *I can feel the bulge struggled against It's rings, the piercings, and the hollow spigot inside.*

Game Mistress advises Elle, "Don't worry if It pops a big load in your mouth; It is able to deliver big load after big load. That, and the size of It's prick, is why It is here."

Beka watches Elle's Porn performance with envy. But not without arousal; her hanging broda continues to accumulate a volcano-shaped pile in her Collection Dish. What Beka wants most is to sixty-nine with Elle, but watching Elle get cammed sucking purple cock only drives Beka to secrete ever-fresh broda that fills the Meatpacking Plant with her scent.

Beka's scent triggers more of Elle's own secretions, and drive Elle to suck harder on the erection deeper inside her mouth. Elle understands her mission: *collect lube and streamers spinning out the hollow sound; I can do that. And if It spurts cum in my mouth, I can collect that, too, although I've never had to swallow before.*

Elle can feel It's cock come alive. *I can taste it, taste the lube.* Elle understands, *my only purpose at the moment is sucking It's cock. I must make it cum in my mouth, get it on my face, and swallow. On Cam. I am a Star Whore now.*

Elle lets go; she abandons herself to a public cocksucking commitment. *I want my dicksucking lips purple with stain and I don't care who watches me anymore.*

Elle pumps It up and down, works her way down the side of the shaft, presses one testicle entirely into her mouth, and then both, purpling much of her face, then returning to the shaft, counting rings all the way down, one, two, three, then bumping It into her throat, and finally grinding her face onto It's purple groin, then rising up off the shaft and hanging streamers of phlegm in the air as she backs away to collect her breath.

Elle spots a Cam watching her and shakes her purple nuggies for it. *Watch me now!*

Game Mistress' Goad, this time ahead of Elle's forehead, blocks Elle from going back down on the shaft. Purple phlegm mixed with It's lubricant hang out of Elle's purple mouth. Elle can feel the Gentian discolor her lips, feel it soak into her face. Her lips are deep purple, her mouth and lips and chin and cheeks and nose are stained purple too. Elle looks around, looks into the eye of one of the hovering Cams, and accepts her mark up, and speak her first words since her gag was removed, "I'm a cocksucker from now on."

§ Game Mistress Trains Elle: Suck Lick Felch Fuck

Elle takes stake of her new self. *Well, I was always very good at sucking cock, but now I'm sucking cock in front of Play Party Patrons, in front of Cams. And wearing evidence all over my face.*

And why is this my Fate? Because of Robyn I'm a Lockdown Lobelia and because of Beka I am a Whore. Well, me too, Elle must admit, *we're both Dong Whores but my taking anal is what qualifies us as Dirty. Next Term at the Nugget, House Mom Janet will insist I beg that blowjobs aren't sex, so practically speaking, I'm a cocksucker from now on.*

Probably Beka too. I hope so.

Cocksucking is a preamble to what Game Mistress shall accomplish with Elle next.

Game Mistress makes a sign and China Doll pivots Gimbled It. GM values commitment, dedication, and abandonment; she directs

Elle, "Use your hands to pull It's butt cheeks apart, then bury your face and lick It's asshole clean."

Elle obeys, follows these directions, but doesn't linger. It's asshole is gaped, and Elle is forced to taste a pipe and not a pucker. Still, just hitting the rim of It's anus sends It into shimmers. Smothering her face in between It's buttock purples Elle's face; she keeps her eyes shut although the Eyepods provide protection. Elle feels the stain soak into her cheeks, her nose, her forehead, lips and tip of her tongue. Now also, Elle's hands: slippery with acquired stain, Elle's fingers will now purple anything they touch.

Elle comes up for air and sees that the tips of her shoulders have also taken on purple. Elle knows the Gentian doesn't wash out and feels alarm at its spread. On one hand Elle realizes, *I need to be more careful about contact.* On the other hand Elle accepts her fate, *It doesn't matter. I must abandon what I want to be, and be what Gamers want me to be. That is my new goal. If Gamers want me to be a purple felcher, then I am a purple felcher.*

Elle constricts her vagina. The thick blob that she squeezes strengthens the streamer already hanging downward, elongated now and almost touching her Collection Dish. Elle's scent tickles Beka's nostrils; Beka fidgets her fingers and takes a deep breath. *Now it's my turn to suck cock!*

Maybe not, because it pleases Gamers to frustrate Beka. She too hangs anticipatory brodeas out of her creamy sex booth.

Game Mistress signals China Doll to reposition It so that It's penis stands upright in front of Elle. GM commands, "Climb aboard, Cowgirl."

Elle climbs aboard It. She stretches her body upward, hesitates before she slithers to balance herself on It's purple torso, accepts the inevitable, braces herself with palms on It's purple saturated chest, wraps her legs around It's purple hips, and then, ever so carefully, Elle lowers her already sloppy nookie onto the long, thick, rings and pierced, purple penis.

Elle blows air out of ovaled lips. It is a lot to take in and her vagina stretches as she settles herself down onto the full volume of It's penis. Elle breathes in, settles the full length of the shaft inside her, rubs her clit on where It's erection meets It's groin, and grinds.

Instinctively, and without thinking, she draws both palms to massage her breasts, purpling them, discovering this as she looks down to watch herself roll her nipples with purple fingers. Elle touches a finger to the top of her head, leaves a mark, touches a finger to her face, but this doesn't make any difference. Elle's face has already been soaked twice. *And now I have a purple nookie too. I'm not just a Player giving blowjobs, I'm a suck and fuck Lockdown Whore, advertising that my mouth and nookie are used.*

Game Mistress reinforces this concept. "Behave like the wanton greedy slut you aspire to be," she commands Elle. "Fuck It, you prick pumping Lockdown Whore."

Elle does like to go wild during sex. *But with an audience?* The suspended Gimbal Armature supports both Elle and It, and the AI inside the Gimble balances It and Elle to perfection.

Now a sublimely pulsating penis deeply cleaved into Elle's fuck nave synchronizes with her squeezing actions, and Elle struggles to go higher. Elle forgets about the audience.

No, I haven't forgotten, they are still there, they matter. They can watch. I want them to watch. I am free to fuck now.

The view inside Elle's Eyepods switches, so that suddenly she sees a view of herself, sitting on Gimbled It's lap, impaled on It's penis. A suspended Plaster Mummy hangs in the background.

Elle watches as the entire suspended Gimble Assembly begins to slowly rotate around its hanging cable, so that Elle, indeed everyone in the Meatpacking Plant, can get a view of Elle fucking It from every angle.

Elle loses whatever last bit of self-control she possesses and starts to go wild, reptile brain unleashed.

Elle grinds her clit on It's pelvis, and It grinds back. Elle presses against her own pelvis with her fingers, rub-a-dubs her clitoris, pants, tries for the climax, and thinks her last thoughts: *Fuck me. I'm fucking for real and on Cam and everyone is watching me. I'm going to cum. Here. In front of everybody. I want everyone to watch. I am a cock nock. And Game Mistress is going to assign me to Madam Nurse Beautician. Or Pimp Cowboy. I no longer fuck when I want to, I fuck when I'm told.*

If before GM's Goad restrained Elle for redoubling her efforts sucking cock, this time the Goad breaks Elle's pant and rhythm, as

Elle feels the penis fall down and away from her, leaving her standing in a squat with her feet on the floor, And with a mixture of It's lube and her own naughty secretions, all thick and purple, hanging out below her parted and purple sex-lips and purple nitro button, all now saturated with It's surplus Gentian Violet.

These will augment spendings already in her Collection Dish.

It takes a second for Elle to come out of the Zone, Elle knows *there is more climax in me, and I failed to gather a vaginal creampie.* But she is still saturated with Gentian Violet: solid purple through the crotch, purple inside the thighs, purple wherever Elle has touched herself, including her breasts and nipples, and with a purpled face, nose, forehead, and especially her mouth, lips and tongue after getting both cocksucking and felching colorations.

And purple up and down the inside of Elle's vaginal pipe.

Game Mistress's Goad encourages Elle to turn around.

Elle obeys; and she has reluctantly anticipated what's next. *First my mouth, then my nookie, now I have to give my nadir away. If I don't do this they will confront me with another hidden video.*

"Pull your butt cheeks apart," Game Mistress commands, "squat down, and slide It's cock all the way into your gaping nadir tunnel."

Elle recall she has been de-gagged. *I can talk.* She does. "China Doll, please help guide It's dick into my nadir. Please go slow. I'll squat down on it. And I *will* take it all the way."

Elle squats, pulls her butt cheek apart, the trolly and gimble whirl, and China Doll guides It's thick, long and very erect penis up into Elle's rectum. There is some resistance at first, but Elle's rectum has recently been widened with an oversize Double Dong that have left her (and Beka) gaping. Elle struggles and manages to work in the head, and then the first ring inside her rectum. She spreads her legs and purples her thighs.

Game Mistress instructs, "You want Gimbled It all the way in."

Elle moans deep in her throat as she settles an inch or two. That's still only a fraction of the length of a long and thick dick. She begs, "China Doll, please slowly give it to me all the way, please China Doll. I *want* it all the way; please China Doll, I am a Dong and Dirty anal Whore."

Elle looks at GM, sees all the Cams upon her, and deploys her hands and weight differently, leans back, and carefully works It's dick further into the recesses of her rectum. The Gimbal adjusts the balance of the weight cradled, and moves It's arms and legs to accommodate Elle's latest positions with majestic efficiency.

A sound comes from Elle's throat as her rectum slowly gives way as she settles her full weight and accommodates more and more of the ringed erection burying itself up to the hilt inside her rectum.

It is not a first for Elle; it is a reenactment. But with a much, much bigger cock, and with this one buried to the hilt.

Elle moans, and has the good sense to make sure the cock sinks all the way home. The Gimble Armature adjusts to balance Elle on her buttocks, with her legs splayed wide and her purple hands resting on It's purple chest behind her. The Gimbled Armature and the cable upward to the trolly now supports both Elle and It.

Elle's purpled and splayed nook has a sopping, "just fucked" look to it, and hangs open with the lips on one side flapped open, the lips on the other side hanging straight, and purple-tinted secretions oozing out, so that everyone in the Meatpacking Plant can smell her scent. Elle thinks she knows what comes next: *I am going to get my nooky climaxed.*

§ Beka Eats Elle Analed on It: Elle Climaxes

Beka's frustration has been building since she saw Elle go first, saw Elle get throated, felch an asshole, saw her eagerly fuck cock, and now rocking rather helplessly on a long pole buried deep in her asshole. Beka may love her Roommate, but she is not without pride, and Roommate rivalry. *I should be first! And make no mistake, I am here to collect cum today. Empty It right out just like I did Rodney, and while I climax myself. No matter how purple I get or how much cum gets on me, or I have to swallow. I'm going to make a video today that is going to make every Gamer pop. So what I'll be purple for days, my* Videos *will play in the Nugget forever.*

Hummm, Gamers will look at Beka's mouth later on and know she is a good pussy eater, for that is Beka's next purpose. Elle, preoccupied with the complications of It's cock pulsating inside her, has not observed that China Doll has removed Beka's O-Ring Gag and Tongue Clamp, guided her hands from behind her head to crossed behind her back, and guided kneeling Beka to position her mouth affront Elle's spread crotch and sopping pussy.

Elle straddles Gimbled It, legs hooked over It's lower limbs, and feels Gimbled It's swollen member totally inside her rectum, it feels very alive, and Elle can feel both the engorged blood and the three steel cock rings. It pumps her, pushing up against her from the inside, balances her on the penis, with Elle's buttocks balancing on It's groin, getting purpled of course, hands balancing behind with palms on It's chest, also getting more purpled.

GM is curt to Beka. ''Bury your face, clean out your Roommate's juice, suck on her clit, run your tongue down her nookie and make this needy notch nizzy trill.''

Beka advances. Elle's pussy lips already hang open. Everything from Elle's belly button down to her plugged anus is saturated with purple stain. Elle doesn't show her pink, Elle shows her purple, and a purple vestibule, a purple pee hole, a purple clit.

"Eat her out, you wannabe Whore," GM commands Beka. "Bury your mouth in her nookie, you Box Gobbler. Make her secrete some nectar for you."

And so Beka plunges her face into Elle's wet swamp, and as Beka licks out the cream she realizes, *I taste traces of It's penis as well.* Beka swallows. Elle's pussy is totally saturated with the stain, acquired from all of Elle's grinding and rubbing around fucking It.

Beka resigns herself to getting a purple mouth second hand and swabs her mouth and lips inside Elle's soaked nectary. But *I must still get a purple face directly! And a purple breech!*

Beka genuinely loves to give pleasure as much as take it; she lifts her head to pleasure Elle's purple clit with a now-purple tongue. Elle moans and simply surrenders herself completely to Beka's lips and tongue. The cock up Elle's ass throbs and Elle wiggles, and bounces up and down. Beka increases her assault. *I love Elle, but I will fuck anybody. So she has to fuck anybody also.*

Elle feels Beka put more heat into her pussy, and she herself puts more heat into the dick up her ass. Enough thinking. Beka is good. Elle climaxes.

Beka doesn't consider she is helping to imprint her Roommate on anal sex.

§ Beka Sucks It: A2OPM & Anals It • Elle A2OPM

Game Mistress doesn't let Elle climax indefinitely.

So be it. In a coordinated gesture China Doll quickly withdraws Gimbled It's cock from Elle anus, and as she moves Elle out of the way, Game Mistress's Goad guides Beka's neck and plunges It's penis, streaming with pre-lube and the flavor of Elle's rectum, directly into Beka's mouth.

"Clean it up, Whore," Game Mistress orders.

And Beka sucks. And qualifies A2OPM.

Beka cleans the taste of Elle's rectum off Gimbled It's erection and commences gathering some first-generation purple onto her own lips and tongue. She can feel the hollow sound and two barbells in It's head, counts the rings as she works her lips down the shaft, gathering purple around her lips as she descends. She breaths in, takes throat, purples her nose, and presses all the way down. Now she can rub her face on Gimbled It's soaked skin.

Beka comes up for a breath, graces It's pee hole with the tip of her tongue, circumnavigates It's head, graces a purple rim with now purpled lips, returns to It's lube hole, and strings a bead of lube away from It's hole with her tongue. Beka know the Cams are watching her and she relishes the moment, letting the streamer extrude and then move in, so it can paint gloss on her lower lip.

Beka eyes a Cam that is watching her, feel many eyes watching her, catches a glimpse of Elle watching and masturbating on the sidelines, and relishes the attention. These voyeurs, coupled with It's dick, now drive Beka's frenzy of arousal; she never asks to move her hands and grasp it's testicles into her hands, or move her now-tainted fingers to press on It's pelvis, and squeezes more lube out of the hollow Sound in the middle of the purple penis head and very sensitive rim and underside.

Beka focuses, *I am going to make It cum in my mouth!*

No, Gamers do not choose to pop It right now, so the Genie inside It blasts Beka with a mouthful of urine. Beka recoils, spills some of her own pee, recovers, tosses her head back, touches her purpled hands to her cheeks, and spills some of It's urine out her mouth.

"Swallow, Piss Mouth," commands GM, and Beka swallows. Out of the corner of her eye she can see China Doll, who never needs to be told what to do, already on her hands and knees and dutifully licking up the spilt urine… and getting it on her long hair. Beka correctly identifies China Doll as a certified Piss Mouth, yet fails to register that she herself has just been given a taste and vision of her own future.

Elle, nearby, and already a certified Piss Mouth, interprets that *Beka has just also been initiated a Piss Mouth. Beka is my Roommate and I'm not sure how this will affect me. She will either dominate the Patrons, or Patrons will want to see which of us cries uncle first.*

For Beka the future is simple: *I need It's cock in my fuck box.*

"Take your hands off It's balls," GM advises Beka, "you're begging handcuffs," she teases, "but now that you've got your fingers and palms purple, how about you turn around, reach around behind you, and use those wiggly fingers of yours to pull apart your butt cheeks, and show everyone your gaping bore hole."

Beka has uncertainty about this request but does appreciate that her fingers are purpled, and does obey to reach around and mark some purple spots inside her butt cheeks, and she pulls her posterior rugage wide open and displays her anus. And gape. Like problem-solving Elle, Beka has been stretched throughout Lockdown, especially by the Double Dong in its various incarnations.

Beka stays bent over and wonders *should I try to reach down and try to also pull pink?*

There is no shortage of Beka pink in the Game. And no time to consider: Game Mistress orders Beka to advance her position. "Put your face on the floor. Keep your knees spread. Keep your borehole open and lifted up. Your Roommate is an anal Whore, that means that you're an anal Whore also. Beg seriously, bonk moll."

Beka stumbles at unexpected knees, flattens her purpled face onto the floor, makes sure her knees are apart but support her, arches her buttocks upward and pulls her butt cheeks apart with purpled hands. "Please fuck my butthole," Beka begs, trying to lean back on one ear so that her mouth is fully functional, "fuck my bore hole right here, right now, then cock my mouth and cum –"

"Shut up," Game Mistress orders, and graces the Goad near Beka's anus to indicate Beka to lift higher, and Beka offers upward.

China Doll aligns Gimbled It's erection with Beka's upwardly offered entrance to her bowels, and then advances the erection forward and carefully. Beka arches her buttocks up and holds her ground, she can feel the end of the caged erection penetrate her brownie and push in ever so bit. *China Doll gives me time to relax, and accept It inside me. If Elle can handle analing It, I can too.*

And so Gamers throughout the Prefecture watch in real time as China Doll inches Gimbled It's cock forward and deeper, watch Beka squirm and accommodate It deeper and deeper into her rectum; Beka has to push up and take it, breathe carefully, ripple-pant, and gasp as the depth and diameter challenges her Dong experiences.

Contact, and as Beka settles down onto the long and thick penis, she acquires heavy glistening purple stain onto her hindquarters, her butt crack, and even inside her rectum. Beka's first anal qualifies not just as a Dong Whore, but a Dong and Dirty Whore.

Settling down causes fireworks to erupt in Beka's bruised buttocks, where paddle marks left blisters from rough treatment earlier at the Party. China Doll navigates Gimbled It upward, and Beka feels the purple Gentian Violet stain seep into her butt crack, then stinging pain as the stain rushes into the bruised area, where it will deepen them and also aid their healing.

Beka finds anal intense. Purple stain transfers from It's immense cock to the insides of Beka's stretched rectum. Beka breathes harder now, and begins her climax as the cock seats itself all the way home, well aware multiple hovering Drones cam her letting go.

Elle, watching from a position inches away from where It's cock buries itself in Beka's asshole, discovers herself masturbating (again), and touches her own anus. *I'm still gaping. And It is going to leave Beka just as gaping as I am.*

I'm a Whore, a natural Whore, I was a whore before I became official. Elle touches herself, parts her sex lips, and examines herself. *No pink, just purple inside.* Elle touches her clit and begins to fingerball herself. It feels good, purple on purple; no one stops her. *It doesn't matter anymore if they watch me.*

Beka's climax lifts her into the trill zone, she sings, and Game Mistress has a special treatment that will endear the most horny Lobelia a thrill she will never forget. The maneuver requires precision, that is correct, and it is also guided by the able skills of Slavesex China Doll and AI deep inside the Gimble.

Beka starts to trill higher as she feels It's cock begin to rotate inside her asshole, her last thought is an image of drill bit reaming a hole. She is correct, the entire Gimbled It Assembly rotates around the shaft of It's penis, so that Beka really is being screwed. China Doll brings Beka up to a steady scream, holds her there, then slows down the rotation and Beka gasps for air, and then guides Beka back down, ending with waves of trills until Gimbled It's rotation comes to a rest where it began and Beka is left in a pant as Gimbled It's ringed, erect penis is withdrawn from her rectum….

And plunged into Elle's nearby mouth, who, positioned on her knees and waiting, swallows the erection, cleans Beka's anal insides off It's cock, and embellishes her purple face and mouth with a third staining.

Elle is not stupid. *Now we are both A2OPM Whores.*

And Elle goes for it; pumps the erection, hands-free obviously, gags on it, vacuums its length, rims and tickles around the sound inside It's pee hole with her tongue.

Once again, (the Genie controlling?) Gimbled It releases a torrent of urine, surprising Elle and flooding her mouth. She retreats, discovers herself stepping in her own urine.

Elle watches China Doll lick up more urine. Mine and It's. Elle assesses how China Doll's lip rings are flush with her surface flesh, *so that her lips can make good suction. Or be sealed tight.*

Yes, China Doll does swallow much of the urine she gathers up from the floor, but she also deposits mouthfuls into a small basin affixed to the side of the Plaster Mummy, so that droplets of the golden water can be raised and dripped into Robyn's encapsulated mouth over time.

The tastes and the smells of It's cock and two assholes linger in Elle's mouth and on her breath. Elle senses that *the aroma, like that of eating pussy, might last for days. I'm a Piss Mouth too, Elle shudders, and I don't need rings in my lips or studs in my tongue in order to lick piss up. Players can piss on me anytime anywhere in front of anybody. I'm a Piss Mouth Stripper begging to Whore.*

V-10 Beka & Elle & Steph: Desires • Suspicions • Exits

§ Beka & Elle: Aftermath & Beka's Desire

Game Mistress take charge of Beka and Elle. "Stand & hug each other," she orders, "face-to-face, press your lips together. French Kiss. Do not let your mouths come apart, or I swear I will stitch the two of you together."

Beka and Elle might now be confirmed anal Whores, but they do not want their lips sewn together, *or our tongues spiked together with a single barbell.* And so they press their lip together, tip their tongues, dingle nose rings, and rub their tits and torsos together. They balance with their feet apart, purple hands leaving finger marks on each other's backs and buttocks, and smear purple stain around. Now, for the first time, as their bodies press together, Beka gets purple on her boobies and buds.

Each compares the foul aftertastes of their own mouth with the foul aftertaste of the other's palette. It's urine dominates and will quelch the inside of both mouths for hours. The tastes of each other's assholes, kindly delivered coating It's cock, are digested; a talismanic bond of unity shared by the Roommates that transcends the fame of a Party Fuck. Beka's mouth also contains a strong scent of Elle's nookie, but the inverse is not true; nobody ate Beka's burrow and nobody fucked it.

Beka sucked, and she got anally climaxed, a first, but she did not obtain cock in her boneroo and that has left her very, very frustrated, and even more horny. Afraid even.

Beka and Elle hears Game Mistress laugh. "I love you both, you are both going to become Porn Whores and maybe even Slavesex someday. You lucky Piss Mouths got to sample It's urine, but the Genie inside It isn't going to let It give either of you any of It's sperm today!

Game Mistress explains. "Gimbled It is primed and loaded with heavy and thick loads, but Gamers are saving It's cum blasts for our Two new Whores. If they are lucky, It's cum will blast out their noses; if they are unfortunate and their eardrums burst, you'll see the cum shoot out their ears."

Game Mistress addresses Beka and Elle, "You needn't worry. Semen is something you shall beg for from now on. You can't be Goo Whores yet, but you can be Goo Girls. More fundamentally you have an opportunity to become Cock Poppers, and once you get to the Nugget you can beg House Mom that handjobs and blowjobs aren't sex. You can argue that A2OPM cleanup and bukkake and gokkun isn't sex either, and show her examples."

Beka and Elle have but a moment to absorb Game Mistress's proposition, amazed at each other's purpled faces, hands, and bodies. Elle has a purple mouth, a purple nookie with purple all the way down her pipe, a purple nadir way and a purple butt crack. Beka has a purple mouth and purple bowels, but her bangbox bears no traces of penis penetration.

Hugging each other and kissing enables two bare-bald-naked Lobelia to look into each other's eyes. Booth ooze valiva. Beka's is natural; Elle's is purple tinted.

"As a matter of fact, you, Beka Broda," Game Mistress graces Beka between her legs with the Goad, "won't be working your bone-socket between now and Midnight; and since you're Stripping next Term, you won't be boning cocks then either. You think you're a Broda Bitch right now? Wait till House Mom Janet tailors your diet, lets you get fondled and fingered, and encourages Patrons to take pictures of you pinking center Stage if not felching in the Camera Lounge; Gamers know that 'not getting fucked' will frustrate you immensely, and you will go wild with desire."

Beka shudders, pulls Elle closer, and pushes her tongue into Elle's mouth. More valiva pushes her sex lips outward.

"You put yourself in this position, Beka Broda, you're a wannabe Whore, you're the one who Free-Fucked, so not letting you pleasure your bonker is a fitting channeling of your desire, now through the end of next Term. At a minimum. You think you pumped out broda at record rate during your first Term in the Game? Wait till House Mom explores getting you to pump more. Just what are you really willing to beg to actually Opt-Whore and get your bonker banged? How about a glass of jizz three times a day?"

Beka begs, "Mistress I'm a Stripper Deluxe, I'll do handjobs, I'll lick and eat pussy. I'll suck cock. I'll swallow all the goo you want to feed me, Elle too, we both want to be Goo Gobblers, Gokkun Gulpers, and Bukkake Babes."

Elle squirms at hearing this, *but I also know this is true. I'm a Whore, now until Midnight. And not just with Beka or Gimbled It. Anybody. And there is no way out. And after a Term on the Strip, I'm not just a Dong Whore, I'm a Dong and Dirty Whore.*

Beka escalates. "Mistress, I want to climax, Mistress. Please, I want cock in my box, I want cum all over me. I'm a Dong and Dirty Super Whore, Elle and me both, we'll eat each other's pussy while we get fucked."

Elle watches Game Mistress take a deep breath, and watches Beka correct herself, "Elle and I, we'll eat any pussy, lick any asshole, we'll suck together, and fuck and anal any cock anywhere anytime in front of anybody. We are already Media Whores, and when you Cam us naked and spread and fucking you are collecting a genuine part of our mind, body, and soul. As well you should, because our ambition is to be Porn Stars, BGG, BBGG, bisexuals, transexuals, DP, TP; gangbang us in the Spunk Pit, face down and then face up, make us Dong and Dirty Porn Whores."

Elle does understand. *My holes belong to the Game now.*

"You can tattoo my skin as much as you want, tattoo Elle too," Beka volunteers, "pierce the both of us, drive my bonesocket crazy with desire, let me eat Elle and I'll make her crazy too. Sell all of our holes; I'll do anything you want to land cock in my breech."

Game Mistress agrees. "Better," she says and blesses Beka and Elle, "May Kundalini share goodness with you! May the Patrons at the Nugget love your dancing and strips, crave your hands and mouths on their dicks, listen to you beg to sell your every hole, and fall in love with you!"

Two Eyepods go black and two Earpods go silent; the transition is so fast that it spins both purple Roommates to break their French kiss and embrace, catch their balance, and reach for, and acquire, the other's hand. Game Mistress allows them to stabilize.

A gentle grace with the Goad across purple lips reminds them to "don't speak unless you are spoken to."

Both quickly discover they are following a lead attached to their nose rings. They continue to hold hands, walk shoulder-to-shoulder. Each craves squeezing the opposite's hand, both treasure rubbing shoulders, and both desire to fuse together into an extended ecstasy of sixty-nine mutual cunnilingus.

§ Beka & Elle: Depart to the Nugget

Beka and Elle's transportation from the Play Party to the Nugget has been arranged. And Elle is not stupid. *I'm still a Lockdown Whore until Midnight, a Stripper Deluxe for a Term, and a Dong and Dirty Whore thereafter.*

Beka and I are going to get oraled continuously, and the Back Door Man at the Nugget is going to let all his friends train fuck me while Beka readies their dicks with her mouth and masturbates.

A correct prediction; Beka will clean up afterwards too.

Beka is fateful and optimistic. *Okay, so Babs gets to Whore next Term, but Elle and I have to wait a Term while we Opt Strip. It won't be easy for Bang Babe, but she doesn't have any choice in the matter. She'll still be at Flesh Ranch when Elle and I arrive. All I have to do is bring Elle along.*

Both future Whores continue to pulse valiva, but they have left their Collection Dishes behind, so that now as they move their vaginal cream just oozes out their shaven slits or swings between their walking thighs. If once upon a time, Beka was the more prolific producer (hence her surname, Beka Broda), now Elle also swings nectar, albeit with a purple tint to it.

The Four Lockdown Lobelia who remain behind (Babs, Tiffany, Kimju, Steph), all blessed with their own Collection Dishes, might wonder what will become of Beka and Elle's spendings. Beka might have the larger accumulation, but Elle's has a purple tint on the top.

Silly Lobelia; they should not be wondering "what will become of the spendings," but considering "what can I sacrifice in order to consume them?"

Beka and Elle's departure fails to provide total closure of their influence upon the remaining Four Naked Lockdown Lobelia. Certainly the Roommates' misbehaviors assures Babs' Whoredom. There exists unrevealed evidence pertaining to Steph's truthfulness. And, if Tiffany really does desire to Double Opt Down and Whore, any relief Gamers might grant to Opting-Whore Kimju, will certainly be expensive.

§ Beka: Fears Impact Her *Fuck Video* Upon Steph

Beka and Elle feel changes in the air, sometimes hands grace their skins. It appears the two nose leads join together ahead of them in the darkness, likely following the trolly above the duo. Beka concludes *we are being lead like a pair of concubines into a palace where....* Elle concludes, *we are being guided by a cable to the trolly above. We are Lockdown Whores advertising our purple holes. We don't dare stumble.*

Both rectums are starting to ache. Both assholes gape.

That Beka shall be denied all vaginal penetration between now and the end of next Term is already driving Beka crazy with desire; but setting aside Beka's prime motivator, now pride and fear complete for Beka's attention.

Pride, because *many Cams collected me eating Elle to climax and my A2OPM blowjob. I would have popped Gimbled It if I hadn't been piss-mouthed! Finally I get twisted to a howling climax getting analed like some Dirty Whore sticking her ass up in the air. Maybe now the* Video *can help me become famous, and with both of us purpled up, things are better now, except I still need to fuck. Be fucked, I don't care, I just need a dick stuck in breech.*

Elle has pride too. *I've purpled my every hole on cam and outdid my Roommate! Except she climaxed my brains out and I know I owe her an on-Cam oral climax. Gamers didn't let me masturbate while I was fellated, didn't let me climax when I was coitaled, and are training me to climax when I am anally possessed, albeit with Beka eating me out, but maybe also while I'm DPed with a cock in my mouth. Or my nookie. Or maybe my nook and my nadir at the same time. I can do that before Midnight, Beka can't, she can only do her asshole and mouth.*

Elle also has submission but not fear of her Fate: *If my nose ring leads me onto a cock that is where my mouth will be. And if my nookie is up in the air? I want someone to fuck it and spill jizz on me.* I'm a Lockdown Whore right now, a Stripper Deluxe at Midnight, and a Dong and Dirty Whore after next Term.

Elle tries to look ahead. *Beka and I are Stripping next Term. I know that once we arrive at the Nugget that we're pretty much committed to check all the boxes that turn a Stripper into a Stripper Deluxe. We are committed to dildos, buttplugs, watersports, handjobs, felching, and not just lollying cum but sucking it right out of cocks and swallowing. If we are smart, we can do gokkun contests and bukkake videos. Beka and I are going to get dunked like Goo Whores Penny and Coco. Besides, we're already begging to become Dong and Dirty Whores. It's not where I thought I would end up, but maybe Fate is teaching me to be humble. And to not be afraid of my sexuality. I'm letting go. I've let go. I'm gone.*

Beka appreciates the wind of Fate that advance her toward Porn Stardom, but Beka alone shoulders a deeper concern. Fear, actually, because *I can tell for sure that Steph is a Free-Fucker. That means that she's an instant Whore, if she gets caught. Just like I'd be whoring right now, if Gamers had not given me Immunity.*

Steph shot daggers into my eyes, and she keeps her fingernails sharp. Beka considers her situation. *It seems likely that Rodney told me the truth when he told me about a* Steph and William Sex Video. *That's because he made it! Just like he voyeur-cammed me. I wonder what William knows? Or Steph?*

In fact, during his attempt to assuage Beka's concerns about the risk of Free-Fucking, Rodney had indeed told Beka that William had secretly sexed with Steph, but didn't tell Beka that his subsequent discovery of that *Video* had fired his jealousy, so when the flirtatious Beka had visited the Peacock House handing out her Pink Page, Rodney had seized on the opportunity and had satisfied himself. *I am able to fuck a Cosmos Pledge just like Monitor William can!*

And I have the proof of it!

Gamers always carefully manage what facts and fictions get presented to which Lobelia, and have ensured that Beka's unconfirmed suspicions about a Steph and William liaison remain unconfirmed. Beka has no clue to suspect that there exists a second *Video* starring Steph and William, and which also includes Rodney making a barging-in, apparently surprise visit. This hidden cam view documents enough double penetration combos for Steph to taste herself twice, and run out of breath climaxing.

It pleases Gamers to keep Beka, and the others, largely ignorant of Steph's transgressions, let alone her potential Fate.

Self-defense motivates Beka to think. *It doesn't matter how Gamers discovered the* Beka & Rodney Fuck Video, *and if Game Mistress knows she didn't let on. It doesn't matter, I'll do anything she tells me to do. Steph doesn't have to know that I gave up Rodney, because that doesn't matter. What happened matters.*

And Rodney? *Certainly Rodney got turned out, copped a plea and squealed. Because if he made a secret* Video *of Steph and William, the Gamers have it now. Or maybe he was just feeding me a line in order to fuck me. Except none of this matters; Steph looked at me with fire in her eyes and that says it all.*

What happened is that Steph Free-Fucked with William, Maybe Rodney made secret a video and maybe not. Or William destroyed it. So maybe she won't get caught. But she's guilty; she is a Free-Fucker and deserves to Opt-Whore on her own.

So if Steph gets discovered, it needs to be because Rodney outed William and Steph. I had nothing to do with it. I'm innocent. What happens somewhere else, stays somewhere else. Not my Karma.

Beka grins to herself. *But if there is a Video of Steph and William, I want to see the part where Steph has her legs spread wide and his cock is pumping inside her. I want to see the part where she is growling and grinding back. I want to see cum running out of her snatch, just like I got shown off. I want to see her swallow.*

Beka wrinkle her nose. *She doesn't like at all that I fucked with Rodney, and that we got caught. I got outed in front of everyone at the* Play Party *as well as the Prefecture. And qualified for Whore Caste. I'd be a Whore now if Gamers hadn't given me Immunity; Elle would be a Whore too, except my Immunity means we both have to Strip a Term before we Opt Whore, and become Porn Stars.*

Beka wonders what Gamers know about Steph. *She was always a haughty who thought she deserved to be served. In fact, she's an opportunistic Free-Fucker, and a liar. I can tell from how she looked at me. Otherwise why would Steph look at me like that? She would look at me like the others do, like I'm some kind of sex-crazed fuck box, which is probably true.*

And it has to be William. Steph would never put out for Rodney; there is nothing he can do for her.

But will Steph get away with it? Rodney can say whatever comes to his mind, but if William denies it, and unless there is proof, Gamers will pierce Rodney's tongue for making false accusations.

Steph is still a Free-Fucker and deserves to Whore. Steph could be a real detriment, especially if she is relegated to selling her slit at Flesh Ranch. She could still be there when Elle and I arrive. She could stop me from getting a full body suit. So could cut me off from cock. She could beat me up and make me her toilet.

Except. I'm okay as long as I keep Elle with me. As long as we stay together Steph doesn't have a chance. Especially now that Elle is recognizing she really is a Whore; and is starting to like people watching her have sex.

But if there is a Steph and William Video, *could Steph become Slavesex? Make a full drop, just like Robyn? She's an Opt Whore for Free-Fucking, but she lied about it as well. That's a tongue piercing for Steph, and maybe another Caste down.*

So if Steph gets caught, then Gamers need to take her down before she can get her hands on me; and if she gets away with it, I'm in danger. She needs to be spread out in chains inside a Dungeon, beaten, pissed on and gangbanged.

Beka might not even know the total on Steph's lame deceptions, but Gamers have counted three strikes.

Elle, unaware of the events driving Beka's concerns, and herself defeated by Steph earlier this Term, continues to assume that Steph would reclaim her Monitor Opt at Midnight. *That's why she was allowed to watch some of us get masturbated to climax. Get depilated. That's why she is the only Cosmos Lobelia not pierced and tattooed.*

Certainly during their transport to the Nugget, both Beka and Elle's mouths are indeed claimed, side-by-side and on their knees, and yes, cammed while they suck and snowball the pops.

They ring the Stage Door Bell, naked, and yes,

The Back Door Man greets their ring of the Stage Door Bell, and promptly bends Elle over the collection box so as to facilitate train fucking from behind, nooky or nadir, and the use of Elle's bent forward mouth.

Being naked, Beka and Elle had no final Garments to surrender before ringing the Bell, and their purple holes advertise their commitments.

Beka readies the cocks, cleans the creampies out of Elle's nook and nadir, and plays with her frustrated and wanton sex box.

Molly watches on a Screen from inside the Nugget. No hiding for Beka and Elle now, or when this *Video* screens while the Roommates are dancing in the new Term. Or their *Videos* sexing with Gimbled It. Or even their *Gonzo Suck and Fuck Videos*.

Beka is sopping. And she also gotten a couple of pops on her own. *I want to be fucked so bad I may have to trade away Elle for cock. This is a crazy thought. And look at Elle moan. She always was a whore, now she has discovered what she is. I've given my skin away, I'll give her skin away too. We're Whores. And we're going to be big Porn Stars.*

Beka especially knows that *there will be no fucking once we pass through the Stage Door, however our purple marks show that our begging to be Dong and Dirty Whores is real. In the meantime, we shall blow or eat every member of the House Staff. Lick every asshole. And suck goo from Patrons in the Champagne Room.*

§ Steph: Beka's Revelation Creates Worry

Four Cosmos Lockdown Lobelia remain following Beka and Elle's exit. Kimju and Tiffany, unsuspecting that Steph may still harbor revelations, continue to assume that *either Steph's Duel victory will guarantee her an Opt Monitor, or Robyn's drag is sufficient for Gamers to accept her begs to Opt-Strip.*

Babs, wiser by Janet's advisory, evidenced by Beka and Elle's *Videos*, presumes Steph's Fate remains undecided. Babs considers, and accepts that *my Opt Dong and Dirty Whore Fate is deserving. It doesn't matter if Steph Free-Fucked, Beka and Elle have made sure that my mouth, burse, and butthole are already appropriated.*

But Babs also anticipates, *Game Mistress now decides if to play, how to play, when to play, the Steph outing.*

Correct, and it pleases Game Mistress to pitch all Four Lobelia into darkness and silence, and contemplate how they might equal or transcend Beka and Elle's Fate.

The isolation only magnifies Steph's ongoing unease. Beka's revelations and the *Beka and Rodney Fuck Video* jangle an otherwise confidant assumption of Fate; that *Video*, coupled with the reality of Beka sucking and analing Gimbled It's cock, keep Steph's mind turning; Steph cannot completely put the matter to rest.

And why should she; Midnight still lies ahead. Yes, Steph has become wary, but she remains confident she reads the power dynamic; *the* Runout *is a charade for me,* and although Steph fails to anticipate any decline of her Caste, she does mentally reconsider what moving pieces might be unleashed which might require damage control.

Steph rewinds. *I was the Cosmos who defeated Elle in the Duel; now she Opts Down and I Opt Up. She's a wannabe Whore. Good. And Beka? Beka might have gotten Immunity, but she's still one horny bonker. She'll fuck anything. Besides, just how do Beka's confessions, after getting caught, qualify her for Immunity?*

Steph affords herself the smallest of smiles. *Beka's a pariah for her Roommate. Elle might be addicted to the Double Dong, but Beka is going to make sure that Elle get addicted to erections and pussy.*

Steph rolls Game Mistress around in her mind with newfound consideration. Steph has assumed all along that *my own nakedness, armbinder, and humiliations are merely temporary gestures to disguise my obvious promotion at Midnight.* Suddenly Steph feels herself overcome with a sudden faint, that *however that stupid Beka got herself on Candid Camera with Rodney, and however the Gamers found the* Video. *that well, er, you know… maybe that is not a good thing.*

Rodney! Steph puts her finger on the weak spot. *If the Gamers pinched Beka they pinched Rodney! What an asshole.* Steph replays in her mind the *Video* sequence of Rodney penetrating Beka. *He shoots his jizz right into her breech and when she stands up it creeps down inside her thigh. And to think the perp fucked me as well! And not just my snatch, he rammed my shithole and fed me. Except I was forced into it, whereas Beka is just a horny bimbo with her bone hole always slippery with want.*

Steph acquires confidence. *So I know what happened, when Gamers showed Beka her* Video *she was happy to confess to her obvious guilt, and commit herself to Whore. And just now she swallowed timber up her bowels and thinks that she is on the road to Porn Stardom. What a bimbo.*

I, however, have been presented with nothing because there is nothing to present! Rodney took William and me by surprise, so William demanded I suck Rodney's cock while William fucked and analed me. I didn't have a choice. Then they switched off and I got DPed and A2Med like I was some kind of a Whore!

Rodney couldn't have cammed that encounter because he didn't expect to find us. And the first time he wasn't around.

And William would never dare to cam himself with a Pledge, because if he ever got found out, unlike Rodney, William wouldn't just end up a Whore, he'd be Slavesex.

Steph revisits Beka's reaction to the *Video* and concludes, *Beka might be a Free-Fuck but she didn't know she was shooting a* Porn Video. *So who shot the scene? William? Rodney? They are both perps and assholes!*

Steph tries to keep all outward appearances calm but the torment won't go away. *I want to know how Gamers found the* Beka & Rodney Fuck Video, *but just like Beka, Rodney is going to make the drop. Rodney's been a Stripper before, now his Whore mouth and ass are about to get sold in an after-hour gay biker bar.*

Steph finds her clamped tongue a great inconvenience. *No, the thought of the Gamers finding any* Video *of me is untenable. There can't be any Videos.*

And besides, I fucked Rodney because I had to, Steph reconfirms to herself. *I didn't break the Rules. I'm an Opt Up,* Steph breathes a sigh of relief. *I was forced into sex by a Monitor and analed by a Pledge. I would never use my body to Opt Up!*

Steph finds herself getting more and more irritated. *I am peeved at Beka. Peeved at her for fucking around, peeved at her for confessing. I am peeved at Rodney, for barging in on William and me. Irritated at him for being so stupid to secretly make a* Video *of his fuck with Beka.*

Steph is additionally jealous that Rodney fucked Beka. *What a prick. So did William fuck Beka also? Are there any other Cosmos he might have screwed? I used to like William and find him hot. But now I'm pissed at him – I already have a guaranteed Opt Up and he let me think that if I fucked him I could get a Double Opt Up at Midnight. I got double penetrated instead.*

Steph craves r*etribution! Fuck Beka and fuck Elle too: Whores. And fuck Rodney: Slavesex. And fuck Kimju for not reporting; Whore. And fuck Babs for letting Robyn escape in the first place. She deserves to be bound and backeye buggered: Whore, Dong and Dirty type.* Anger reels, and Steph jangles her cuffs. *Fuck everybody.*

Steph will; but she didn't know it quite yet.

V-11 Tiffany & Kimju: Trade Places & Depart (LD8)

§ Game Mistress Appraises Four Cosmos Lobelia: Fates

Beka and Elle's departure (and Robyn and Molly's earlier exit) leave behind Four Cosmos Lockdown Lobelia in the confines of the Meatpacking Plant: Babs, Tiffany, Kimju, and Steph.

All Four are blind-deaf-mute, bare-bald-naked, kneeling-spread-armbound. So yes, Tiffany has been moved from a sucking, kneeling fuckee on the Risen Cocks Lineup, to sharing a position with the remaining three ex-Cosmos.

Babs and Kimju both beg to be Dong Hoes, Babs also feels compelled to beg to take on the backdoor trade.

Tiffany, currently Opting to Strip at the Nugget, seeks ways to ride the destruction of Robyn's Charm downward, but understands that trades, might they even be negotiated, could require forfeits.

Steph continues to believe she shall Opt Monitor at Midnight.

Vision and sound return to their Eyepods and Earpods, providing them however, not their own view of the Meatpacking Plant, but the view of what Game Mistress sees and hears. Realtime. These Four Naked Lobelia should be grateful to see anything.

Four Lobelia watch a closeup of Babs' boobs; Bondo Babe's boobs still bear cinch marks, where ropes binding her breasts have only recently been removed. BB watches herself but also feels the fingers rub the goo into her crescent d'areolage. She transudes fresh brodeas immediately, then watches the view of herself descend and reveal her bursting butterfly and hanging stalactite of creamy batter.

Watching herself squeeze burgoo out of her burke encourages this naked-kneeling-armbound Lobelia to pump another helping.

Babs will keep transuding from now on, but the view in Four Lobelia Eyepods shifts to Tiffany; Tiffany also watches herself as a finger reaches from behind and rises up into her twirly, swabs her trigger with fresh tang, and masturbates Tiffany into a pant, and settles her into the Zone. Tiffany accepts the pleasure, but seeks to move faster in the direction she is already heading, and replace the finger with cock.

Kimju finds Game Mistress looking down at her and watches herself while she feels a cock rub on her cheek. Real and coordinated with the picture she sees of herself. The cock graces itself around Kimju's O-Ring Gagged lips, and the tip of the cock tickles the tip of Kimju's double-pierced and clamped tongue.

Whore conditioning?

Must I whore both my mouth and my kunny at Flesh Ranch?

Yes, that is my beg, and with two tongue studs I'll be kept busy.

But Steph, Steph seems to shake off hands which attempt to fondle her scones or pinch her spouts on top; and because the Four Lobelia are indeed looking through Game Mistress's eyes, Babs and Tiffany and Kimju interpret that Steph is given a pass.

Watching themselves and each other is a *very* disorienting experience to all Four Lobelia. Do they see themselves occasionally? Yes. Do they see each other? Yes also. Do they silently compare, scheme, surrender?

Yes, but their goals in the Game are all different.

Are these Four Trophies too self-indulgent, too creamy, too zoned?

Probably, but certainly prizeworthy.

Four Misfortunates?

Perhaps, but also the careless, the opportunistic, the weak, the deceitful.

Worthy of training?

Worthy of love.

But also the most fortunate?

Four Cosmos Lockdown Lobelia present themselves naked and depilated so their nipples, buttons, and slits show out, deep pinkers all, gapers every one, pissers for sure and Piss Mouths… but no purple holes.

Has adequate attention been bestowed upon them?

Indeed, none of these Four Cosmos Lockdown Lobelia have earned any purple stain, let alone any purple plundered holes, like Beka and Elle departed with (five out of their six). The Four remaining Lobelia observe the deeply stained Gimbled It with varying degrees of desire, fear, promise, and compromise.

Babs accepts *I deserve to Opt Whore, Tiffany certainly seeks an avenue to Whoredom, maybe Kimju should not have been so quick to seek sanctuary and beg to Opt Whore, and Steph continues to convince herself, "I am a Monitor next Term. And I will be paddling my Pledge every morning, noon, and night."*

Game Mistress still presides, and the Lobelia continue to see not her, but see what her eyes see, and hear what her ears hear, directly into their very own Eyepods and Earpods.

Might Game Mistress deem to look, all can see that Bab's hands continue to collect goo. Aside from the already-departed Molly, Babs is the only Cosmos Lobelia who has enjoyed her hands free of mittens, and over time not only coated her hands with semen, but also her outer thighs and hips. Party-goers have accelerated her valiva production by swabbing her crescent d'areolage with fresh goo, and contribute to her diet by scooping the endless goo running down her body and feeding her O-Ring-Gagged mouth.

Babs is not so stupid she would use her free tongue to push jism out of her mouth, or try to sneak it out with drool; BB knows what to do; she swallows. And swallows and swallows and swallows.

Babs' O-Ring Gag has enabled her to lick clits and the insides of pussies, consume goo while continuing to beg penis oralation, and provided unencumbered access to pee holes. Some Lobelia believe that Party Players may already have sampled BB's mouth, if not also her lower parts.

Two other Lobelia, Kimju and Steph, also wear O-Ring Gags. Like Babs, these remain tightly secured behind their teeth, and are so big around there is absolutely no give, no chaffing of the mouth. Custom fits. Mouths totally taken, O-holes, jaws stretched almost to the breaking point, immobilized, no play. And producing hideously distorting and contorting faces.

Kimju and Steph's tongues also remain tightly clamped. A pair of parallel horizontal rods continue to squeeze the tongue from above and below; the rods are wider than the O-Ring, so the tongue can't retract inside the mouth. One Lobelia, Kimju, enjoys the prestige of double tongue studs, one in front of her Tongue Clamp rods, and one behind it, centered about the O-Ring. Kimju isn't sure if they are a blessing or a curse.

Tiffany's mouth is unencumbered by a gag or a clamp. It does retain a deep scent with semen, and Tiffany's face and head, and indeed much of her body, remain splattered with jizz; not just facials, but side shots, pinkeyes, goo that now creeps down her now-kneeling body, and vaginal creampies in quest of a Collection Dish.

Tiffany knows that *wanting to be cleaned off is part of my humiliation,* but Tiffany is experienced enough to keep the flavors of cocks inside her closed mouth. Tiffany also can see, via Game Mistress's eyes, *I am the only Lobelia absent a Gag.*

This is why Tiffany, alone among the Four, doesn't drool.

Bondo Babe drools, unlike Kimju and Steph her Tongue Clamp has been removed, leading to speculation that her drool is diluted by jizz fed into her O-Ringed mouth; and besides, BB has a free tongue and is encouraged to swallow. Lacking free tongues, when Kimju and Steph drool, it is pure drool, and yes, they make a mess out of themselves. Sticky drool creeping down their chins, spilling onto their knockers and spouts, pooling in freshly pierced and tattooed belly buttons belly buttons, tickling clits.

Besides, Tongue Clamps hurt, and if not managed right, can make the tip of the tongue go numb after a while.

Babs and Tiffany's tongues remain unencumbered. In Babs' case she is able to move her tongue around inside her mouth or protrude outside the Gag hole, and doesn't have a Tongue Clamp blocking access to her mouth.

Tiffany, fresh from her recent stint on the Risen Cocks Lineup, is no longer gagged nor tongue clamped; O-Ring Gags are great for training recalcitrant throat Whores, but a fellatrice of Tiffany grade knows to apply a full brace of tongue, lips, teeth, the insides of her cheeks, and yes, her throat, to the pleasures of a penis.

At the moment, Tiffany's mouth remains awash in semen, her face is splattered with semen, her vagina overflows with creampies, and her body drips goo.

Slavesex Gimbled It hangs around, testicles swollen, penis huge, glistening with deep purple stain.

Slavesex China Doll has cleaned up any spilt urine, brodeas, or jizz that has reached the floor. This is what a Slavesex mouth is for.

Slavesex Robyn, blind-deaf-mute and bare-bald-naked, remains encased in a Plaster Mummy suspended from the trolly sitting on the rail overhead. Slavesex China Doll, she who anticipates all problems, has watered Robyn, lightly soaped her rectum, put her on a slow but steady urine drip, and tuned her runnel production.

All Four Lobelia remember Game Mistress proclaiming that "Robyn's Fate goes deeper than total immobilization and life support, and shall focus on total reconstruction of her mind, body, and soul."

The hanging reality of this potential outcome helps ensure that none of these Four Cosmos Lobelia wants to take this particular route to nirvana.

§ Game Mistress Advises Four Lobelia: Consequences

The Four Naked Lobelia need not know (at least in the short term) the Fates of Beka and Elle after they exit the *Play Party* and pass through the Stage Door at the Nugget. Conversely, Beka and Elle will not get to witness the outcome of these Four Cosmos Lockdown Lobelia who remain behind, despite the fact that their Free-Fucking is advancing their ex-Monitor Babs to a stall at Flesh Ranch.

"You and you," Game Mistress curls her word to Babs and Kimju, "appear to be Whores next Term. Lucky holes." GM turns to Babs, "word is you beg the Dong and Dirty type, is that true?"

Babs hesitates, unsure of the necessity, then knows to affirm, "Aaha-aaha." BB also knows, *I am already a Pee-Camer, Piss Mouth, Goo Gobbler, and pussy eater. I begged to Whore on Cam, and I knew about the Dong, but I didn't know what Dirty meant. Now I do. Every hole, any cock, many cocks at the same, anyplace, anytime, in front of anybody, on Cam, live show, private client.*

"Good, so you're settled," GM states, "you're a Dong and Dirty Whore from now on. Until Midnight, after Midnight, and as many Terms as the Gamers want you to beg."

It's a slight shift; Game Mistress does not ask for an answer but BB responds anyway, "Aaha-aaha." *I am going to get cocked during Lockdown and I'm going to keep getting cocked after Midnight too. I'm going to eat pussy and get my pussy eaten. I'm going to be double penetrated in my mouth and ass, my pussy and ass, and my mouth and pussy. None of that is normal. I'm sure to be spread and fucked in the Spunk Pit, banged face up, buggered face down. I'm sure they will make me a Goo Gal, and mark me with purple as a Dirty Whore.*

Game Mistress has already told me I'll be fucking Gimbled It, and now I know I'll also be sucking It and sodomizing It's erection. "So goes a Pledge so goes her Monitor."

GM turns to Kimju with a movement and look that strikes fear into Kimju, "You've been a Stripper before, now you beg to Double Opt Down and Whore for a Term? Is that true?"

Kimju slowly affirms through the Ring Gag, "Aaha-aaha." *I am not sure why I am agreeing to this.*

Game Mistress finger scoops Kimju to make sure her kootch is empty, and to test for wetness.

"I bet you'd like to clean my pretty finger off, wouldn't you, Whore wannabe?" GM inquires.

Kimju whinnies. Then grunts twice, "Aaha-aaha."

"You want your Tongue Clamp off so you can lick my finger clean." GM states.

Is this a question? Kimju hesitates.

Time up; GM provides. "I totally understand. You want the Clamp off so you can lick cock with your double-pierced tongue, don't you." GM states.

Is this a question? Kimju feels she must agree, "Aaha-aaha."

"You want if off so you can get mouth-fucked." GM advises.

Again, Kimju reluctantly agrees, "Aaha-aaha."

"You want some deep throat practice." GM states.

Kimju agrees more slowly this time, "Aaha-aaha."

"Then take your Gag off completely so you can bury your face and eat pussy."

Another statement, another affirmation, "Aaha-aaha."

Game Mistress takes a deep breath. "You're a lot of work, you know that? But you need not worry. Gamers have confidence in you. You have Two Terms to break out from a typical suck-fuck-facial Whore, offer up your asshole, and gain Dong and Dirty status."

Kimju remains silent at this proposition.

"You," GM points to Tiffany, "appear to be Stripping after Midnight. Sorry, although everyone knows you qualify to Opt Whore. Certainly you can beg to be a handjob and blowjob Stripper, tell House Mom 'it's not sex.'"

"But look at you, you are already a 65% Goo Whore. Gamers will have to decide whether to send you into the Nugget like that and have some Strippers lick you off center Stage, or clean you up before you leave the *Play Party*.

Certainly Tiffany's mouth has been shot full of jizz many times today, and certainly her stretched twister has been fucked and creampied. Both mouth and twat are wrought of overuse.

Yes, Tiffany has climaxed, and at times almost continuously with one cock eruption followed by another immediate penetration.

But always Tiffany has enjoyed the luxury of the Ass Hook that held her tush up and ensured that her sex organ got vertically displayed and easily fuckable, and, more importantly in Tiffany's mind, *that my anus remained inaccessible.*

But now as Tiffany kneels in a part of the Plant occupied by the Four Cosmos Lobelia and their Superiors, Tiffany considers *what I might have to do to achieve a swap with Kimju?*

"You," Game Mistress points to Steph, "appear to be Opting Monitor at Midnight, although with the Clock stopped, maybe you can get screwed before then. Something to show your Pledge next Term.

Steph grits at the possibility of getting screwed during Lockdown, *between Robyn casting us here and Beka and Elle providing role models, I do not need any cock in my slit. William exploited me, and he'd better keep a secret, so that my Opt-Up is not jeopardized!*

Yes, the revelation of the *Beka and Rodney Fuck Video* does disturb Steph. *The fact that Beka looked at me with fear in her eyes was not a good sign.*

I hope that with Beka gone that the Rodney matter is gone also. I hope Rodney is sucking cock and getting analed. Probably William too, because "so goes a Pledge so goes the Monitor." That's why they weren't part of the Sedan Chair Bearers. William is simply too good a hunk of meat to pass up, so wherever Rodney is sucking and getting sodomized, William is right next to him.

Probably still opposite and upside down on the Wheel.

Steph draws conclusions. *But there is no Video of William and me. Beka and Rodney got caught, Beka and Rodney are guilty Free-Fuckers, and Babs and William are Whores by entailment. Being the Boss Bitch and the Big Bugger have a price.*

Still, Steph increasingly finds herself tormented by a growing nagging worry; in particular Steph to wants to touch where there remains lingering pain in her nose and her navel. Steph is well aware that all the other Lobelia have rings in their noses and decorations in their belly buttons, even Babs. *I want to engage in compulsive behavior and check myself, even though I don't need to because there is nothing there and any pain is artificially induced.*

Steph takes a deep breath and lets her air out. *Come Midnight I will Opt Monitor. But until Midnight,* Steph understands, *because of this Lockdown business, unless I am careful I will have to suck cock, and that's just unacceptable to me. I'm not even about to get my hands purple! There is nothing they could do to me to force me to suck cock on camera. I would never do that.*

Maybe Steph hasn't considered that climaxing Cosmos Lockdown Lobelia while sodomizing them might be a trend.

§ Kimju: Resigned to Whoring

Kimju has abandoned all hope of promotion. She remains O-Ring Gagged and Tongue Clamped, bare-bald-naked, kneeling-spread-armbound. She drools on her 35C "knockers," and ponders her old nickname, "Knock Knock Kava Kava," because the kava is gone and *I overhead myself called "Knockers Kopperkunt," which pretty much describes my predicament.*

Kimju has a reputation for being practical and forthright, but eager to please and easily manipulated by expressions of power. Right now she sees what Game Mistress sees, hears what Game Mistress hears, and feels what Game Mistress desires she feel.

Kimju understands where she is headed, *but I doesn't know why. Somehow I have fallen from Opting Monitor to Opting Whore. I don't deserve that.*

Actually Kimju knows why. *I'm a Whore because I begged to Whore during* The Runout. *Madam Nurse and Pimp Cowboy suggested that if I didn't beg to Whore I might end up Slavesex. What did I know? I was secured to my Post with my arms behind my head, my armpits open, and my legs spread, and I thought it was the only way for me.*

It was the only way.

Then in the Amphitheater, Game Mistress made be beg to Whore right in front of Robyn, after Robyn had been captured, and knowing

Robyn was the reason I was a naked, spread, secured Lockdown Lobelia begging to Opt Whore.

Now I know I was duped.

So now not only is my body being taken away from me, but so is my friend, and my former Nugget Roommate, Molly. Molly has weaknesses, for sure. And for sure Molly's fresh begs to offer her mouth will be honored the moment she arrives at the Nugget, if not before she goes through the Stage Door. And me? I'm going to have to suck cock too from now on too, only not in the Champaign Room at the Nugget. I'm going to suck cocks at Flesh Ranch. And I will not just be getting fondled and fingered, and doing handjobs and blowjobs, I am also going to get fucked.

Which might be okay, except things could go worse than that.

Kimju does consider what Gamers design she observes. *I watched Beka and Elle suck and fuck. And anal. And clean the other's asshole off Gimbled It's penis, A2OPM. So they are correctly tagged Dong and Dirty Whores, now and whenever. I saw them take on purple stain all over their faces and mouths, inside their butt cheeks and rectums. Elle even has a purple crotch, purple inside her sex lips, purple on her clit, and purple all the way down her nautch.*

Kimju projects, *Bondo Bangho is already begging Dong and Dirty Whore, and from the way she's hanging I suspect she has already been throated through her O-Ring, balled, and buggered. I'm begging to Whore so after Babs gets cocked, I take it for real. I'm going to arrive at Flesh Ranch with purple stain all over my body, my holes stretched, and dripping.*

That leaves Tiffany and Steph, if Steph is for real.

Game Mistress watches Kimju react as Kimju's remote eyes take a long stare at the hanging Plaster Mummy. "Don't worry," GM conjures, "Slavesex Robyn will get to replace her Anal Intruder with real cock up her ass once Gamers decide how they want to imprint her personality upon reentry. Until then maybe it is convenient to feed her anally, pump her stomach, and feed her purge to any recalcitrant Lobelia among you.

"Or do I have that backward, Whore?"

To agree or disagree, that is the question.

Kimju struggles to hold her spread position. Earlier this Term, Kimju had retained a self-confidence that *my intelligence and statuesque figure would guarantee me an Opt-Up. I had earned the Two Garments, when suddenly I was runout naked.*

Kimju tries to steady her thoughts. *Robyn Runaway turned us all into Naked Cosmos Lockdown Lobelia, and I was singled out and condemned to Whoring because I didn't see her missing!*

I know what's happening. I'm a very good Stripper. Top tier. I know more ways to doff a bra than Vasudhara has arms. I've practiced pullasides and pinkings, had to suspend my kloop all the way to a Collection Dish on the floor, I've climaxed and peed center Stage. Peed stark naked in public too. The last time I was a Stripper I was on Cam 24x7, no exceptions. I changed tampons center Stage, then sucked on the one I took out.

But this isn't enough for them is it? They want more of me. And they are going to take it out of me, even if it's not fair.

Who said the Game is fair and balanced?

It's not fair that I'm begging to Whore. I don't deserve a fuck stall at Flesh Ranch, and I don't even want to return to the Nugget, even if it is all mostly solo work without any Stripper Deluxe extras. And I've played all the parts: full-nude, pink pussy masturbation, dildos and buttplugs, poured shots onstage.

I had two Garments and an Opt-Up before Robyn Raghole Ragabash Ragazze ran away. Disappeared. Kidnapped. Whatever. Cancelled my Opt-Up. Charmed me. All nonsense.

Gamers just want an excuse for me to suck cocks. Handjob cocks and swallow the goo. And fuck me. And watch me fuck. Absolutely no privacy, Suck Fuck Facial on Cam. Leading Man after Leading Man, eating pussy with another Leading Lady. Threesomes, BBGG, gangbangs, orgies.

Gamers could have picked any Cosmos Pledge, or no Cosmos Pledge, and they pick me. I deserve to be a Monitor next Term; but they set me up and broke me to Whore, because they intend to turn me into a Porn Star.

So that's what's right for me now. This is what is best for me. That must be my way.

Kimju twists a lip. *I got my knockers played with endlessly last time I danced at the Nugget, and I long ago got over getting fingers inside my kooch. As long as they were clean and didn't have sharp fingernails. That hardly qualifies me as a handjob artist, although cocks might even be easier to handle, at least they can't scratch me.*

So once I'm a Whore I shall jerk off cocks, suck them, explode them on my face and in my mouth, and swallow? Yes, I can do that. I had to watch Beka and Elle suck and I'm as good as they are. I shall eat pussies, lolly creampies out of pussies and assholes, snowball, gokkun, bukkake, and everything else?

Well, yes, I am a very good fuck!

Except. Except, I'm not begging to be an anal Whore! Like Beka and Elle. And I will not be lining up behind Babs and Tiffany and Steph to get my rectum reamed by a purple erectile monster.

My ass is all I've got because I don't control my skin, my mouth, or my kunny.

Kimju considers. *I accept I can be good at the Whoring. The one-on-one of it. The sexual excellence. I don't want to Whore, I never have, but I can master it.*

I might even prefer it to Stripping, because I do like to help people and I'm understanding of their needs. Although I am good at the tease.

What's happening might be unfair. But it does advance my chances of expanding into a full body suit.

Kimju considers the deeply colored circles that radiate from around her nipples and down her knockers, from her kypsey and kawazoo as an outward oval, and her belly button, her sacred Cosmos spot. Collisions are unavoidable.

My piercings still carry the pain of the piercing needle, and double nipples are next. My body continues to appreciate the sting of ink. I have hit the ink jackpot. I am going to keep adding ink until my concentric rings collide and no part of me is left uncovered.

I just could become an alt-Porn Star!

And I've got one more tattoo coming. And it's on top of everything else. Maybe I can beg they tattoo circles around my pee hole, patterns across my vestibule and sink ink into my keystone.

Kimju takes a deep breath. *Using my mouth is only half of it. I understand I will now be expanding my repertoire. I will no longer be doing just solo acts. I will be doing girl-girl, boy-girl, boy-girl-girl, boy-boy-girl, girl-girl-girl and all combinations beyond. I shall learn to handle the splosh parties, win gokkun contests, and fit endless cocks into my pussy. On premises, or outcall. More than one at a time.*

Kimju's concept of Whoring keeps evolving. *Whoring is more than just getting handsome guys to fuck me. It's them paying me to fuck me. It could be wild. I am going to be taken to exclusive parties wearing a dress with no panties and a scoop neck so when I lean over everyone can look at my knockers. I'm not shy, and I am a showoff. And I've done strip-pink-toy parties by the score. Now I am going to get party fucked, I am going to get cammed on a Yacht, suck and fuck in public at a Porn Convention, and escort politicians.*

But there is a wrinkle which worries Kimju mightily.

I know I must confront the implications of losing control of what's between my legs. and my mouth. What I'm afraid of is that Madams and Pimps may well take me into an addictive state of arousal, perpetual arousal, where I need cocks in my mouth and pussy all the time.

I saw Steph get Zoned following her defeat at The Greatest House Roar. I saw Elle surrender to the Double Dong, Beka finally climax, only now she is chastised and will be driven crazy as Elle gets train fucked.

Kimju tries to consolidate. *I'm at a disadvantage. I'm already a Whore looking at Double Terms. Gamers are going to control my kunny, put cocks into it for sure, but also deny me so that I get very horny, and I'm afraid that I am going to beg Gamers to tie me down and sex me. And that sooner or later I will beg them to be a Whore-for-Life, or even a Slavesex.*

Right now, Kimju realizes, *I must deal with the present. I need to be a Lockdown Whore right now. I need to collect facials and swallow, and after Midnight be the best Whore at Flesh Ranch, or wherever I'm sent to fuck.*

Kimju rushes. *Tattoo me, cream me, climax me, fuck me in any position, private, bachelor party, hovering Drone Cam. Spread me naked and work me flat on my back.* Kimju confides to herself, *because I will do anything to avoid being cast into plaster.*

Kimju grunts. GM understands, and lets Kimju feel the Goad on her clit, just enough so that Kimju can freshen herself. Kimju accepts, *Might as well get slippery for cock, cause it is coming my way. But at least my kawazoo is safe.*

For now.

§ Tiffany: Porn Star Seeks Way to Flesh Ranch

Tiffany waits patiently. Since being moved from the Risen Cocks Lineup to the kneeling-spread-armbound position like the other Three other Cosmos Lockdown Lobelia, and seeing herself through Game Mistress's eyes, Tiffany confirms that even her eyebrows have been shaven off, her eyelashes trimmed, and her lips rouged and stained so as to make her look like a cheap whore.

All this underneath a head and face 100% coated with thick goo.

The fat Ass Hook is gone, but Tiffany's gape remains, Tiffany knows, *advertising the only thing I can offer.*

Tiffany's mouth remains unencumbered; Tiffany knows to remain silent unless spoken to.

Like the others, what Tiffany sees through of her Eyepods and hears via her Earpods are Game Mistress's view of the vista of the Meatpacking Plant; these include the hanging Gimbled It and Plaster Mummy, and the Four Lobelia, including herself. No secrets, and just like the others, Tiffany hangs valiva and is honored with a Collection Dish.

Tiffany, alone among the Four Lobelia, does not have any Gag in her mouth; it had been removed while working the Risen Cocks Lineup. Needless to say, Tiffany's mouth has been splooged, indeed her entire face and head remain coated with semen, as does much of her body, and of course semen oozes out of a tormented toaster that has been fully loaded via many, many penetrations.

Unlike Whores Penny and Coco, Tiffany can't claim any anal creampies. Only vaginal ones, like also newbie Whores Hottie and Odee, presumable still getting broken in on the Lineup.

Tiffany reviews the avenues that *might deliver me to Flesh Ranch.* Pragmatics? *Trading places is the only way, and trading places will also require sacrifice. Just Opting Down won't be enough. Here in Lockdown, Gamers are collecting assholes. They have already collected Beka and Elle, Babs has already promised hers, but Kimju has not. And Steph may get a pass if she Opts Up.*

I need to get ahead of the Game and start begging the inevitable, the time has come to start collecting dick up my tailpipe, especially *if I can trade my asshole in exchange for switching Opts.*

But Tiffany is also not stupid. *I was made to see Beka and Elle both get analed and climaxed at the same time. They are anal Whores and they are taking Babs with them, whether BB knows what she's begging or not. We are Four Lockdown Whores and we are all going to get analed.*

I need to offer to trade places with Kimju and surrender my asshole; it's an offer she wouldn't refuse and the Gamers won't refuse. She can Opt-Strip and give away everything except her kunny and kawazoo, which is not allowed for Strippers anyway. Net plus for her and further away from Slavesex. And I can advance my Porn Star career immediately.

Tiffany continues her evaluations. *Babs is a Dong and Dirty Whore now and after Midnight, and Steph will become either a Stripper or a Monitor next Term.* Tiffany smiles to herself. *It's not like Steph's pink hasn't been put on display while she was a Pledge this Term; still, I hope GM sends Steph to the Nugget, Charm over Duel. It would be Steph's first time! And would be good training for her. Humanize her some, perhaps, if that is possible.* Tiffany wets her lips with her tongue. *Prepare Steph to Opt Whore.*

Little does Tiffany know the Karma Steph actually confronts, but then Steph doesn't know either. No problem, Tiffany evaluates her own exposures. *So far today I have failed to collect the attention that has been lavished upon Robyn, which I guess I should be grateful for. Beka and Elle showed us the future.*

Tiffany's anus has been excessively pleasured by the Ass Hook all during the Play Party. Getting buttplugged while sucking cock or getting fucked while sucking is not a new experience for Tiffany; more than one of her Porn Star scenes feature her double penetrated, tongue and twat, and showcases A2M thereafter. Another features a lesbian sharing with a Double Dong ass-to-ass switching to mouth-to-mouth, A2OPM.

The Ass Hook has left Tiffany gaping. *I need to combine what I want, that is to trade places with Kimju, and the inevitable, that is to get analed as a consequence of Lockdown.*

I need to make Porn Movies again.

I'm great at having sex, and Gamers love to watch me, and so from now on I'm going to get buggered as well. I have to beg the Dong and Dirty route.

But hey, once a Porn Star, always a Porn Star, and I am proud of my work and my contributions to the Art. My oral skills are excellent, and I know how to twist cock in my pussy and in my mouth at the same time.

Hey, I've double penetrated before, with the Leading Men swapping off between my twat and my throat. but now when two guys take me, it will be all six ways. They can even warm their cocks up in each other's asses before they throat me the first time. I'll take the facials, I'll snowball, I'll swallow, and while I'm in Lockdown I need Gamers to bind me, beat me, bang me, and bugger me; I can't stop it, I'll just beg for more and more, because Lockdown has no Rules, and I probably don't want any Rules to apply to what they do to a gangbang Whore.

When I was a Whore before, some of the Gamers had wanted me to Opt Slavesex. And some of them are still lurking. So they have until Midnight to trick and treat me, after all, bondage sex doesn't exist in my catalog, and my fans will love it. And during Lockdown I can Star in a short burst of bondage porn without a long-term Slavesex commitment.

Tiffany has watched Kimju and Beka acquire bodyart, but she herself has escaped the more extensive pleasures of the tattoo gun and piercing needle. *Yes, beside surrendering my asshole, I must considers how a swap with Kimju might involve bodyart, as well as any Obeisances, and Terms in the Game.*

Tiffany considers her own bodyart; her three pieces document her past Whoredom. *Kimju is still begging double nipple studs. She can keep them. I already have implanted nipple stims and ultraviolet ink tattooed into my areolas, an ultraviolet tramp stamp descending down the crack of my tush and becoming visible as it circumnavigates my tailpipe, finally I have the words "Porn Star" tattooed backwards inside my inner lower lip so I can read it in the mirror, and remind myself of what I am and what I aspire to be.*

Lockdown has added a nose ring, and a navel stud and tattoo, to Tiffany's inventory. The first of these, bestowed upon her by Robyn

Runaway, provides a securement point, and the navel jewelry is another asset shared by all the Cosmos Lockdown Lobelia.

And given all shall beg navelage 24x7 forever, then, these assets shall remain on display.

Tiffany has been proud to see that many of her *Videos* have gotten screened at the Party. This series of *Tiny Tit Suck Fuck Facial Videos* were made during her Whoredom one Term ago. They show Tiffany performing explicit hardcore sex acts, fucking, fucking while sucking dick, and getting bukkake with rich creamy facials… until her face and long hair are totally soaked in semen, semen running down to her breasts. Tiffany knows, *Penny and Coco have nothing on me. I've been a Goo Whore before.*

I know how it works around here. The first time I was a Stripper I broke the Rules, and because a Stripper caught sucking cock is automatically a Whore, that was perfect for me.

However Tiffany knows, *if I becomes a Stripper again, and pull the same stunt again, Gamers will identify me as a repeat offender, so instead of Opting me Whore, like the last time, Gamers could double me down and Slavesex me, which I definitely do not want. Being a Stripper, or better yet a Porn Star, has dignity. But begging to become a bound beaten banged buggered Slavesex for many Terms has no dignity at all, and is not for me.*

A Slavesex does require a different kind of courage and strength.

§ Kimju & Tiffany: Trade Places & Pay Gratuity

Game Mistress organizes her Four Naked Lobelia. Already blind, already mute, all Four hear the sound of the Meatpacking Plant – and GM's voice – cross-fade, and this is where their paths separate.

For Babs and Steph, the complex audio waveforms that caresses their ears, coupled with their blindness, encourages them to ooze valiva into their Collection Dishes.

Game Mistress, always a guardian of secrets, has no motivation to let Babs and Steph see or hear the Fates of Tiffany and Kimju. It might be harmless information, and Babs and Steph may find out eventually, but for now, GM's modus operandi is to keep these Two Lobelia in blackout. One of them continues to do handjobs, and is serenaded with goo. One of them, her mouth guarded with a Tongue

Clamp and her hands encased in mittens, is allowed to shake off fondles. But blackness and silence moderate both.

Tiffany and Kimju continue to see and hear the Meatpacking Plant through Game Mistress's eyes and ears, via their Eyepods and Earpods. At the moment Game Mistress appears to be examining a shaven pubis, a vertical kleave, and some oozing kunny juice.

It's me, Kimju appreciates.

Kimju never sees who removes her Tongue Clamp (it is China Doll actually), and who carefully unlocks and unbuckles her O-Ring Gag, and helps gentle it out of her mouth.

Kimju feels her mouth go entirely free. Pain erupts as her pierced tongue collides with her teeth as she draws it into her mouth. She tries to rotate her jaw; it is so stiff she can't even close it; she yields to China Doll's gentle hands massaging her jaw so it may close eventually. China Doll pinches Kimju's lips together with her fingertips then draws the back of a finger across Kimju's lips.

Kimju understands, "no speaking unless spoken to."

Tiffany finds herself watching a cam view of what she determines to be *my own tawdry twat. I like it, and I have good lines and details. And I don't care how much purple I get. And I don't care anymore where I get purpled.*

That is not correct.

I want to get purpled everywhere, and then I want to show off my purple in the Show Ring at Flesh Ranch.

Tiffany has not worn any mouth prosthesis since her latter time on the Risen Cocks Lineup, but Tiffany is also a trooper and knows to not speak unless spoken to.

Tiffany is almost totally covered with semen, her mouth is sopped, her skin besotted, and she continues to ooze semen out of her vagina. She somewhat chaffs at the fact her arms have now been secured behind her back and that her folded up fingers rest inside a mitten that seems like they had been filled with goo before she made a fist for the glove to fit over.

Tiffany and Kimju's Eyepods present views of the hanging Plaster Mummy and the Gimbled Armature with a humanoid folded into an immobile position, and rotated so Gimbled It's huge erection points upward from the purple mass of articulated flesh and bone.

When you are a Lockdown Lobelia one sees what one is shown and one hears what one is told, and Tiffany and Kimju are no exceptions. Both can see, via Game Mistress's eyes, that Babs and Steph also kneel-spread-armbound nearby; and both assume, incorrectly, that Babs and Steph share the view and the audio, when in fact Babs and Steph see and hear nothing.

Tiffany and Kimju can quickly ascertain that Babs remains a handjob artist and goo canvas; Babs has been a Goo Gobbler ever since Penny and Coco shaved her bush and fed her goo at the Post Henge. They have no reason to suspect that Steph, equally naked, kneeling, and armbound, remains equally unaware she is awaiting her paint.

Two Naked Kneeling Lobelia watch themselves be addressed by Game Mistress, who also pitches her head to the larger surround of Party Players. "Honored Gamers, Tiffany and Kimju, pay attention: Members of the Prefecture, Running Agents, even Players at this very Party, have urged a reconsideration of your two Fates!"

"Lobbyists for each of you have made arguments that your Fates should reverse, others argue that your outcome at Midnight should stay the same.

"It is argued that Tiffany is an already experienced Whore, a turbo-suck twat-twister with Porn Star credits. During her recent stint at Flesh Ranch, Tiffany dazzled with suck, fuck, and sharing the Double Dong, but she's hasn't yet qualified for the Dirty work.

"A contingency of do-gooders argue that you, Kimju, were miss-appraised as to the severity of your failure and you deserve leniency. I believe the record shows that you have confessed to your misdeeds and begged to accept punishment. Is that correct?"

It is. Kimju responds. "Aaha-aaha."

"You are begging to Whore, is that not a fact, Kimju Knockadoodle? Speak."

Kimju wets her lips and speaks her first words in a long time. She discovers her tongue heavy with the two studs weighing her words down. She speaks carefully. "Mistress, I begged to be a Whore before Robyn got caught, but now she's inside a Plaster Mummy."

"Are you begging to trade places with Robyn?" GM leans back.

"Mistress, no, Mistress!"

"Are you still begging to Whore?"

Kimju takes a deep breath and considers carefully, "Mistress, please I'm a Lockdown Whore until Midnight, and a Whore after Midnight, Double Terms, may it please you Mistress."

Game Mistress acknowledges, "You please me, Whore, and I shall sell your kunny and mouth."

Game Mistress turns and addresses Tiffany, "You were a Whore once before, and you're a Lockdown Lobelia at the moment, and you want to be a Whore again. Do you like being a Whore, Whore?"

Tiffany opens her mouth and speaks. Speaks carefully. "Mistress, I love being a Whore, and I wish to be a Whore all the time. The arguments for trading Fates with Kimju are persuasive, Mistress."

Game Mistress gives thought; she scans the Players who watch, she responds. "Interesting proposal; Tiffany Opts Whore and Kimju Opts Stripper. Perhaps Kundalini can help balance your Fates, so allow me to question you both, and let's see if trading places might appeal to both of you, a win-win.

"So let me understand what you two are begging of me. You want to switch Castes?"

Tiffany and Kimju sound an ill-timed unison, "Mistress, yes, Mistress."

"You understand you will both have to make adjustments?"

This affirmation comes slower, *What adjustments?* Both answer out of sync, but both affirm, "Mistress, yes, Mistress."

"Let's make sure you both understand the basics of what you are begging for, regardless of whether you are begging a Stripper Deluxe or a Whore."

"Who said anything about begging to be a Stripper Deluxe?" Kimju interjects.

Game Mistress frowns upon this intrusion, and speaks in very matter-of-fact matter to Kimju. "You have a choice. You can either Opt Whore, go to Flesh Ranch, and sell your mouth and kunny; or you can Opt Strip, go to the Nugget, and beg to be a handjob and blowjob Stripper. So what are you, Whore or Stripper Deluxe?"

Kimju licks her lips.

Game Mistress lightens, "Maybe we aren't trading after all!"

Kimju begs, "Mistress please I beg you –"

Game Mistress silences Kimju. "I love you. I suggest you beg me to decide if you want to be a Stripper Deluxe or a Whore."

Kimju stays confused only for a moment. "Mistress please I want to be everything a Whore can be, minus selling my kunny and keelway, or you can decide to put my mouth and kunny for sale."

Tiffany watches herself through Game Mistress's eyes, and Tiffany watches herself beg, "Mistress, I'll be your Whore or your Stripper Deluxe, however, I'm already a Porn Star, and I'll be an Anal Star and Dong and Dirty Whore next Term; every hole, one at a time, two at a time, three at a time; double pussy, double anal, double mouth, facials, creampies; anyone anywhere anytime in front of anybody. Private, on Cam, booth at a Sex Show. I'll eat twats; I'll suck creampies out of twats and tailpipes. I'll swallow anything you put in my mouth. Please make me a Dirty Whore and take my last hole away from me."

"Well, at least one of you knows for sure what you want." Game Mistress summarizes, "we shall first agree on the privileges of the Caste of the Strippers Deluxe, since they are a subset of Whoring."

Your Pink Pages advertise you are both Pee-Camers and Piss Mouths and fully Watersports certified?"

They are, and mumble together, "Mistress, yes, Mistress."

"Louder!" Game Mistress instructs, and looks back and forth at them. "So I gather that no matter where you end up, you are both going to eat pussies, on Stage, on Cam, any pussy anyplace anytime.

This seems reasonable and both agree, "Mistress, yes, Mistress."

"I gather that no matter where you end up, you are both handjobbers?"

Handjobs are not sex; so a Stripper Deluxe does handjobs.

Both together, "Mistress, yes, Mistress."

"You are going to collect cum in your hands?"

Again together, "Mistress, yes, Mistress."

"Good. You can lick it off and swallow it."

It's not a question but Tiffany leads anyway, "Mistress, yes, Mistress," and Kimju follows, "Mistress, yes, Mistress."

Hesitancy? Game Mistress scowls at the hesitator. "You'll lick Tiffany clean, you'll lick Babs clean!"

Kimju tries not to panic. "Mistress. Mistress, I'll lick every blob of goo off their bodies, I'll clean creampies out of Tiffany's twat, suck jizz out of BB's butthole, I'll snowball any cum left in their mouths. I'll swallow it all."

"You'll suck cock with or without a Hole Gag." GM admonishes.

Another statement or a question? Tiffany affirms, "Mistress, yes, Mistress," but Kimju hesitates.

Game Mistress tilts her head and explains, "All Whores get mouth-fucked. Impress me, Whore, beg."

Kimju sees herself tilt in her Eyepods; she understands and catches up, "Mistress, I have begged to be a suck and fuck Whore and, please, I want to trade, I want to be a Sucking Stripper Deluxe. I'll blow and eat everyone on the Nugget Staff. And if Patrons want me to take their dicks out and jerk them off I will suck too. And if they cum in my hand or my face, I'll clean up and feed my mouth."

"Are you begging cum in your mouth?"

A delay, and Tiffany leads, and Kimju rushes to catch up. "Mistress, yes, Mistress, yes Mistress."

"Snowball?"

This time they answer in unison, "Mistress, yes, Mistress."

"Swallow."

"Mistress, yes, Mistress."

"There is lot of competition to be a Stripper Deluxe, so let's make it clear for the record what you are begging for:

"Clean cocks that come out a pussy, one that is definitely not yours?"

A round-about for a Stripper Deluxe, who after all, is forbidden cock in her own stash. Kimju doesn't quite have time to process the implications, but slowly stumbles along with Tiffany's commitment. "Mistress, yes, Mistress."

Tiffany takes a breath. *I know where this is going and I know I have an opportunity to follow and stay ahead.*

Game Mistress presses onward. "Clean cocks that come out of an asshole, one definitely not your own?"

Not my own because even a Stripper Deluxe is forbidden coitus and anal. Tiffany knows the answer, and knows the answer to the next question, when it will come. *But if I'm a Whore it doesn't matter to me.*

Kimju answers, but takes offense at this suggestion. She stumbles, forms mental images, blurts, "Mistress, a Stripper Deluxe might suck cocks, but she does not fornicate nor anal them. So presenting secondhand cocks to a Stripper's mouth should be forbidden."

Tiffany trades eyes with Game Mistress. Confidence, patience.

Game Mistress raises an eyebrow. "Excuse me, Kimju Klute, did I hear you correctly? '...a Stripper Deluxe *might* suck cocks.'"

Kimju backtracks, "Mistress, please let me be a Sucking Stripper Deluxe and I *want* to suck cocks. I will suck any cock, anywhere, anytime, in front of anybody. I'll swallow the jizz."

Kimju pauses. Game Mistress tilts her head, and allows Kimju to augment her answer. "Okay, Mistress, I'll suck any cock no matter where it has been, I'll eat any pussy, I'll clean any creampie, I'll snowball any mouth. I want to be a Cocksucking Goo Gobbling Stripper Deluxe, Mistress."

Game Mistress looks at Tiffany and Tiffany begs. "Mistress, please let me suck cock no matter where it has been. P2M, A2M, P2OPM, A2OPM. I want to be a Dong and Dirty Whore. Please sell my mouth to cocks big and small, black and white, cut and uncut, new and used. Please sell my twat, please sell my tailpipe; please secure me spreadeagle in the Spunk Pit, open my mouth, spread my twat, gape my tailpipe. Blow me, bang me, bugger me, beat me over and over again; I'll do whatever it takes to trade places and become a Dong and Dirty Whore, now and many next Terms."

"Excellent, it shall come to pass!" Game Mistress proclaims.

Game Mistress smiles at Kimju. "A Stripper is forbidden to use her kunny or kawazoo. But you can beg to put them into play *after* your Stripper Term."

Kimju lets out air at this suggestion, then advances slowly. "Game Mistress, please, I'll get on my knees in the Champaign Room, rub my naked knockers all over the Patrons, I'll suck them and let them grab my hair and force my head down. I'll pop them, and I'll swallow too."

"And?"

"And I'll do Double Piercings, Double Tats. Double Stripper Terms and then beg to Opt Whore."

"Excellent." GM commends. "You'll wear cum on your face if that pleases your House Mom. May your pierced tongue not only remind you to be forthcoming, but also not speak unless you are spoken to."

"Gamers have decided that your planet tattoos shall continue to multiply all over your body, and your rings will continue to expand until they collide and cover your skin completely. You want this?"

Kimju does, "Mistress, please, Mistress."

"You shall retain the three piercings that you earned begging to Whore, including your clithood and your navel, which count, and your nose and tongue, which do not, so I calculate you are owned one more piercing. Is this correct?"

Kimju must agree, "Mistress, yes, Mistress."

"You beg double everything," Game Mistress states.

Kimju does. "Mistress, yes, Mistress."

"You want to beg all your piercings get double stretched?"

Kimju opens her mouth wide. *What! Painful!* And closes her mouth and speaks. "Mistress yes, Mistress, some are already gauged larger, Mistress."

"And you are already begging your double nipples?"

Kimju knows the answer, regrettably, "Mistress, yes, Mistress."

"And Double Terms?"

Surprise. Kimju stumbles, recovers. "Mistress, yes, Mistress. Please let me be a Stripper for Two Terms, not just One."

"However you shall beg a full complement of Whore tattoos," Game Mistress provides, "just like you beg a full complement of piercings."

Kimju knows to beg. "Mistress, please tattoo me on the vestibule inside of my sex lips. Ink patters around my pee hole, and around my clit."

"A worthy goal," GM proclaims, "may three marks on your body constantly remind you of the Fate awaiting you, a Fate you are delaying. So tell me, Stripper Deluxe, what is the Fate awaiting you?

Kimju is startled by the question. "I'm a Lockdown Whore. After Midnight I'm a Stripper Deluxe for Two Terms, then I'm a Whore." Kimju adds clarification. "A regular suck-fuck-facial Whore."

Game Mistress advises. "I think since you are destined to Whore, and since your dick-sucking lips will be busy during your Terms at the Nugget, that you should ask nicely that your third tattoo be on your face."

Kimju takes a deep breath. "Mistress," she begins, "please put like a mole near one side of my lips, so that Gamers will know I'm a cocksucker from now on."

Game Mistress agrees, "And when you look closely, it is the head of a penis, yes Stripper Deluxe?"

Kimju agrees, "Mistress, yes with a magnifying glass, Mistress."

Game Mistress seeks consensus. "Certainly you don't want to suggest that your mouth favors only one sex?"

Kimju agrees, "Mistress, please tattoo another mole somewhere else on my face which is really a vulva or a tiny open pink, I'm a cocksucking pussy-eater from now on. Those who know how to read Marks will know I'm a Stripper Deluxe begging to Whore."

"Perhaps they will interpret that the open pussy mole symbolizes your kunny, and that cock is welcome." Game Mistress suggests.

Kimju response is spontaneous. "Mistress I will tell them I am serving Two Terms at the Nugget and after that they can fuck me."

"You are going to be seasoned for Two Terms, then you will be turned out, turned on, and turned klute. Thank me," Game Mistress orders.

Kimju offers thanks, "Mistress, thank you for reminding me that that I'm a cocksucking pussy-eating Stripper scheduled to Whore after Two Terms. Please double pierce my nipples and put double Whore marks on my face to enshrine my destiny."

Game Mistress acknowledges. "You're welcome."

Game Mistress closes out her Kimju book. "Your transportation to the Nugget has been arranged. Assure me you look forward to orally satisfying those who transport you?"

Kimju hustles, "Mistress, I'll suck any cock put into my mouth. Any color, any size, any taste, young or old, cut or uncut, lubing or dry, new or fresh out of any vagina except my own."

Game Mistress lifts a chin and shares a private, knowing glace with Slavesex China Doll, and focuses back on Kimju.

Kimju augments, "and fresh out of any asshole, except my own. I'm a Stripper Deluxe now, and I'll suck cock any cock anyplace, anytime, in front of anybody, and I'll suck cock P2OPM and A2OPM, and just as soon as my time Stripping at the Nugget is over I'll suck cock out of my own pussy and ass, P2M and A2M.

"Lucky you get to Strip, but remember, Lobelia" Game Mistress wags a finger, "when you get to the Nugget Stage Door, and you beg the Back Door Man to let you in, you must remind him that your Clock remains stopped and won't strike Midnight until you pass through the Stage Door, so that if he want to use you, or share you with friends, that you remain a Lockdown Whore until Midnight. Think you can remember that?"

Kimju thinks she can. "I'm a Lockdown Whore until Midnight, and if the Back Door Man and his Patrons want to throat, fuck, or anal me before they let me in, I will beg them to use me as much as they want, and as long as they want."

§ Game Mistress & Tiffany: Closing Remarks

Game Mistress turns and addresses Tiffany. "You've pledged, you've stripped, you've whored, but really now, you don't really think you're heading back to Porn Stardom just so Kimju can get out of working her kunny? Beg me, Whore."

Tiffany begs, "Game Mistress I'm already begging to surrender my tailpipe. A Dong and Dirty Anal Super Whore. Any hole, every hole all at once, anywhere, anytime, with anybody, in front of anybody. On Cam, private outcall, adult theater performance.

"And please, please bondage gangbang me before Midnight, while it can happen."

"Tell me about what is tattooed inside your lower lip." Game Mistress commands.

Tiffany answers, "The words 'Porn Star' only backwards so when I pully my lip down I can read it in the mirror and know what I am."

"And inside your upper lip?" Game Mistress inquires.

"Mistress, nothing is there, Mistress. I need the words 'Porn Star' tattooed only normal, so when I pull my lip up I can show to the Game what I am."

"Maybe you should also beg a stim get implanted in your clit."

Tiffany leans back. "Mistress!" she exclaims.

Game Mistress doesn't give Tiffany more time to answer. "Why don't you beg to take on Kimju's Double Terms? That could extend your Whoring to Six Terms, and Kimju wouldn't have to linger at the Nugget as long before her kunny goes on sale."

Tiffany agrees, 'Mistress, yes, please, Mistress."

Kimju, hearing this, feels her breath run out, as her time-until-Whore time just got cut in half. She widens her eye, *so unfair,* catches Game Mistress's fingertip in her eye as she open her mouth, halts and watches GM address Tiffany. "Your wish to promote to Super Whore is granted and shall be fulfilled.

"Your wish to be bondage gangbanged before Midnight is granted. China Doll will escort you to the Spunk Pit, where you will be secured spread-eagled for a performance where you will be beaten, balled, and buggered incessantly. First you will be taken lying on your belly, then following intermission, taken lying on your back, double mouth, double twat, double tailpipe.

"After your throaters, fuckers, and buggers have exhausted themselves, you will be unshackled and lead to your stall at Flesh Ranch, just as the Clock strikes Midnight.

Game Mistress blesses both departing Lobelia. "May your Terms at the Nugget and Flesh Ranch provide pleasure to the Patrons. And may Kundalini infuse your mind, body and soul with the force of desire, passion, and fulfillment!"

Tiffany knows. *My* Spunk Pit Bondage Video *is going to be a huge hit, and with anal I can now become a Dong and Dirty Super Whore, a Super Porn Star, not just another* Suck Fuck Facial *Cam Whore. Life is good.*

Kimju knows. *I'm stripping again. This time I've lost my hands and my mouth, and after one Term, my kunny goes on sale. This should not be happening to me, but I can't stop it.*

And that's the last that Tiffany and Kimju see and hear inside the Meatpacking Plant.

Babs & Steph & the Peacocks: Wheel of Fortune (LD9)
s
V-12 Babs & Steph Greet: William & Rodney & Pushers

§ Babs & Steph: The Last Cosmos Lockdown Lobelia

Ex-Cosmos House Monitor Babs, and ex-Cosmos Pledge (and former Monitor) Steph, remain the only two Cosmos Lockdown Lobelia illuminating the Play Party here in the Meatpacking Plant. Unless one also counts Robyn, currently embedded inside the hanging Plaster Mummy, suspended from an overhead rail trolly, on a spur not far away.

Both Babs and Steph remain blind-deaf-mute, bare-bald-naked, kneeling-spread-armbound, their forearms parallel behind them, secured from the elbow to wrist. Steph keeps her chin up, her unacknowledged nose stud still connects to the trolly above.

Steph's hands continue to be shrouded in mittens; Babs' hands are both exposed, and BB continues to provide handjobs to anyone who doesn't mind sticky fingers on their dick or clitoris.

Babs feels exposed. *If Molly were here she would be giving handjobs too, but right now I'm the only handjobbing Goo Gobbler. Semen shall be a part of my diet from now on. I am going to beg that everything I eat get spunked first. And next I'm going to be getting pops directly, so the Cam can catch the ejaculate as it flies through the air into my open mouth. Gamers need to cam me with a cock buried in my mouth, so that when it blasts me the jizz shoots back out my nose. I want to be Gokkun Goo Gobbling Whore.*

Both Lockdown Lobelia are mute because they enjoy huge and extremely tightly strapped-in O-Ring Gags in their mouths; Steph also enjoys a Clamp on her Tongue, and drools beautifully. Babs has no such encumbrance to discourage cocks straight into her gorgeously lipsticked mouth, but she doesn't so much drool, she just swallows the jizz that friendly hands from time to time scrape off her fingers and hips, slather onto her garish face, and feed into her Goo Gobbling mouth hole.

Babs, still BB, and now Bondo Ballcocker, accepts, *I am being groomed as a Goo Whore. I am already a handjobbing Goo Gobbler, and I am destined to become a Dong and Dirty Whore at*

Midnight. All holes gone, just like how Elle got used. And until Midnight I remain in Lockdown, which is even a worse place to be because even Slavesex rules don't even apply.

Babs has witnessed Robyn's final plaster. BB had watched China Doll licking up spilt urine, knowing, *that's me too, I'm also a Piss Mouth.* But one reality had stood out: *Beka and Elle's consumption of It's huge purple penis into their gaping assholes.*

Gamers are turning "the hidden fuck slut inside Elle" loose so we can all watch her let go in a howling climax. And now, after breaking in Beka's asshole, Gamers have decided to chastise Beka's bonker. I know Beka, and I know that will drive her wild.

Beka has given away all her skin, become an anal Whore, and promises to bring Elle along. Maybe now via-versa.

The only thing Beka can still give away in order to obtain coitus is to beg Slavesex. She will do this once she understands that is her only path, but she must also ensure that Elle begs first, so that she can then follow, and not risk Elle staying behind.

Babs has become aware that her vagina is being slowly penetrated. She can't look or hear, can't speak, and hesitates to move her head least her nose ring be secured to something. But she can feel something small and round slowly easing upward into her slippery sex bushing. BB rolls her tongue around the inside of her O-Ring and pays attention to keeping her knees spread wide.

During her blindness and silence, ex-Monitor Babs has not only handjobbed many cocks, her body has also been a free-fondle. Kneeling Babs has taken it: fingers smearing goo onto her face, pinches of her nose to cut off her air and make her breathe through her mouth, caresses on her neck, squeezed boobs, bitten nipples, grabbed buttocks, finger tasted asshole, and yes, her open crotch endlessly finger-fucked. Babs understands, *I'm a fondle, finger-fuck Lockdown Lobelia;* still BB faithfully retained her kneeling spread position. *And handjobbing cocks is only the beginning.*

Babs had come to crave the touches, tremble as her buzzer gets fingerballed, and might two fingers rise into her vagina, crave two fingers more. *I crave a fist. I want more finger scoops; I want to be fed. I want to suck cock on Cam.*

If before BB hung her brodeas into a Collection Dish, she now coats her vaginal intrusion with fresh slippery. But, *this uplifting intrusion into me feels different, mechanical? A hand holding a dildo? Half of the Double Dong?* Babs lets out a sigh. *I can do this. I wore the Pear in my bajango and hung burgoo out the stem. After all, I am a filthy anal A2M A2OPM Piss Mouth Dong and Dirty Whore. Gamers should tie me down to a fucking machine and then walk away. I deserve Gamers to fuck me however it pleases them. I deserve punishment that is more harsh than I can imagine.*

Whoring just is. I failed and it is important I be made an example of. My redemption is embracing my total sexual surrender. I need Gimbled It to spunk my blower, spunk my burse, spunk my bung.

And then they should tie me down in the Spunk Pit and release a gang of sex-craved prison convicts to plunder me. Face up; face down. My blowhole, my buck-twister, my buggery.

And hey, Beka and Elle just showed me a taste of what is going to happen to me: my blower, my bangbox, and even my bunghole are about to get stretched. I don't decide anymore who uses my holes, or when, or where I have sex, or who watches me. Any hole, any combination. I'm a public Whore, I have no privacy of my body, not even my body functions. I'm a Cam Whore, Brothel Whore, Escort Whore, 12x7: 12 hours on, 12 hours off, seven days a week, no exceptions, next Three Terms.

BB resigns, *and my media will stay on Automatron forever.*

BB concludes that the round probe penetrating her vagina is in fact the Pogo, the intrusive dildo on the end of a rod that, during this Term, has variously penetrated Beka, Kimju, and especially Steph.

Babs remains unaware of the many times the Pogo climaxed Steph at a moment when a Cosmos got painfully pierced; including when the Pogo climaxed Steph as BB got her navel pierced.

Cams document how BB's pussy lips stretch back and forth around the slow-stroking, up and down Pogo stick, with its mechanical penis on top. The Pogo tweaks Bang Bauble up just a notch, and BB coats the Pogo with fresh brodeas. Would providing BB a sneak view of her own shaven and penetrated vagina stimulate more abandon? Is the Pogo able to tip BB into that place where she stops thinking and Gamers play tunes out through her Ring Gag. Yes and yes, most certainly, but just because Bondo Babe is cradled in the saddle of sensuality does not mean she must be immediately given a rise.

More and more BB wants to go higher, but she accepts, *I will now climax when Gamers want me to, with machines or humans they choose, where they choose, and on-Cam or not they choose. I'm a full model release.*

And soon I will beg anything to get sexed.

Steph Sorostitute continues to assume her Fate at Midnight is to Opt Monitor, and with all of the privileges of that Caste. Steph doesn't challenge her blind-deaf-mute, bare-stubble-naked, kneeling-spread-armbound position.

For Steph, the armbinder and mittens have yet to come off, and Steph interprets this attire positively. *The reason they don't take my mittens off is because I am not a handjober like Bondo Bauble. I'm too important to get my hands gooey.*

Like Babs, Steph wears an O-Ring Gag that stretches her jaw just as wide open as possible. Steph rebels against the Tongue Clamp but knows *the reason they don't take my Tongue Clamp off is because I'm not a suckface cum repository like Blowho Bitch, and my Tongue Clamp is the only obstacle to Gimble It's enormous erection fitting through my O-Ring Gag and my mouth getting splooged.*

The connection between Steph's nose and the trolly overhead tilts her face upward just enough to enable liquids to be poured into her O-Ring atop her stretched out tongue, and to compel Steph to swallow. *Aphrodisiacs? Laxatives? Diuretics? Purgatories?* Steph fumes but the embers don't go out. *Gamers wouldn't dare,*

The downside of Steph's Gag, Clamp, and nose suspension is that Steph has no control over her drool. When Steph's head tilts forward, she is deeply humiliated by drool spilling and coating her chin, spilling down to her spigots, with rivulets down to her slit.

Steph continues to have confidence she shall Opt Monitor at Midnight. *Gamers have to be very careful with me, because after I Opt Up there are some Players I am going to get even with*, like Bondo Bitch.

Steph calculates status. *I got a glance at Bondo Bitch earlier, all slippery with handjob goo, with a bunch of it scooped up and fed into her Whore face. I want to watch her work the Spunk Pit; she failed Robyn, she failed Beka and Elle, and most importantly, she failed me, and all of us are paying for her brainless, careless failure of leadership; there is only one destination for her: Flesh Ranch. On the way she can work for tips at a shoeshine stand; she can buff shoes with her bazoombas, and buff cocks with her buggery.*

Ha ha ha!

Gamers appreciate Game Mistress's compartmentalization of information relative to the Cosmos Lockdown Lobelia. Babs and Steph, the two remaining miscreants, might be aware of Molly's departure; of Penny and Coco's visit and collection of the Double Dong; of Robyn's final Fate; of Gimbled It's arrival and Beka and Elle's various oral, vaginal, and anal enrichments.

But neither Babs nor Steph know that Tiffany and Kimju traded places, and that both now-Whore Tiffany and now-Stripper Kimju have departed, with Whore Tiffany begging anal and Stripper Kimju begging "blowjobs aren't sex."

In fact, neither Bang Babe nor Steph Sorostitute know who is missing or present as they kneel in the dark and silence. Babs is grateful for the many penises placed into her hands, and increasingly proud of her goo consumption. BB's swinging hanging breasts are fondled constantly, and she can feel that the cylindrical Pogo rub her sex lips back and forth, and can feel fingers push her buzzer against the increasingly bigger-around internal protrusion.

Steph's thoughts return to her own self-interest. *I'm protected. Players know better than to touch me. I have a guaranteed Opt-Up. And, unlike all the others, I don't have a stud in my nose or ink in my navel. That's because I'm important.*

But enough already. Give me something to wear, give me a House to take over, and I'm on my way. But don't tell me to sit naked on the Front Porch, pull pink with a Pledge, and count to one thousand.

Both Babs and Steph hold their positions. They have nowhere to go. Babs kneels on the Pogo; Steph's uplifted chin balances drool and accommodates fluids poured into her mouth accommodation.

Babs can't decide *if I have actually had the head of cocks in my mouth or if I'm getting jizzed.* Babs is not stupid. *It doesn't matter when all I have to do is swallow.*

Open Season is near.

Steph plots retribution.

§ Babs & Steph: See Each Other After a Long Time

Vision and hearing return to Babs and Steph, but both mouths remain restrained.

Babs and Steph look at each other for the first time in a long time. Babs sees a subdued, but still rebellious Steph, drooling helplessly out her O-Ring Gag with her painful Clamped Tongue, but not broken. Steph sees *an open-O-Ring cum hole repository*, baneful eyes, and a compliant Babs.

Yes, BB has been fed many fingers of goo into her O-Ring hole, and yes, she has swallowed. Swallowed a lot. She has been gooed on her crescents d'areolage and surged uncontrollably.

Steph canvasses the rest of Babs displayed naked body and her eyes come to a rest at BB's shaven crotch. *So, Bondo Bitch is a Pogo Whore!* Steph exclaims.

Steph vacillates between jealousy and rage, but holds her kneeling-spread-armbound position. Part of her rants, *That's my Pogo! I climaxed the Pogo watching you get your belly button pierced. I love how you screamed. Now you think you own the Pogo? I hope Gamers tie you down, turn up the power until you are screaming in pain, then walk away and leave you.*

The Steph that Babs sees remains bare-bald-naked, stubbly, but otherwise pristine and clean. BB self-evaluates. *I've bruises on my butt from paddle discipline, I have cinch and whip marks on my bazoombas. Yes, Steph is Gagged and Tongue Clamped, but her body has not been touched, not been fondled, not flogged, not nipple bruised, and most evidentiary, Steph is not a goo mess.*

How little Babs knows; she knows her experience – handjobs and goo – but her eyes and ears were cloistered during periods when Steph had been clandestinely handled, and been allowed to shake off the clandestine feels made upon her naked body. This has helped build her confidence that her Fate is secure.

And it is.

Steph does have a predatory horniness, and she derives pleasure watching Babs dance on the Pogo, shake her bazoombas, and not be able to control her sexual vulgarity and panting goo mouth.

Babs observes that Steph hangs a stalactite of sexual lubricant out of her bare sex slot, and warrants a Collection Dish. Steph would like to control her secretions but she can't stop herself from squeezing on the Steel Sphere and Cylinder, and pumping more sop out, especially watching Babs. *I love that now-Whore Bargain Bundle can't resist liking the Pogo encunting her bald burse. I hate the bitch, ultimately this is all her fault, and it's worth a certain degree of inconvenience to have a ringside seat when it is time to watch Gimbled It's purple pole stretch BB's mouth, buck-socket, and bung-chute.*

Steph's thoughts are relentless. *I hope Gamers tattoo a whore mark on BB's face. Like Marilyn Monroe's mole, only when you look close what you see is Bondo Bitch' asshole! So you get warned about who you are dealing with and at the same time know what is available for penetration.*

Babs doesn't consider the politics of Steph's secretions, or consider to what extent the vaginal and anal components of the Shaving Kit stimulate Steph's thick secretions. But Steph's plight fades from BB's mind; increasingly it is all BB can do to keep up her breathing and not fall behind the Pogo. *I know I'm on display. I am coating the Pogo with my burgoo, I want my burgoo seeping down the shaft. I'm a Pogo Whore.*

Moaning sounds resonate from BB's O-Ring; the Pogo responds and BB warbles the pitch of her singing, then is quieted back down.

Yes, the Pogo is deep, it can swell; it can also vibrate, tingle, stroke, wiggle, and transmogrify into an AI learned shape and sensation that maximizes attraction. And manages arousal.

Babs used to have a Collection Dish, but it was taken away when the Pogo was first inserted upward into her vagina. BB can't see that her burgoo coats down the sides of the Pogo, but worries, *what if Steph might have to lick it off while the Pogo stays in me?*

This is not a "what if" that Steph ponders. Steph compares her pristine self to BB's gooed and Pogoed body, and Steph's confidence widens, as might be expected.

Both break from looking at each other to panning the Meatpacking Plant, locks, stocks, Lineups of cocks, Lineups of pussies, dunking mechanisms. But their quick visual canvas is interrupted....

§ The Peacocks Arrive: Their Condition & 1st Reactions

Eight Peacocks arrive at the Play Party. They are unannounced and unanticipated and unappreciated. Technically speaking, they are no longer Peacocks, they too have become Lockdown Lobelia, stripped, secured, erected.

The Two remaining kneeling-naked-armbound Cosmos Lockdown Lobelia – Babs and Steph – watch Six Naked Wheel Pushers roll a giant Wheel into the Meatpacking Plant. The Wheel is not quite as tall as the overhead track.

The Wheel supports Two naked and spread ex-Peacocks who are secured to the four wood and iron spokes of the wheel: former Monitor William and former Pledge Rodney.

Babs and Steph react sharply to the intrusion. Apprehension thickens. Do both consider that William and Rodney's arrival is… disruptive? orchestrated? threatening?

Gamers hope so.

Babs and Steph attempt to deconstruct what they witness. Reality overcomes disbelief and sears both of their brains. The two Lobelia recognize familiar faces and identify the totally naked and shaven Wheel Pushers as ex-Peacocks.

The Six Pushers had been the Lineup of cocks Tiffany had to "talk-pop," in order to gain entrance during *The Arrivals*. The Poppers had provided a jerk-off Lineup at the Greatest House Roar. They had been the Mermen pulling the Parade Float that the gaily body-painted Cosmos Mermaids rode. They had been the Sedan Chair Bearers who bore Game Mistress to review the Cosmos Lobelia at the Amphitheater during *The Runout;* and while they had waited they had prostrated themselves on the ground into a six-figured position, each with the next's cock in their mouth, a "Benzine Ring," complete with each cocksucker's free hands arousing the asshole of the cocksucker adjacent.

Most Cosmos lobelia had read William and Rodney' absence from the Sedan Chair Bearers as significant, and that William and Rodney were cocksuckers too, albeit elsewhere.

Well, here they are, except that William and Rodney's cocksucking is far more severe.

William and Rodney are affixed to the Wheel so both face inward, spread-eagle, upside-down to each other, so they are face-to-groin, cock-in-mouth. Both waists are secured to the Wheel at its center; their opposite arms and legs are tightly secured to the same spokes, and with their wrists chain-cuffed to their opposite's ankles.

Both necks and heads are rigidly mounted, and not only do Rodney and William's ringed cocks penetrate each other's mouths, but each mouth and dick is connected by thick stainless steel studs that penetrate through a cheek, the penis inside the mouth, and through an opposite cheek back outside, so that each penis is firmly secured in the opposite's mouth. Each views the Meatpacking Plant looking through the opposite's crotch, facing the opposite direction.

There is more to this too, later.

The two culprits get a free ride, and view a world which turns over and over as they rotate head over heel. Sometimes they are parked straight up and down, but angles torment them more.

The Naked Wheel Pushers roll the Wheel three to a side: one leading each side, one flanking each side, and one on each side bringing up the rear. All stretch their arms upward in splendid repose as they roll the wheel forward like Olympians, with all cocks strenuously erected and swinging hanging lube in the air.

BB and Steph observe that the Wheel Pushers have all been given a fem-butch look, with pretty faces, mascara, eye liner and lashes, rouge, lipstick. Tinted nipples, engorged penises. Perfumed. And unlike Rodney and William, no cock restraints. All hold their mouths firmly closed, and Babs imagines that *all of them retain hollow, perforated gold balls in their mouths that contain time-release chemicals, drugs, for erections, to make lube, create itch. For feminization.*

Gold balls or not, the Pushers shall keep their thoughts to themselves, just like Rodney and William do, albeit with a more strident methodology.

The Pushers bring the Wheel to a rest, and then slowly pivot it around in a circle: BB and Steph see that although William's butt is firm and pristine, that Rodney's butt has been paddled, caned and beaten with thorns. The one Cosmos who would most appreciate this, Beka, doesn't get to see her lover's triumphant arrival.

The 360 degree pivot provides both rigidly immobilized Peacocks on the Wheel a full panoramic sweep of the Meatpacking Plant, with its many alcoves, operating tables, fucking machines, retraining devices, cages, and instruments for the infliction of pain and pleasure, and the secretion of brodeas, lubricant, and cum. Elsewhere they see a line of standing men, all cock caged and being serviced by male and females, and glimpses of beatings, blowjobs, balling, and buttfuckery.

The panning view include a glimpse of the Risen Cocks Lineup with its row of kneeling, bowing, cocksuckers, including the fresh Whores Hottie and Odee, whose sloppy wet, creampied, and overflowing pussies continue to be fucked.

The pivot ends with Rodney facing the wall away from the Two Naked Lobelia with his stripped rear end facing them, and an upside-down William looking at them with two eyes beneath Rodney's penetrating cock and hanging testicles.

Rodney and William and the Six Wheel Pushers take in the scene, and William convulses as he assimilates the naked, kneeling, spread, armbound, and gagged, Babs and Steph. One of them is encunted on a Pogo, and the other hangs sex sauce with her chin lifted up.

It will take William a minute to get his mind turned around, *but in general what I see concerns me. More than just Rodney's cock in my mouth.* William views the world upside down and through the truncated V of Rodney's shaven and spread legs. Ahead his attention is drawn to boobs that seem inflated and floating up in the air, and two slits. One of them, Steph, extends a stalactite of splurt that hangs upward (in William's view) and maintains a wobbly balance as it grows toward a Collection Dish on the ceiling. The other shaven vulva supports a Pogo that plunges downward (in William's view) into Babs' shaven burse and pushes her sex lips wide, while at the same time secretions crawl up the Pogo.

Might William learn to interpret an upside-down world he can always be rolled right-side up again to disorient him.

The Pogo inside BB's vagina has widened, it can't go any deeper, and it produces a stimulus that face-painted Babs can't exactly identify, one that encourages her to gyrate her body in a taut, wanton, and vulgar abandonment, while coating the Pogo with freshly-scented balm, mingled with goo left over from a finger or two. And might it be necessary, the Pogo has a rich palette of substances it can release also.

The Pushers study BB, and Bang Bauble feels ashamed she can't stop panting and exposing herself, worse, *I can't stop displaying myself to the Pushers in a sluttish manner that is just as wantonly carnal as is possible.* BB's face flushes, her areolas respond, and more burgoo pumps out and oozes down the Pogo. *They don't deserve to see me Pogoed, spread, and embarrassing myself.* But then BB realizes, *I have no secrets from them. Not now, not ever. I have no secrets from anybody anymore.*

And I don't care about control anymore. I can't. I can't stop quivering and if it gets more intense I am going to start vocalizing. Babs accepts, *I am starting to crave the Pogo and I* want *it to take me over the top. So if I want to climax I must reveal myself completely in front of William and Rodney and all the Wheel Pushers, in front of Steph, and in front of the Cams. In front of the entire Prefecture. In Automatron, forever.*

The Wheel Pushers have come to rest, and Babs can see that now they hang lube out their cock holes. BB squeeze her penis-shaped end of the Pogo, suddenly aware that *the Pushers watch a feed from a Pogo-cam deep inside my vagina. I am a vagcam Whore. I have no secrets; my body is cammed inside and out.*

I'm a Dong and Dirty Whore because I failed. I have to start at the bottom. Streetwalking, pimped, lucky to have a bunk with hay at Flesh Ranch. I know I'm going to have to suck-fuck-anal Gimbled It, and I am probably going to have to clean It up after William and Rodney get analed. I might even have to suck-fuck-anal with William, because we are both broken Monitors. But nothing could be worse for me in the world than being given to Rodney. Before and after they turn him into a tranny.

It is Gamers, not me, who possess my burse, and who decide if and when to climax me on the Pogo, or just build me up to my tipping point, make me grovel like a homeless Whore, screw me with Gimbled It's purple prick, and park me in the climax Zone.

Babs' plight is of little concern to William and Rodney. But Steph's presence is alarming. Does Steph feel alarmed that the outing of a *Beka and Rodney Fuck Video* increases the odds that Rodney recorded other scenes? Steph has convinced herself no such recordings exist. Babs has been told about one that exists but BB isn't talking, can't talk. And William and Rodney know both *Videos* exist, or existed, for sure, because they made them and watched them together.

And laughed.

Deep down these conspirators fear there is a small hope that when the *Beka and Rodney Fuck Video* was discovered that, however unlikely, that their two *Steph and William Videos* were not found. William and Rodney might be sharing cocks on the Wheel, but no charge have been made, no questions asked, no confrontation with any evidence concerning Steph has been raised.

Babs wonders if *pinning the cocksuckers together on the Wheel might be too harsh a treatment, compared it to Beka's lax punishment for the same misdeed. Certainly Free-Fucking does invite cock restraint, but this is over the top! And harsh on William for just being entailed in Rodney's Free-Fucking? Well yes, and harsh on me too for Beka's getting her box creampied. Okay, so I'm a Whore, I deserve it, but I don't have a cock spiked in my mouth. No, this is something more; Janet told me the truth about Beka and Rodney, and I believe her more than ever that William and Steph fucked. And there is a* Video *of that too.*

I think maybe William is in big trouble. Steph too, and everything she did as a Pledge entails me too. Except it doesn't matter to me anymore. Every one of my holes already awaits ballcockery.

William's muscular body, fastened safely against the Wheel, lacks the lacerations that decorate Rodney's rear end. William interprets this as a hopeful sign, *punishments melded out for the* Beka and Rodney Fuck Video. *Rodney and Beka got revealed to everyone,* William understands, *but there is no indication that Steph's transgressions have been found out. If they had been, Steph would be cast in Plaster just like Beka is. So why is Steph here?*

William may not understand the physics nor the Karmic effects emanating from the Plaster Mummy, but he does understand his primary problem. *So Rodney fucks Beka in the Garage, and I, as his Monitor, get equal treatment. So he's a Whore, so I'm a Whore; it's the best I can hope for now.*

But why is Steph here? And Babs, she's an ex-Monitor like I am; if she is smart she begs to Whore. She has to, because of Beka.

But William also knows, *if Steph gets found out, then Steph Opts Whore and I'm Slavesex, Whores because we fucked, and Slavesex because a Monitor coupling with Pledge violates a Caste Rule.*

Except it's Steph's fault. She forced me to have sex with her.

And made a *Video* of it?

Please, why doesn't matter. Gamers need not concern themselves with power motives: if a Pledge tries to assuage a Monitor, or if a Monitor tries to coerce a Pledge, or if the parties really are equal: oral, vaginal, and anal sex is forbidden between the Caste of Monitors and the Caste of Pledge.

William would like to talk, drool runs out his cock-gagged mouth and onto his face. Rodney, facing away from where Babs and Steph kneel, drools around Williams cock.

Game Mistress observes Babs and Steph's contemplation of the two Wheel Wenches.

"Nice touch, yes?" states GM to the Two remaining naked Lobelia. "What you can't see are the multiple rings around both dicks, and a second, vertical barbell that spikes each intruding penis and flattened tongue together. As they say, 'a tight connection is a safe connection,' so double bonds for these Two Homo-Bondo-Whores is de rigueur."

William doesn't approve of what is happening. *All my Pledge are being feminized. Rodney and I are Lockdown 69x24x7. We are being fed with tubes at both ends. Gamers are already feminizing us, and this is all because of Rodney. And if Gamers find out about Steph and me, they will feed me hormones, grow my breasts, and turn me into a she-male.*

Sounds like a plan.

Steph's eyes flash. But she can't read William's eyes. Hard when they are upside down and Steph has her chin lifted, and her O-Ring Gag, tight behind her teeth, unceremoniously holding her mouth wide open. But with her Tongue Clamped. And drooling all down her kneeling body.

Rodney is sure about the Mummy and its consequences. *I got a glimpse of the Plaster Mummy and can tell it's Beka inside. She's missing but is here. We Free-Fucked, got exposed, and now Beka is a Lockdown Lobelia. She seduced me, she deserves to Whore, but no plaster for me, please!*

Rodney feels himself tickle for a moment; Piss Mouth for William. *Stop! I'm just a victim. But if Gamers need me to I'll start working cock in my mouth, I'm your Boy. And you can sell my ass, and milk me. I'm your Whore. I want to be your Whore. And you can feminize me, make me wear makeup, perfume me, Turn me into your fembitch. But Beka is the instigator, I'm just the victim, the plaster is right for her, but not for me.*

Gamers agree it is wonderful for Rodney to envision himself in the art of Plaster. And to think that feminization is a way out.

Rodney does correctly interpret ex-Monitor Babs *as a Pogo encunted, handjobbing, goo-guzzling Whore. Beka did that to BB by seducing me,* Rodney asserts to himself, *too bad for Boss Bitch, and I like how Gamers put a ring in Babs' nose and decorated her belly button. I hope that's just starting her out, she's got some Whore freight ahead. A whole lot of Pledge lost out today because she allowed Beka to Free-Fuck.*

Rodney pushes Steph out of his mind. *I'm already a Whore, Beka has made sure of that. So if anything goes wrong, it's William who will Opt Down. And maybe Steph too. No maybe. Maybe if I'm lucky Steph and I will both end up at Flesh Ranch, and will get to perform live sex shows together.*

Neither William nor Rodney are able to identify the folded-up purple humanoid bundle with a huge penis protruding, which Gamers call Gimbled It. At the moment Gimbled It is angled back with a cock vertically uprisen. The impact of Gimbled It sears the Peacocks; certainly some have seen deeply stained Pledge before, but never a body so totally secured, so totally manipulated, so totally controlled, yet so totally committed to penis penetration.

William and Rodney can see each other's assholes, and determine that they are already commandeered by tubing, T-connectors, and bags which can feed as well as take away. Both bowels had been flooded before their roll, leading to sensations which mortified their helplessness. Head-over-heels as the Wheel rolled. Total primal scream. Total loss.

BB can't make out the details but can tell that all testicles have been separated and pressed.

And another observation: *Both assholes are taken.* Babs shudders. *This is heavy duty. I've had the Snake up my ass, I think it was a Python or a Boa Constrictor. I'll beg a Snake again if I'm told to. Whenever I'm told to. I'll beg the Centipede, all the way around my intestine, and cam me all the way.*

But what I really want is Gimbled It's purple penis inside my every hole. I want It to discharge in my burse, discharge in my buggery, and discharge in my blowhole.

I deserve to be on the Wheel. I want Gamers to enema me and clean me out; I'll beg rectal feeding. I need to be a total suck-fuck-anal-A2M-facial Whore.

§ Babs & Steph and William & Rodney: Agendas

Babs feels a trickle of fear. *I might be a Stripper because of Robyn,* BB concludes, glancing at the Mummy, *but I am a Whore because of Rodney. And Beka. And anal because of Elle. Janet tipped me off about Steph, but whether Steph is innocent or gets outed as an anal Whore doesn't matter to me anymore, I'm already fully impacted. Tagged.*

I need to be totally crushed. And if I have to beg Slavesex I will. Gamers will take my skin, Gamers will guide my actions, and Gamers will harvest my soul. I need it hard, I need it rough, I need to be beaten and permanently marked. Branded.

Such confidence!

Babs considers, *Rodney and William are naked, spread, and cock-gagged on the Wheel because…? Because Beka and Rodney were Free-Fucking, that's why, we've seen that* Video. *So William is a Whore like I am.* Babs concludes, *"So goes a Pledge, so goes his or her Monitor."*

Except what I see is beyond "like me," which makes me wonder. Am I about to replace Rodney on the Wheel?

Because Janet told me there was another Video, *"one starring Steph, and that Steph whored every hole." That's why I begged Dong and Dirty in the Amphitheater, because Dirty included anal, and I deserve the worst. Even Slavesex.*

Babs feels a temporary kinship with the fellow fallen Monitor. *Monitor William is being forced to Whore. Harsh. Except I'm not being forced; I volunteered. I had no choice, my Pledge really did misbehave, they dishonored themselves and our House, and so I, as Monitor and leader deserve to be demoted, prostituted, and punished. Except I am not really being punished, I'm being trained. Welts on my body. Remediated. Brainwashed.*

BB also forms assumptions. *William and Rodney are not going to be taken off of the Wheel and sexed any time soon, for the time being they shall continue to embrace their... mutual oral homosexuality.*

And not only that; they are also being feminized!

Babs is amazed she can see humor ahead. *And after they grow breasts they can be lesbian cocksuckers. Or she-males sucking each other's tits and cocks and cornholing. Or whatever.*

The Pogo commands Bongo Babe's attention and breaks BB out of her thoughts. Babs becomes aware of William's eyes following her boobs, *watching me grind my pelvis like a ballum rackum Whore working It's giant erection. I can't stop myself, even with you watching me. I want It's dick first and I can't stop you watching me get purpled up.*

William finds BB's eyes and reads a wildcat helpless in quest of sexual release. Goo oozes from her mouth, BB pants, she can't stop her drool, can't stop moving her pelvis, and she slathers the Pogo with her own thick burgoo. Lower down the Pogo stick vacuums the brodeas back into itself, so that Burgoo Babe doesn't spot the floor. And her secretions continue to be Collected.

William interprets, *Bondo Babe wants hard purple cock. BB is not all Whore yet, but BB is going, going, ...* William concludes, *BB's becoming a Whore and Robyn is already Slavesex.*

William's asshole itches and whatever invades it seems to grow longer and fatter. Both mouth cheeks hurt from when the piercing went through, his tongue hurts, and his dick hurts double, having been pierced twice. William doesn't care that Rodney also shares a left and right cheek, one tongue, and two penis piercings.

William dreams his best nightmare: *So Rodney could well be a Plaster Mummy next. Like Beka, probably also a repeat offender. But where does that leave me? A wanton Whore like Babs? Bad. But Whoring may be my best option; it may be my only option.*

Again William studies the naked-kneeling-spread-armbound ex-Cosmos House Monitor unable to stop grinding her bucket on the Pogo. *BB and I are both sex victims, both entangled Whores next Term, all because Beka and Rodney Free-Fucked.*

Some of William's analysis is correct.

Steph evaluates the arriving Peacocks with premonition, observes the fear build in BB, senses it build in herself. Yes, Steph considers

William and Rodney's arrival an ominous sign. *Two connivers.* The kneeling Lobelia squirms, and tries to control her bare bald and naked, knees apart, splurt-oozing sex cavity. The stainless Sphere inside Steph's snatch, and the hotdog-shaped hollow Tool Cylinder inside Steph's stern tube conspire to reinforce Steph's sex sauce production; Steph has little choice but to hold her chin-up, hold her kneeling-spread-armbound position, and pump enough sauce that it finally reaches her Collection Dish and begins to pile up.

I get it, Steph concedes optimistically, *Rodney, unlike Beka, didn't get Immunity from Free-Fucking and is a Whore. William is like Bang Bitch, and is corollary damage, a Whore.* "So goes a Pledge, so goes a Monitor," Steph assures herself. *And that little fucker Rodney now shares his randy behavior with William, just like Beka and Elle have turned BB into a Whore. Entailment theory; Karma at a distance.*

Hostility toward Rodney bubbles into Steph's thoughts. *Maybe Rodney give Beka a line, or maybe that horny Bimbo teased his cock out. It doesn't matter. What matters is that today we discover that Rodney made a secret* Video *of his tete-a-tete with Beka Bonesocket; Rodney deserves the Wheel,* Steph declares to herself, *and William gets to roll with him. Entailed just like Bondo Bitch, courtesy Beka. Ha ha ha.*

But Steph should know her laugh has overhang. *If indeed Babs no longer controls her constrictions, I no longer control my sex sauce. I have been show in my Eyepods how my sweet syrup hangs all the way down to a Collection Dish. That is so rude of Gamers to do that to me; it's so unfair! They are using* my *Shaving Kit to take advantage of me.*

Note to Steph: It is not "your" Shaving Kit, indeed, you belong to the Shaving Kit, not the other way around.

Unheard notices are not in Steph's mind, but Steph also admits to herself, *I'm also getting realty horny. I climaxed on the Pogo watching Bondo Bitch get her button pierced and inked. I liked that.*

Steph glowers at BB. *Now I want to watch you get climaxed with Gimbled It deep up your asshole, just like Beka and Elle did, after all,* "so goes a Pledge, so goes her Monitor," *doesn't it, Bauble Bitch!*

Steph projects her own pleasure. *I am going to climax from the time Gimbled It violates BB's backeye, sinks all It's inches up BB's back hole, and keeps climaxing while BB is forced to climax out of all control. I hope getting buggered is most unpleasant for BB, but I am going to enjoy the show, and masturbate myself to my own climax, thank you!*

Steph takes a very slow and deep breath. *I've already figured out that Gamers have nothing on me. Besides, I was taken advantage of. William is a lot better off staying entangled with Rodney and Opting Whore, than Gamers discovering he sexed me. That's instant Slavesex for him.*

Steph clenches her fists inside her mittens; she would clench her jaw except that is impossible. Still, *I love how William and Rodney's assholes are possessed, but sooner or later China Doll is going to disengage their rectal plumbing, drive Gimble It's cock all the way in, set the Gimble on pump and grind mode, and plunder one of their assholes over and over, and then turn and plunder the other.*

Rodney blocks most of William's body, but Steph can see Williams's head; she finds his upside-down eyes disconcerting. Steph has had little use for William beyond what William might do for her; at the moment William can only do negative. Steph dares to dart her eyes toward William's upside-down eyes, framed beneath Rodney's spread crotch, with Rodney's cock pinned in-between his cheeks, and also pinned to his tongue.

There is not a lot of fire in the eyes that look back. Steph squints and this time drives arrows into William's agonizing position, *You fucked me, not only into my mouth and screwhole, but also my spice gate. And then you made me taste myself.*

Steph's eyes harden on William. *You made me come back to you, and when Rodney surprised us, you let him use me. You let Rodney fuck me in the ass, and you fucked me in the ass, like you owned it. Maybe now it's your turn to get your rectum stretched, you are both cock-throating anal Whores from now on.*

And still even more forceful daggers at William, *You had better be grateful your mouth is cock-gagged, because if Gamers ever find out you fucked a Player of lower Caste, and then allowed Rodney to participate, you won't be a Whore next Term, you're Slavesex.*

It is hard to scowl when your face is distorted and made hideous by a huge O-Ring Gag and one's Tongue hangs down with the weight of a Clamp, but Steph daggers hate. *I hope your cheeks and dicks and tongues are in pain.*

They are.

Steph spikes out a message to William, darts out of her eyes. *I want to watch you get your butt paddled, caned, and thrashed with thorn bushes. I want to watch you get circumcised and your foreskin hung from a ring in your nose. I want to see you spread out in the Spunk Pit and buggered over and over again!* Steph makes an ever so small tilt of her head. *I'm a guaranteed Opt Monitor after Midnight and I intend to keep it that way!*

William offers little reaction to Steph's darts; her eyes dart as she studies more closely how Rodney's cock is spiked into William's mouth. *Very compact. Not a laughing matter.* William's mouth drools, and the drool runs down his upside-down face, covering one eye, then down his forehead. Upright Steph considers that the cane marks across Rodney's rump ooze blood, and that the thorns from his thrashing with berry bushes have left pits, so that as Rodney was rolled, the trail of blood made spirals.

Steph admires the pits in Rodney's rump; Babs finds the spirals of blood artistic.

William also has no choice but to consume the lube that Rodney drips into his mouth. William knows *I am in Lockdown,* and at Midnight, Rodney entails me to Opt Whore. *First, I'm going to get ass-fucked with Gimbled It's giant purple cock. Next Term, at a minimum, I'm going to be a cocksucking buttfucked facialed Dirty Whore. I'm going to give and take facials, bukkake, snowball, gokkun. I'll do guy, gals of course, and any threesome you want.*

Yes, yes, yes. All male Whores suck cock and collect anal cock, whereas lady Whores suck cock and collect cock in their vaginas; ladies must beg to be Dong and Dirty Whores if they want to be cast for anal performances.

William detects fresh Rodney lube in his mouth. He can't turn his head, can't push Rodney's cock out with his tongue. William swallows, shutters, feels his Procto talk to his prostate and his cock rings tickle his dick, and shares some of his own lube with Rodney. To whatever extent Kundalini possesses them, Kundalini's fields of

Force resonate between their two bodies, and helps enhance their arousals and their pain.

V-13 Two Cosmos & Two Peacocks: Show Time

§ Game Mistress: Two Lobelia Plus Two Peacocks

Game Mistress allows Two kneeling-spread-armbound Lockdown Lobelia – Babs and Steph – and Two Wheel Wenches –William and Rodney – to observe her. She addresses all Four clearly. "You may all know each other, and you may think you know why you are here; but what you think no longer matters. I shall decide your Fates."

Game Mistress gestures toward Babs. "The naked Lobelia astride the Pogo, with her shaven, spread-wide-open, slippery sex bushing, used to be the Boss Babe."

Babs' boobs bounce as she gyrates on the Pogo impaling her, she grinds her pelvis uncontrollably, shamelessly. So shameless many are embarrassed to watch.

Game Mistress advances, "That's still BB, but she's begged to be a Dong and Dirty Whore, so we call her a Blow Bang Bugger Babe when we are nice, and a Blow Bang Bugger Bitch when the Whore craves correctional training.

Game Mistress draws Bondo Babe out of a trance. "You're a Dong and Dirty Whore, now, on your way to Flesh Ranch, and after Midnight, Three Terms. Is that correct?"

Babs understands, "Aaha aaha." *It's all true. And I know how Gamers work, they won't let me become Slavesex until they have Whored me out for multiple Terms.*

"BB took the fall for a wayward girl. Too bad." GM looks at the hanging Plaster Mummy.

Game Mistress tilts her head down and focuses her eyes upon William's upside-down eyes. "BB's a Whore because her Pledge Beka Free-Fucked your Pledge Rodney, just like you're a Whore because your Pledge Rodney Free-Fucked her Pledge Beka."

Game Mistress graces the Goad on Rodney's abused buttocks. "Obviously you and Beka are Whores too," she pronounces.

There is a rustle of the two anointed Whores on the Wheel, acceptance as well as the safety of Whoredom, as William knows, *especially for me.*

Game Mistress addresses the many Players here in the Meatpacking Plant. "Some of you have demanded to see the evidence of Beka and Rodney's Free-Fucking, as justification for these two ex-Peacocks free ride on the Wheel. They have no shame breaking the Rules, so Gamers have no shame exposing their fornication to full public view." GM lays the Goad across one of Rodney's blisters. She doesn't need to push a button, it stings.

Game Mistress muses, "Tell me, Rodney, that you like to star in your own clandestine selfie videos?

Rodney knows he must agree, hard with his tongue pinned to the cock in his mouth, but he manages. "Aaha-aaha."

GM muses, "Tell me, Selfie Whore, do you like that your Hidden Camera Lady didn't know she got filmed having sex with you?"

Gurgles emit from Rodney's penis-gagged, tongue-tied mouth.

Game Mistress tilts her head, raises her eyebrows, turns to William, and interprets. "He says he liked showing the *Video* to you."

And like a cat GM lays the Goad between Williams two uplifted, separated, and presented testicles. "Yes?"

True. William affirms. "Aaha-aaha." *We laughed about what a silly slut Steph was.*

"Did you masturbate together, did you jerk each other off while you watched?"

More gurgles abound from Rodney's throat, about as strenuous as possible given that the tip of William's cock, pinned inside Rodney's mouth, tickles the back of Rodney's throat when Rodney gurgles too much.

Game Mistress laughs. "Just kidding, you two can bugger each other another time. But tell me, Rodney, you do want everyone here to watch you fuck Beka, yes?

"Aaha-aaha."

"You want it uploaded to Automatron, so the entire Prefecture can watch? Available in perpetuity to all Gamers?"

Asking a lot, but with William's cock affixed to his mouth, and a long something deep into his rectum, Rodney takes the easy way out. "Aaha-aaha."

"You want to show off Beka as a Whore too."

"Aaha-aaha." *She deserves it.* And then some gurgles.

Game Mistress translates. "Rodney said Beka seduced him and deserves to Whore."

GM addresses Rodney "Remind me you are a Whore."

Rodney accepts this, "Aaha-aaha." Rodney knows, *Three Terms of Whoring beginning at Midnight. They will turn me into a pretty boy, shave and twink me, pretend I'm a girl, plunder my asshole. Gamers can put me in a glory hole, or in a booth at an adult entertainment expo with a Cam on me and glass walls.*

"What you deserve is your own Plaster Mummy."

Rodney saw the hanging Plaster Mummy earlier and can see it now on the Screens. Rodney knows he must agree. "Aaha-aaha."

Babs feels the Pogo advance her breathing rate, her heartbeat, her blurt production; the Pogo commands more twist, a bump and a grind, a locomotion, she feels her burgoo gush, and starts to moan, and surrenders her last thought before she zones. *I give up. I must surrender. I have no choice. I've seen* Beka and Rodney's Fuck Video *before,* BB confesses, *only this time I am going to be masturbated while reminded about my incompetence for allowing it to happen. I am going to be forced to climax in front of the very Peacock, Rodney, responsible for my demise.*

This is total humiliation, even for a Whore. I can't stop being shamed. And the more I'm reduced the more humiliating it gets. There is no bottom, only a spiral down that is turning me inside out. I am a Whore now, I'm a Handjobbing Dong and Dirty Watersports Goo Whore, and anything else Kundalini wants me to be.

The many screens around the Plant spring to life, and Babs is brought out of her fantasies by shouts and cries by the Patrons of the Meatpacking Plant, because? Because something is wrong! *This is not Rodney fucking with Beka!*

§ Steph & William: *Suck Fuck Anal Video* & Reactions

No, it is not the *Beka & Rodney Fuck Video* that Babs and others have seen before; the *Video* wrestles BB out of obtaining climax.

But it is a *Video* that William and Rodney have seen before, viewed together and laughed about....

Steph's recognition of herself comes slowly. First there is the decoding of the room and the Players from a different perspective, and finally the disbelief at seeing herself, and.... *I demand this stop, suspend, terminate! Enough!*

And, as if upon Steph's gurgled command, the image on the Screens freezes, and Game Mistress feigns surprise. "My goodness! What's this? This is not the *Beka and Rodney Fuck Video!*"

It is not, and the gasps of surprise and a stirring of bodies and souls in the room are quite genuine.

William also looks at the freeze frame. *That's Steph with her mouth around my cock. That slut is using me.*

Steph, still Ring Gagged and Tongue Clamped, still armbound behind her back, visually convulses. *That is me! And this is a privacy violation! This should not be happening! This is outside the Cosmos House; this doesn't count!*

And besides, I have a guaranteed Opt Up. I took Elle Down in the Duel and that guaranteed my Opt Up.

The *Video* starts to run again. GM acts confused, "Where did this come from?"

Now images flood the Screens and show a naked Steph aggressively sucking up and down William's cock. William's shirt comes off, his pants are down to his knees. Steph's tongue licks William's nipples, the head of his penis, then pushes forward and takes his penis all the way into her mouth.

There is actually a murmur of appreciation throughout the Meatpacking Plant. Steph hears it too, can't do anything about it; her nose remains connected to the trolly above, she keeps her chin level and drools out her O-Ring Gag. She squeezes her rectum around the Shaving Kit's steel sausage inside her stern tube; she squeezes her snatch around the Soap Sphere inside her sex gear, and widens her pool of sex juice accumulating in her Collection Dish. Steph's scent is not the only one inside the Meatpacking Plant, but to those nearby to her, it is overpowering.

For Babs, the flash of recognition of what she is witnessing brings great relief, because *it unburdens all remaining uncertainty about the credibility of Janet. Janet is my friend, even if she turns me into her toilet and I turn tricks in her Club. So I know how this ends, Steph sucks-fucks-anals, and lucky me, I'm ahead of entailment, I'm already begging the Dirty Whore, Three Terms, 12x7.*

Steph watches the screen, gurgles but no one in the Meatpacking Plant quite understand what she tries to say, "Help! I am being forced to give William a blowjob!"

And what a down and dirty piece of cocksucking: up and down with the mouth, rim job, twisting down and swallowing William's head all the way into her throat, coming up with so much suction that Steph's cheeks cave in, then out with phlegm streaming out, another twisting down and another throating, this one followed by phlegm and purge bits, and had Steph not laid back and spread herself open as William, phlegm-dripping erection wagging, drives his penis into Steph's already sopping sex socket. The fucking might be termed brutal were it not for the fact that Steph so releases herself into a wailing climax.

There are audible gasps from the Partygoers. And a consensus that Steph just committed to Opt Whore and head to Flesh Ranch.

May Free-Fuck Steph be so fortunate.

On screen, the lovers switch positions and Steph rides on top, and sweat glistens on her naked body. Here in the Meatpacking Plant, Steph can't stop squeezing her Shaving Kit, meanwhile the Pogo compels Babs' attention, and surfs her onto the higher altitudes and outer orbits and waves of the Zone.

Sexual congress and sexual stimulation harmonize.

Rodney, like William, is too immobilized to speak or even turn his head. Rodney faces the opposite direction, but there are Screens in his view and he can hear, he knows what he listens to and relaxes. *If Gamers have this Video they have the second one too. I'm double fuckmeat. I can't save myself. William can't save me either.*

This is a correct assessment. William can't even save himself. William can see the Screens, and reliving the experience upside-down drives this once-muscular, ex-Peacock House Monitor into despair. William convulses in his tight bondage to the Wheel, and manages to ripple pain through his cock, his cheeks, his tongue. Manages to cause Rodney pain too. *Damn Rodney. Damn Beka. Damn Steph. I hope that Gamers make them all Whores.*

William's wish shall be granted.

Babs quickly calculates. *Steph is my third Pledge off screwing around. I can guess why she went there, she wanted more Caste, and she whored William to try to get it.*

Babs feels remorse and penitence. *Steph is just another example of what a failure I was as a Monitor. I should never have been promoted after my first Term, I should have been sent to the Nugget right away, now I'm bypassing the Nugget, which is good actually, because I deserve to start out on my back, pinking my baldy, soaked in oil, and train fucked in minivan.*

Steph watches the on-Screen Steph fuck on her back, fuck riding the saddle, and watches as William pushes her off and onto her face and knees, parts her butt cheeks, but instead of mounting her sex socket from behind, doggy style, elects instead to bury his cock inside Steph's stern tube, amidst much squealing and objection, eventually silenced when William grabs Steph by her ears, rotates her mouth around onto his cock, and tells her the obvious, "You're an A2M Whore." There is applause in the Meatpacking Plant as William backs out so Steph's mouth is in point blank position, and launches a stream of jizz that piles up inside Steph's mouth.

Babs deepens her gratitude to Janet for sagely advice. *Thank goodness I'm already a suck-fuck-anal Dong and Dirty Watersports Goo Whore 12x7 for Three Terms; I'm fully tapped, and nothing more can happen to me. Gamers are turning me into a Porn Star. That's more than I deserve and I owe them the insides and outsides of me. All my skin, all my holes.*

And is there not a finale to this *Video?* There is:

"Swallow, you dirty scumbucket," William commands in the *Video*, and Steph swallows the scum.

The *Video* stops after Steph exits William's bedroom, stark naked, gooey, angry she let her asshole be taken, but somewhat confident that *whatever benefits William might confer upon me are well in hand.*

Or well in Steph's mouth perhaps. She had gathered her Garments back from where she had hidden them, and during her return to the Cosmos House, and despite trying to wipe cum out of her mouth, Steph had had little choice but to swallow the residual.

The Meatpacking Plant acquires a hush after the *Video* concludes; Steph steels a glance at BB. *Bugger Bitch. BB's been a Goo Gobbler ever since the Goo Whores, Penny and Coco, depilated her bang box and helped her get her barrel expanded, that was early on in* The Runout.

Instinctively, Steph attempts to reach a finger to her lips and test any imaginary droplets of cum. Stimulus from the *Video* proving that media can affect behavior. But neither Steph's arm nor the balled fist inside the mittens, moves.

Post-cinematic revelations start to sink into Steph's brain. *Ex-Monitor Babs is already a Goo Whore and has yet to fuck anybody. She's a mess. I'm an on-Cam Triple Dipper, and although I managed to get most of the jizz and the taste of my ass out of my mouth after I left William, I have to remind Game Mistress I hold a guaranteed Opt Up.*

§ Steph & William: Beg Changes of Fates

There is a gathering of minds here in the Meatpacking Plant following the Screening of the *Steph and William Suck Fuck Anal Video* (a.k.a., *Steph Sex Video I*), however the thoughts of these witnesses largely concern the implications upon themselves.

Hard core? Pretty obvious. And two new aspirant Porn Stars.

Opt Whores? Well at least one of them.

Steph squirms, flexes her folded-up hands inside her mitten, clangs her Tongue Clamp against her O-Ring gag in a demand to speak, and curls fresh sop on top the small volcano that has been piling up in her Collection Dish.

Game Mistress addresses a wayward Steph. "Are you trying to tell me, Slut, that you want your Tongue unclamped so that Players can use your O-Ring mouth for target practice."

Now is not the time to discuss Players' practices. "Aaha-aaha."

"You want jizz poured into your mouth by the pint!"

Huh? Maybe getting my promotion requires I do this. "Aaha-aaha." *I need to tell you to stop.*

Steph can see in front of her the chain that rises up to the trolly above her. Steph can tilt her head and look upward, see the trolly above even, and if she keeps her chin up she can cast her head from side-to-side. But there is not enough slack in the chain to look down.

China Doll appears; she is indeed one of Game Mistress's favorites, and calms Steph with her movements, puts her hands on Steph's body, takes liberties with her, and quiets her.

Steph discovers that her nose has been disconnected from the chain and she watches as the bottom of the chain ascends upwards until it hangs above the heads of the Players.

Steph tilts her head downward; there she observes China Doll lifting her Collection Dish upward so as to collapse the hanging stalactite up into the Dish, the naked Slavesex then breaks the hanging flow level with Steph's engorged sex lips, and then removes this Collection Dish to a secure location.

China Doll's long slender fingers reach into Steph's stubbly vulva, fetch the stainless steel Soap Sphere out of Steph's socket with a slurp, and feeds this useful Prop into her own compartment. China Doll licks her fingers clean.

China Doll next extracts the stainless steel Tool Cylinder with its rounded ends from Steph's stern tube. China Doll wipes this second component of the Shaving Kit across Steph's upper lip and into her nostrils, then across her clamped tongue behind where the rods cross. Then China Doll kisses the round end of the cylinder with her own mouth.

Steph appreciates that *China Doll tags me A2M then tags herself A2OPM. I don't have a chance when she is around.* Steph concludes, *China Doll will seize any opportunity to accelerate debasement. Right now I need to hold my position,* knowing *I just practiced A2M using a Prop,* and worrying that *fingers and real cocks could be next.*

China Doll appropriates the Cylinder into her own rectum, and with it, possession of both halves of the Shaving Kit.

Gamers who track such things observe that although Steph carried the Shaving Kit for a long period of time, that she never gained an opportunity to make use of the Prop to achieve her own goal of smoothing her pubis and sex lips.

Shaving was not something Steph would ever have done to herself before she had been stripped, spread, and shaved bare and bald, center Stage at the Nugget (D23), with the Patrons going wild. But ever since, Steph has realized the power of her shaven slit. As her stubble has grown itchy, the frustration of losing the Shaving Kit intensifies Steph's resolve for payback.

Steph tries to quantify her loses. *First, Gamers are trying to Whore me for Free-Fucking. Except I never Free-Fucked; William and I were buddies when we were both Monitors last Term, and then he Hovered and I got Opted Down. And that changed things, suddenly he has Caste that I want, and I have a body he wants.*

William made it clear, when I crossed paths with him on my way to the Bachelor Party during The Arrivals, *that I would need to secretly fuck him if I expected to guarantee an Opt-Up. When he made Rodney piss in my mouth at the end of* The Runup *I knew he had Monitor power and I really did need to fuck him.*

William is not just another mouth-cocked, cock-mouthed Wheel Wench like Rodney; William broke Caste Rule; he's Slavesex.

And I just lost my ability to shave and manage my body hair. I am now bare-bald-naked, kneeling-spread-armbound; and, although I am O-Ring Gagged and Tongue Clamped so my mouth can't be dicked, both my snatch and stern tube are now empty, and there is nothing to stop China Doll from lining Gimbled It up with my every hole, drive It's drill bit all the way into me, and turn me into a screaming, climaxing, howling purple mess. And I know, we all heard, that It has huge loads stored up, at least six blasts, one for each of us begging Whore holes.

Steph feels GM's Goad grace the center of her back, and as she leans forward the Goad descents to her butt and buzzzzz!! It is a deep shock with significant voltage at high frequency, right between Steph's anus and vagina, but tingling outward around and into Steph's satchel, adding floors to her skyscraper, and circling around her stern star. Before finally coming to a rest.

Ouch! Automatic reactions. China Doll catches Steph just before she would smash her face onto the floor. And not coming to a rest, as Steph's body continues to tingle and pulse.

It is rare for the Goad to actually be pressed into action; the shock follows Steph down and she discovers herself flat on her face and belly lying in her own fresh urine. The fresh contribution has splattered the floor and gets her thigh and knees and feet wet. Steph has difficulty getting it to stop, and *I am unsure if my bladder is empty or not. Or if I've been given diuretics!*

"Oh my," GM looks down at her: "It looks like we have more than one Cosmos who likes to sneak out and fuck Peacocks."

Steph gurgles. Something about a guaranteed Opt Up?

GM chooses to translate. "You're a Free-Fucker begging to Whore? Accepted!"

More gurgles.

And again GM translates. "You beg for Slavesex? Under consideration."

Here in the Meatpacking Plant, Steph makes another gurgle, deeper in her throat.

Game Mistress considers, interprets. "Yes, Whore, you may have your tongue pierced for lying. China Doll shall arrange."

More gurgling.

Game Mistress squeezes Steph's breasts and vocalizes. "You say it's not fair unless William gets his tongue pierced too? You're not paying attention, Skank. By happenstance your lucky fuck boy is *already* tongue pierced, that's because when Gamers secured Rodney's rambunctious rod inside William's mouth, they spiked it and William's tongue together. Likewise, Rodney's tongue got secured to Williams's wandering wonker."

Quieter Steph gurgling.

"It's very sweet, not too elaborate, but when you have two perverts fastened to a Wheel, you definitely want them firmly secured together. Do you like how they end up?

Steph does actually, but tries not to sound overly enthusiastic. "Aaha-aaha."

"That's good, because after *your* tongue gets pierced, we shall pierce your clit hood, so that you can take somebody's place on the Wheel. Beg me you want your tongue pinned to a cock, and your snatch chained to a tongue, Whore."

Steph obeys and begs, "Aaha-aaha."

And feels badly disoriented. *Right-side up or upside down?* And gurgles what she thinks is akin to "My guaranteed Opt Up trumps Free-Fucking!"

Apparently not. Game Mistress translates, "Yes, you certainly qualify to be a full-fledged anal Whore. You'll beg Dong and Dirty Whore when I give you the opportunity. Or perhaps you want to beg the alternative?

Steph knows what the alternative is, and although *Free-Fucking doesn't qualify one for Slavesex, multiple infractions, plus lying about it, may permit Game Mistress to bend the Rules.*

What a silly Whore, Game Mistress makes the Rules!

Game Mistress turns, draws BB back to reality, and addresses her. "It would appear your triple-hole Free-Fucking A2M Pledge Steph

Sorostitute entails that you also reduce yourself. But aren't you already begging to be a Dong and Dirty Whore?

Babs is; she whimpers. "Aaha-aaha."

"You like your Pogo, Whore?"

Babs knows the correct answer. "Aaha-aaha."

"You like how it stretches you lips back and forth?"

Yes, that and more things. Slower now. "Aaha-aaha."

"You'd like cock instead, wouldn't you, Banggo Butterbox."

A statement or a question?

It doesn't matter. I want to be what you want me to be.

"Aaha-aaha."

It's not just about liking cock, you wannabe fucked!"

Yes, more all the time. BB grinds. "Aaha-aaha. Aaha-aaha."

Game Mistress's attention (and perhaps the gentle guidance of BB's Pogo) encourage Babs to grind in a slower rhythm. Burgoo that runs out of BB's burse and down over the Pogo is collected at the bottom. BB rotates as if with music in her head, and then counterpoints, thrusts, rotations and up and downs. BB doesn't stop grinding. Can't stop grinding.

BB again drifts into reverie as images of Beka and Elle getting anal-climaxed flow through her head. *Yes, I am a Dong and Dirty Whore and I am going to have to be just as dirty as they want me. I failed. I need to be paddled, paraded, and pimped. I need intensive correctional training. Gamers have already controlled my bladder, my rectum, my mouth, my nose, and my sex. I need more restriction, more pain, and total sexual surrender. And not just my sexual physical self, but letting go with my mind, body, and soul so I can become shaped into what Gamers want me to be.*

I'm a Dong and Dirty Whore, Three Terms, Twelve on twelve off, seven Day a week. 12x7.

I need to be a Chamber Pot Girl because that what a Slavesex is. And then I want to become Slavesex.

Gamers know I really need to be Slavesex, because that's what Robyn is and "so goes a Pledge so goes her Monitor." And besides, there is nothing more harsh. I saw what happened to Robyn. I need it worse than that.

Game Mistress scratches her chin, hoists her breasts, rubs the material that covers her sexual parts, and again invites BB back from outer torrents of the Zone. "Whore, let me ask you," GM says to BB, "it appears that your slut Pledge here," Steph gets a shoulder tilt, "has not only whored her mouth, pussy, and asshole, but also collected an A2M tag. That will play very sweet on Automatron. Congratulations for her contribution, Whore.'

Babs finds it convenient to remain silent.

"And of course you do want to equal her performance?"

Not really, and the answer comes out reluctantly. "Aaha-aaha."

Anytime a dick comes out of your ass you want it in your mouth."

When you put it that way. "Aaha-aaha."

"Actually, you want to exceed Steph's performance. Tell me it doesn't matter whose asshole a dick comes out of, you want it in your mouth, you want to be an A2OPM Whore."

Babs takes in a breath.

Game Mistress teases, "Like some of your other ex-Pledge?"

Babs closes her eyelids for a moment and remembers Beka and Elle, *yes,* and begs A2OPM. "Aaha-aaha." *Now I know why I'm a Dong and Dirty Whore from now on.*

Game Mistress turns her attention to the Wheel and places the Goad between Rodney's anus and his cock and buttons some juice. Urine, quite uncontrolled, shoots out of Rodney's cock and floods (upside-down) William's mouth, and spills down across his face and onto the floor.

GM walks around to the other side of the Wheel, and places the Goad in the same place on William's body. "That shock to Rodney was to make sure *you* know you're a Piss Mouth from now on. If Rodney is lucky he can Whore for bunk and board in the basement of a Gay Biker Club and beg to be pimped out to leathermen.

"But your Fate, William, is different, you are not just another Free-Fucking ex-Pledge opting to Whore, you're a Monitor fucking a Pledge, so your Fate is Slavesex, now, after Midnight, and Six Terms thereafter. Total recalibration: mind, body, soul. May you so love your indoctrination that you never come out."

Game Mistress buttons the Goad, William quivers and holds back, so GM increases the voltage. It is hard for William to scream with his tongue pinned to Rodney's dick inside his mouth, easier to let go with the urine, and flood Rodney's mouth. Game Mistress makes sure she holds the shock into Williams sensitive parts double the seconds that William held out; and it is only thereafter that William regains control of his bladder.

GM feels a beg should be done when the culprit is calm. "You Slavesex?" she queries?

William is. "Aaha-aaha. Aaha-aaha."

William can still feel the shock long after the Goad is removed. William's pee, spilled upside-down and overflowing into (the right-side up) Rodney's mouth, drain back down both of their naked chests and pelvises. Some pee even makes it all the way down and finds its way into its maker's mouth. Some drips on the floor.

Game Mistress looks at prostrate Steph with a feeling of distain. Her thigh-high boots let her wade through deep contamination, the tips of the toes come to a sharp point, and the heels adjust from wide with hammer-like percussion, to a quarter of that size, so that the full impact of the stomp gets concentrated into dangerously smaller crush areas.

GM graces Steph with the Goad on her inner thigh and Steph instantly spreads her legs just as wide as possible. She would spread her arms too were they not armbound behind her back with her fingers mittened. Steph tries to find a comfortable position with little success. She rests her head on her chin and the tip of her nose.

More gurgles.

"Crawl forward," Game Mistress commands Steph, "rub your face in that puddle of piss. Rub your tits and belly around in it."

Steph obeys; she cannot avoid getting her Clamped Tongue in the puddle, can't avoid getting the denser yellow liquid all over her face, her chest, her brown nipple stalks, …. *This is not good; I stink. I got pee up my nose, in my mouth. GM is trying to turn me into a Piss Mouth Watersports Whore. She can shock the piss out of me, but there is no way I am volunteering to lick up pee. I am no China Doll.*

Volunteering may not be necessary in Lockdown.

Pee-camming and Piss Mouth commitments are things that Steph has washed away in her memory banks. But the smell and the oiliness of the urine trigger a memory of *lying on my back, rolling my bare snatch up over my head and pissing into my own mouth. Robyn made me do it and Darleen cammed it.*

What I don't know is if she uploaded it to Automatron before she got taken Down, and where it might be now.

Steph has another recall: *Penny and Coco visited the Play Party and left behind bags of urine dripping into my mouth. Now I'm groveling in piss. I already got my own pee all over the insides of my thighs, and my feet are already damp. And I need to know whose piss gets into my mouth, up my nose, all over my body. William's? Rodney's? My own?*

No, Steph doesn't need to know, past, present, or future.

Steph scratches her stubbly pelvis in warm urine, feels the pee touch the top of her slit, and lifts her buttocks upward to avoid the squish. Steph's action of avoiding foreign pee touching her sex entrance causes Steph to confront the new reality that *my snizzaroo is empty now, and my Shaving Kit has been taken from me.*

But Gamers are going to keep my tongue clamped because I'm not really a piss mop, although I smell and taste like one. And my Tongue Clamp ensures I don't suck cocks.

Steph pauses to catch her breath and feels Game Mistress step onto her back, kneading her naked back and buttocks with the bottom of her boots. Steph can feel the pointed tip of the toe, Mistress's sharp heel on her dual semi-globes, and she splashes her vulva down into the urine on the floor.

More gurgles. "You don't need to do this to me," and again Game Mistress tilts an ear and answers, "I'm honored you also beg me to piss in your mouth; later Piss Mouth. Perhaps in the meantime you want to stand in for China Doll, and lick these Wheel Boys clean?"

Steph feels it is wise to agree, "Aaha-aaha."

"You'd like your Tongue Clamp off so you could better lick up all the pee."

Steph would. She tries to take a full breath of air. Hard when GM is standing on top of you. "Aaha-aaha."

Game Mistress steps off Steph, collects Steph's head between two boots, and squares it with the floor, so that her head rests on the tip of her nose and the tip of her clamped tongue lies in a puddle of pee.

"You want to swallow pee."

Not really. "Aaha-aaha."

"You want fresh piss, right out of the hydrant."

Yes, I must want this now, "Aaha-aaha.

"Silly Whore," Game Mistress teases, "you don't fool me, I know why you want your Tongue Clamp off! Off, so you'll be better able to suck cocks! You like that idea, you sniveling suckface piss mop?"

Steph must agree, "Aaha-aaha."

"You Free-Fucked, skank."

Impossible to deny the *Video*. "Aaha-aaha."

"You're a suck-fuck-facial Whore, now and next Term."

Okay, if Game Mistress says so. "Aaha-aaha." *No anal on the list!.* "Aaha-aaha."

But Steph's head doesn't realign. *It's not fair. Game Mistress* knows *I have a guaranteed Opt Up. She is deciding that my Free-Fucking qualifies me to Opt Whore and overrides my guarantee.*

Not correct. Game Mistress has decided that lying about the guarantee voids the guarantee; not only will Steph be demoted to Whore, she shall also be marked for lying about Free-Fucking. Steph Free-Fucking twice and lied about it three times.

It is not necessary for Game Mistress to tell a Whore anything, explain actions, present evidence, or justify means.

Steph feels fingers loosen the nuts which hold her tongue clamp tight. China Doll performs this service skillfully, opening the space between the two horizontal rods so that the pain of the blood running back into to a purple tongue causes Steph to cringe. China Doll understands; she is an expert at extracting pain from a body.

"Lick, Toilet Whore" Game Mistress commands, "the floor, my boots, Rodney's nuts."

Steph licks. Gamers appreciate this is not the first time Steph has collected piss. Licking is hard with the big O-Ring Gag still tight behind Steph's teeth, but Steph does manage to accumulate some urine into her mouth, and the acidity of it bitters her palette.

Steph angers. *I played along during the Term even though I wasn't really a Lockdown Lobelia. It shouldn't matter to the Game that William fucked me. First of all, the Rules can't apply to me when a higher Caste Player chooses to fuck with me!*

Besides, showing an unauthorized Video *of me having sex under duress infringers upon my privacy. Then, making me beg to Whore is a ruse to convince other Players of something that is not real.*

Still, when one's body is secured, and there are pendulums swinging that are out of one's control, the mind can go wild with imagination. *Everyone is taking advantage of the fact that my defenses are disabled right now. But once that changes, retribution will occur. I want to see William and Rodney get circumcised, and their foreskins hung from their noses, instead of hiding the heads of their dicks.*

§ Steph: The Consequences of Lying

It is not easy to move from a flat-on-your-belly position to a kneeling-spread-armbound position, but the tip of Game Mistress's shoe provides inspiration, and China Doll provides the additional muscle power to rotate Steph upright. Steph shakes her shoulders, makes sure her knees are spread, and faces forward. Pee runs off her face and body.

Babs watches China Doll lick up the runnels of urine on Steph's naked body and face, and squirt these mouthfuls of urine into the inviting space inside Steph's big O-Ring Gag. Oh, rude!

China Doll trades eyes and the softest of smiles with Babs, and BB understands, *not all of the pee that China Doll cleans up gets redeposited. Whatever is left over she swallows. And she knows I'm a Piss Mouth too, that I've swallowed too, and I deserve to get watered. And a lot or a little, the taste stays with you.*

It does. Babs can still taste Penny and Coco's pussy and pee in her mouth. Both linger on her palette; the former as some kind of impression taken into the body and also smeared onto her face, and the second leaving a lasting bitter aftertaste in her mouth.

And a third contributor seemed familiar, more tart, *anonymous and a harbinger of new essences – including those of men – which will soon augment my palette. I am a Piss Mouth,* BB resigns, *I failed, I deserve all my food be dumped on the floor, pissed on, and I have to stick my face in it and eat it all up. While I am being paddle stroked so I don't dally too much.*

Gamers need to hook me onto the bottom of Robyn's urine bag; they need to punish my failure, If Robyn is broken out of her shell, I will have to humiliate myself immensely and beg to lick her asshole, eat out her rag hole in the middle of her period, and make her climax. Kimju had to humiliate herself in front of Robyn and beg Whore, and I'm going to have to as well. It is not possible to humiliate me more than having to beg to service the one Pledge most responsible for my demise.

Babs marvels at China Doll's *total confidence, total submission, total control. China Doll is a role model I can aspire to, she will teach me how to gargle and spit out – or gargle and swallow – whatever I'm given; teach me to surrender and trust. She will help me to become a Super Whore.*

Steph sees the negative in her new (old) position. *I am now in a kneeling, cocksucking position, with my legs spread wide and my snatch hanging open.* Steph misses the Shaving Kit. *China Doll is going to move Gimbled It over in front of me, and I'm going to beg It's cock in my waiting, wide-open, O-Ring Gagged mouth, "Aaha-aaha." I hate this Game.*

I know what Game Mistress is trying to do, she is trying to make a Whore out of me. I couldn't stop William and I can't stop Gamers now, because since everyone has seen me suck and fuck on Video *they are going to want to watch me live. Okay, so after I get holed, I still have my guaranteed Opt-Up whenever Midnight arrives.*

Sounds like a plan.

China Doll reappears. She holds a Tray in her hand; she stops midway between what Gamers may rightly assume are two bare, naked, kneeling Lockdown Whores.

One of them is a Dong and Dirty Whore by entailment of the misdeeds of several (former) Pledge. The other has revealed herself to Whore for advancement, and shown herself willing to use every hole in her body to conquer and control others.

Each in their own way has failed. One of them admits her failings and desires to be turned inside out so her mind, body, and soul are totally exposed. The other holds others responsible for her own sexual misconduct, and rebels against her restraints.

Gamers intend to sexually manage the both of them, but do debate among themselves how to best train them, so they will develop so much creative sexual horniness that they will infect others.

There is a gesture unseen by either Babs or Steph but Three Naked Pushers break from supporting the Wheel to forming a tight, closed, cocksucking triangle on the floor between the two Whores. As the Three Pushers form into a triangle, each Pusher collects, first catching on the tongue the dangle of lube hanging from the dick of the next, then following the streamer up onto the head, wiggling downward with the lips, going up and over and down into the valley behind the rim, then down the shaft, and finally stopping when the cock bangs into the back wall. This is not throat practice time, or collecting upchuck, this is forming a table, and a "tight oral formation" is expected.

China Doll sets the Tray down on the table of three uplifted shoulders. The Tray contain piercing instruments, sterilizing necessities, Pennington clamps, and barbells.

The Three remaining Pushers are adequate to support the Wheel, still with its right-side-up Whore, and upside-down Slavesex occupants. GM signs them to balance the Wheel with one arm and shoulder, and masturbate with the free hand. These Three Pushers also have total erections, and they shall now extend their hanging streamers of lube.

Babs watches as China Doll approach Steph, and for an instant BB and Steph trade eyes; Babs sees the hardening of Steph's eyes, and breaks eye contact. Steph sees Babs' eyes glaze over in helpless anticipation of what is about to happen. Babs accepts, *I am going to get tongue spiked because of Steph's lies. It's okay, I deserve it.*

Game Mistress addresses Steph. "You Free-Fucked and lied about it, when it mattered. When we had a Runaway loose. That's not covered in any Option!" GM sounds like a schoolmarm.

Steph gurgles louder, translation, "I need to explain! I'm a Monitor next Term!"

Game Mistress accepts words from Steph's mouth, "Yes, I agree, you lied to us three times!" GM states a fact, "And three-time liars get their tongues pierced three times. Congratulations."

Steph tries to argue. "Ummmagggghhhfff," she says and rustles her armbound hands still behind her back and moves her tongue around inside her spread wide-open O-Ring Gagged mouth.

Game Mistress calms. "This is not a matter of simply adding soap or castor oil into your diet for routine lying, this is a matter of how many studs Gamers shall put in your tongue."

Steph gurgles again, and again Game Mistress translates, this time speaking to Babs. "She says you're the Monitor and it is you, not she who should bear any Pledge burdens."

GM leads Steph. "You are advocating that Bondo Bangho take on your tongue piercings?"

Steph feels relief, brightens, "Aaha-aaha!" And scowls toward BB. *I like how Gamers are marking you up. 12 gauge nose ring, and your swinging boobs still imprinted with rope marks when you got hung by your blaaters not too long ago. I hope they expand the tattoo around your 12 gauge navel piercing, and beat your butt every day so that it is always too painful to sit.*

And beat the soles of your feet so it is always too painful to stand. Make you Bastinado Bitch led around by her nose ring. Every step hurts, hurts to sit down. Ha ha ha.

Game Mistress turns to Babs, "The Skank tells me you should take on her tongue piercings."

Yes, plural. Babs knows the Rules, and BB does what she's told, and begs, "Aaha-aaha." BB runs her tongue around the inside of her O-Ring Gag. *Won't be long now. Maybe I don't deserve this, except that I do. I want it so harsh that my neural circuits are seared forever.* Babs looks at Steph and sees Steph lift her chin. Steph's huge O-Ring Gag distorts her face.

My face is distorted too by my O-Ring, Babs accepts, and predicts what is going to happen next. *We are both going to take Gimbled It down our throats. Then we will work It's cock together, and It's balls and asshole and nipples and neck and lips ectaras, and get facialed and creampied fore and aft. And share cumdumps and snowball and eat cum out of each other's vestibules, inner lips and vaginal ways, and felch cum-collect from each other.*

I still have pain in my nose. I still have pain in my button. And I deserve to have pain in my tongue. I saw Kimju get her tongue punched, twice, Steph looks to get three, so I need at least five studs in my tongue. It has to hurt.

Babs can't always get what she wants.

Steph watches as China Doll approaches Babs, looks BB in the eye, and gestures with two fingers. Babs sticks her tongue out through the O-Ring Gag. China Doll grasps BB's tongue with two fingers, top and bottom, then draws forward from the back of the tongue to the front, scooping goo off. China Doll cleans her fingers in her own mouth, reaches carefully and plants the Pennington Clamp, with its round center at the end, centered on and midway into Babs' tongue. China Doll gently lets go, and the weight of the clamp hangs BB's tongue out of her mouth. More cum and drool follow it out.

"You beg for it, you get it," Game Mistress advises. And the Pogo quickly lets BB know she shall now pay for pleasure with pain.

Help! I forgot how much the Tongue Clamp hurt! This piercing Clamp is worse!

And is made worse. Babs' Pogo ensures that BB is unable to stop grinding her butt and bouncing her heavy boobs, but the more she bounces the more the Pennington Clamp hanging off her tongue flops and bounces, shooting pain and whipsawing BB between coital arousal and tongue pain. Babs resigns herself to the pain. *I need pain in my tongue in anticipation of the piercing needle. I had my nipples clamped during Lockdown and I know they will be pierced too.*

BB's painfully pulled and distended tongue encourages drool, which in turn oozes down to BB's hanging and wagging tongue, coating it, coating the bouncing Pennington Clamp, and dripping onto BB's already painted bamboochas, with their splotchy blaater tops and upstanding bacillars. Babs entire body is hot.

I can't stop grinding on the Pogo. I'm sopping wet. I'm a bawdy bangbox blurt bitch. I'm a Dong and Dirty Lockdown Whore. I am really not in control at all. And I am in a place past Rules. I will beg away Rules. China Doll is going to pierce my tongue, drive It's purple penis deep into my asshole and surf me; I am going to squirt, lose all control of my bladder, and sing out my O-Ring Gag for as long they keep climaxing me.

Sounds like a plan.

"You're a mess," Game Mistress observes to the helpless grinding Whore, "and yes, you are destined to be a Star! There is not a person alive who will not pay to squeeze your bazoombas, bite your bullets, and partake in a gangbang. You are an instrument to be played, different strokes for different notes, and if Gamers are nice they will have you sing notes that balances your carnal stimulation vs. the pain from your weighted-down and flapping tongue.

"Now sing for us, Bauble Babe!"

Bauble Babe blow air out her O-Ring Gag. And takes pain.

China Doll returns to her tray, picks up another Pennington Clamp, and Babs watches as China Doll reaches into Steph's O-

Ring Gagged, wide-open mouth with the open forceps, grabs Steph's restless tongue, and snaps the clamp tight onto her tongue. Now Steph's tongue also hangs out of her mouth with the weight of the dangling Clamp.

The gagging and gurgling noises from Steph are almost continuous (and Steph doesn't even have a Pogo to contend with).

"Yes, yes, I hear you," Game Mistress explains to Steph, "But there remains a small difference between Beka's Free-Fucking and your Free-Fucking; Beka confessed to her sins, whereas you lied about them. Over and over. Three times."

"Let me show you what happens to liars."

China Doll appears into Steph's field of vision and Steph's eyes suddenly dilate wide with fear; the Cams see the whites in Steph's eyes as she recognizes what China Doll holds between her thumb and first finger.

China Doll grasps the dangling, painful Pennington with one hand, pulls Steph's tongue forward, stretching it, and with the other hand drives the piercing needle through Steph's tongue. 12 gauge. Armbound Steph screams from her throat, and again pisses herself. Pain pulses with every heartbeat in Steph's skewered tongue, it's on fire and can't be put out. *Damn William! Damn Rodney! Both of them deserve the Wheel. Both of them deserve to Whore. Both of them deserve Slavesex!*

Maybe both deserve, but only William will serve.

BB squints her eyes and sees China Doll follow on with a barbell stud through Steph's tongue. A long one. One long enough that Steph will have to open wide to navigate her tongue in and out of her mouth, that is, might her O-Ring Gag ever come out.

Babs has no choice but to masturbate in a narrow range as Steph curls in pain. The Pogo vibrates in response to BB's constrictions and her sloppy wet interior, the pain in her bouncing tongue throbs, and Bondo Babe lets go and loses herself into the heavy-eyelid Zone.

Pain rages inside Steph's head. Steph's arms are still bound behind her back. Steph feels lightheaded, the pain spins around, and she desperately gasps for air.

Starbursts erupt as Steph clangs her new tongue stud against her O-Ring; Steph sees the Meatpacking Plant through a gray haze. And another burst of urine. *I am in big trouble and it is not over yet. Game Mistress is going to try to use this opportunity to whore me. What she needs to do is whore Babs double instead. Whore Babs double Terms, double hours. It's not my fault.*

Steph presses her barbell against the inside of her mouth. *It feels long*; it is long. *Game Mistress thinks I'm going to slide this inside the end of pee holes and stimulate dicks from the inside. GM is crazy to think that.*

Game Mistress is not crazy and such thoughts are disrespectful. Tickling the insides of pee holes with the ball on one end of Steph's long stud will be just part of Steph's basic Whore services.

Steph might be contemplating the loss of her tongue, and will need to learn that her spigots, snatch, and skin are also relegated to Flesh Ranch. Or maybe Steph's destination hasn't sunk in yet.

Babs does not read Steph's thoughts but daggers in Steph's eyes leave no doubt as to pent up retribution. Ironically, Babs feels inoculated. *I'm a Whore, a Dong and Dirty Watersports Goo Whore. I'm going to fuck the President.*

Steph might be down but she is not without spite. *I hope Gamers put a ring in BB's buzzer, march rings down her sex lips, then tie her lips wide to her thighs, so that her fuck hole is waiting to get stretched. Then drive Gimbled It's purple shaft down her bushing, and possess her.*

But Steph does not confine her spite to Babs. *Bondo Bitch is especially getting what she deserves; she failed to control her House. But me? I'm being exploited. I'm a naked-spread-pink fondle toy at a Play Party where I am being taken advantage of!* Steph flushes. Her body feels warm. Thoughts rush through her mind. *What's happening is not my fault! What's happening to me is because of William and Rodney's actions!*

Gamers enjoy watching Steph's collapse.

Steph digests. *William has just gotten revealed for the ass-fucker that he is. He is not my friend. And he is no longer able to protect and advance me.*

Protect me? Steph gets a grip on herself. *William told me that if I fucked him I would get "preferred Monitor treatment." Okay, so I fucked him. But he didn't have the power. Not even the power to not get caught. He's either in on the voyeur Cam with Rodney or not; it doesn't matter. He's guilty. Even better, he's Slavesex.*

William and Rodney need to be put on a diet of hormones, grow tits and be feminized. Rodney should be shaved and turned into a she-male. And William should be castrated and turned into a eunuch or trannie, or get stubbed completely and left with a working mouth, anus, and pee hole.

And his detached dick can get turned into a dildo gag for his own mouth. Ha ha ha!

Harsh.

Conversely, William also lacks fondness for Steph. *An empty-hole, bare-bald-naked Cosmos Lockdown Lobelia kneeling before me. Actually, hanging from the ceiling like some kind of vampire.*

Yes, in William's upside-down, spread-eagled Wheel view of the Meatpacking Plant, as he looks through Rodney's crotch, Steph hangs from the ceiling.

An inverted world does not stop William's antagonism toward Steph. *Fucking slut deserves to Whore,* William escalates. *Deserves to be a Dong and Dirty Whore. Was a whore when she seduced me. I kept the* Video *as evidence. She's still a Whore. And she gave me away. Just like Beka outted Rodney, I bet.*

Saving evidence of seduction, evidence of favoritism, evidence of coercion, ectaras; reasons don't matter when Rules are broken and sentences are already defined. William no longer needs to plan his future, his Fate has already been defined, and his future will be planned for him.

William looks at the hanging Plaster Mummy. *That is where Free-Fucking got Beka; and that's where Rodney's got to go.*

GM turns her eyes toward William, "Seems like you and your Roommate both love venery with women. And now you practice venery with men! I know I know, you both love having each other's cocks in your mouths and you don't want to give them up." Game Mistress grasps upside-down William's balls, where they ride just above his cock in Rodney's mouth, and teases, "Don't worry, you shall learn to love having men in your mouth. Or up your ass. You'll service anyone. Right?"

William can't move much. "Aaha-aaha."

Game Mistress squeezes William's balls tightly, "You won't need these to suck and get analed, right?"

Correct, and William must reluctantly agree, "Aaha-aaha."

Babs tries to close on what is happening. *I'm already a Dong and Dirty Watersports Goo Whore. I just begged a tongue piercing but GM pierced Steph instead. And the Pogo climaxed me on Steph's pain. Except I'm the one who really deserves the pain. This is all my fault; I am lavishing marks and pain upon all the Pledge around me that I'm supposed to protect.*

Steph's optimism has reached a point of conflict with the still pulsating pain in her tongue. The Pennington Clamp is gone. Really deep pain, genuine, witnessed pain that invokes a reconsideration of pain in Steph's nose and navel. *Could those pains be real too, and not just fakery?*

Steph also evaluates. *What's happening can't be real. At Midnight I have an Opt Up; the Eyes told me my Option wasn't jeopardized by Robyn Runaway. I'm innocent and can explain everything. I got tricked at the Greatest House Roar, got forced to cum like a worthless masturbator, and had to piss into my own mouth during the* Beach Day.

But then I won the Duel, made Elle beg to Opt Down, and claimed my promotion. My getting forced to have sex with William doesn't matter. Can't matter. I'm still going to Opt Up. Maybe they all resent it, but I am going to get back at them double.

As they say in the Opera, it's not over until the Fat Lady appears.

V-14 Bang Babe & Steph: Another Surprise Video

§ Steph with William & Rodney: 2nd Surprise Video

It has been said that the Fat Lady is a descendent of Mother-of-Calamity, where at the Palace of King Hardub in Cesarea she earned a reputation for castrating her young male lovers after they ejaculated into her.

The Fat Lady was last seen on Day 23 and although she shares a similar disgusting appearance of her ancestor, complete with the warts, ambiguous sexual organs and lube hanging from a proto penis, the Fat Lady lacks her ancestor's unusual impulse to ensure that sperm donated to her shall not be donated elsewhere.

On Day 23 of *The Runup,* the Fat Lady had brought an envelope to the center Stage of the Nugget; an envelope that contained an Option. Tiffany had first choice, but declined the offer, so it passed to Steph, to took it, and which enabled Steph to pick a Duel with Elle, and Opt Elle to the Strip, and Opt herself to Monitor.

Once again the Fat Lady brings an envelope, announces itself with a giant melodious fart, hands the message silently to Game Mistress, and exits.

Game Mistress reads the message in silence.

Perhaps there is more to the show.

Game Mistress turns from reducing Bang Babe to reducing Steph. Steph looks at GM with pain in her face but daggers in her eyes.

Bad idea.

The last time the message in the envelope had enabled Steph to claim power. And Steph had, carelessly perhaps. And this time?

Game Mistress shrugs. "Resistance is futile," she says, and waves a finger.

And another *Video* appears on the screens. Another surprise *Video* – to Babs and the (ex-Peacock) Wheel Pushers perhaps – but the *Video* is not a surprise to William and Rodney. (It is a surprise to Babs because it got made after Janet had revealed to her the existence of the first *Steph and William Sex Video,* just seen.)

And is it a surprise to Steph? Steph now with a long stud in her tongue, pain pulsing through her head? Steph is no longer Opting Monitor, Steph has cast herself as a Whore.

The *Video* playing is another *Video* that Steph had convinced herself didn't exist. Steph has rationalized that *because Rodney interrupted our sex, Rodney never recorded my second scene.*

Excuse me Steph, but Rodney never recorded the first scene either.

Steph watches herself. *There I am climbing on top and fucking William again.*

Game Mistress addresses Steph lazily, "Seems like once is not enough for you. You really do want to be a Porn Star, yes?"

The Steph here at the Play Party must agree, "Aaha-aaha."

Yes, there Steph is on the screen, sixty-nining with William, and cleaning his cum and her juice off his cock, while he eats his own cum and her juice out of her pussy.

But then, something happens on the Screens which startles Bondo Bauble and the Six Pushers: Rodney barges in! Gasps among the Players here at the Meatpacking Plant! Steph sneaks a confirming look at helpless cock-sucking, cock-restrained, buttocks bloodied Rodney on the Wheel, as the on-screen Rodney take his pleasure with her.

Steph knows for sure *they DPed me, swapped the cock in my asshole into my mouth, and pleasured my other hole. I know I climaxed out of control,*

I cleaned cock A2M twice, but at least I recycled myself.

That can change.

§ Game Mistress: Fates of Babs Steph William Rodney

Game Mistress smiles as she approaches the kneeling Steph.

"It appears you not only like to make more than one movie, you also like to fuck with more than one guy."

Steph gurgles. "This is not the way it happened!" Steph recalls, *William let Rodney anal me!*

Things start happening to Steph at a rate faster than she can absorb.

"Tell me you're a double penetrating anal Whore!" GM commands.

Steph agrees, "Aaha-aaha." *True! The Video is my witness.*

"Very well, Whore, the time has come for you to beg to be a Dong and Dirty Whore. Is that your goal, Whore?"

Steph hesitates, *I know when I'm being rung up*, but the *Video* confirms. "Aaha-aaha."

"You are an ass-licking, pussy-eating, cocksucking, cunt-fucking, anal-gaping, A2M, A2OPM, Dong and Dirty Watersports Goo Whore."

Steph agrees, "Aaah-aaha."

Game Mistress professes sympathy, "We were all so proud of you when you got your Option and crushed Elle. Committed that naughty nympho to her natural Fate. Now you are a three-hole Free-Fuck Dirty Whore, you entail your ex-Monitor Babs to the same Whore Fate."

"Aaha-aaha." Steph agrees.

Fear strikes into Babs as Game Mistress turns to her, smiles to her, and assuages her fear. "Lucky you. You're already a three-hole Dong and Dirty Whore 12x7 because your Pledge Elle whored her asshole. Besides Elle's Karma is your Karma, isn't it. You sent Pledge Elle on a mission that forced her to either fail or put out on your behalf. She's begging to be an anal Whore after one Stripper Term. You're responsible, and I trust you will welcome that little nympho when she joins you at Flesh Ranch after next Term?"

Babs blinks. *Me at Flesh Ranch, and more than one Term? Yes, me, Flesh Ranch Whore, so yes, I will welcome Elle.* "Aaha-aaha." *Beka too, although all she whored was her bone hole and mouth.*

Game Mistress tucks in one cheek, relaxes, and speaks. "These *Videos* indicate that another one of your Pledge went rogue. And whored her holes not just once, but twice! My inclination is that you too need to double your commitments, yes, Whore?"

Wait! Babs stabilizes. *Yes, I want what you want for me. Double Dong and Dirty?.* "Aaha-aaha."

"Double mouth, double pussy, double anal," Game Mistress explains. "All at once, plus double both hands. Ten cocks at once. You want to be a gangbang Whore from now on?"

Bang Babe gurgles through her Ring Gag. "Aaha-aaha."

Game Mistress delights in pressing. "Whore, beg me that you want it Double time. You can do Three Terms 12x7 for Elle and another Three Terms 12x7 for Steph, but what you are going to do is Double up and do Three Terms 24x7. How does that appeal to you?"

Babs startles, she doesn't want to, she take in a breath, falters. *Six terms instead of Three?*

Not quite. GM smiles. "Beg, Whore, no more 12x7, no more 12 on and 12 off, beg Dong and Dirty Whore 24x7. Quickly now!"

Babs begs. "Aaha-aaha." *Different.*

Wait! Babs gathers her thoughts. *No! Yes, 24x7 is necessary; it makes me a total Whore for Three Terms. It's almost like Slavesex but without being tied down and sexed, without forced cosmetic enhancements, or being a breeder. I shall beg what GM wants. So from now* on, *I am never off duty. I'm a three hole! Whore 24x7.*

Correct.

I will have to sleep on cam with a cock in my mouth. I deserve it as rough as they need to give me, even rough beyond what I deserve; some Players are even genuine sadists who just want to hurt and humiliate me for their own pleasure. Except it doesn't matter if they are sick and twisted and want to beat me. I failed. I deserve whatever madness the Game can dish out to me, and my humiliations cammed and saved in Automatron.

A worthy goal.

Game Mistress steps back. "We love you, and love your acquiescence to your Fate. You try hard, and we shall help turn you into a world-class courtesan, concubine, and Porn Star. You're going to do great! You shall escort generals, sheiks, and ministers, and I shall help make you a Super Whore, with fans throughout the Prefecture who will all fall in love with you!

"I shall advise you might the time be ripe to beg Slavesex. Right now, with your Clock Stopped, you're a helpless and venerable Lockdown Bondage Whore. You like?"

Babs likes, "Aaha-aaha."

"You lucky Pogo Princess. Stay," Game Mistress commands a stunned Babs, and turns to Babs' nemesis, Steph.

"And you, Whore," Game Mistress targets kneeling Steph, you Free-Fucked twice, analed twice, and enticed men to double penetrate you. Tell me you also want to be a Dong and Dirty Whore Double 12x7. Beg 24x7! Double Terms.

Steph whimpers, feels the Goad, and agrees, "Aaha-aaha."

If Rodney and William didn't fully realize the night they were run out that they are Opting Down, they certainly know it now. The piercings through their cheeks, penises, tongues, noses are 10 gauge. Heavy duty. William assumes a future in which the cheek piercings will expanded to gromets; Rodney doesn't think past the now.

Game Mistress bows to Rodney, "You're more than an accomplice. I trust you understand by now that you are twice a Whore, and like Bang Bucks and Satchel Skank, you too shall double your Whoredom to 24x7. Still Three Terms. Beg me, you Rimjobber Rodhole."

Rodney begs, "Aaha-aaha."

Game Mistress philosophizes to Rodney. "You can be Ramho. Your mouth will suck cock, no matter where the cock has been, collect facials and swallow, eat pussies no matter how filled with jizz, and felch anal creampies. Your cock shall be milked, injected with prostaglandin and forced into a state of constant erection, or limpness, and your asshole shall be sold and flooded with creampies. You want this, Rodney, don't you. Beg me."

Rodney agrees, "Aaha-aaha." And leaks a little pee into William's mouth.

"You grateful?" Game Mistress inquires.

Rodney is. Slavesex is far worse. "Aaha-aaha."

"Lucky boy."

GM bows to William. "Slavesex don't deserve bows, but I want you to know that you shall start begging that anal creampies decorate any and all food that you shall eat. But don't worry, everything about your body will be managed for you. You shall be rectally fed, rectally enemaed, rectally sexed. Your mouth shall work as a washing machine. Your stomach is a food source for privileged Slavesex."

Game Mistress scans. "Good. Now all Four of you pay attention, because I am about to tell you what your Fates shall be."

§ Babs & Steph and Rodney & William: Final Solutions

Game Mistress prepares some rearrangements. "First, congratulations. Gamers have accepted the Three of you who are begging to be Dong and Dirty Whores, next Three Terms, 24x7.

Furthermore, Gamers have accepted the One of you begging to be Slavesex, next Six Terms, 24x7.

"You are all Goo Gobblers, whether you know it or not, and you shall beg that everything you eat gets spunked first. And you are all Pee-Camers and Piss-Mouths, and you are allowed to beg that everything you eat gets watered first. You are Dirty Whores of the lowest common denominator. The only thing beneath you are Slavesex; Dirty Whores are fucked in every hole; Slavesex are bound, beaten, and fucked in every hole, and bound and beaten some more."

Game Mistress continues. "Whores possess nothing. You shall remain naked except when you are instructed to dress. You shall be made up and perform as it pleases Pimp Cowboy. You will of course service him, all of the Flesh Ranch staff, and Patrons who are placed into your care. You shall not discriminate as to the Patrons you fellatte and fornicate, or who sodomize you, even if they reek of perfume or body odor, or demand for you to get gangbanged in the Mudpit or enter you into a cocksucking cum collection contest.

Game Mistress bows to Babs and Steph. "You Whores will beg whatever I want you to beg, and since you have *both* already begged Slavesex, there is no need to repeat yourselves."

This statement produces gasps of air. Game Mistress reads minds and reminds the two Whores about another Rule, "What you beg you beg forever."

Game Mistress continues. "After you arrive at Flesh Ranch, Gamers will arrange for Seven Contests between both of you to determine which of you Two Whores will have your beg honored and turned into Slavesex, and which of you will remain a Whore. Whoever wins four or more Games remains a Whore. Whoever wins less than four Games is a Slavesex. You shall compete for your climaxes, reveal yourselves sexually, and surrender all self-control. We want you both to enjoy the winning, as well as the misery of losing these competitions. And in at least in some of the contests, you will not actually get to know the outcome. You will find if you remain at Flesh Ranch that you have won the Contest.

"The Games are designed to remove your last vestiges of socialization, if not your humanity, and allow you to grovel and showoff and expose your most base Whorish and Slavish tendencies. Some of the Games will require you exceed the other in humiliation. Some of the Games will require you exceed in disgracing the other. May your predicaments force you to choose between pain and humiliation, or between inflicting pain and humiliation upon the other.

"Many require self-discipline. Gamers have gathered the contents of all of the Lobelia Collection Dishes together, yours included as well as some others, and divided the thick mass into two equal drinking containers. Down the hatch, each of you, center Stage; the winner who collects their last drop first, the loser gets one paddle stroke for each second it takes her to complete.

"You shall play a Dice Game blindfolded, and not be told if you win or lose. It is important you know that the Game can come to decisions about you that you don't observe. That lack of transparency makes cheating possible.

"The stakes are high. For example, as long as you are a Whore, breast augmentation (or reduction) is always an option; but once you make Slavesex, breast, indeed all body modification, is an option one's Superiors enjoy; breasts can be made like balloons, or removed entirely. Slavesex have no rights, none own their mind, body or soul. Slavesex can be infested with AIs and Running Agents, females can be bred like in Gor; some male penises have grown to farm animal size, other males been known to beg castration, stubbing, and breast implants."

§ Game Mistress and Babs & Gimbled It: Cock Tease

There is another unseen signal and Babs discovers herself being rotated around the Pogo so that she faces away from the Wheel, the table and Tray, and away from Steph. Steph can still see Babs, so too can the Pushers, so too can the upside-down William, but Rodney, who faces in the wrong direction, might only witness Babs via a Screen.

Mission accomplished; Babs sees none of them. The unseen hands that rotate BB belong to the always naked China Doll, who next propels the bound bundle called Gimbled It, still hanging from the overhead rail, around a curve and onto a siding so that It's erection directly faces the kneeling-naked-armbound Pogoed Bondo

Babe, with her large, hideously O-Ring Gagged tightly-cinched mouth and contorted face. No Tongue Clamp.

Gimbled It's immense purple penis is closer now; Babs observes and struggles to make the Pogo go faster. Babs contemplates the huge purple erection, the rim around the head, the hole in the middle, and a ripple of lube oozing out the hole, creeping down the side of the head, hanging off the rim, and then swinging in the air, some of it swinging back and coating the huge purple erection.

Bang Babe pants. *I want to catch that on my tongue!*

China Doll reads BB's mind, gathers Gimbled It's hanging bead of pre-cum into three fingers, and with her other hand loosens the Pennington Clamp hanging BB tongue out, takes it off, wipes drool off BB's tongue with two fingers, inserts the fingers wet with Gimbled It's pre-cum into BB's O-Ringed Gagged mouth. Babs swirls it around with her free tongue, swallows, and releases a blob of her blurt onto the Pogo.

China Doll carefully swipes more of Gimbled It's thick lubricant into Babs' two nostrils, and then carefully dabs just one of BB's crescent d'areolage with the remainder.

China doll departs with the Pennington Clamp. With this damper being removed, the taste and the smell of Gimbled It's pre-cum, and the accelerant on Babs's areolage, tip Babs past any point of self-respect. BB vulgarizes the Pogo with her movements, she pants, she drools, she is barely able to control her urine. Babs tries to control her flush, her erect nipples, and her oozing burgoo. *I can't. I'm a Whore. I'm a Cam Whore, and everyone wants to watch me lose control. And I want everyone to watch me fuck Gimbled It. In my mouth, in my barrel, and deep in by butt.*

But before the Pogo and Babs can settle into a relationship unhindered by the tongue-pain factor, somewhere off in the Zone no doubt, Game Mistress probes to the heart of the matter. "Tell me, Whore, you like that Pogo in your burse?"

Babs does, "Aaha-aaha."

"But you'd rather have cock."

Babs would. "Aaha-aaha."

"You want Gimbled It's big purple prick in your sloppy bald bushing."

BB wants. 'Aaha-aaha!"

"In your mouth."

"Aaha-aaha."

In your bunghole."

Again a statement, and a slower answer. "Aaha-aaha." *I saw what happened to Beka and Elle. They got anal climaxed.*

"Possibly Gimbled It's penis is too big to fit through your O-Ring Gag hole. Maybe if we take it off you could suck better?"

Yes. "Aaha-aaha!"

"Patience, Whore. Keep grinding your barrel on the Pogo."

Babs worries but doesn't stop. Maybe can't stop. *What if It's cock is too big for my mouth? Too big for my throat? What if Gimbled It's cum-blast inundates my mouth, and blows out my nose? What if It pisses in my mouth and I can't swallow fast enough and I drown?*

Babs lets out a sigh. *Except Gamers don't want me to die. I am an embarrassment machine. Gamers don't want to watch my Pledge pee into my mouth because they need to learn how to pee, they watch because they want to see me be degraded. And then degrade myself, like when Steph had to pee into her own mouth on the Beach. Self-humiliation, I will do it. Gamers can't punish me enough.*

I need to be a cocksucking cumdump repository. I need to swallow. I need to gokkun, I need to be a bukkake Whore. A totally-covered Goo Girl; I need to live in a clear glass stable where there is goo on every surface, goo dripping from the ceiling, thick warm goo covering a water bed.

The Pogo talks to BB; a high frequency pulse runs up and down the thick insertion and takes BB's breath away. BB fixates on Gimbled It's purple penis, dances with Pogo in her bone socket, finds a steady rhythm of constrictions and a sustainable heartbeat, catches a wave, and surfs the Zone.

Not a screaming high climax where one goes over the top and runs out of breath, but a steady trot, Kundalini enabling, running on the pleasure and peace of Nirvana.

§ Babs: Overhears William and Steph & Rodney Depart

As if in a dream, behind her, Babs can hear GM direct China Doll: "William... keep him upside down... chain his feet to the overhead rail... unfasten him from the Wheel... send him down the line to a branding station… shave his body… tattoo a bar code on his neck… yes, hood him… yes, through a lashing line… deport him to the Dungeon."

Babs hears noises behind, finds the steady bounce on the Pogo compelling, and contemplates It's cock, not far from her face, pulsating, pumping fresh lube out. Bondo Burse can smell it now, it's inside her nostrils, *inside my mouth, seeping into the skin of my areola. I can smell Gimbled It in the air. I want Gimbled It.* BB thinks less; and she needs more. *I want It in every hole in my body. In front of everybody. On Cam on Automatron. I want to be saturated with purple stain, I want a load of It's jizz dripping out of my bangbox, a load hanging out my bunghole, and I will swallow a load fed into my mouth.*

I will collect It's creampies out of my holes and eat them. I will eat It's creampies out of anybody's holes. I will eat anybody's creampies out of anybody's holes. I'm a Dirty Whore now.

Babs does not see Game Mistress bow at William, but she does hear GM speak. "Goodbye Slavesex," and hears the trolly roll out.

Babs is correct to assume that William's Eyepods and Earpods go black. Yes, of course Slavesex William's mouth will service more cocks than pussies from now on; and, yes, his asshole will service more cocks that his cock will service pussies, might he service pussies other than with his mouth.

Furthermore, Bondage Whores – Slavesex – are always a leading attraction. If William is lucky he will only lose his foreskin, have his dick turned into a permanent pincushion, or be turned into a transvestite. If he is less fortunate, well….

Babs does not see GM bow at kneeling Steph. Creaking noises follow, and BB can overhear GM's directions to China Doll, "Fasten Steph to the Wheel where William was…," the sound of an armbinder and mittens being undone, and of a naked Steph being fitted, upside down, onto the Wheel.

More sounds and Babs again hears GM giving China Doll directions. "Take off Steph's Ring Gag… use the barbell to fasten Steph's tongue piercing and Rodney's cock piercing together… so they are very secure."

More noises. Babs still anticipates that her own tongue, like Steph's will be pierced and that the two Whores would be led by their pierced tongues to Flesh Ranch. This is not happening, and BB envisions Steph, now behind her being affixed spread-eagle to the wheel, facing it and upside down, *looking at me from between Rodney's thighs, and with her spread sloppy snatch pointing upward. And with her tongue, and upright Rodney's cock, on the other side of the Wheel, pinned together.*

This is a correct assessment.

The sound of suppressed scream is unexpected, as China Doll operates like a surgeon and strikes a piercing needle through Steph's clithood, following with a 12 gauge stud and a U-bolt that swings and will forever dangle and arouse Steph's clitoris.

Game Mistress narrates. "You have two more spikes coming into your tongue, but piled up lies don't increment your Whore piercing count. Your nose doesn't count either, but your button work does and so does your fresh clithood stud and dangle. So, Whore, plan on your nipples getting punched after you arrive at Flesh Ranch. And, lucky you, Janet has decided to bequest you her vaginal rings. I've decided they don't count either because you demanded them, besides you've demonstrated your snatch needs to be managed for you." And in seconds China Doll marches three needles down both sides of Steph's fleshy outer sex lips.

This time Bouncy Babs is brought out of reverie by Steph's gasps and sobs; they are not pointed muffled screams, more like a cascade of pain. Babs shudders.

"You like Janet's rings on your sex lips, Whore." GM states.

Not a question; Steph must like. "Aaha-aaha."

"You probably want them pulled open so your pink snatch is wide open to fuck."

All right. "Aaha-aaha.'

"You probably want them laced shut so your snatch is totally chastised."

Steph surrenders. *Ok, control my snatch now.* "Aaha-aaha."

"You probably want Rodney's tongue chained to your clithood, but with enough reach he can suck your stamen into a hard ball and lap up all your satchel sauce inside your round ripe ratchet."

"Aaha-aaha."

"Your wish is granted."

Babs hears Rodney gag as Game Mistress yanks his tongue forward and secures it to the stainless adorning Steph's sex.

Babs does not see Game Mistress wave the Three cocksucking Pushers, who comprised the table, back to their positions supporting the Wheel, and for the others to cease masturbating.

Nor does Babs witness China Doll collect all the hanging lube, vanish the Tray of piercing supplies, and install a bidirectional rectal feeding/enema system deep into Steph's anus, and feed her stern tube some thick gruel diluted with soap flakes.

Rodney already enjoys total rectal violation. And certainly also William, last seen dispatched toward the Dungeon, possibly already with his foreskin hanging from a nose ring and testicles in a vice.

Babs has heard a certain kind of moan that accompanied Steph's rectal flooding. And again she correctly conjects, *both rectums also possessed. I know, Gamers put a Snake up my butt, and I know next time I have to beg for a Python or Boa Constrictor or the Centipede. Or whatever they want inside of me, that's what I want. I've heard that Slavesex must sometimes harbor nests of asps in their cavities. I will do anything to avoid that.*

BB does hear Game Mistress's final instructions to the Wheel Pushers, "Roll these two Whores over to Flesh Ranch, transfer the Wheel to the Ranch Hands at the Main Gate, then hold hands together into a circle so all your dicks are pointing outward, and comport yourselves back to the Peacock House, form a Lineup in the Backyard, masturbate, and beg to Pledge a Term all over again. But save your pops.

"I'm advised a pair of femdoms will take over as House co-Monitors, and that they plan on turning you into sissy boys. Lipstick, blush, mascara, eye liner, nail and toe polish, shaven completely, permed hair. You don't deserve it, but it's what they want, you're convenient, and your mouths suck."

Babs hears the Wheel creek into motion and GM speak, "Goodbye, Whores. Beg Pimp Cowboy to pimp you out to a facial abuse website. You'll be fed breakfast, double penetrated and face-fucked until you puke it all out, get fed each other's puke, double penetrated again, and then face-fucked until you upchuck all over each other, And then things will really get scary.

"Goodbye Wheel Pushers. Enjoy blowing, butt-licking, and getting beaten next Term."

Steph loses her head during the head-over-heels rotations; Rodney appreciate being fastened tightly to the Wheel as it goes round and round. His balls hurt, his pierced penis hurts, his tongue hurts, his welts hurt.

The Plaster Mummy is barcoded and switched from a siding to a main line, and not seen again.

§ Babs Confronts Gimbled It: Midnight Ravage

Game Mistress reappear in Babs' field of view. The Pogo has relaxed its pace, but not so much that Babs can hold still.

"If you're a Dong and Dirty Whore after Midnight you shouldn't need to be a bound and gagged Lockdown Whore, right?"

Don't need gagged and bound. "Aaha-aaha.

Babs feels hands on the Pogo; it's China Doll gentling it down and out of her body. BB tries to widen her spread knees and lower her bucket, but her knees are already spread wide and there is no "lower to go."

The Pogo is a stimulus BB doesn't want to lose and the feeling of it inside her stays with her after its extraction. Babs feels the armbinder being unfastened, loosened, gone. BB wiggles her fingers but keeps her arms crossed behind her back; her hands and hips still sticky with goo. BB's face is sticky too, goo even sticks to the remains of one eyelash, suspended above one eyelid.

"A good Whore knows to keep her mouth closed unless she is spoken too. Are you a good Whore?"

Babs breaths easier now. "Aaha-aaha."

Bondo Bangho feels China Doll's hand unbuckle the straps holding the O-Ring tight behind her teeth, feels China Doll's able hands slide forward until they encounter the ring inside the widely-spread teeth, feels her able hands exert purchase on the Ring, gently tilt it back into her mouth, and then guide it carefully out between still-parted teeth.

China Doll gently massages the sides of BB's cheeks and jaw, and Babs start to feel sensation return. China Doll gives her a most gentle and loving kiss, and a grace upon BB's navel art which comforts Babs and helps bond her to this magnificent Slavesex.

It is a goodbye for now, but not a goodbye forever, and China Doll departs.

Game Mistress address the now totally unencumbered, bare-bald-naked, kneeling-spread Lobelia. "A perfect Whore masturbates when she is told, stays horny all the time, and must beg in the most vulgar and wanton manner to ravish any cock, and the body attached to it. Are you a good Whore?"

Yes! "Aaha-aaha!" *I want to climb all over Gimbled It and fuck. And everywhere I fuck It's dick, purple stain will mark my naked body. I need to be branded.*

"Tell me what you are. Answer me with words."

Babs blinks, and speaks her first words, "Mistress, I am a Dong and Dirty Whore, Mistress."

"Fixate your eyes upon It's cock and masturbate. Use one hand on your burse and buzzer, and use the other hand to swab goo onto your crescents d'areolage. Don't stop. Work up a pant for us. Keep your bone socket wet and dripping burgoo. Keep your bdellium standing out of its hood, and make sure your areolas stay bubbled up and your bullets stay hard. Your Clock has been started! And it is counting down from 100 to Midnight. Beg it down, Whore. Impress me. At Midnight, Gimbled It is yours!

Babs obeys, and begins masturbating a very sensitive set of intimate parts. It doesn't take much to pop both nipples up.

Babs chants. "One hundred, I'm a Dong and Dirty Watersports Goo Whore. I want It's cock to fuck my every hole. Fuck my cocksucking mouth, fuck my bangbox, fuck my bugger hole. Facial me, creampie me, I swallow, I felch, I'm an A2M, A2OPM total everything Whore."

Babs masturbates.

"Ninety-nine, I'm a Dong and Dirty Watersports Goo Whore. I want It's cock to fuck my every hole. Fuck my cocksucking mouth, fuck my bangbox, fuck my bugger hole. Facial me, creampie me, I swallow, I felch, I'm an A2M, A2OPM total everything Whore."

Babs masturbates.

"Ninety-eight, I'm a Dong and Dirty Watersports Goo Whore…."

Game Mistress pronounces. "At Midnight I will return to watch you ravish It. And extract It's loads inside your goo-gobbling mouth, your breached barrel, and your soon-to-be gaping bunghole cum repository.

"Come Midnight for you, Whore, and the end of the Term."

V-15 The Cosmos no More: Midnight & the End of Term

§ Our Cosmos Cease to Exist: The End of the Term

And so our story about the Cosmos House and its eight Cosmos comes to an end with the end of a Term. The clock strikes Midnight and the Gamers have the satisfaction to know that each of their former Cosmos arrives at their destinations safely. And that is a good thing for our four Strippers, three Whores and one Slavesex. Some are ready to rock 'n' roll, some still need their bodies tagged. Some of them will play the line, some will hedge their bets, and some will go for broke. Some of them will excel, some of them will act stupidly, and all of them shall be jostled with luck – good, bad and otherwise. May they be happy, and healthy, and learned in the arts of love. May the prudes be taught to cum uncontrollably, and may the horny ones be driven mad with desire.

Kundalini blesses the Cosmos, and blesses them with the pleasures of love.

Reference Materials

Description of the Various References Materials

§ Introduction

Gamers who have followed the Cosmos throughout *The Arrivals, The Runup, The Beach Day, The Runout,* and now *The Play Party* may draw upon the following Front Materials and Appendix to refresh their histories. These pages include Floor Plans, Garment and Prop inventories, a Glossary, Manifests, and an Index. Together these provide rich entry points into the Cosmos Saga.

§ Cosmos Front Pages: Preface, Table of Contents, Plans

This section details the various front materials that are part of *The Cosmos Book V: The Play Party.*
The **Preface** contains a story from the *1001 Arabian Nights*.
The **Table of Contents** includes the Chapters, as well as the Scenes (§). Scene names are frequently in "GamerName & GamerName: Actions that Take Place" format.
Gamers are reminded that **Plans & Elevations** at the front of the Book detail the Cosmos House, including the surrounding Front and Backyards and Doors, the Cosmos House's first and second floors, and reaching further away, a floor plan of the Nugget.
The **Chant and Dialog** are a discourse between Game Mistress and Slavesex China Doll.

§ Cosmos Back Pages: The Appendices

Appendices are located near the back of the book, following this last Chapter and before the Index. They include:
The Frame of the Eight Castes compares each Caste versus its properties (e.g., their residence, forms of address, the number of Garments, task responsibilities, and their Caste Options.

The Rules of Engagement by Caste detail what contact including sexual contact, is permitted by members of the same and/or different Castes.

The List of Capital & Lower Case Words details words that are capitalized; these include all of the Players, Props, Locations, and certain Events. All Capital Words are also Indexed. Many specialized words, words with precise meanings, are not capitalized. These include most Obeisances (e.g., "coitus" or "lapdancing"), Exposures (e.g., "areolage" or "hairage"), and Garments ("bra" and "panties."). Many of these lower case words are also found in the Index, but unlike Capital Words, they are not mandated to be there.

The Location List provides a hierarchical list of all Locations with capital letters. All Locations are also found in the Index in the form *Location: GamerName* and *GamerName: Location.* However because *The Play Party* occurs at a single Location, Locations are not cross referenced.

The Props List provides a list of all Props with capital letters, as well as a few objects included in the Index that do not have capital letters. Props starting with capital letters are bidirectionally indexed, whereas props that are lowercase are only indexed *GamerName: prop.* Some of the motive behind this schema is that Props are shared by Gamers; Gamers do not possess Props. A separate section of Prop histories is found following the Manifests.

The Event and Time List provides a list of all Events and time-related words with capital letters. All of these are indexed thus: *Event: GamerName.* This list also includes a few specialty words, including 'Clock,' which tracks the morning and afternoon action of *the Days*, and the word 'Midnight,' which defines the end of the last Day of the Term, Day 28 (D28). Because the Clock is stopped for the Cosmos Lobelia during *The Runout*, Days are now identified as Day LD1 through Day LD3, whereas other Players, for whom Midnight has passed and the Clock is still running, they are on Day ND1 through Day ND3. In book V, The Play Party, still with the Clock stopped, the Cosmos Lobelia are timestamped LD4 (Introduction), LD5 (Penny & Coco), LD6 (Robyn, Molly), LD7 (Beka & Elle & It), LD8 (Tiffany & Kimju), and LD9 (only Babs & Steph). All other Players, with Clocks running, are timestamped ND4 through ND9 and any subsequent times.

A List of Obeisance and Opts identifies related Capital Words but does not list individual Obeisance; a complete list is found in Index: Obeisance.

A List of Exposure Codes identifies how to read the six letter codes for what skin a Player exposes. These codes are limited to use in the Manifests.

The List of Positions and Hand Signs recommends a minimum visual vocabulary that every Cosmos should know. Signs which are commands are indexed under *GamerName1: GamerName2: orders:* and the opposite, *GamerName2: GamerName1: orders:* syntax.

An Inventory of Chants (lest Gamers need reference for training) is also found in the Appendix.

A Summary of Garment Exchanges logs all costume exchanges between individual Cosmos costumes during *The Arrivals* (D01-D14), *The Runup* (D15-D27), *The Beach Day* (D28), *The Runout* (LD1/ND1-LD3/ND3), and *The Play Party* (LD4/ND4-LD9/ND9), although there are no exchanges during *The Play Party* because all Cosmos are always naked.

Infrequently Asked Questions provides answers to questions you probably don't need to ask unless you are playing the Game.

§ Cosmos Back Pages: The Manifests

The Manifests detail the Garments, Exposures, Obeisances, and Props associated with each Cosmos (and each other Player) throughout the narrative, from Day 1 through the end of the Term.

The first two Cosmos volumes included separate Manifests for opening positions and the changing position. This volume (and since Volume III) consolidates them into a single Manifest that contains much of the same pattern of information but in a single narrative that begins with each Cosmos' opening position and continues onward with any changes that occur.

Opening positions are retained, if only because they are useful entering one of the Books, but they are inline.

Because the Manifests bear witness to different points in time the Manifests detail positions as well as directionality. Certainly, on the morning of this *The Play Party,* Kundalini and Karma possess momentum, forces already in motion, the flow of the Game. Physics determines that if you snapshot the Garment positions perfectly you can't know anything about their directionality, whether they are more seductive or more sedate. If you monitor their blur, then you know less about their identity details, but more about where they are heading. The Manifest data tries to be revealing in both attributes of momentum.

Following the Manifests of the Players, a short new section is included with recounts histories several significant Props.

All of the Gamers, Garments, Exposures, Obeisances, and Props changes documented in the Manifest are found in the Index also, as is the media they fabricate, especially if Automatron digests it and feeds the Prefecture.

§ Cosmos Back Pages: The Glossary

A Glossary defines many Capital Words, as well as some of the specialized language used throughout. Most of these Glossary terms are also Indexed, and the Glossary will occasionally provide examples that contain italics for where a Cosmos name would go (e.g., *GamerName*: body & exposures: figure). Note that Lady Part Words are not included in the Glossary nor the Index.

§ Cosmos Back Pages: The Index

Finally, an Index provides ways for Gamers to search out individual Cosmos, Locations, Props, Obeisance, and Exposures (body parts), as well as other themes germane to our Game of Karma and Kundalini forces. Individual plot lines, and the back and forth dynamic between Cosmos may also be indexed.

§ Acknowledgments

The Professor wishes to thank a small cadre of readers and editors for their invaluable contributions to this series. These include Louis Peluso, whose insight into character relationships and wordplay has been unrivaled; Riley MacLeod, whose editorial reviews contributed much to strengthening the plot, lightening the touch; and finally the management and line editing staff at All Ivy Writing Services, who provided consultation and clarity early in this project, Maria Garcia for help in preparing the Index, and Samantha Acquaviva, for her insightful corrections of the manuscript.

Appendices

The Frame of Eight Castes

Caste	Residence	Proper Address	Garment Count	Tasks, Requirements, Restrictions	Movement Potential
Game Mistress / Master	Mansion	Mistress Master	5	Owns Slavesex, manages Madams	Hover, Opt Slavesex
Madam Pimp	Whorehouse (e.g., Flesh Ranch)	Madam Sir	4	Leases Whores, manages MomCaps	Hover, Opt Up, Opt Down
MomCap DadCap	Strip club (e.g., the Nugget)	House Mom, el Capitan	3	Bosses Strippers, manages Monitors	Hover, Opt Up, Opt Down
Monitor	House (e.g., Cosmos House)	Ma'am Mister	2	Manages Pledge	Hover, Opt Up, Opt Down
Pledge	House (e.g., Cosmos House)	Pledge	0, 1, or 2 (total 8 in House)	Beg pink, cream, climax, solo toys, lesbian acts, share Double Dong	Opt Up, Opt Down
Stripper	Strip Club (e.g., the Nugget)	Stripper	0	Nude dancing, lapdancing, solo toys, pinking, cream, climax, ALL sex acts forbidden, Double Dong forbidden	Opt Up, Opt Down
Whore	Whorehouse (e.g., Flesh Ranch)	Whore	0	All Pledge tasks, all Stripper tasks, all sex acts, Double Dong	Hover, Opt Up, Opt Down
Slavesex	Dungeon	Slave, Slavesex	0	All Pledge, Stripper, and Whore tasks, plus bondage and pain	Hover, Opt Up

Rules of Engagement by Caste

Inner-contact means within a Caste, e.g., Pledge-to-Pledge.
Fondling is defined as physical contact outside of one's Caste.
Sex is defined as lesbian, homosexual, or heterosexual genital-genital contact.
Bondage is defined as restraint, possibly coupled with physical punishment (*Discipline*).

Pledge: lesbian-contact allowed, fondling forbidden, sex forbidden, bondage forbidden.
Strippers: lesbian-contact forbidden, fondling allowed, sex forbidden, bondage forbidden.
Whores: lesbian-contact allowed, fondling allowed, sex allowed, bondage forbidden.
Slavesex: lesbian-contact allowed, fondling allowed, sex allowed, bondage allowed.

Capital & Lower Case Words

Capital Words are used in the Cosmos to denote a series of proper nouns relevant to the Game. A comprehensive list of them will be found in the following four sections, which detail capital words for Gamers, Locations, Props, and Events. Also detailed are other classes of words that tend to not be capitalized (e.g., individual exposures such as 'areolage' or 'hairage')

§ Players & Others List

All the following "who's" deserve capitals:

Names of Gamers / Players
Names of Houses, e.g., Cosmos House, Cosmos
Madam & Pimp, Game Master or Mistress, GM
Monitor, House Mom el Capitan a.k.a. MomCap
Pledge, Stripper, Whore, Slavesex
Roommate, Roommates
Crowd
Gamer(s)
Player(s) appears in the Virtual World
Prefecture
Revelers
Automatron
Kundalini
Drone Cam and Cams in general
You, you are among the Prefecture

§ Locations List

Cosmos House
  Downstairs
    Kitchen
      Tiffany Porn Star Calendar
      Screen
    Dining Room
      Dining Room Pictures
      Screen
    Parlor
      Washroom
    Living Room
      Screen
  Upstairs
    Bunkroom
      Three bunks over three bunks
      Minxy Mirror / Screen
    Bathroom / optional Pee Cam
    Bedroom
      Desktop
      Bunk over floor
      Private bathroom
  Backyard
    Bell
    Doghouse
    Garage
    Mudpit
    Post Henge
  Transitions
    Front Door & Porch
    Back Door & Landing
  Cams
    Front Door Drone Cam
    Back Door Drone Cam
    Bathroom, a.k.a. Pee-Cam
School
  Quad
  Library
  Lecture Hall
  Laboratory
  Medical Room
  Gymnasium
  Amphitheater
Village
  Beauty Salon
  Figure Drawing Studio
  Bachelor Party Restaurant
Nugget
  Stage
  Dressing Room
  Camera Lounge
  Champagne Room
  Inner Sanctuary
Mansion
Meatpacking Plant
Jail

Not Capitals
  alley (behind the Cosmos House Backyard)
  flagpole, stocks, hitching post (on the Quad)

§ Props List

See Index. Prop: *PropName* for more complete list. Props with uppercase follow

Alabaster Flask
Anal Intruder
Ass Hook
Cart (w/Stroking Rod, Drildo)
Cath
Centipede
Cravat (something to sit in)
Crawlers
Dice (two different colors, not seen during *Runup*)
Dining Room Pictures (not seen but alluded to)
Double Dong
Double Penetrator (DP) Ben Wa-Balls & Procto
Drildo
Earpods
Eyepods
Glass Bull
Goad (*see* Swagger Goad)
Makeup Case
Monkey Fist
Measuring Cup & Logging Chart (left behind)
Measurement Nudes (*see* media)
Pear
Pink Pages (*see* media)

Pogo (shared by several Cosmos)
Porn Star Calendar
Prod (tool of the Eye, not seen at *Play Party)*
Shaving Kit (scissors, razor soap) in two pieces
Snake
Speculum
Stims
Stroker Rod
Swagger Goad (tool of Game Mistress)
Watering Can (not seen at The Play Party)
Wheel

§ Events & Time Words List

Greatest House Roar (at Peacock House D18)
Mansion Open House (D27)
Day
Term
Clock
Midnight

§ Obeisance and Opts List

The following words are capitalized in the Cosmos and may be found in the index:

Option, Options, Opt Up, Opt Down,
Opt Strip, Opt Monitor, Double Opt Up, etc.
ALL of the above with hyphen, e.g., Opt-Up
Garment
Obeisance
Exposure
Redacted
Charm
Duel
Fate
Karma

See Index Obeisance: *ObeisanceName* for full list of Obeisances. These include solo body activities (e.g., pinking, streaking), as well as activities performed by couples and groups (e.g., handjob, coitus). Most Obeisances are not capitalized), but two are:

Pee-Cam
Piss Mouth

Further definition of an Obeisance is found in the Index Introduction.

Exposure & Exposure Codes

A list of Exposures is incorporated into the list of "body & exposures" found in the Index and not duplicated here. Tactically, this grouping is indexed for each Cosmos Player (e.g., "Janet, body & exposures, hairage)." No exposures are capitalized (e.g., hairage, navelage). By definition an Exposure is a part of the body that is partly, fleetingly, or ongoingly exposed. See a more comprehensive list in the Index.

Exposure codes are a shorthand for what parts of a body are exposed. They are used in the Manifests, but nowhere else. Here is their meaning:

T = Top (cleavage)
M = Midriff
L = legs
B = breasts
A = ass
P = pubis
C = male chest

The order is always in sequence, TMLBAP for a nude female, or TMLCAP for a nude male. For example, TML is the exposure produced by a bikini, or a bra and panties. L usually flags as above the knee. Obviously, the world is more complicated, so this is a first approximation.

The N- code is the inches of waistline below the navel.

Exposures relate to flashings, a word used herein which indicates that an Exposure is intermittent and is not logged as an Exposure Code, which implies some permanence.

Many of these tactical exposures have Glossary definitions, Cleavage is the partial exposure of breasts, nippage is flashing of nipples, hairage is the exposure of pubic hair, posterior rugage (or just rugage) is the exposure of butt crack, pubage is the exposure of the pubis, slitage advances the top of a (shaven) vulva, lipage leaks out the sides of a thong, and buttage is the exposure of the butt cheeks. All these terms and many more are found in the Glossary.

Standard Positions & Style

Positions are frequently described by a triad in the following format: bodyPosition-legPosition-armPosition. An example is stand-spread-surrender, which defines an upright standing position, legs wide apart and feet firmly balancing the body, and the fingers clasped together behind the back of the head.

The positions are built out of following three clusters of elements, breaking the rules sometimes when a situation yields itself to a varied description.

§ Standard Body Postures

Stand
Sit
Kneel
Belly, also Prone
Back

§ Standard Leg Positions

Crossed (forbidden for Pledge)
Touching (forbidden by Cosmos House Rule)
Ajar (Apart)
Open
Spread

§ Standard Arm Positions

Surrender > Hands behind head
Present > Wrists crossed behind back
Attention > Hands at sides
Horizontal > Held wide away, horizontal
Veed > Hands held away & upward
Handbra > Hands crossing breasts (3 ways)

§ Hand Signs for Legs

Legs Crossed > Cross fingers
Legs Together (Touching) > Close fingers
Legs Apart (No touching) > Two fingers open
Legs Open > Two fingers midway
Legs Spread > Two fingers held wide
Kneel > two fingers bend at knuckle

§ Hand Signs for Movements

Walk > two fingers walking
Crawl > palm rubbing horizontal
Grovel > palm up with active fingers
Stop > steady hand
At ease > circle in the air and drop

§ Signs for Mouth & Eyes

Oval mouth > Thumb and 2nd finger
Close eyes > Thumb and 2 fingers together
Open eyes > Double snap
Present tongue > Two adjacent fingers extended
Lick tongue around mouth > circle in air w/finger

§ Hand Signs for Arousal

Leanover > Two fingers waving downward
Nipple play > Roll thumb & 2nd finger
Pullaside > Thumb & 2 fingers, sweep
Pull pink (butterfly) > Thumb & 2 fingers apart
Clit play > Roll thumb & finger
Finger Fuck > Wiggle middle finger
Rub Masturbation > Rub thumb atop 1st knuckle

Inventory of Chants

§ Gamer Chants

In the Game stay the Game.
What you beg you beg forever.
Once a Cath, anytime a Cath

§ Pledge Chants

Hot hot hot. Titters and twat. 98.6 in my anus.
Please let me Pledge naked and cum be a Stripper next Term.
Please let me Pledge naked and cum be a Stripper next Term. Titty titty, clitty clitty, hole mouth.
Please let me shave bare bald naked, stay pink wet ready, eat pussy & juice the Dong & cum be a Stripper next Term.
I love you, Post. Hug 'n' kiss. Rub my tits. Masturbate.
Please let me shave bare, bald, and naked.
I'm pink wet and ready to Strip. Titty titty. Clitty clitty. Hole mouth.

§ Stripper Chants

Please let me pullaside, pink, and finger my holes.
Please keep me pink-wet-and-ready. I'll cum on cue.
Please let us share the Double Dong and become Whores next Term.

§ Whore Chants

I've done everything explicit, all holes, all sexes!
I'm a cocksucking, cunt fucking, ass-to-mouth cum-dump Whore.

Garments

§ Garment Inventory

A Garment inventory is not included in these Appendices, however all Garments are indexed at Garments: *garmentName*, and by individual Cosmos, *GamerName:* Garments: *garmentName*. The number of Garments is finite, and the index may contain Garments which do not appear.

§ Exchange Equations

< indicates single costume trade to the party on the left.
> indicates single costume trade to the party on the right.
<> suggests an exchange (balanced, but not necessarily equal in terms of exposures).
<< >> indicates two pieces (more nuance).
> Trash implies destruction of Garment

§ The Garment Exchanges

From *Book I: The Arrivals:*

Molly > Steph. Topless Molly gives Steph her panties, which Steph dons under minidress.
Steph > Molly. Steph gives naked Molly panties back and wears minidress sanpan.
Tiffany <> Kimju. Voluntarily nude Tiffany borrows Kimju's tanga during Post Henge; returns them afterwards.

From *Book II: The Runup:*

Beka <> Elle. Flip-Flop. Beka's croptop & miniskirt are exchanged for Elle's halter & shorts. Beka now titter and hairage; Elle titter and vagflash (Nugget D20).
Janet <> Louise. Louise strips off maillot and bandeau, which Janet acquires in exchange for Spiderweb Bikini (Nugget D20)
Steph > Molly. Steph, wearing an undershirt, forfeits it to Molly at Greatest House Roar. Molly dons over panties. Steph shall remain naked (Peacock House D22).
Molly > Babs. Molly, wearing undershirt and panties gives Babs her undershirt in exchange for the Watering Can; when Babs dons the undershirt it transforms to a minidress, which Babs now wears over her bra and nombril Black Bikini; Molly again topless with panties (Bedroom D22).

Tiffany <> Elle. Tiffany, wearing a transparent croptop & slacks, and Elle, who wears a croptop and minidress, trade the slacks for the minidress. When Tiffany dons the minidress it becomes transparent. The skintight slacks on Elle guarantee hairage, rugage, and cameltoe (Bunkroom D23).
Tiffany > Robyn. Tiffany, wearing a transparent croptop & miniskirt, gives both to Robyn, who dons them overtop her strapped maillot. This leaves Tiffany naked (Nugget D23).
Kimju <> Beka. Beautician gives Beka's shorts to topless Kimju, and Kimju's g-string to haltered Beka. (Beauty Salon D24)
Beka > Tiffany. Babs orders Beka loan halter to naked Tiffany, leaving Beka topless, and Tiffany bottomless. Tiffany returns wearing a bra bottomless instead of the halter (Backyard D25)
Elle > Steph. Babs orders Elle give croptop to Steph, leaving Elle topless w/miniskirt sanpan; Robyn hacks the croptop to a bib rendering Steph bib bottomless (Backyard D25). The bib will become a collar.
Tiffany > Kimju. Tiffany gives her what used to be Beka's halter to Kimju as a bra, leaving Tiffany naked; Kimju now wears the bra & shorts (Bunkroom D25).
Elle > Steph. Topless Elle forfeits her slacks to Steph; Elle is now nude, Steph wears the collar & slacks, which become crotchless (Kitchen D27).

From *Book III: The Beach Day:*

Beka <> Beka. Beka exchanges micro g-string for transparent nano g-string, soon worn inside anus (Mudpit AM D28).
Robyn <> Steph. Robyn demands that Steph, wearing an opaque short sleeve croptop, exchange it for her transparent long sleeve. They swap, however the transparency sticks to Robyn and the opacity to Steph. (Bathroom AM D28).
Robyn > Tiffany. Robyn gives transparent croptop & miniskirt to Tiffany, leaving Robyn w/one Garment, Tiffany w/two Garments (Beach D28). Tiffany > Elle. Tiffany gives transparent croptop to nude Elle; Elle now dons transparent croptop bottomless, Tiffany now topless and transparent miniskirt. (Mudpit PM D28)

From Book IV: The Runout:

Babs > Trash. Forfeits cutout minidress, bra, panties, becomes nude.
Tiffany > Trash. Is topless, forfeits transparent miniskirt, becomes nude.
Kimju > Trash. Abandons bra & jean shorts, runout nude.

Robyn > Trash. Forfeits maillot cutout, arrives nude.

Molly > Trash. Forfeits panties, becomes nude.

Steph > Trash. Abandons croptop & slacks, runout nude.

Beka > Trash. Forfeits micro g-string worn around neck, becomes nude.

Elle > Trash. Forfeits transparent croptop, becomes nude.

From Book V: Play Party:

There are no Garment exchange among the Cosmos Lobelia because all are naked 24x7.

There is an exchange between Kimju & Tiffany in which Kimju trades an Opt-Whore to Tiffany in exchange for an Opt-Strip to Kimju. The inducements for the trade to be approve include Kimju committing to Stripper Supreme (blowjob, fondle, finger, handjob), and Tiffany committing to Dong & Dirty Whore (oral, coital, anal, A2M, A2OPM, etc.).

Infrequently Asked Questions

Where is the School? Cyberspace? Metaverse? Heaven? Purgatory? Earth?

What is the purpose of the School? To gain knowledge, to learn about oneself, to discover Kundalini, to explore power exchange, to achieve harmony with romance, power, and suffering.

What are the Rules of the Game? There are many of them, some secret. Start your search in the Index under Game Rules. But just remember, when you break a Rule you didn't expect, you're guilty.

What are some of the Games? The Roommate Games began during *The Runup,* and they pit pairs of Roommates Together against another pair of Roommates Together; or they pit Roommates against each other, Roommates Apart. Other Games alluded to include: Dice Games (not witnessed during *The Runout*), the Mudwrestling Contest (which resonates during *The Runout*), The Greatest House Roar, and the Duel, which, during *The Runup*, let Steph defeat Elle without even a fight.

Robyn's escape stresses the Cosmos, some of whom reveal secrets that tumble further revelations.

Is Kundalini real? Gods are expressions of Forces in Nature. The Forces of Nature give rise to existence, to space and time and momentum, and the structures the Natural Forces forge throughout the Universe, from the subatomic to planets, and galaxies to Gamers. So of course Kundalini is real, it is a force of sexual selection, and the Nature of our DNA to propagate and build symbiotic environments. Kundalini works differently in different species. Dragonflies mate while flying in the air, one of the couple flies upside-down, and the lovers can coital for long periods. Trees scatter nuts that can nurture in soil and reproduce. (Trees extract solar energy and deploy it along with building materials from the soil to grow forests, and combat with other trees for a place on earth. They migrate slowly but they do migrate.)

Is Karma real? Expressions of good and ill will, both far and near, require memories, human, as well as the animals and plants around us. And certainly even rocks keep themselves in their place. Our brains and our neurological memory and processing units, although biological in construction, are indeed the manifestation of energy flowing through structures built of matter. So Karma has a physical presence.

Which Pledge have danced at the Nugget in the past? Cosmos Tiffany (two Terms ago), Kimju and Molly (last Term); Corvette Monitor Janet (two Terms ago), and Corvette Pledge Ginny and Lee (last Term).

Which Pledge were Monitors last Term? At the Cosmos House, only Steph is a fallen Monitor. At the Corvette House, both Darleen and Louise were Monitors last Term (of different Houses).

What is navelage? Areolage? Each 'age' corresponds to an exposure of a body part, like cleavage, leggage, bellage, buttage, areolage, hairage, pubage, slitage, lipage. Index directs you to *GamerName:* body & exposures: *-age.* There is a long list at "body & exposures" in the Index.

What are the sizes of halters? Assume triangle halter, the area of a triangle is equal to one-half the width times the height (Area = ½ width x height).

Mini soutien-gorge: two triangles plus string 2.83 x 2.83 inches = 4 square inches each.

Micro soutien-gorge: two triangles plus string 2 x 2 inches = 2 square inches each.

Nano soutien-gorge: two triangles plus string 1.41 x 1.42 inches = 1 square inch each, or pasties 1 square inch each.

Pico soutien-gorge: neck and torso strings to tie together using knots. Can be tied as halter or bra, but is never more than the torso string (bow tied front or back) and the two strings ties to it, and which either rise upward to tie behind the neck, or ride over the shoulders to tie back again to the string around the torso.

What are the sizes of G-strings? A g-string always has three edges: a waistline, and two leglines that expose the buttocks arising up the posterior rugage before parting in order to cross the hip, descend down the inguinal to meet in the crotch again.

Table of sizes available to the Cosmos and other Pledge follows. (Similar sizes may also be applied to tanga. In crochet bikinis, sizes may also be by stitch counts.)

The area of a triangle is equal to one-half the width times the height (Area = ½ width x height).

Mini g-string: 2.83 x 2.83 inches = 4 square inches.

Micro g-string: 2 x 2 inches = 2 square inches.

Nano g-string: 1.41 x 1.42 inches = 1 square inch.

Pico g-string: .22 x .22 inches = ½ square inch (more like one knot near the anus and two cords up across the vestibule and up to both sides of the clit (or parting and riding outside the sex lips, or between the inner and outer), with the three strings joining at the top to a waistband string. The only way for a Pico to get smaller is for the strings to miniaturize, e.g., monofilament fishing line.).

Femto g-string. Similar to a Pico g-string except composed of composed .01 inch monofilament line. It's strong and can dig into the skin.

Atto g-string. Similar to Femto except composed of material smaller than .001 inch, comporting to the body so it leaves no imprint, and is invisible to the eye. Players with at least one Garment and who seek good graces presenting bottomless yet carrying a Garment are encouraged to beg Attos.

How do Gamers acquire piercings & tattoos? Pledge who Opt-Strip earn one tattoo & one piercing. Strippers who Opt-Down and become Whores earn two additional tats and piercings; Whores who become Slavesex earn three additional ink & steel. Thus, ink & steel in a body sometimes provides history, but tattoos can be big or small, and piercings sometimes come in pairs, or quadruples, or sextets.

How do Gamers piercings get stretched? When a Gamer Opts Down to a Caste previously occupied, and marked with a piercing(s) and tattoo(s) these existing piercings and tattoos may be enlarged in gauge, mass, area.

Does a Monitor have special Options? Yes. A Monitor with a third Garment shall Opt Up to MomCap. A Monitor with one Garment shall Pledge next Term. But a Monitor may also elect to retain two Garments and Hover, that is, to be a Monitor again next Term. (Pledge and Strippers cannot Hover and must Opt Up or Opt Down.)

Is Navelage only a Cosmos House Rule? Yes. That is why Monitor Babs and Seven Pledge all comport. The Corvettes have no required navelage. Certain Gamers of higher Caste also bare navel, but explanation is absent.

If Monitor Babs is required to display navelage is MomCap required also? What about Madam Nurse Beautician? What about Game Mistress? If you have to ask these questions your Caste indicates you needn't be supplied with answers.

What about Strippers, Whores, Slavesex? You may ask about them and the answer is simple: navelage is not an option for them. They possess no Garments, so being stark naked qualifies them as navelage 24x7. Qualifies all exposures.

Hovering versus Ops. A hovering is defined as remaining the same Caste next Term as this Term. An Opt implies that choices are limited to moving to an adjacent Caste. Certain Castes may Hover or Opt, certain Castes may only Opt.

Madams and Sirs, MomCaps and DadCaps, and Monitors may choose to Hover or Opt. Pledge must Opt Monitor or Opt Strip, Strippers must Opt Pledge or Opt Whore next Term. Whores may Hover or Opt Strip or Opt Slavesex. Game Masters and Mistresses, and Slavesex, have more complicated Rules.

("Although there are exceptions.")

Does who reports to whom follow the hierarchy of Castes? Sort of, but upper Castes usually have two reports, one immediate and managerial, the other disciplinary. (Only the feminine aspects follow):

Madams (& Slavesex) report to Mistresses.
MomCaps (& Whores) report to Madams.
Monitors (& Strippers) report to MomCaps.
Strippers (& Monitors) report to MomCaps.
Pledge report to Monitors.
Whores (& MomCaps) report to Madams.
Slavesex (& Madams) report to Mistresses.

What are the five cleavages? Exposures of the top of the breasts are cleavage décolletage. Under breast is cleavage neathage. Side is cleavage côté. Middle is cleavage centros, and all around (e.g., w/pasties) is cleavage cleavy. (Don't confuse décolletage, a noun that describes the exposure, and décolleté, the adjective.)

What does it mean to be 'bare bald and naked? 'Bald' is absent hair on the head, 'bare' is absence of pubic hair, and 'naked' equals zero Garments. A BBN Pledge can only Opt Down, and collect tattoos, piercings, and Obeisance.

Are their required readings at School? Yes, the Beauty Books, O, de Sade, John Willy, Eric Stanton, Enig, Insex, 1001 Nights.

Are there great femes in history to study? Certainly. The Queen of Sheba, Cleopatra, Juliette & Justine, Mata Hari, Hedy Lamarr, Marilyn, Madonna, Paris, Jenna.

Must Slavesex aspire to learn about some of the great harems? Indeed, for their studies span the globe and time, from the Grand Seraglio, to those of Tamba of Banaras, Kublai Khan, King Solomon, Harun al-Rashid, Montezuma, and Amenophis III.

Why is this novel indexed? And why not? Study by characters, costumes, bodyparts, Props, locations, events, fetish/Obeisances.

How many Cams are in the Cosmos House? Three. Front Door, Back Door, Bathroom (activated by Pee-Cam Pledge). Monitor controls via Desktop.

Who made the Rule that Pee-Camers can only use the Bathroom naked? MomCap? Monitor Babs? Babs once controlled the Desktop switch that determines which Cams get fed to the Prefecture and recorded for posterity in Automatron. All Cams are active.

That is the difference between Gamers, Players, Automatron, and the Prefecture? Automatron is a giant storage system that keeps data, video & images about the Cosmos. The Prefecture are all the Gamers who watch and follow the events at the Cosmos House and related locations; you too are a Gamer. A Player is Gamer who appears in the Book.

Are Pledge and Strippers allowed to handle semen? Restrictions on the handing of semen, pre-cum, valiva, and urine do not necessarily follow Caste; there are Rules pertaining to lollydors, Collection Dishes, qualifications for Pee Cams and Piss Mouths; gokkun strictly speaking doesn't require cocksucking, it needn't even require physical contact. Goo Gobblers need not be Whores, or even Strippers for that matter. But genital-oral contact is against the Rules for Pledge, and for Strippers, unless they have begged wavers.

Do Slavesex have to volunteer to be Piss Mouths, just like Strippers and Pledge have to? Slavesex don't volunteer, Slavesex just do. Every Slavesex is a Piss Mouth because there is nothing a Slavesex isn't.

Is the penalty for Free-Fucking different for different Castes? Please who Free-Fuck are considered Whore applicants. A Monitor who engages in sex with a Pledge is guilty of a Caste exploitation, and is relegated to Slavesex.

How do I find out more information about the Players and the Game? Consult the Index; the introduction to the Index will help make it valuable to you. Read the Gamers' Reference Materials in the Appendix; you might also want to examine the Manifests, which detail the Garments and activities of the Cosmos throughout the Term (and the Five Volumes). The Glossary may also be useful, as well as the Rules of Engagement by Caste Table.

What's the difference between a Dong and Dirty Whore and a Slavesex? Slavesex are subject to bondage and imprisonment, Whores are not. Whores are not required to do anal, although Dong and Dirty Whores do anal. Slavesex have no sexual restrictions

Do Slavesex need to beg for Caster Oil? No. Whores and Strippers and Pledge must beg for laxatives, diuretics, purgatories, enemas, but Slavesex has no Obeisance to beg away because a Slavesex possesses nothing at all.

Is it true that a Master or Mistresses can become Slavesex? Yes. Masters and Mistresses may hover, so the Caste is sort of Locked in. However, might a Slavesex vacancy occur, one random Master or Mistress is transferred to Slavesex. Total subjugation, inability to not beg Slavesex-for-Life. At the same time, a second Master or Mistress randomly Opts-Down to Madam/Pimp Caste. And two Madams and/or Pimps may become a Master or Mistress. And one

Slavesex becomes a Whore, often begging to be a Whore-for-Life.

The Manifests: Books I-V

Overview, Style, How to Use

§ Overview

These Manifests harbor the Garment Descriptions, Exposures, and Garment Counts of each Cosmos from the beginning of the Term at *The Arrivals,* continuing throughout *The Runup, The Beach Day, The Runout,* and the newly described, *The Play Party.*

These Manifests may be useful to Gamers who wish to recall the status of a Cosmos at a particular point in time or place.

In addition to the Cosmos, these Manifests also detail the Corvettes, Peacocks, certain Nuggets, and certain Madams and Pimps, Game Mistresses, and Slavesex.

The style of these Manifests proscribes one Manifest for each Cosmos, for each Player. The Manifest begins with a physical report of each Player, followed by their opening positions and Garments worn at the beginning of *The Arrivals, The Runup, The Beach Day, The Runout,* and this volume, *The Play Party.*

The Garment exchanges which occur during *The Arrivals* (Days 1-14) are detailed in The Manifests of that book and are recapitulated herein (the Garment Exchange equations also provide this information).

Likewise, the Garment exchanges which occur during *The Runup* (Days 15-27) including the Mansion Open House, are recapitulated herein and also detailed in that Manifest.

Likewise, the Garment exchanges which occur during *The Beach Day* (Day 28) are detailed in that Manifest and are recapitulated herein.

The opening and closing Garment positions during The Runup and this Volume, The Play Party are also found following.

§ Notes on Style & Using

Style Rules do exist for composing this reference, but their rule is not always rigorous. There is an attempt to describe costumes from the outside layer working down layers, and to describe Garments, and the body, from the top to the bottom. The Manifest still includes body measurements and physical descriptions of each Player; Cosmos are fully detailed; others less so.

The Garment and body descriptions may be complemented with: Props, Obeisance (skills and forfeits), body hair and shaving details, Exposures (which parts of the body are visible), as well as the critical Garment Count, which defines Options.

The Manifest contains a condensed review of Garment, including acquisition and loss of Props and Obeisance, body hair styling and loss, and occasional media Events.

If there is no change in the costume then the Garment description will not contain a doff or a don, and Gamers may assume the Garment remained unchanged throughout *The Runup.* Given that most Cosmos spend the Runout naked, they have little Garment variance.

The order of the individual Cosmos Lobelia (and other Houses) remains that of the paired Roommates at the beginning of *The Arrivals,* despite some reshuffling. Babs and Tiffany (D1-D24), Babs and Robyn (D24-D28), Robyn and Kimju, later Tiffany and Kimju, Molly and Steph, and finally newbies Beka and Elle. This is also their alignment in bunks, Lineups, at the Post Henge, in the Amphitheater. This order is consistent through the Manifests.

The status of body hair is logged throughout the Manifests, and it is assumed that all Cosmos expose their navels 24x7. They have no Garments other than the Garments described.

These descriptions sometimes include Exposure Codes (e.g., TML, TMLB); these are described in the Appendix at "Exposures & Codes." Help for the many exposure and teaser terms might be found in the Glossary.

Occasional descriptions in curly brackets "{}" are provided for reference only. It includes information not currently visible to the Cosmos. Examples include physical descriptions of Cosmos body parts where that body part remains covered, secrets withheld from the Cosmos, and changings that are not yet deduced. It is unlikely that any Cosmos retains any hidden anything.

The use of the vertical bar character "|" connotes the end of a Gamer's opening position at the beginning of a *Volume,* and the beginning of changes which transpire thereafter.

Throughout this document the time descriptions "1 Term ago" and "last Term" may be interpolated to mean "1 Term before Term ending at Midnight."

The Cosmos Players Books I-V

§ Cosmos: Garments Props Obeisance Exposures

Monitor Babs (BB, Bikini Babe, Boss Babe, Boss Bitch): Long black hair, olive skin, eyes black as pearls, 5' 11", 140 pounds, 37D-24-36, hourglass figure, full bust, {deep maroon areolas with milk glands and puffy nipples}, cratered remains of a center-knot navel, {full black bush}, full butt, shaven legs and armpits, {deep purple vagina}. No tattoos or bodyart. Monitor of the Cosmos House.

Was newbie Pledge last Term & Roommate with Janet.

This Term Roommate was Tiffany, then Robyn since D24.

At the beginning of *The Arrivals* Babs wears a bra & culotte nombril bikini (the Black Bikini); TML; N-4; cleavage, areolage (crescents d'areolage).

During *The Runup*, she acquires navel cutout minidress (from Molly D22) over bra & nombril. Freedom of silhouette of the dress enables M (cutout navelage), ML, TM, or even TML exposures. Occasional cleavage; upskirt but nombril underneath.

Begins *The Beach Day* wearing cutout strapped summer dress over bra & nombril bikini/lingerie; TM (cutout navelage); cleavage, optional TML, upskirt but nombril underneath. | Carries Makeup Case in shoulder bag.

BB Commences *The Runout* as a Monitor prepared to Opt Up to House Mom el Capitan next Term, in a companionship with fellow Monitor Janet. Cutout strapped summer dress over bra & nombril panties lingerie; TM (cutout navelage); cleavage. | Upon Robyn's disappearance, BB is stripped nude; TML > TMLB > TMLBAP; hairy, spread, pink, asshole. Panty gag taped in; tape blindfold applied. Volunteers Pee-Cam. Handcuffs. Leg irons. Doffs panty gag. Begs to Strip next Term. Creamed, Cammed.

BB forfeits the Makeup Case to Madam Nurse Beautician.

BB is questioned by Madam Inquisitor & Pimp Interrogator and soon finds herself wearing an electrified and computerized speculum Pear dildo, an electrified and computerized hollow buttplug Snake, and electrified and computerized Catheter. A size Large rubber Ball Gag with a variable hole is held in place with a tight head strap and a locking roller buckle that keeps the Gag Ball tightly behind the teeth. Fed aphrodisiac; fondled; creams.

Pierced with 12 gauge nose ring; forced to cream, tiny climax. Eyepods provide blindfolds. Public nudity; nose ring locked to first Henge Post; ponytail secured, spread. Earpods. Restrained hands behind head and behind Post, armpits and legs spread. Shaven bare by Goo Whores Penny and Coco and fed goo-bush while climaxed. Shaven bald except for long braided ponytail with loop end (also by Penny & Coco). Shaven eyebrows, Gentian stained.

Janet tells BB about Whore Fate (courtesy Beka & Steph), suggests BB needs to beg to Whore. Handjob, blowjob Stripper at the Nugget insufficient, goal is Flesh Ranch Whore. Janet finally force-cums BB while Piss-Mouthing her.

Restrained spread eagle and by nose ring. Collects 12 gauge navel ring, navel tattoo. Creams. Pees. Secured to Stool in Amphitheater. Ball gag changed to O-ring gag with tongue clamp. Eyepods and Earpods fade in reality. Witnesses Robyn Restrained. Retains Pear, Snake, Cath. Last presents blind-deaf-mute, bare-topknot-naked, sitting-spread-secured.

More than once BB begs to be a Dong and Dirty Whore and this wish shall be granted.

Babs arrives at *The Play Party* blind-deaf-mute, bare-bald-naked, and suspended from tightly bound breasts from a trolly on a rail above. She is actually suspended from a balance beam with Molly suspended on the other end, also swinging helplessly from her bound breasts). A 12 gauge nose and navel rings offer sturdy support might lead chains need be attached. A filigree of ink around BB's navel is her first ever, and as a Whore BB is entitled to two more. (The ring in the nose doesn't count; it is a Robyn convenience.)

BB's diet includes aphrodisiacs, diuretics, laxatives. Begs enemas, rectal feeding, cybernetic Snakes, anal sex with real dicks, anal creampies, and of course valiva from any vagina and cum from any cock. She continues to beg to be a Pee-Camer, Piss Mouth, Goo Gobbler, and Dong & Dirty Whore, Three Terms.

O-ring gag with tongue clamp, armbinder (behind back), mittens, a spreader bar at the knees, ankles crossed, breasts tightly bound and yes, BB's entire weight hangs from bound boobs.

Spanked and caned by unseen Players have left marks, bruises, welts.

Babs discovers her mittens removed and that she adds handjobs to her repertoire. The ejaculate that she quickly accumulates will eventually get smeared all over her body, and fed to her, reprising her Goo Gobbling at the Amphitheater.

During *The Play Party*, Babs is eventually lowered from her suspension, knees-spread-armbound, and pleads for more humiliation and sexual surrender. The screening of the *Beka & Rodney Fuck Video* confirm Janet's claims to BB, and confirm Babs' commitment to Whoredom.

During *The Play Party* Babs receives sexual conditioning designed to stimulate a quest for arousal, including a prolonged stint impaled on the Pogo. She is still impaled when only she and Steph remain at the Party, and William and Rodney are rolled in.

After the screening of Steph & William's *Sex Video*, Babs entailment to anal was guaranteed. Babs gets surprised when, after Steph's second *Sex Video*, GM escalates BB's Dong & Dirty Whoredom from Three Terms 12x7 to Three Terms 24x7. (BB's peer, another ex-Monitor, William shall be dispatched to Slavesex, and Steph and Rodney shall Opt Whore.)

Following their departures, Babs remaining encumbrances are removed, including the Pogo, armbinder, and O-Ring gag. Babs now has all her limbs free and all her holes empty. A free Whore at ease.

Except. BB's goal in the Game, her desire, is to ravish the purple-stained Gimbled It suspended afront her. BB masturbates as she counts down to Midnight, Gimbled It belongs to her as the Clock strikes Midnight, then BB can consume It's huge erection, collect six loads of cum, two in every hole, and travel to Flesh Ranch with It's stain all over her face and body and inside every hole.

I am Bang Bucks now.

Tiffany Transparent: Longhaired redhead, milk-white skin, blue eyes, 5' 10", 105 pounds, 32A-23-33, flat chest, a deep curvy concave belly, small butt, round carnation-colored areolas with cylindrical nipples. Navel is a vertical slit inside a harder, firmer rim, and with a question-mark dot at the bottom. Thinnish red pubic hair, shaven legs and armpits, burgundy-colored vagina. Three tattoos: {Tattoo of words "Porn Star" on inside of lower lip, reversed so she can read in mirror.} Second, an invisible ultraviolet ink tramp stamp that descends from rugage into her trough and becomes visible as the ink surrounds her anus. Third, deeply set ultraviolet ink tattooed nipples. No piercings, but Eraser Head nipple implants count for three piercings and are linked to Automatron.

Stripper two Terms ago, Porn Whore last Term, and a Double Opt Up to Cosmos Pledge this Term. Roommate was Babs (D01-D23); then Kimju since D24-D28.

Tiffany is the first Pledge to arrive at the Cosmos House at the start of *The Arrivals* (D01). She wears a translucent silk sleeveless croptop and low-rise stretch slacks, | which she will exchange for a clear vinyl long sleeve croptop and miniskirt.

Keeps thighs apart. 1st to beg Opt Strip next Term. 1st Pee-Camer, formerly Piss Mouth. She models topless tanga and begs nude; spreads, pinks; creams, climaxes.

During *The Runup*, Tiffany doffs croptop and miniskirt (gives to Robyn at Nugget) to become nude (D23); TMLBAP; hairy; spreads, pinks, creams. climaxes; pees. Naked 24x7 now. Cunnilingus and shares Double Dong with Steph (Nugget Stage D23); also Kimju, Molly, Steph (again), and Ginny Corvette, where she abandons it. Spreads, pinks, creams at Beautician's; purple dyed hair (D24). 3rd Cosmos to be masturbated to climax (Backyard).

Commences *Beach Day* naked (since D25); TMBAP. Hair on head and pussy dyed purple. | Sits, spreads, pinks, masturbates, creams, chants, and begs Opt-Strip. Made-up and perfumed by Robyn. Oiled, sanded. Shaven bare and bald except for two topknots; spreads, pinks. Dons clear vinyl see-through sleeveless croptop and miniskirt (from Robyn); ML; TMLBAP in see-through. Gives transparent croptop to Elle. (TMLB, TMLBAP in see-through) Fastened by topknot with Molly in the Mudpit, end of Day.

Tiffany begins *The Runout* as a Pee-Camer and Piss Mouth, yet scheduled to Opt Up to Monitor next Term. Has spread, pinked; creamed, cum; donged. Topless and clear vinyl miniskirt; TMLB; TMLBP upskirt, TMLBAP and bare in see-through; bald with two braided pigtail topknots with loops. Oily and sandy and muddy. Fastened by pigtails to Molly in Mudpit using Molly's panties. | Severed pigtails. Stripped nude, TMLBAP; bare, bald, spread, pink. Cloth gag (Babs' bra parts) taped in; handcuffs, asshole, also locked to Henge post. Pees. Inquisition chair in Basement. Acquires switch marks on inner thighs. Begs to Strip next Term. Blindfold, bridle with a hard ball gag, 14-gauge nose ring. Earpods. Nose and wrists secured to Post; legs spread and secured to stakes. Restrained hands behind headfirst behind post, armpits, hands later spread. Steph watches Tiffany acquire 14 gauge navel stud and tadpole tattoo. Secured to Stool in Amphitheater. Bridle gag changed to O-ring gag with tongue clamp. Eyepods and Earpods fade in reality. Witnesses Robyn Restrained. Face to blackness and silence.

Last presents blind-deaf-mute, bare-bald-naked, sitting-spread-secured.

Tiffany is first seen at *The Play Party* in a bow-spread-suck position on the center cock of a Risen Cocks Lineup. She remains bare-bald-naked, elbows and knees on the floor, buttocks held up by an Ass Hook connected to the trolly overhead.

Tiffany remains a Pee-Camer and Piss Mouth, and a recent 14 gauge nose ring, and a navel stud and tadpole tattoo, augment her nipple implants and tattoos, and a tramp stamp which descends to surrounds her anus, and her tattooed inner lip. |

Vision and sound return slowly, eventually Tiffany's O-Ring Gag is removed so she can suck easier, and her pussy is left unfettered, so it may be pinked, fingered, masturbated, and fucked by any and all. A collection Dish below Tiffany's uplifted pelvis collects not just valiva, but endless creampies.

Tiffany's Eyepods and Earpods see and hear what Gamers decide she sees and hears. Sometimes it is a view of *The Play Party*, sometimes it is a view of her cocksucking mouth, sometimes she matches the video with the cock pounding her torrox; disconcerting when Tiffany recognizes herself, disconcerting when the picture follows the sensation of the cock inside.

Tiffany gets slimed, overflows Collection Dish w/creampies.

Following the departure of Beka & Elle, Tiffany is moved to a kneel-spread-armbound position. Tiffany, currently slated to Opt Strip, offers her asshole and Dong & Dirty Whoredom to trade with Kimju, who is slated to Whore. The trade is approved, with adjustments to bodyart and Terms. Tiffany exits to Flesh Ranch, also managing to double her Whore Terms to Six. (Kimju who had begged Double Term Stripping before Opting Whore, may now anticipate Stripping only one Term before she Opts Whore.)

Regarding bodyart, Kimju gets to keep her three tattoos (and projected full body suit), and three piercing, complete with her pending double pierced nipples. Tiffany gets to add an upper inner lip tattoo, a wet pussy monitor, and stims round and about her body.

Robyn Runaway: Big hair streaked blonde, skin that tans easily, green eyes, 5' 6", 108 pounds, 34C-25-34, curvaceous figure, modest butt, rose-colored areolas, outie navel, {trimmed blonde bush}, shaven legs and underarms, {raspberry colored vagina}. No tattoos or bodyart.

Pledge last Term, but Redacted and is Pledge again. Roommate was Kimju (D1-24); Babs since D24.

Begins *Arrivals* (D03) wearing stretch-fabric strapless maillot with navel cutout; TML (M is cutout navelage). | Acquires straps (D07) and maintains throughout *Arrivals*.

During *Runup* dons clear vinyl long sleeve front-button see-through croptop and see-through miniskirt (from Tiffany at Nugget), over strapped maillot cutout (D23); M (skin in cutout); TML in see-through. Carries Shaving Kit from Penny and Coco at Nugget to Cosmos House on behalf of Steph (D23), and gives it to Kimju (D24). Yellow

dyed hair at Beauty Salon (D24); yellow bodypainted at Mermaid Parade also with buttage flashing (TMLB), and maillot straps lost (D25).

Through *Arrivals* and *Runup* Robyn frequently controls the Cosmos Drone Cam.

Begins *Beach Day* wearing clear vinyl long sleeve front-button see-through croptop and see-through miniskirt over stretch-fabric strapless maillot cutout; ML; TML in see-through (M is cutout navelage). Yellow dyed hair. Faded yellow body paint. | Croptop exchanged for sleeveless croptop (from Steph) that becomes see-through. Fleetingly TML. Maillot de roulè tangá; TMLA in see-through and flesh. Then de roulè to topless tanga underneath croptop and miniskirt; TMLBA; N-4 in see-through. Doff croptop and miniskirt (to Tiffany) leaving topless tanga; TMLBA; N-4, rose-colored areolas. Cammed. Then allowed to roll up, TMLA, and roll down the butt resolving to strapless maillot cutout; TML (M is cutout navelage).

Robyn goes missing near Midnight, and so begins *The Runout*. As a result, all other Seven Cosmos, including Monitor Babs are stripped naked, pinked, and secured in Lockdown. Robyn was seen wearing strapless maillot cutout. Capture details redacted, although subsequently Robyn has been secured, stripped nude; TMLBAP; shaven bare and bald, spread, pinked, fingered, and masturbated by men, women, and machines. | Arrives Amphitheater (LD3) blind-deaf-mute, bare-bald-naked, sitting spread secured and affixed to Bondage Cart pushed by Naked Negro. Eyepods, Earpods, Cyber Gag, feeding tube and gas mask. Hands and feet cast in plaster. Electrified and computerized hollow Stroking Rod connected to Cart penetrates rectum. Electrified and computerized stroking Drildo connected to Cart penetrates vagina. AI's embedded everywhere. Pressure sensitive vibrating electrified Catheter with remote valve. Electrodes on neck, belly, armpits, insides of thighs; also electrodes on palms of hands and bottom of feet (inside the plaster), clamps on opposing pussy lips pulling outward expose vestibule and vaginal canal. Crawlers. All controlled by the Cybernetic Control Program, a.k.a. the Cybernetician, which coordinates the many Running Agents, and full duplex with Automatron. Begs Slavesex 6 Terms; 6 piercings; 6 tattoos ("with the first being a full body suit"). Creams, cums, perfumed, auditions Pee-Cam. Confronts Lobelia. Masturbated by strange man. Game Mistress transfers clamps from pussy lips to clamps on nipples with swinging weights. Climaxed while watching Kimju get pierced, Janet and Nuggets observe. Rolled away in Cart, blind-deaf-mute, bare-bald-naked, sitting spread secured and impaled.

Robyn arrives at *The Play Party* encased in a white Plaster Mummy suspended from the trolly above. Slavesex 6 Terms; credit for 6 piercings; 6 tattoos ("with the first being a full body suit"). She is blind-deaf-mute, bare-bald-naked within the plaster; when she arrives only her front torso (breasts, belly, pubis) remain exposed. |

Robyn's bondage totally immobilizes her. Eyepods and Earpods are buried inside the plaster, Robyn's mouth gag extends out through her plaster cast, and a feeding tube and breathing tube vanish into the plaster and through her nose, one to the stomach allowing the Plaster Mummy to be fed or stomach pumped, and the other providing gas to the lungs.

Bags connect to tubing which passes through the plaster to other locations within Robyn's body. Tubing and a bag hanging from the Mummy collect secretions from a vaginal speculum; in reverse, Robyn may be douched. Another tube connects to a catheter which can irrigate as well as drains the Mummy. A third connect to a deep hollow rectal procto, also bi-directional.

All feature variable electricity, vibration, and warmth, bi-directional valves, and many body monitoring functions. Robyn is also blessed an intravenous cannula in a vein to monitor her blood, and a brain scanner imbedded in the paster around her head.

Electrodes on Robyn's neck, belly, armpits, insides of thighs; palms, foot bottoms, opposing pussy lips, clit, and nipples; all monitor and stimulate with electricity, vibration, and temperature.

Much of Robyn's behavior is entrusted to an Artificial Intelligence manifest by the Cybernetic Control Program, a.k.a. the Cybernetician, described in detailed during *The Runout*. Certainly Cybernetician analyzes inputs and behaviors, and might Gamers want to optimize, for example, urine production, or more likely, valiva production, Cybernetician learns from experience.

In a display of possibilities to the other Seven Cosmos Lockdown Lobelia, the Naked Negro returns to ejaculate on Robyn's still bare belly button, seal her up completely in the plaster, and exit. Later the Lobelia witness Robyn get certified as a Piss Mouth.

If and when Gamers decide to crack the Mummy open, they intend to hatch a sex machine.

Kimju Kickshaw: Not quite shoulder-length brunette hair, polyglot mixture of Hispanic, Asian, African, and indigenous Indian, brown eyes, 5' 8", 117 pounds, 35C-24-35, stacked figure, taut butt, beige silver-dollar sized areolas with puckered and knob-like nipples with lines in them. Navel is vertical oval with a custard swirl inside. Shaven armpits and legs, trimmed brunette bush, deeply pigmented inner lips surrounding a rosy pink vagina. 14-gauge clithood ring hidden beneath pubic hair, and an astrological sign tattoo (Pallas) secreted in navel. Was a Stripper & Molly's Nugget Roommate last Term. Recent Roommates include Robyn (D01-D24) and Tiffany (since D24).

Kimju arrives topless with a solid color stretch-fabric tanga; TMLBA, N-1, inguinal; which she continues to wear throughout *The Arrivals*, although sometimes gathered into the crotch, hairage. During *Arrivals* keeps thighs apart, pullaside, naked in Backyard, spreads, masturbates, pinks, creams; 2nd Cosmos to climax.

During *Runup* earns Pee-Camer, Piss Mouth; begs Opt-Strip. Spreads, pinks, creams, climaxes. 3rd Cosmos to beg Pee-Cam (D17), 5th Cosmos to beg Stripper (D20); kisses, mutually masturbates, cunnilingus, creams, borrows and shares Double Dong with Molly to be 2nd Cosmos to climax; TMLBAP; pees. Private Piss Mouth with Molly, tanga reduced to micro g-string (still Nugget D20); TMLBA; N-7; hairage, and sometimes with handbra TMLA. Robyn returns with the Shaving Kit on behalf of Steph, stores it inside Kimju (D23) who gives it to Beka (D25). Shares Double Dong with Tiffany, and acquires Piss Mouth. Temporarily naked, spreads, pinks, creams at Beautician's; orange dyed head and pussy hair. G-string exchanged (with Beka) for ripped shorts, still always worn topless (D23); TMLB; hairage, buttage. Followed by acquisition of Beka's halter turned into a tattered bra, TML, cleavage, ectaras, but in fact the first time that Kimju has covered her breasts since she arrived (D24). Orange body paint with heavy grease (Mermaid Parade D25). She uses both Garments as a pillow at night, leaving her to sleep naked but retain her Garment Count (2), which ensures her Opt Monitor next Term.

Kimju continues to wear the bra and shorts, and by *The Beach Day*, they have disintegrated to TMLA, cleavage, full buttage, flashing hairage, TMLAP, flashing TMLBA, TMLBAP; N-4; Orange dyed hair. Faded orange bodypaint and Vaseline remnants. Pee-Camer, Piss Mouth. |

During the *Beach Day*, and largely upon Robyn's orders, Kimju titters and hangs boobage for the Cams, spreads and pinks, makes cream, shows off her 14-gauge clithood ring, displays her asshole, masturbates, finger-fucks, and climaxes. However, she retains both the hair on her head and her pubes.

Kimju transfers her Piss Mouth to Beka.

And the astrological sign (asteroid Pallas) remains secreted in her navel. | On the morning of Robyn's disappearance Kimju, scheduled to Opt

Monitor next Term, is run out of the Cosmos House naked and joins the Lineup in the Backyard; TMLBAP; spread, pink; asshole. Kotex gag taped in; eyes taped shut; handcuffs. Dons legirons. Inquisition chair. Doffs panty gag and blindfold. Confesses to ignoring Robyn's absence. Begs double tongue piercings and eventually begs Whore. Begs three tats and three piercings, all doubles, all double in size and diameter. Begs three Terms Whore. Awarded 12-gauge nose stud through center of her nose (during interrogation) and soon to extended through both sides of the nose to support U-bolt. Dons large hole gag and blindfold. Returns to Post Henge, and pees (on Babs, unbeknownst to both). Public nudity handcuffs and nose ring locked to a ring in a Henge Post and impaled upon hollow tubing up her rectum, the Centipede, which seems able to crawl deeper, stimulate up and down its body, expand and contract, squirm. Imagines fed aphrodisiac. Acquires electronic Catheter with wireless valve. Eyepods. Earpods. Enema. Hairy, spread, pink; shaven bare and bald; cream, cums. Restrained hands behind head and behind Post and spread. Acquires Pogo from Steph. Circular tattoo in and around belly button, then 12-gauge navel stud with opposing holes across navel. Existing 14-gauge clithood ring expanded to 12-gauge and augmented with second, vertical bar in behind the ring. Circular tattoo around pussy. Zodiac around navel. More circles of ink around breasts, navel, genitals. Secured to Stool in Amphitheater. Bridle gag changed to O-ring gag with tongue clamp. Eyepods and Earpods fade in reality. Witnesses Robyn Restrained in Cart. Acquires double 12-gauge tongue studs, to constantly remind Kimju "if I see something say something." Tongue Clamp removed. Circular ring tattoos around areolas, navel, and pussy shall continue to expand.

Last presents blind-deaf-mute, bare-bald-naked, sitting spread secured.

Kimju arrives at *The Play Party* blind-deaf-mute, bare-bald-naked, TMLBAP, suspended from the trolly above so that she is horizontal, floating on her back, with her knees folded and her legs spread back, and her arms folded and secured in surrender position so her armpits display. Kimju's head hangs down, hangs upside down, her tongue clamped with parallel rods nestled between her double tongue studs. Kimju's head hangs at the right height, that, might the tongue clamp be removed, she is ideally positioned for cocksucking duties, and her shaven kleave flushes her lips, and shows Kimju is wet and level for fucking.

Players have had the option of adding ink into Kimju's body during *The Play Party*. Kimju continues to beg to Whore next Three Terms and

acquire the bodyart commensurate with that Caste, which she believes is the only positive aspect of the commitment. She arrives at the Party with a small astrological sign (Pallas) tattoo secreted in her navel and a 12-gauge U-bolt in nose. The navel planet tattoo counts as one of her three Whore tattoos, and will expand. The nose stud is a permanent Runaway consequences reminder. Now, in anticipation of her Whore destination, Kimju's other piercings, in her tongue & clithood, have all been stretched; all double in size and diameter. Double nipple piercings are in the queue.

Already Kimju's navel tattoo has expanded into circular rings around her belly button, another set of rings encircle her kleave and anus and also grow outward, and a third set of rings, a pair actually, encircle both areolas, tickle Kimju's nipple, and already begin their descent down Kimju's 35Cs. Over time, as these rings expand they will collide with each other and color in Kimju's body. They will bifurcate for the arms and legs, and eventually Kimju will be covered.

Certainly during Lockdown and while transported and suspended Kimju could hardly object to fondles and feels, pinches and fingering, tasting this or that on the tip of her clamped tongue.

Kimju suffers little during *The Play Party*, like others when she was fed aphrodisiac, aroused, and had a Collection Dish assigned. All hopes of Opting Monitor are dashed. After observing Robyn's sealing of Fate, Molly's fortune of heading back to the Nugget, and the purpling of Beka and Elle, Kimju assumes that among the four remaining Lobelia (Babs, Tiffany, Steph, Kimju), her Fate was a forgone conclusion.

Her position is moved to kneeling-spread-armbound. Much to Kimju's surprise, she gets an opportunity to strike a bargain. and trade her Opt Whore to Tiffany, and get Tiffany's Opt Strip in return... with a few caveats. After all, Kimju did error by not reporting Robyn not being where she was supposed to be. The caveats are that Kimju shall become a Stripper Deluxe, and that is everything a Whore does except coitus and anal. And she shall keep all the piercings and tattoos she had been accumulating, meaning her rings will continue to expand, and that she will indeed collect double nipple piercing.

Kimju agrees, knowing that from now on she jerks cock, sucks cock, gobbles goo, works the bukkake circuit, and competes in gokkun contests. And yes, she will eat pussy, pee on-Cam, and get pissed on, besides all the normal getting boobs felt if not sucked on, and tasting her cream on a finger that has just knuckled her.

Gamers trust that Kimju will find a ride to the Nugget, and that she will keep a cock in her mouth during the entire ride to the Stage Door.

If not walk backward into the Club with a cock already in her mouth.

Molly Mammoth: Long black hair, Irish-Spanish skin, gray eyes, 5' 3", 140 pounds, 38DD-30-37, a square face, a fleshy Rubenesque figure, rolliosis, large splotchy sepia areolas, deeply set navel, a full black bush, big butt, unshaven armpits and legs, copious body hair, and a deep brown vagina with purple deep inside. 14-gauge clithood ring and small alchemy sign tattoo (phosphorus) hidden on her body. Was Stripper last Term when Roommate was Kimju. Current Roommate is Steph.

Arrives topless during *Arrivals* wearing pale-rose cotton panties underwear; TMLB; N-3, sometimes gathered into her moon shadow or crotch or both; TMLBA, hairage. Streaks, spreads, gapes anus, pinks, creams. Keeps thighs apart. 1st Cosmos to cum. 2nd Cosmos to beg Pee-Cam, acquires Piss Mouth at Bachelor Party and is 2nd Cosmos to beg Piss Mouth.

During *Runup* eyebrows, armpits, arms and legs are shaven. Continues to spread, pink, cream, cum. Cunnilingus, dongs with Kimju, Tiffany, Steph. 4th Cosmos to beg to Opt-Strip. Kisses, mutually masturbates, cunnilingus, and shares Double Dong with Kimju to climax (Nugget D20); TMLBAP; bare, bald, spreads, pinks; creams; cums; pees. Acquires smaller, see-through panties, also gather back-side tanga style (also Nugget D20); TMLBA; N-6. {Secretly shares Piss Mouth with Molly,} Panties also yanked, in the front, essentially TMLBAP. Reconfirms Piss Mouth by pissing into own mouth at Greatest House Roar, victorious, acquires undershirt cutout minidress from Steph, and dons over panties; TML; but doffs it (to Babs D22) and becomes topless with see-through panties (again); TMLBA; N-6; TMLBAP in see-through. Reacquires Watering Can; wet. Besides Kimju, also shares Double Dong with Tiffany, Steph. Temporarily naked, spreads, pinks, creams at Beautician's; eyebrows, arms, armpits, and legs shaven; red dyed hair, both on her head and pussy, red body stain (D24). Red bodypaint with heavy grease (Mermaid Parade D25). Ordered move panties to mouth (D26); full-frontal, TMLBAP; full pubic hair. Faded red bodypaint, red body stain, and grease remnants.

Arises the morning of *The Beach Day* wearing soiled transparent see-through panties in her mouth; TMLBAP, hairy. Long hair on head dyed red, full pubic hair also dyed red, faded red body stain and Vaseline remnants. Keeps thighs apart. Still Pee-Camer & Piss Mouth. | Made up and perfumed. Watering Can, packed with ice. Sits, spreads, pinks, masturbates, creams, chants, and

grunts to beg Opt-Strip (Beach Lineup). Oil and sanding; masturbates, creams, cums. All body hair shaven, bare and bald except for topknot braided into a loop (Beach Lineup). Surrenders Piss Mouth to Beka (Mudpit PM). Panties are used to fasten topknot to Tiffany (Mudpit PM). Assumed that at Midnight both will Opt-Strip.

The morning of *The Runout* finds Molly, residing in the Mudpit, with her ponytail bound to Tiffany using her panties. Molly remains gritty with oil and sand and mud; nude, TMLBAP, bare and bald except for topknot braided into a loop, and fastened by her panties to Tiffany's topknot.

Now her 14-gauge clithood ring is visible, since it is no longer hidden in hair. The small alchemy sign (phosphorus) tattoo hidden deep in navel is scheduled for expansion might Molly Opt Strip again. | Upon awakening, Molly observes the Lineup of BB and the House Pledge and watches them all get stripped naked. Her ponytail is severed from head and she is parted from Tiffany, parted also with her irredeemable panties. Now nude; TMLBAP; bare, spread, pink; bald. Cloth gag taped in; handcuffs; asshole. Locked to Henge Post. Lockdown Lobelia.

Inquisition chair. Ungagged, begs to Strip, accepts Lockdown. Eyepods, Earpods, 14-gauge nose ring (augments preexisting clithood piercing) Cloth gag replaced with Pump ball Gag. Re-secured to Post Henge; pees. Restrained hands behind head and behind post, spread. Existing alchemical sign in navel (phosphorus) augmented with element signs tattooed into areola, foot, vagina, and armpit. Steph watches her acquire new navel ring and fire tattoo erupting from navel. Penny and Coco give her the Double Penetrator, consisting of the Ben-Wa Balls and the Procto.

Secured to Stool in Amphitheater. Exchanges pump ball gag for O-ring gag with tongue clamp. Eye & Earpods fade in reality. Witnesses Babs equally helpless and begging to Whore, and Robyn Restrained.

Last seen blind-deaf-mute, bare-topknot-naked, sitting-spread-secured. Molly makes cream, cums on arousal, and Pee-Cams. She likes to eat and shall gain weight.

Molly arrives at the *Play Party* blind-deaf-mute, bare-bald-naked, and hanging by her bound breasts from the end of a beam to which Babs hangs on the other end. Like others, she is armbound w/mittens, and her legs are kept apart so her crotch is aired out. Pee-Camer, Piss Mouth; scheduled to Opt Strip next Term. 14-gauge nose ring, new navel ring, clithood rings. Five alchemical signs of elements (including an older tattoo hidden in navel pit) are now tattooed on her body, plus fire erupts around her navel. O-Ring

Gag with Tongue Clamp, armbinder (behind back), mittens.

Molly still retains the Double Penetrator, consisting of the Ben-Wa Balls inside her merrymaker, and the Procto, up her mawkport.

Most certainly Molly begs her mittens off, begs to be a handjob Stripper next Term. She is permitted both hands, and joins Babs in collecting goo, prior to her early exit Besides just lapdancing the cloistered cock, Molly shall now take it out and handle it too. Bring it to climax. Consume the goo, possibly by using her mouth. Maybe Molly tasted goo that popped through pants during her last stint at the Nugget, but next Term Molly will beg that "blowjobs aren't sex," and collect goo from a cock already deep in her mouth.

Molly finds blackness and silence comforting following video of her own gape, pink & drool; she discovers her armbinder removed, her hands brought in front of her, and secured near her navel, unable to touch either her breasts or vulva.

A Voice in Molly's Earpods tells her to march, turn left, turn right, stop. Molly obeys.

Molly is the 1st Cosmos Lobelia to leave *The Play Party*. She expects she will have to fully service the Back Door Man to gain entry at the Stage Door, and know that whatever compromises she makes that they will surely get played on Screens while she dances on Stage next Term.

Molly's good fortune is that she still bears the Ben-Wa Balls and Procto in her moo and mawk, with orders to deliver them to the Nugget. Even the Back Door Man doesn't want to quibble about if "to means into" so Molly must do with her mouth.

Steph Sorostitute: Long blonde hair, white skin, blue eyes, thin lips, 5' 7", 105 pounds, 32A-23-32, slender figure, brown nipple stalks on beige areolas that burst forth like fruit. A small, puckered navel features a round crater with a fleshy rim, and a hard outie bulb in the middle. Medium butt, thin blonde pussy hair, shaven armpits and legs, scarlet vagina with distended clitoris.

Was Monitor last Term, but broken to Pledge for covering her navel. Roommate last Term was Robyn Redacted. Roommate this Term is Molly.

Steph approaches *The Arrivals* wearing only one Garment, a tattered strapless minidress with the belly ripped out; TML (M is cutout navelage). During *Arrivals* she wears a variety of minidresses (always sanpan of course) that ensure titters, upskirts, and extends vagflash, but never pinks. Keeps thighs apart.

Demonstrates rectal thermoprobe, produces one drop of cream (D14).

During *Runup*, Steph reduces her minidress into a belt, displays full-frontal TMLBAP (D15). She trades her minidress for a men's undershirt.

She spreads, pinks, creams, cums (3rd Cosmos to do so); 6th Cosmos beg to Opt-Strip. After losing Greatest House Roar to Roommate Molly, she surrenders her minidress and becomes nude (D21); TMLBAP; spreads, pinks; creams, cums. Pees. 4th Cosmos begs Pee-Cam. Begs Piss Mouth. All Cosmos participate in extended forced climax (4th Cosmos). Zoned. Pees. Muddy, messy, and wet. Naked 24x7 now.

Taken to Nugget for an Audition with Tiffany, Penny & Coco let Tiffany ride the Double Dong w/Steph (D23), then Penny and Coco pee on Steph and shave all her hair off while climaxing her center Stage.

She becomes the 1st Cosmos bare-bald-naked, that is, the 1st shaven bare, 1st shaven bald. Full-frontal; TMLBAP; bare, bald.

Steph also acquires a Duel Option and the Shaving Kit (D23), but streaks back to the Cosmos House absent the latter, masturbated to climax by the Rachmaninoffs on the way. The Shaving Kit is hand carried by Robyn (on behalf of Steph), who inserts it into Kimju back at the House (D23)

Tiffany retains the Dong, takes it to the Cosmos House where it is widely shared, including Molly sharing it with Steph in the Doghouse (D24).) On the morning of the Mermaid Parade, Steph surrenders the Dong to Tiffany; Steph announces she shall Duel with Elle (D25), and Elle surrenders her croptop. Elle will display topless in the Mermaid Parade.

{Steph avoids Mermaid Parade, streaks to the Peacock House, and secretly sexes William; oral 69, vaginal, anal; creams, climaxes, collects cum (D25). Steph would be appalled to discover that William secretly cammed their tryst, or that Rodney discovers the secret, possibly making copies.}

The Shaving Kit bounces from Kimju to Beka (D24) to Steph (D26).

On the last Day of the *Runup* (D27), Steph acquires a Piss Mouth via Rodney in the Bathroom, with Tiffany and Molly aiding the swallowing. Elle shall acquire all of Steph's Obeisances, including water rights.

That night, Steph takes Elle to the Mansion Open House (D27), where Elle surrenders her stretch slacks and forfeits the Duel. Penny and Coco extract Steph's Shaving Kit and use it to shave Elle bare and bald; Elle shall now remain bare-bald-naked 24x7 and Opt Strip next Term; and Steph shall retain two Garments (croptop & slacks, TML) and possesses a guaranteed Opt Monitor.

After Steph piss-climaxes Elle on the Glass Bull, Whores secrete the Shaving Kit inside Elle & send her streaking to the Doghouse. Steph thinks the Whores have taken the Shaving Kit.

On the Morning of *The Beach Day*, Steph's initial costume is an open-armhole scoop-neck croptop and low-rise but now crotchless slacks; TMLP; N-5, titter, pubage. Five Days stubble on both a bald head & bare pubis. Still a Pee-Camer and Piss Mouth; was although once begging to Opt-Strip; now has guaranteed Opt-Monitor. | Sleeveless croptop exchanged for long sleeve front-button croptop (from Robyn) acquires opacity and low-rise slacks; M, N-5, rugage. Required to display herself topless, bottomless, and rolled up so she could drip secretions into her own mouth, and wash them down with her own piss. Piss Mouth. Transfers pee from China Doll to Elle. At times controls Cosmos Drone. Escorts Corvette Pledge home. {Sexes with William and Rodney; BJ, coitus, cum, anal, BJ, double penis penetration, mouth & pussy, mouth & anal, A2M facial, creampie. Also secretly cammed by William.} Returns Cosmos Cam to Backyard.

Steph is awoken on the morning of *The Runout* and ordered out of the Cosmos House naked, leaving her croptop and slacks behind on her bunk. | Steph shall remain naked now, TMLBAP, bare with stubble, bald with stubble. And although Steph has spread, pinked. creamed, cum, and peed like a good Pledge, all know her defeat of Elle in the Duel has earned her an Opt Up to Monitor next Term. Thus, despite any guarantees, Steph is treated like all the other Cosmos Lockdown Lobelia, except perhaps for ex-Monitor Babs, who is treated worse.

Cloth gag taped in, handcuffs; asshole. Locked to Post. Paddled, pees. Inquisition room. Throats Sybian, lies, shocked, cloth gag removed, agrees that Lockdown for her is a sham only, and has no real consequences; she shall still Opt Up next Term provided she tell the whole truth. Fitted into a gag harness, Earpods. Invisible 14-gauge nose ring. Un-gagged and re-gagged during second questioning in which she incriminates herself totally, yet her guilt and conviction is not revealed to her at this time. Sits spread with hands restrained behind head and behind post. Eyes temporarily uncovered to witness three other Cosmos (Tiffany, Molly, Elle) get ink and steel.

Steph may choose to deny reality, but the invisible nose stud is 14 gauge, the navel stud is likewise 14 gauge, and the navel tattoo is an ultraviolet ink starburst that to Steph's eyes is invisible. Certainly Steph is adept at pinking and displaying her asshole, and has creamed, climaxed, and shared the Dong. She is a Pee-Camer but avoided Piss Mouth.

Steph acquires the Shaving Kit (from Penny and Coco) while secured to Stool in Amphitheater (LD3). Harness gag changed to O-ring gag with tongue clamp. Eyepods and Earpods fade in reality. Witnesses Robyn Restrained. Then ending with blackness and silence.

Last presents blind-deaf-mute, bare-bald-naked, sitting-spread-secured.

Steph arrives at *The Play Party* confident in the belief she shall Opt Monitor at Midnight, and that her harassment is only for show. Like the other Lockdown Lobelia, she presents blind-deaf-mute, and bare-bald-naked, albeit with several days of stubble. She walks into the Meatpacking Plant following her a lead that connect her nose stud with the trolly above, and her arms bound behind her back and her hands mittened.

Later in the Party Steph shall kneel-spread-armbound, confident that her mittens & Tongue Clamp are prophylactics that prevent handjobs and blowjobs. Steph still conforms to the lead from her nose to the trolly above, and keeps her chin up.

Steph's kneeling-spread-armbound position doesn't mask the contrition she feels, and despite begging to Opt-Strip, she knows that is really a sham and that come Midnight, *I will indeed Opt Monitor*. The removal of the lead connecting her nose to the trolly above, and her recent experience at being allowed to watch others get pierced, confirms her self-assessment of invincibility.

None the less, the screening of the *Beka & Rodney Fuck Video* whiplashes Steph, who considers that her sex acts with William might be similarly captivated, concluded they have not been. Steph's confidence builds as Game Mistress appears to give her special consideration after Beka and Elle depart.

Neither Steph nor Babs witness the Tiffany and Kimju's trading places, nor the sweeteners offered.

As the Term draws to an end, Steph and Babs discover themselves kneeling-spread-armbound and the only Cosmos Lockdown Lobelia still at the Play Party. It makes Steph jealous to watch Babs, impaled on the Pogo, be forced to cream and convulse, or in Steph's thoughts, *a Burking Bunghole parked in the Zone because of Beka and Elle's Free-Fucking. Ha ha ha.*

When William and Rodney are rolled in on a giant Wheel, spread-eagled, cocksucking each other, and rectally taken, Steph's Shaving Kit Soap Sphere and Tools Cylinder kindle excitement, and increase Steph's secretions, harden her nipples, and flush her faee and neck.

Steph's Fate instantly advances when Game Mistress screens a *Video* which displays Steph & Peacock Monitor William: blowjob, cunnilingus, coitus, anal, A2M, facial, nude departure. It is indeed a recording of Steph's sneaky visit to the

Peacock House while the other Cosmos attended the Mermaid Parade.

Game Mistress shocks Steph with the Goad, flattens her to the floor in a puddle of piss, operationalizes this now instant Whore as a Piss Mouth. GM sits her back up, feints Babs, and China Doll pierced Steph's Clamped tongue with an extra-long barbell. Proclaimed Whore, Three Terms.

The Fat Lady arrives with a message to Game Mistress and surprise, there is a second *Steph and William Sex Video*, this one also with Rodney. Following this screening, Steph begs Dong and Dirty Whore. William is detached from the Wheel, dispatched to Slavesex, and Steph is attached, spread-eagle and upside down, with Rodney's cock in her mouth and her pierced tongue fastened to Rodney's pierced cock.

GM commands China Doll to pierce Steph's clithood and install a stud and a swinging U-bolt, and install three rings down each side of her spread vaginal lips, a bequest from Janet, and therefore not exceeding her Whore Count (navel, clithood; nose, tongue, and Janet's rings don't count; nipple promised & would be 3rd piercing). Rodney's pierced tongue is chained into Steph's genital stainless.

China Doll installs a bidirectional rectal feeding/enema system deep into Steph's anus. (Rodney already enjoys a similar violation.)

Steph and Rodney shall be Rolled to Flesh Ranch, where they shall begin their service.

Beka Broda: Longhaired brunette, half-Asian, brown eyes, 5' 7", 105 pounds, 33B-25-33. Shallow conical breasts, beige areolas have a dark brown circumference and pigmented dots, and nipples that indent when excited. A flat belly, a long and narrow vertical ovaled navel that suggests a lightning bolt, smallish butt, shaven legs and underarms, trimmed pubic hair, a vagina with inner lips tinted dark brown and darker pigment around her anus. Newbie; 1st Term in the Game. Forbidden masturbation, creams constantly. Roommate is Elle.

At her *Arrival* Beka wears a sleeveless cotton open-armhole croptop and miniskirt; TML; N-6; able to flash nippage, titter, upskirt hairage, and vagflash. Keeps thighs apart. She will continue to wear this during *Arrivals*. She practices the rectal thermoprobe while Elle practices a suppository (Corvette House D11), and collects a suppository while Steph enjoys the thermoprobe (D14). 4th Pledge to beg to Opt-Strip (D11)

During *Runup*, Beka pees nude in Backyard; TMLBAP; 5th Cosmos to beg Pee-Cam (D19-D24). Boobage, spreads, pinks, creams, begs Opt-Strip (Nugget Camera Lounge D20). Exchanges croptop and miniskirt for Elle's halter and ripped and jean shorts (Nugget D20); TML; N-1; nippage, hairage, buttage; boobage, pink (Nugget Stage D20).

Temporarily presents naked; spreads, pinks, creams at Beauty Salon; green dyed head and pussy hair; Beautician reduces halter to size micro; exchanges shorts (with Kimju) for matching micro g-string; green hair to Mohawk and Hitler pussy hair styling, visible above the g-string (D24).

On the Morning of Mermaid Parade, Beka donates halter toTiffany, reducing herself to topless with a micro g-string (D25), TMLBA; crotch; trimmed, spreads, pinks; creams. Green bodypaint (D25); Acquires Shaving Kit from Kimju (D25), gives to Steph (D26). Passes out her Pink Page to all Eight Houses {and secretly sexes Rodney; coitus, creams, climax together (D26)}.

Arrives on the *Beach Day* topless and micro g-string; TMLBA; N-7, trimmed with dyed green Mohawk on head and dyed green Hitler above crotch, with faded green bodypaint remnants. | The micro g-string becomes a transparent clear vinyl size nano g-string; TMLBA; N-7; TMLBAP in see-through. Green goth makeup, green stain on lips and nipples. Perfume. Sits, spreads, pinks. creams, chants, repeats beg Opt-Strip. Oil and sanding, excessive lipstick; asshole; cream oozing out pussy inside clear vinyl. Moves g-string into asshole; TMLBAP. Shaves bare and bald; spreads, pinks; creams. Begs Piss Mouth from Kimju. Begs to play *Gonzo Suck and Fuck Videos* but only Elle gets screened; both are rewarded Double Dong from Ginny and Trixi; shares Double Dong with Elle in Mudpit, Doghouse. Cums with Elle.

The morning of *The Runout* finds Beka and Elle still in the Doghouse, still sharing the Double Dong, and scheduled to Opt Down to Stripper next Term. Both have spread, pinked; creamed, cum, donged, toyed assholes. {Beka sexes with Rodney) coitus, creams, climax.} Nude with nano g-string worn around neck; TMLBAP; bare; bald; messy with mud, sand, oil, and faded green bodypaint remnants. Excessive creamer. Shares Double Dong with Elle; cums. Begs to play *Gonzo Suck and Fuck Videos* (with Elle). | Nude and Double Donging with Elle. Beka and Elle witnesses *Runout* from Doghouse. Moved to Mudpit while sharing Double Dong with Elle in mouth. Blindfold, handcuffs. Shares the Dong anally. Complete *Nine Dong Combos* with Elle.

During the Interrogation Beka confesses to her transgression with Rodney, gets Immunity, and begs Opt-Strip next Term. Begs to be Dong & Dirty Whore Term thereafter. O-ring gag, 14-gauge nose ring. Eyepods, Earpods. Locked to Post Henge. Restrained hands behind head and behind post and spread. Armpits. Zoned while 14-gauge navel ring piercing, temporarily watches the beginnings of a sprawling belly tattoo begun at her clit and extending to her nipple. Creams. Secured to Stool in Amphitheater. O-Ring Gag augmented with Tongue Clamp. Eyepods and Earpods fade in reality. Witnesses Robyn Restrained in Cart. And subsequently fade out.

Last presents blind-deaf-mute, bare-bald-naked, sitting-spread-secured.

Beka arrives at the Play Party blind-deaf-mute, bare-bald-naked, suspended-spread-secured from an overhead trolly, and coordinated so that her bound body is butt-to-butt with Elle, sharing the Double Dong rectally; TMLBAP, pink, cream. Pee-Camer; Piss Mouth. 14-gauge nose and navel rings. Large belly tattoo outlined from neck and nipples to clit, inner thigh, and around to asshole starts to get filled in. Eyepods, Earpods, O-ring Gag with Tongue Clamp, armbinder, mittens.

Penny and Coco arrive, separate Beka & Elle, and collect the Double Dong from them into their mouths and depart. Separated, Beka and Elle disappear into the bowls of the Meatpacking Plant where they are fondled, fingered, and beaten. Both later reemerge in a kneel-spread-surrender position, bearing marking, and with their mouths ungagged and their hands free.

Game Mistress screens the *Beka and Rodney Fuck Video* to the assembled Cosmos Lobelia (LD7). The screening most certainly would reduce Beka to Whore status, had she not previously been given Immunity for her confession. It is a revelation to Elle, absent any Immunity if only because it entails her as a Whore; it is not a revelation to Babs, but it is a confirmation of a secret shared by Janet, and an omen about another shared secret. Rodney isn't here.

Elle, whose confessions also involved anal, also entails Beka & Babs; Beka and Elle will beg Dong & Dirty Whore from now through their Stripper Term. And Babs is ruined.

Elle is now three-hole sexed on the purple Gimbled It; Beka will first get a purple mouth, as the sucks on Gimbled It's cock coming out of Elle's asshole, A2OPM, and a purple face as she gets throated. Beka is put onto her hands and knees and acquires more purple stain as she is analed. Elle is fed It's cock out of Beka's anus, A2OPM, but Beka's vagina is left wanting.

Both new Strippers are risen to their feet, ordered to embrace, rub their breasts together, and French kiss. They obey and share purple stain. Their Eyepods fade to black, their Earpods go silent, the twosome are separated, encouraged to sit side-by-side and hold hands, leads are attached to both nose rings, and they are led by the trolly to the transport to their next destination. Beka will continue to service cocks all the way to the Nugget Stage Door, prepare them for Elle as Elle is train-fucked on her way through the Door, and beg to service cocks afterwards (as will Elle).

Elle Lollydor: Curly-haired brunette, olive Middle Eastern skin, brown eyes, 5' 10", 115 pounds, 34B-24-34, small bone frame. Nipples and coffee-colored areolas resemble a weathered volcano, with crevices that run from the tip of the nipple down to the very edge of the pigment. The navel is a horizontal oval with an overhang, buttocks of medium proportion, legs and underarms shaven, however a full growth of bush extends into her inner thighs and is partly visible inside her shorts, Darker brown vagina and inner lips and a violet-hued vaginal canal.

Newbie; 1st Term in the Game. Roommate is Beka.

Arrives wearing and continues to wear front and neck-buttoned halter and ripped jean shorts; TML; N-1. Keeps thighs apart. During *The Arrivals* nippage, titter, hairage, buttage. 3rd Cosmos to beg Opt-Strip. Begs Flip-Flop. Lollydors Beka.

During *The Runup* unbuttons halter, titter, nippage, hairage, and boobage before exchanges halter and shorts for croptop and miniskirt (with Beka at Nugget D20); TML; N-4; nippage, upskirt hairy spreads, pinks (including Camera Lounge D20). Pinking reveals dark brown vagina with a violet vaginal canal. Trades miniskirt to Tiffany for low-rise slacks (D23); ML; N-7 titter, hairage, cameltoe. Cammed naked, spread, pink, creaming at Beauty Salon, inverse Mohawk and hair butched, inverse Mohawk of pussy hair, blue dyed haircut and pussy hair (D24). Like Beka, she must pass out her Pick Pages to all Eight Housesn. Many also got live pink.

After Steph announces that Elle shall be her Dueling partner, Elle surrenders first her croptop, so she may go to the Mermaid Parade topless (D25). There a Bodypaint Artist paints an indigo blue-black stripe dividing her body, and blue bodypaint; TMLB; N-7; hairage; rugage. Afterwards, Elle has no choice but to forfeit the Duel; she gives her slacks to Steph (D27) and shall stay nude from now on; and be guaranteed Opt Stripper next Term; TMLBAP; hairy, spread, pink; creams; pees.

Begs Steph to not play *Gonzo Sex Videos*. Lollys cum and pussy cream off the floor. Taken to Mansion Open House where Penny & Coco shave her bare & bald; and Steph piss-climaxes her on Glass Bull (5th Cosmos to officially climax), (although her pee awaits official Pee-Cam certification to officially become 6th Cosmos Pee-

Camer).

Now begs to play *Gonzo Suck & Fuck Videos*.

Acquires Shaving Kit from Steph via Penny and Coco (Mansion Open House D27), and streaks it to Doghouse.

Begins *Beach Day* bare-bald-naked; TMLBAP. Faded blue bodypaint remnants. Vertical black indelible stripe divides body vertically into left and right halves. Shaving Kit hidden inside as DP. Dirty from Doghouse. | Overdone makeup, heavy black dividing line bifurcating her body gets complemented with blue indelible writing on body. Stain on nipples, navel, clit. Perfumed. Purple stain on lips, nipples, navel, pussy and asshole. Sits, spreads, pinks, creams, chants, again begs Opt-Strip. Bronze tanning dye; oiled, sanded; excessive lipstick. Asshole; cream, climax. Shares Shaving Kit with Beka, Molly, Tiffany and gives to Penny and Coco. Pees and begs Pee-Cam (6th Cosmos to make it official), pees; snowballs It's ejaculate with China Doll; shares Mouth with Steph.

Begs to play *Gonzo Suck and Fuck Videos* and her wish is granted. First *Gonzo Suck and Fuck Video* with only Elle in it is screened.

Rewarded (with Beka) with Double Dong from Ginny and Trixi; shares Double Dong with Beka in Mudpit, Doghouse. Cums with Beka.

As the loser in the Duel (to Steph), Elle has a confirmed Opt Down to Stripper next Term, and will awake on the morning of *The Runout* as a Pee-Camer & Piss Mouth who has spread, pinked; creamed, cum, donged, displayed asshole. Lollydor. Clear vinyl croptop bottomless, MLAP, TMLBAP in see-through; nude TMLBAP; bare; bald; messy with mud, sand, oil, and faded blue bodypaint remnants. Fading vertical black indelible stripe divides body vertically into left and right halves. Blue indelible writing and bronze tanning dye cover her body. Fading Gentian Violet stain on lips, nipples, navel, pussy and asshole; excessive lipstick. Shares Double Dong with Beka in Doghouse; cums. Begs to play remaining *Gonzo Suck and Fuck Video* (with Beka).

| Like Beka, Elle confronts the morning of *The Runout* to witness, not the start of a new Term, but a Lineup of Naked Cosmos outside the Doghouse. Soon to also include a naked ex-Monitor Babs.

The twosome are moved from the Doghouse to the Mudpit while sharing Double Dong with Beka in mouth. Eyepods, handcuffs. Share the Dong and handcuffs anally. The Eyes insert O-ring gag. 14-gauge nose ring. Retains Opt Down and begs to be Stripper next Term. Begs to be Dong & Dirty Whore Term thereafter. Eyepods, Earpods. After they are questioned they finish a *Nine Dong Combinations Video*. Locked to Post Henge;

spread, pink; asshole; creams, cums; pees. Restrained hands behind head and behind post and spread. Armpits. Steph watches Elle acquires 14-gauge navel ring and tattoo (vine with flowers). Secured to Stool in Amphitheater. O-Ring Gag augmented with Tongue Clamp. Eye and Earpods fade in reality. Witnesses Robyn Restrained. Eye and Earpods fade out reality.

Last presents blind-deaf-mute, bare-bald-naked, sitting-spread-secured.

Elle arrives at *The Play Party* blind-deaf-mute, bare-bald-naked, suspended-spread-secured from an overhead trolly, and coordinated so that her bound body is butt-to-butt with Beka, sharing the Double Dong, nadir and bogey; TMLBAP. Faded body marker and stain. pink, cream, asshole. Has spread, pinked; creamed, cum, kissed, donged; Lollydor. Pee-Camer; Piss Mouth; Opt Stripper next Term. 14-gauge nose and navel rings. Navel tattoo (vine with flowers). Fed aphrodisiac? Lockdown. Eyepods, Earpods, O-ring Gag with Tongue Clamp, armbinder, mittens.

| Penny and Coco separate Beka & Elle and collet the Double Dong from them into their mouths & depart. Separated, Beka and Elle disappear into the bowls of the Meatpacking Plant where there are fondled, fingered, sometime with sweetness and arousal and sometimes with hurt. Both are paddled hard enough to leave red marks, and cropped hard enough to leave welts. Both later reemerge in a kneel-spread-surrender position, and with their mouths ungagged and their hands free.

After Game Mistress screens the *Beka and Rodney Fuck Video* to the assembled Cosmos Lobelia, Elle confesses to Whoring twice to get the *Measurement Nudes* and the *Gonzo Videos*. Beka's misbehavior ensures that Babs will also Whore, and Elle's anal confession ensures that Babs shall anal as well, as will Roommate Beka. Beka and Elle shall Opt Strip at Midnight, and beg to Opt Dong and Dirty Whore until that comes to pass.

Elle now solidifies her commitment to oral, vaginal, and anal sex by fucking purple Gimbled It: blowjob, coitus, anal, passing It's cock to Beka after analing It, and reclaiming the cock following It analing Beka, A2OPM.

Both new Strippers are risen to their feet, ordered to embrace, rub their breasts together, French kiss. They obey. Their Eyepods fade to black, their Earpods go silent, the twosome are separated, encouraged to stand side-by-side and hold hands; leads are attached to both nose rings, and then led by the trolly to the transport to their next destination. Elle will be train fucked all the way to, and until she passes through the Stage Door, marking Midnight; like Beka, whose mouth prepares cocks for Elle's nooky, Elle will claim cocksucking isn't sex, so she can suck during her Nugget Term, and not have to wait until she is a Whore.

§ Others: Garments & Props & Obeisance & Exposures

From the Corvette House:

The occupants of another of the Eight Houses at the School, the Corvette House, are also identified and tracked below, albeit in less detail than the Cosmos. Their full histories are unknown to us, and they are only of interest when they interact with our Eight Cosmos.

Important among them is Janet, at the time of *The Arrivals* the Monitor of the Corvettes, a peer of Monitor Babs, and a former Roommate.

Interactions with Corvettes include Beka and Elle's anal training during *The Arrivals,* Tiffany's transfer of the Double Dong during *The Runup,* a visit during *The Beach Day* including Darleen camming Steph's humiliation, and visits to the Amphitheater during *The Runout.*

Janet becomes a House Mom el Capitan at Midnight; her former Roommate Darleen also makes a reluctant appearance at *The Play Party.*

The individual biographies follow with an emphasis on Garments, Props, and Obeisance.

Ex-Corvette Monitor Janet (Janet Jintoe): Dark hair, beige skin, dark brown eyes, 5' 7", 180 pounds, 40EE-34-46, plump figure, heavy bust, large brown areolas with bubbly milk glands, very full pubic bush, large buttocks, shaven legs and armpits, long outer sex lips. {One hidden tattoo, the name "Janet Jintoe" on the inside of her lower lip, which reads reversed so it can be read in a mirror.} Pierced inner labia, consisting of three holes on each side, worn with whatever stainless Gamers might let Janet wear, including rings (currently jangling), and a chastity if needed.

Was a Cosmos Pledge last Term (was Babs' Roommate), Nugget Stripper two Terms ago (was Tiffany's Roommate). Monitor of the Corvette House; Roommate is Darleen. Exhibitionist.

During *Arrivals* wears crochet Spiderweb Bikini, size mini halter and g-string; technically TMLA; N-7; nippage, areolage, cleavage, buttage, hairage, slitage; although in practice the open-mesh qualifies as full-frontal and is essentially TMLBAP.

At the start of *The Runup* Janet reduces to a size micro halter and g-string Spiderweb Bikini; TMLA; N-7; nippage, areolage, cleavage, hairage, slitage, lipage; full-frontal TMLBAP in open

mesh. Ring in long labia lips display (D15). Exchanges for size nano Spiderweb halter and g-string (Yacht D17). Exchanges (with Louise) for bandeau and T-front maillot tangá (D20); TMLA; cleavage, buttage.

On *The Beach Day* continues to wear bandeau and T-front maillot tangá; TMLA, cleavage, buttage. | Takes Louise's g-string and wears it over bandeau and maillot, providing three Garments, and lets Louise and Lee share the string halter, worn as two micro g-strings.

The Clock never freezes for Janet and at Midnight she Opts to House Mom el Capitan, MomCap for short, and becomes responsible for the Nugget and two Houses, the Cosmos and Corvette House (via two Monitors, former Corvette Pledge Caroline and Wendy).

During *The Runout* Janet visits the Post Henge wearing three Garments: a T-Front maillot tanga & pushup bra, & shoes, TMLA. Cleavage, hairage, buttage, and if Janet is careless, areolage, slitage. Later she returns to the Amphitheater wearing a size nano string halter & deep V-front g-string maillot & shoes. TMLA, cleavage, hairage, buttage, and if Janet is careless, nippage & slitage. She deliberately exposes her asshole.

Janet visits *The Play Party* and joins the fun by eating out a blind-deaf-mute Babs to climax, then forcing an unknowing BB to eat her in return. Janet constricts, pisses in BB's mouth, and departs.

Ex-Corvette Pledge Darleen: Slender brunette. 33A-25-32. Monitor last Term, Pledge during Term ending Midnight and Roommate of Monitor Janet. Stripper since Midnight.

During *Arrivals* and continuing through *The Runup* continues to wear long sleeve pullover top & tight slacks, flashing bellage, no navel requirement, but always flashing M.

Arrives on *Beach Day* still wearing long sleeve pullover top and jeans; flashing M. | Commands Corvette Drone Cam. Flashes M.

Midnight has cast Darleen into a new Term and a new Caste. During *The Runout,* Janet introduces Darleen Dilator as a Stripper (Backyard); Darleen is topless with skin-tight capri pants already stained in the crotch, TMB. Janet orders her into the Mudpit naked & pink, TMBAP. She departs wearing nipple clamps with her capri pants, and is expected to present herself naked at the Nugget Stage Door, TMLBAP.

Later Janet visits the Amphitheater again and brings along now-Stripper Darleen Dilator, topless & crotchless g-string & one shoe (the other shoe is worn by Pacmo Pinky), qualifying full-frontal and TMLBAP. During her visit she (along with the unfortunate Pacmo Pinky) she will be formed into the stamen of a Nugget Burka Flower, pink, cream, and suckle Pinky's nipple (and visa-versa).

Darleen is spotted at *The Play Party*, topless tanga, sucking on the Risen Cocks Lineup. She is a Stripper now and begging to be a Stripper Deluxe.

Ex-Corvette Pledge Ginny: Slender brunette, 33B-26-34. Roommate is Trixi Tubes. Was Nugget Stripper last Term (and Roommate of Lee Lollydor), and Whore two Terms ago, and committed to be a Whore-for-Life.

Arrives nude; TMLBAP; racing stripe, {clithood ring}. Whore-for-Life. Gamers have rights to two additional piercings, and (unless already hidden), three unique tattoos. Streaks, spreads, pinks, creams, cums. Practices Cravat (on behalf Trixi), buttplug, dildo; Beka & Elle hear perform blowjob, coitus, anal (D11). Pees, peed on. Later *Video* confirmation.

As Whore-for-Life experienced at oral sex, coitus facials, snowballing, swallowing, etc.

During *Runup* reveals clithood ring. Spreads, pinks; creams, cums; pees. Cammed sexing w/William; BJ, coitus, facial (Yacht D17). Shares Double Dong with Tiffany (D25) who brings it and leaves it behind to share with Trixi Tubes. Trixi, entranced by the Dong, shares her 2" wide orange Tube, which Ginny hangs on her hips, TMLBAP. They share the Dong (D27)

Arrives on *Beach Day* wearing 1" wide magenta stretch-fabric tube worn as belt (acquired from Trixi Tubes); full-frontal, TMLBAP; shaven bare. Carries the Double Dong in hand with Trixi | Sits, spreads, pinks. creams, chants, and begs Opt-Strip. Gives Dong to Beka and Elle (Beach D28).

Ginny is not seen during *The Runout*, she remains, of course, a Whore-For-Life, no matter what Caste she resides in. Ginny's professional credentials interest Gamers in promoting her. Elle fears Ginny is one of the Burka Nuggets, and that once she herself arrives at the Nugget, Ginny will become a tricky instructor.

Ex-Corvette Pledge Trixi Tubes: Slender brunette, 34A-26-35. Newbie; 1st Term in the Game. Roommate is Ginny. May wear any two of the Six Tubes; the bands around the body, doubling from one inch to 32 inches wide, worn any two at any one time, such as a green bandeau and red miniskirt. (The widths and colors are: 1" magenta, 2" orange, 4" green, 8" blue, 16" violet, 32" red).

During *Arrivals* when Trixi wore the violet & red Tubes together she logged a TM, she demoed many combinations to TML, and with just the magenta & orange she accepted a double belt & presented full-frontal, TMLBAP. Her Roommate Ginny gets punished in the Cravat after Trixi puts her legs together (Corvette House D11).

During *Runup*, Trixi watches Tiffany Double Dong Ginny while Ginny sucks cock, again a situation where Ginny pays penitence for Trixi's carelessness, however when Tiffany leaves the Dong behind, Ginny soon shares it with Trixi (D25). The Dong soon persuades Trixi to share her Tubes with Ginny, so that instead of Ginny streaking to the Nugget and Trixi Opting Up, both will travel safely to the Nugget with one Garment each. The first Tube she shares is the 2" orange.

Babs witnesses Ginny and Trixi perform the *Nine Dong Combinations*, no doubt rich in Tube sharing as well as "all holes in" on Day 27.

On the *Beach Day* Trixi and Roommate Ginny arrive wearing one Tube each; Trixi wears a green 4" wide green stretch-fabric tube worn as a belt (or a feeble attempt at a topless miniskirt, or bottomless bandeau) so able to form various TMLB, TMLAP), but for all purposes full-frontal; TMLBAP; shaven bare. Trixi carries the Double Dong hand-in-hand with Ginny. | Trixi sits, spreads, pinks; creams, masturbates, chants, and begs Opt-Strip. Trixi wants to retain the Dong but she and Ginny are guided to hand it to Beka and Elle, who acquire it this afternoon.

Assume nothing intervenes, after Midnight Trixi may join Ginny, drop her last remaining Garment into the Collection Box near the Stage Door, knock on the Door, and hope it opens. If indeed Ginny sucks and/or sexes the Backdoor Man on her way through the Stage Door, then maybe Trixi, no longer with Tubes, might also make some gonzo Cam footage while she lingers in the parking lot. Footage she can't make inside.

Trixi is not seen during *The Runout*, and it is possible she is another naked Nugget Stripper, possibly one of the Burkas.

Trixi is not seen during *The Play Party*.

Ex-Corvette Pledge Lee Lollydor: Black-haired Italian with full figure. 36C-24-35. A Lollydor. Was Nugget Stripper last Term (and Roommate of Ginny). Roommate is Louise.

No details from *Arrivals*, except we believe Lee is nude; TMLBAP; racing stripe. Possibly one tattoo; clithood ring.

Started *Runup* nude; spread, clithood ring. Nude at Greatest House Roar (D21). Receives Crochet Spider triangle halter (from Louise) and wears it as topless g-string (Corvette House D25); TMLBA; N-6; hairage; TMLBAP in open mesh. From now on, both Roommates are topless g-string Pledge. White painted nipples (Mermaid Parade D25).

On *Beach Day* wears same orange Crochet Spider halter as topless g-string; TMLBA, TMLBAP in open-mesh. (Roommate Louise wears the g-string.) | Sits, spreads, pinks, masturbates, creams, chants, begs Opt-Strip. Janet demands Crochet Bikini that Lee & Louise share; Janet keeps the g-string, and returns one halter triangle to each, and the long string that they connect to them together. "Tie the triangle around thigh as tip garter and tie the torso string finger-to-finger, so you are connected together." Full-frontal; TMLBAP; bare. They both know that one Garment they share between them raises concerns about if they will be streaking or not.

Lee is not seen during *The Runout*, and is believed to be no longer a Corvette Pledge but now a Nugget Stripper, probably because of Babs' deal with Janet. Elle fears she is one of the Burkas in the Amphitheater, and a Lollydor competitor.

Lee is not seen during *The Play Party*.

Ex-Corvette Pledge Louise: Curvy black-haired Portuguese, 36D-28-36. No piercings or tattoos, purple areolas, full bush. Was Monitor last Term. Roommate is Lee Lollydor.

Believed to have been wearing a bandeau and T-front maillot during the *Arrivals*.

During the *Runup*, Babs requires Louise strip naked on Nugget Stage, then exchanges her bandeau and t-front maillot for a size pico Spiderweb Bikini halter and g-string, courtesy Janet, and one size smaller (Nugget D20); TMLA; N-7; areolage; hairage; TMLBAP in open mesh. Janet demands she donate her triangle halter top to naked Lee; who repurposes as a topless g-string (D25); TMLBA; N-7; hairage; TMLBAP in open mesh. White bodypaint for Mermaid Parade doesn't hide much (D25).

Begins *Beach Day* topless with orange crochet open-mesh g-string; TMLB; N-6; hairage; full-frontal, TMLBAP in open mesh. No bodypaint. | Sits, spreads, pinks, creams, masturbates, begs Opt-Strip.

Janet gathers the halter and g-string from both Lee and Louise, retains the g-string, and returns the halter as two triangles and a long string, so that the Roommates may tie the triangles as garters and fasten themselves together with the long string, and thus share the single Garment. Whatever their quantum state, both are full-frontal; TMLBAP.

Louise is not seen during *The Runout* and is believed to be no longer a Corvette Pledge but now a Nugget Stripper, possibly one of the Burkas in the Amphitheater.

Louise is not seen during *The Play Party*.

Ex-Corvette Pledge Caroline: Petite blonde, 33B-22-34; crimson areolas. Newbie; 1st Term in the Game. Has Lingerie Kit like Roommate Wendy; each may wear any two of six Garments (bra, panties, slip, thong, hose, heels) at one time.

Not seen during *Arrivals*, during *Runup* spotted topless and lingerie panties with heels; TMLB; N-3, with white bodypaint w/red lips & nipples (Mermaid Parade D25).

Arrives on *Beach Day* wearing bra bottomless with hose; TMLAP. | Change to full-frontal w/heels over hose; TMLBAP; hairy, spreads, pinks.

During *The Runout*, Caroline is promoted to Monitor of the Cosmos House in the Term starting Midnight, committed to wearing only hose & heels, TMLBAP, shaven. Receives Makeup Case from Madam Nurse Beautician. Required to pink on Front Steps daily.

Caroline is not seen during *The Play Party*.

Ex-Corvette Pledge Wendy: A very randy brunette, 34B-24-34; ruddy areolas. Newbie; 1st Term in the Game. Has Lingerie Kit like Roommate Caroline; each may wear any two of six Garments (bra, panties, slip, thong, hose, heels) at one time.

No details on *Arrivals*. Spotted during *Runup* topless with lingerie thong and heels; TMLB; N-3, with white bodypaint, red lips and nipples (Mermaid Parade D25).

Arrives on *Beach Day* wearing topless tanga and hose TMLB; N-3. | Changes to full-frontal with hose and heels, TMLBAP, hairy, spreads, pink.

Not seen during *The Runup*, but at Midnight is said to be promoted to Monitor of the Corvette House, and committed to wearing hose & heels, TMLBAP, shaven.

Wendy is not seen during *The Play Party*.

From the Peacock House:

Ex-Peacock Monitor William: Dark brunette, an all-over light coverage of body hair, brown eyes, 5' 10", 160 pounds. Was Monitor last Term, Hover this Term and still Peacock Monitor. William and Steph free-fucked last Term and continue to flirt. Roommate is Pledge Rodney.

During *Arrivals*, wears black shirt and slacks, shoes. Demands Tiffany titty strip and excite his Peacock Pledge to climax (D01). She obeys, but declines to break the rules and blow William.

During *Runup* sexes Ginny (Whore-for-Life); BJ, coitus; lube and cream, climaxes (Yacht D17). Together with Janet he advocates the Greatest House Roar between Molly and Steph (Backyard D18), later hosts the Roar (Peacock House D21). {Secretly sexes Steph; oral 69, vaginal, anal; oral; lubes, cums (D25).} Last seen in three Garments, a long-sleeve shirt, slacks, and moccasins (Bathroom D27).

William is not seen during *The Beach Day*. Except at the end of the Day when {William secretly sexes with Steph; BJ, coitus, cum; also, with Rodney three-way BBG (Peacock House D28).}

Following Beka's admittance during *The Runout* about a *Video* with Rodney, the Peacocks are placed in Lockdown. The *Beka & Rodney Fuck Video* is screened to the Peacocks, and William, guilty by entailment, is stripped nude; TMLCAP, and secured spread-eagled on Wheel w/Rodney; each are tongue and penis pierced, and penis gagged with the other's cock.

William & Rodney are rolled into *The Play Party* by the Six ex-Peacocks, now Wheel Pushers, where they confront the only remaining Cosmos Lobelia, Babs and Steph. Certainly William and Rodney both drip pee and lubricant into their companion's mouth; both rectum are plugged so as to facilitate both rectal feeding as well as enema extraction.

The 1st *Steph & William Sex Video* plays, with severe consequences for Steph, and after their second Sex *Video* plays, William is condemned to Slavesex, removed from the Wheel, and dispatched to the Dungeon.

Ex-Peacock Pledge Rodney: Blonde, blue-eyed, wiry, 5' 10" 140 pounds. A totally shaven body, chest, back, arms, armpits, legs, buttocks, privates. Was Stripper last Term. Roommate is Monitor William.

During *Arrivals* wears jockstrap or thong; TMLCA. Tiffany induces him to ejaculate and spot jockstrap (Peacock House D01).

Status unchanged as *Runup* commences. | During much of the *Runup* Rodney stays bare-chested and wears either a black jockstrap or thong; TMLCA, and prone to spotting it with lubricant (e.g., Yacht D17). Bare-chested and thong; TMLCA (D21). Black muscle maillot tanga & boots; TLA (Mermaid Parade D25), where he flirts with Beka. Discovers William's tryst with Steph (D25). Bare-chested & shorts {secretly sexes with Beka; coitus; lube and cream, climax together (Peacock Garage D26).} He is brought to Cosmos Bathroom, bare-chested with jockstrap; TMLCA. Must lower jockstrap, TMLCAP, masturbate. Elle lollys his jockstrap. Rodney pees into Steph's mouth to confirm her Piss Mouth. Tiffany and Molly assist in the swallowing (Bathroom D27). Steph assumes this Obeisance shall transfer to Elle.

Rodney is not seen during the *Beach Day*. Except at the end of the Day when {William secretly sexes with Steph; BJ, coitus, anal, cum; when Rodney barges in for a three-way BBG (Peacock House D28).}

During *The Runout*, Rodney is caught with his secret *Sex Videos* with Beka; like William, he is stripped nude; TMLCAP, shaven bare, and secured

spread-eagled on Wheel w/William; mouth and cock pierced; forced cocksucking (w/William). The *Beka and Rodney Fuck Video* is shown to all the Peacocks, now in Lockdown, but the existence of two *Sex Videos* starring William and Steph, one also featuring Rodney, is kept secret; not even its creators know whether it has been discovered or not.

And Steph doesn't even know it has been made.

Rodney & William and Rodney are rolled into *The Play Party* by the Six ex-Peacocks, now Wheel Pushers, where they confront the only remaining Cosmos Lobelia, Babs and Steph. Certainly both drip pee and lubricant into their companion's mouth; both rectums are plugged so as to facilitate both rectal feeding as well as enema extraction.

The 1st *Steph & William Sex Video* plays, with severe consequences for Steph, and after their second Sex *Video* plays, William is condemned to Slavesex, and Rodney confirmed as a Whore. William is removed from the Wheel (and sent to the Dungeon), and replaced with Steph; Rodney's cock is affixed inside Steph's mouth to her pierced tongue, and Steph's clithood and vaginal piercings are chained to Rodney' tongue. The two are rolled to Flesh Ranch, and Three Terms of Whoring.

Ex-Six Peacock Pledge: Nude, TMLCAP. Names, Roommates, bodies not detailed. During *Arrivals* all Lineup, form erections, masturbate, lube, ejaculate (D01). Called Poppers. Why the Peacock House is short on Garments is not explained to them, and they should not be asking questions.

Seen during the *Runup* at the Greatest House Roar, nude with erections; TMLCAP, lube, climax (D21).

Six Peacock Pledge are not seen during *The Beach Day*.

During *The Runup* we learn that they are in Lockdown and have been stripped naked, TMLCAP, shaven completely including bare, bald; spread, erection, lube, cum. We see them at the Amphitheater when they, now naked Sedan Chair Bearers, deliver Game Mistress, then prostrate themselves into a Benzene Ring of cocksuckers and penises while they wait.

Still naked, the ex-Peacocks appear at *The Play Party* pushing the Wheel containing William and Rodney. The Wheel Pushers are naked; TMLBAP; feminized; erections; lube. While they await the Fate of others to play out, they are variously ordered to masturbate themselves and hang lube, form into a cocksucking trio as the support for China Doll's piercing tray, and care for their ex-Monitor and his Roommate. After Steph substitutes for William on the Wheel, the Pushers shall roll the Wheel, now bearing the naked, spread-eagle, 69ing Steph & Rodney to Flesh Ranch, and after delivering it, streak back to their Peacock House, where they shall Pledge again, allegedly under the care of a pair of Two Prodoms.

From Rachmaninoff House:

The Eight Rachmaninoffs, with their hockey masks and sticks are sometimes spotted in the alley behind the Cosmos House and are believed to prowl the Village, especially at night. During *The Runup,* Step spots them while streaking to the Cosmos House following her defeat at the Greatest House Roar (D21), and again while she is forced to display herself naked and pink publicly on the Back Landing (D22). She encounters them streaking back from the Nugget and is climaxed out of her body (D23).

The Eight Rachmaninoffs, with their hockey masks and sticks, are not spotted during *The Beach Day* or *The Runout.*

The Rachmaninoffs are presumed to be among the audience of strangers who watch and mingle with the Cosmos Lobelia during *The Runout.*

None of the Cosmos Lobelia at *The Play Party* recognize the Rachmaninoffs; they have been face stripped of their hocky masks & present naked, standing-secured-surrender, with wrists secured to collars and penises & testicles secured behind clamps on floor poles. Getting their cocks sucked is painful, getting buggered just is, and all eat what they are fed. Their Fate is undefined.

From the Nugget:

Ex-MomCap (Now Pacmo Pinky): Body details previously redacted are revealed forthwith. During *Arrivals*: Front-button shirt tied bare-midriff and cargo pants plus casual shoes. Navelage; M, 24x7.

During *The Runup*, House Mom greets two contingencies of Cosmos at the Nugget. She has no costume changes.

She does not appear during *The Beach Day*, although her presence behind Strippers Penny and Coco, and the future Cosmos Strippers, is heartfelt.

During *The Runout* we are informed that because of Robyn's escape and Babs' failure, that MomCap has been demoted to Stripper, renamed Pacmo Pinky, and is currently modeling naked in the Camera Lounge. She is replaced by the newly promoted former Monitor Janet.

Body details will no longer be redacted. Pacmo Pinky is a brunette, 5' 10", 130 lbs., 35B, 26, 35, splotchy areolas, shaven, nude, TMLBAP.

Pacmo Pinky arrives with Janet at the Amphitheater. She is full-frontal and wears one shoe (Darleen wears) the other. Pubic hair is shaven bare. TMLBAP. She will become the statement of a Nugget Burka Flower, pink and suckle nipples with Darleen.

Pacmo Pinky appears at The Play Party topless, wears a thong, and sucks cock on the Risen Cocks Lineup; she has argued that blowjobs aren't sex and is demonstrating her commitment.

New MomCap: See Janet.

Ex-Nugget Stripper Penny: Full-breasted brunette. 36C-24-36. Always naked; TMLBAP; shaven bare. Freckles on her inner lip. Roommate is Coco. See "Both" just below.

Ex-Nugget Stripper Coco: Full-breasted brunette, 36C-25-35. Always naked; TMLBAP; shaven bare. Keloid adjacent to anus. Roommate is Penny. See "Both" just below.

Both Penny & Coco: Nude 24x7 since the beginning of this Term; TMLBAP; previous heart-shaped trimmed pubic hair trim has been shaven bare. Both are scheduled for one piercing and one tattoo and have already had their clithoods pierced and ringed. Cosmos Pledge and Roommates last Term, defeated by Babs and Janet in a Mudwrestling Contest. Following defeat, they shared the Double Dong before departing for the Nugget and it made a deep impression on them. They remain Roommates this Term.

Penny and Coco take the Dong with them when they streak to the Nugget during *The Arrivals*, but are forbidden to share it. They stay naked 24x7, and spread, shave, pink, work toys, cream, and climax center Stage. The fact that the Dressing Room with its attached glass toilets is completely cammed doesn't forbid Penny and Coco from peeing into a cup or a shot glass on Stage.

During *The Runup*, *Videos* of Penny and Coco lapdancing and soloing the Dong circulate the Cosmos House. A deeper impression is made when the Cosmos watch the Roommates beg to share the Dong next Term, knowing that Whoring is a likely outcome. Penny and Coco do loan the Dong to guests Kimju and Molly to ride on Stage (D20), and again three Days later to Tiffany, who shares it in both pussy and ass with Steph (D23).

Before the Cosmos depart the Nugget, Penny and Coco give the Dong to Tiffany (who takes it to the Cosmos House); they give the Shaving Kit to Steph (Robyn will take to the Cosmos House); in return Penny and Coco acquire a right to share the Double Penetrator, very intelligent Ben-Wa Balls and a Procto, along with a Piss Mouth, via Robyn, which actually relieves Tiffany,(D23).

At the Mansion Open House (D27). Penny and Coco briefly acquire the Shaving Kit from Steph, and use it to shave Elle bare bald and naked. Then after Elle is piss climaxed on the Glass Bull and before she is sent to streak to the Doghouse, Penny and Coco secret the Shaving Kit inside Elle's vagina and rectum.

On the *Beach Day*, Penny and Coco are discovered by the Cosmos during their Beach Hike (D28). Both present bare and naked, on their backs, X-spread. They are commanded to pink and masturbate, cammed, then put at ease to join the group. At various times they are ordered to join the Lineup and chant, pull China Doll's butt cheeks apart and kiss her ass, and make out.

When at ease Penny and Coco may seek their own payback, like tormenting their former Monitor, Steph; Steph is lucky to hold her shirt in her teeth, so she is unable to beg Penny and Coco to pee on her. The Strippers also have grudge with Monitors Babs and Janet, and make a power play.

Throughout the day they are tormented about their begging for the Dong, and eventually agree to Opt-Whore to get it.

They leave the Beach first, and are seen one final time as the Cosmos pass by on their return. This time they are face down with their assholes presented to the radiant sun. They will not be returning to the Nugget; anything they might think they possess they don't. Eventually a handler from Flesh Ranch will arrive to transport them in a pickup truck to the Nugget.

They share the Double Penetrators (Ben-wa Balls and Procto) and the Shaving Kit (Sphere and Cylinder). Both retain credit for one tattoo.

| During their transport from the Beach to Flesh Ranch, and subsequently, both of their mouths, vaginas, and rectums are sexually used; this is accomplished by moving the Insertions around.

During *The Runout,* now Dong and Dirty Whores Penny & Coco, are brought to the Post Henge and allowed to haze Babs & Six Cosmos, now all Lockdown Lobelia. Both Whores are naked and covered with goo, TMLBAP. Goo seeps out of their mouths, vaginas, and rectums, it saturates the hair on their heads and gets on their faces. At the Post Henge they shave Babs bare and bald and cream her, and feed her goo & trimmings. Donate the Double Penetrator to Kimju; donate Shaving Kit to Steph, and remain TMLBAP, bare. Absent these Props, Penny & Coco may now be double penetrated, triple penetrated, and gangbanged. Other cocks deposit semen all over their naked bodies.

Dong and Dirty Whores Penny & Coco make two appearances at the *Play Party*. Fist, bare-bald-naked, bow-spread-sucking on the Risen Cocks Lineup; TMLBAP. Their uplifted buttocks are repeatedly coitaled & analed, both accumulate prolific vaginal & anal creampies as well as their own valiva. Collection Dishes overflow, both get heavily cumdumped. Positioning prevents the Cosmos Lobelia from identifying these transient party favors. They lick each other clean for the Cams, but not the eyes of the Cosmos Lobelia.

For their second appearance Penny wears what was once Babs' Black bra & low-rise nombril Bikini, and Coco wears what was once Steph's front-button croptop and low rise capri slacks. The gaining of Two Garments each spooks the remaining Cosmos Lobelia; the naked but still confident Steph notches revenge for the insult, Babs correctly interprets the omen as a humiliation now and of more to come.

Penny and Coco both drop their bottoms so they enable Babs to lick creampies out of their assholes, creampies out of their pussies, and practice keeping up with a stream.

They separate Beka & Elle, collect the Double Dong from their rectums into their mouths, rise & exit. Some Lobelia are unsure where they go next.

Ex-Nugget Stripper Odee: Racing stripe. Nude; TMLBAP; shaven bare. Roommate is Hottie. Pinks in Nugget during *The Runup*. Not seen on *The Beach Day* or during *The Runout*. At Midnight either she or Hottie will Opt Whore and the other will Opt Pledge.

At *The Play Party* it turns out that both Odee & Hottie have Opted Whore, evidenced by their naked bow-spread-suck position on the Risen Cocks Lineup. Both are fucked endlessly, both pussies hang spunk down to Collection Dishes. Both are buttplugged, certainly to prevent anal sex, and because the buttplug is very able to tease through the membranes and modulate cocks penetrating deep into Odee's vaginal pipe.

Ex-Nugget Stripper Hottie: Tattoo around anus. Nude; TMLBAP; shaven bare. Roommate is Odee. Pinks in Nugget during *The Runup*. Not seen on *The Beach Day* or during *The Runout*. At Midnight either she or Odee will Opt Whore and the other will Opt Pledge.

At *The Play Party* it turns out that both Odee & Hottie have Opted Whore, evidenced by their naked bow-spread-suck position on the Risen Cocks Lineup. Both are fucked endlessly, both pussies hang spunk down to Collection Dishes. Both are buttplugged, certainly to prevent anal sex, and because the buttplug is very able to tease through the membranes and modulate cocks penetrating deep into Hottie's vaginal pipe.

Other Ex-Nuggets: Bodies not described. Nude by default, TMLBAP. Assume they pink and pee in the Nugget, lapdance, face-rub, get bare boobs fondled, and lolly up after the Patrons. All of course are Pee-Camers, all are cammed 24x7, even in infrared if the lights are out. Janet brings Seven of them to the Amphitheater during *The Runup*, nude underneath burqas; no exposures, except for slits for eyes, barefoot as always.

Certainly many Nuggets aspire to Opt Whore, but only half make it.

From the Beauty Salon:

Madam Nurse Beautician: Body details redacted, although believed to be 36C-25-36 5' 10". She is one Caste superior to House Mom el Capitan, two Castes superior to Monitors (e.g., Babs, Janet, William), three Castes superior to Pledge, and four Castes superior to Strippers. Believed to reside at the Beauty Salon.

During *Arrivals* she gives Molly a medical exam (D08).

During the *Runup* she wears a low-cut white nurse minidress over panties, rubber hose, shoes; TL; cleavage. She is spotted at the Greatest House Roar (D21), detailed as she dyes and shaves Six Naked Cosmos (Beauty Salon D24). She attends the Mansion Open House (D27).

She is not seen on *The Beach Day*.

During *The Runout*, Beautician continues to wear the low-cut white nurse minidress over rubber hose and panties, shoes; T. Acquires Makeup Case from Babs, and will present to full-frontal, now-Monitor Caroline.

Beautician visits *The Play Party*, checks on some of her handywork, but is never seen by any Cosmos Lobelia.

Madam Inquisitor: Redacted.
Pimp Interrogator: Redacted.
Pimp Cowboy: Redacted.

From the Dungeon:

Game Mistress (GM): Body details redacted Fredacted. Owns Slavesex. Five Garments include black full or décolletage leather or rubber bodysuit with many zippers and cutout holes around navel, nipples and clit. Clithood ring. Navelage 24x7, so always M, sometimes MB, sometimes MP, sometimes MBP.

Game Mistress remains abstract in the mind of newbie Cosmos, so her appearances during the *Runup* impress. She is a guest of honor, joining Babs and a sack at her feet, the night Four Cosmos perform at the Nugget (D20); she watches the

Greatest House Roar sitting on a human table while her pussy is eaten (D21); finally, Elle does spot her dark Garments and masked face, but more fundamentally the cane-marked naked beauty with her, China Doll at the Mansion Open House (D27).

Game Mistress does not appear during the *Beach Day*, but her presence is expressed by China Doll, Slavesex extraordinary (D28).

Game Mistress answers Monitor Babs' alarm when Robyn is discovered, and upon arrival in the Cosmos Backyard wears a leather & rubber bodysuit, boots with cleats & spikes, thigh-high hose, panties, & a hat; there is cleavage & a hole for the navel, ML.

She wears a similar outfit during *The Runout*, when brought to the Amphitheater in a Sedan Chair born by Six Naked Peacocks, except she wears gloves and is sampan, still ML. She will transfer clamps on her nipples and weights from her pubis to Robyn, MLB, MLAP.

Game Mistress awaits the Cosmos Lobelia at *The Play Party* wearing a cape, gloves, boots, and two Garments hidden under the cape (5 total). She carries the very powerful Swagger Goad.

When Babs arrives, hanging by bound boobs, GM fondles her, shocks her, confirms BB's begging to Whore. GM fondles Molly, shocks Robyn & supervises her final casting in Plaster Mummy, introduces Gimbled It, gets Elle to reenact her sex scenes with It, and makes sure Beka gets analed. She approves a trade between Tiffany & Kimju so Tiffany can Whore & Kimju can strip, and she oversees the arrival of William and Rodney on the Wheel, torments them, sends William to the Dungeon and replaces him on the Wheel with Steph, departing them to Flesh Ranch, and priming Babs to ravish Gimbled It.

Slavesex China Doll: Long black hair, slender, Asian; 5' 8", 100 pounds, 31A-24-32. Nude; TMLBAP; vulva shaven bare. {Assume shaves, spreads, pinks, gapes; creams, cums, dildos, dongs. All sexes all holes.} Heavily pierced and tattooed. Total surrender includes Mind, Body, and Soul, including but not limited to all skin and holes, all body functions, all control over eyes, ears, mouth, nostrils, rectum, vagina, urethra, skin, movement of muscles and limbs, and the mind inside. Slavesex has been owned by Game Mistress for many Terms.

Seen during the *Runup* at the Greatest House Roar, nude with a braided ponytail and her mouth buried in Game Mistress's vagina, and with older cane welts on her buttocks, more recent cane welts on thighs (D21).

China Doll presents herself on *The Beach Day* after the Cosmos, Corvettes, and two Nuggets are gathered near the Hanky and Hat. She is naked; TMLBAP; bare with braided ponytail. Piercings including nose ring, ear loops with plugs, five lip rings above and below mouth, double tongue, and double studs in both nipples, double navel, large clithood ring, and five studs between opposing pussy lips. Tattoos include phases of moon under eyebrows, a mole on her cheek, and a line around her lips on the outside, an outline around both areolas, and dollar signs around her asshole. Not seen today is her name, rank and number inside the lips of her mouth, Cane marks on buttocks and back of legs.

She presents herself in spread prone position. She Pee-Cams into It; blowjobs It, snowballs with Elle. Piss Mouth à la It, with transfer to Steph and who transfers to Elle, who pisses on China Doll. Abandoned in place.

China Doll is not seen during *The Runout*.

China Doll, always nude; TMLBAP, body detailed above. Assists Game Mistress during *The Play Party*, including piercing Steph's tongue, licking up spilt urine, and manipulating Gimbled It's penis into Beka & Elle's holes.

Slavesex It a.k.a. Gimbled It: Not seen during *Arrivals* or *Runup*, possibly in a sack beneath Game Mistress' feet (Nugget). On the Beach Day penis revealed under hat. Male no other body details. Assumed nude; TMLCAP, totally shaven; totally violated; totally immobilized. Assumed to be Piss Mouth, Ejaculates, pees.

Slavesex It is not seen during *The Runout*.

Slavesex It is brought into *The Play Party* secured in a Gimble Armature suspended from the trolly above. Nude with purple stain; TMLCAP, totally shaven including bare and bald. Double piercings in head of penis. Secured to Gimble Armature, Eyepods, Gag, Earpods, buttplug, erected; stimulus controlled by the Program Genie The armature allows all of Gimbled It's body to be folded in any fashion, and in this presentation, It is secured in a tight bundle, blind-deaf-mute, bare-bald-naked, and suspended. It's entire body has been stained purple w/Gentian Violet, and It's penis is fully erect and dripping with pre-cum. Game Mistress represents that It contains enough stored semen for at least six massive ejaculations.

China Doll manipulates It's gimble; Elle is sexed orally, vaginally, anally; Babs collects It's cock out of Elle ass A2OPM, and is sexed orally & anally but denied vaginal intercourse. Elle cleans It's cock following Beka's anal A2OPM. Elle will carry It's purple stain for days, marking her mouth, pussy, asshole as deflowered. Beka will carry It's stain for days also, marking her mouth and asshole as "gone commercial," and her extremely horny pussy in chastisement.

Throughout It is never permitted to ejaculate. Following the departure of all but Babs, Babs faces It, masturbates and begs to ravish the Gimbled erection. When the Clock strikes Midnight, this Term ends, and Dong & Dirty Whore Babs – Blow Babe, Bang Babe, Bugger Babs – shall ravish It. And when she is done with It, drained at least six loads, she shall carry purple stain all over her naked body, and move to Flesh Ranch. BB's proof of Caste shall include creampies leaking out her butt, creampies dripping out her breach & butthole, and cum all over her face and down her throat that is firsthand.

§ Garment Counts

Former Cosmos House

Ex-Monitor now Whore Babs: 0.
Ex-Pledge ends Whore Tiffany: 0.
Ex-Pledge now Slavesex Robyn: 0. (or 1)
Ex-Pledge now Stripper Kimju: 0.
Ex-Pledge now Stripper Molly: 0.
Ex-Pledge now Whore Steph: 0.
Ex-Pledge now Stripper Beka: 0
Ex-Pledge now Stripper Elle: 0.

Total Garments for Eight former Cosmos: 0. All remain naked throughout *The Play Party*. They are in fact, bare-bald-naked. If Plaster Mummy counts as a Garment, Robyn gets 1, although for Slavesex, Garment Count has no definition.

Former Corvette House

Ex-Monitor now MomCap Janet: 3.
Ex- Pledge now Stripper Darleen: 0.
Ex- Pledge now Monitor Caroline: 2.
Ex- Pledge now Monitor Wendy: 2.
Ex-Pledge Lee Lollydor: No Data.
Ex-Pledge Louise: No data.
Ex-Pledge Trixi Tubes: No data.
Ex-Pledge Ginny: No data.

Total Garments for Eight former Corvettes is unknown. At the end of *The Play Party* one former Corvette has three Garments, two have two Garments and one is known to be naked.

Note that Midnight has come & gone and that all former Corvettes are now in a new Term. Lee is believed to inhabit the Nugget if only to provide Elle w/lolly competition. Louise is suspected to be working the Nugget, and there is a concern that if Trixi is not dancing there that somehow Ginny has found a way for her to progress to Flesh Ranch.

Former Peacock House

Ex-Monitor now Slavesex William: 0.
Ex-Pledge now Whore Rodney: 0.
Six Ex-Peacocks to repeat Peacocks: 0.

Total Peacocks Garments is 0.

The revelation of the Beka & Rodney Fuck Video produced Lockdown for all Peacocks, including a stopped Clock. Midnight occurs when William departs to the Dungeon, Rodney (& Steph) are rolled into Flesh Ranch, and the Six Pushes return to the Peacock House to repeat the Term.

Nugget, Ranch, Dungeon

Ex-Monitor now MomCap Janet: 3.
Ex-Stripper now Whore Penny: 0.
Ex-Stripper now Whore Coco: 0.
Ex-Pledge now Stripper Darleen Dilator: 0.
Ex-MomCap now Stripper Pacmo Pinky: 0

Madam Inquisitor: 4.
Pimp Interrogator: 4.
Madam Nurse Beautician: 4.
Pimp Cowboy: 4.
Game Mistress: 5.
Slavesex China Doll: 0.
Slavesex Gimbled It: 0. Stained.

Garment Counts 3, 4, 5 match w/Caste. Counts of 2, 1, 0 can be possible for several Castes. Midnight has come and gone for all of these Players; they play in a new Term, whereas the Cosmos Lobelia still approach Midnight

Props Histories: Books I-V

§ Props Introduction

Props are anything a Cosmos might "possess" other than their Garment(s). Props do not belong to a Cosmos and do not contribute to Garment counts; more correctly, a Cosmos "belongs" to a Prop.

There are Props which are static, Props which are soloed and can move from Player to Player, and Props which are shared. We shall detail this shortly, with further expansion upon Props which are shared.

Props which are soloed can move from Player to Player, or be ordained upon one Player at a time. Some of these Props have been enjoyed by only a single Player (e.g., only Robyn carries the Monkey Fist), but most Props migrate (e.g., the Pogo), and all have that potential

Examples of solo Props include the Alabaster Flask, Anal Intruder, Cath, Cravat, Crawlers, Dice, Makeup Case, Monkey Fist, Pear, Pink Pages, Pogo, Shaving Kit, Stims, Skeleton Keys, Snake, and the Watering Can. Static "Props" include the Dining Room Pictures, the Tiffany Porn Star Calendar, the Glass Bull, and the Centipede. This list is not exhaustive and more complete lists are found in the Props List elsewhere in this Appendix, as well as the Introduction to the Index, which addresses indexing concerns.

At least three Props are distinct because they may be shared by two Cosmos simultaneously: they are the Double Dong, the Shaving Kit, and the Double Penetrator. Detailed histories of these three Props as they are detailed shortly as they migrate during *The Arrivals, The Runup, The Beach Day, The Runout,* and *The Play Party.* There is also a detailed chronology of the Pogo and the Cath.

Props which are in Upper Case, are carefully indexed, by a) both the Upper Case Prop and the Player, or b) by only the Upper Case Prop, or c) only by the Player. There also exist many Lower Case Props; these include many pieces of medical equipment, feeding tubes, also buttplugs, dildos, clamps, and other items. They may come and go in the Game, and when indexed only follow the c) rule above. It could be argued that some of these should have their case elevated.

Previous Volumes of the Cosmos may treat different Props in different Volumes with different approaches (a, b, c), and that indexing guidelines are not always strictly followed, although the indexes have always strove to make every attempt to direct the searcher toward where that index item is resolved.

§ Double Dong

The personality and features of the Double Dong are recounted throughout The Cosmos Saga. Suffice to say the Dong seeks to promote love and harmony, and that it seeks to make itself welcome no matter what orifices it inhabits of the Donger: mouth, vagina, or rectum. It swells and locks into place on its own, takes a moment to stabilize, and evaluates what might be needed to stimulate bump 'n' grind, valiva production, and bond its two participants in the pleasure Zone.

Or calm them might they panic.

And allow them to communicate, perhaps the only way for them to communicate.

Besides shape-shifting & rippling vibrations, the Dong can also tingle and shock, get hot and cold, and sluff of enzymes which can effect either or both Dongers' biochemistry.

The Dong doesn't like inserted in just one Donger, and will sink into the first empty hole offered. Dong commitment depends upon Caste. The Dong has total memory of all Dong carriages. It knows the time of day, the geo-location, the DNA of each participant, and throughout their encapsulation of the Dong, their vital, including their heartbeat, respiration, blood oxygen level, and it most certainly knows of all climaxes

Cheating, that is unauthorized sharing of the Double Dong (e.g., by a pair of Strippers), is detected immediately by the Dong, reported upward through a network of Running Agents, and will result in a decision to let the rogue behavior build to climax, or short circuit it, literally. Either way, the Rule violation dictate an Opt Down.

Although Strippers may not share the Dong, the Rules do stipulate that Strippers may hold the Dong together hand-to-hand, and hand the Dong from one to the other. There may be times when, may it please the Patrons, and only if House Mom commands, that one Stripper grasp one end of the Double Dong firmly, guide it upon and into an orifice of the other, even masturbate the other, parking her in the Zone, and leaving her with the Dong embedded in her body and quivering center Stage. But even House Man cannot demand hole-to-hole sharing; this remains strictly forbidden under all circumstances for Strippers, is monitored by the Dong for violation, and entails harsh repercussions for any miscreants.

Some Double Dongers get addicted; addiction has consequences. Players who are addicted should discover that the Double Dong will cooperate with them to deepen their addiction. See former Pledge Penny and Coco, they donged, became addicted, spent the Term ending Midnight Stripping, and have successfully begged Dong & Dirty Whores. Now Beka and Elle face similar consequences.

Certainly the AI's inside the Dong and the network of sensors and responders that adorn many Dongers remain sensitive to Kundalini, one of the component of the Life Force and the spirit of the creative and the art of Love.

History. The Double Dong is not seen during *The Arrivals*. Its pre-history is alluded to, in particular an encounter in the previous Term in which then-Whore Tiffany dong-climaxed then-Pledge Janet, center Stage at the Nugget. Janet got promoted to her current Monitor Caste, and Tiffany acquired a Piss Mouth and an unusual Double Opt Up. It is speculated that then-Monitor Steph secretly witnessed this and made *Videos*, which got lost when she was Locked Down.

Penny and Coco, then Cosmos Pledge, acquire the Dong after losing a Mudwrestling Contest to then-Cosmos Pledge Babs and Janet, who promote to Monitors in the Term that ends at Midnight. The Dong infects the loser-Strippers before they arrive at the Nugget; they are instantly addicted to the levels of climax the Dong enchants them with. Stripper Rules forbid sharing of the Dong at the Nugget, so Penny and Coco will be driven to beg to become Dong-Hoes in order to regain access.

During *The Runup*, Strippers Penny and Coco loan the Double Dong to Kimju and Molly to climax center Stage at the Nugget (D20). Kimju and Molly are the first Cosmos Pledge to share the Double Dong, and its first physical appearance. They leave it behind, enabling Penny and Coco make solo *Videos*.

During a different visit to the Nugget, Tiffany and Steph borrow the Dong for their on-stage performance: Tiffany rides the Dong with Steph, center Stage, shaves her bare, and creams, climaxes, and pisses her in front of the Crowd at the Nugget (D23).

Tiffany does not return the Dong, she retains it on behalf of Steph, and returns with it to the Cosmos House, with the toy encunted.

At the Cosmos House Tiffany shares the Double Dong with Kimju (Day 23-24), then with Molly (Day 24), who passes it to Steph (Day 24-25), who passes it to Tiffany's anus on the morning of the Mermaid Parade (Day 25).

Tiffany takes it to the Corvette House, shares it with Ginny's rear end, and leaves it behind in Ginny and Trixi Tube's mouths at the Corvette House (D25.

Corvette Pledge and Whore-for-Life Ginny shares the Dong with Trixi Tubes (D25), and Babs observes this twosome perform a *Nine Dong Combo Vide*o in the Cosmos Backyard (D27).

On *The Beach Day* Corvette Pledge Ginny and Trixi Tubes bring the Dong with them and join a Lineup of sitting spread surrendering, pinking, and chanting Cosmos & Corvette Pledge, and occasionally Nugget Strippers. The Two Corvettes are persuaded to give the Dong to Beka and Elle, who retreat with it to the Cosmos Doghouse, and spend overnight awaiting their Stripper Fate at Midnight.

Beka hopes that the Doghouse interior really is mediated to a similar-sized, life-looking display located throughout the Prefecture, and she never hesitates to lead Elle through four possibilities of oraling and encunting the Double Dong, but by morning Elle is no longer a follower and has eaten Beka to her first climax so far this Term. The Dong addicts them, and both will beg to become Dong-Hoes.

On the morning of *The Runout*, Beka and Elle naively believe these four combinations of encuntment and oralation exhaust their Dong possibilities, But once they are moved to the Mudpit, and to and from their Interrogations, Gamers make sure that their anal and mouth and pussy combinations, their *Nine Dong Combs*, are added to their media.

"Negative reinforcement bonding," works on this duo.

Following Beka and Elle's physical separation the Double Dong remains with them, initially in a form where each of them believe they have sole possession, but eventually revealed to them that each harbors one-half of a CyberDong.

The detached CyberDong cooperates with Beka and Elle, enabling them to stimulate arousal, demand attention, but also conscious of their valiva production. Meanwhile, Penny and Coco connive to get what they believe is rightfully theirs. They brought the Double Penetrator and Shaving Kit to the Post Henge and left with three empty holes.

Beka and Elle revert to a singular, long and fat Double Dong to *The Play Party*, carrying it in their stretched rectums, bound and suspended, secured butt-to-butt, bare-bald-naked, hanging from the trolly above. Creameries. Both beg Dong & Dirty Whores at Midnight. During the Party they are separated with the Dong transferred to Penny and Coco's mouths, ensuring both A2OPM. Penny and Coco are in their new Term, and the promise to give them the Dong has been fulfilled.

§ Shaving Kit

The Shaving Kit is a Prop and consists of two parts: a watertight hollow Sphere worn in the vagina and containing soap, and a hollow Cylinder worn in the rectum containing a razor and folding scissors. Both the Sphere and the Cylinder unscrew in the middle.

The Shaving Kit qualifies as one of the Double Penetrators, meaning that two orifices may be simultaneously penetrated, typically the vagina and rectum. The Rules dictate that a single Player can carry both parts, or that Roommates may share the Prop. A single Player carrying both parts qualifies for a double penetration obeisance (two orifices are simultaneously penetrated)

Rarely half of the Shaving Kit may be carried in the mouth.

Note that the Shaving Kit prevents penetration

The Shaving Kit should not be confused with the Double Penetrator, likewise its Ben-Wa Balls and Procto may be soloed and enables a Player to carry DP, or shared with a Roommate.

The Shaving Kit is alluded to during *The Arrivals*, but never seen.

Upon their arrival at the Nugget, then-Strippers Penny and Coco shave bare (D06), suggesting the presence of the Shaving Kit there. In fact Penny and Coco shall shave every day, live feed, center Stage at the Nugget. Armpits, legs, pussy, asshole.

During *The Arrivals,* Cosmos Pledge Tiffany, Molly, and eventually Beka and Elle (D14), all beg to shave bare; Tiffany and Molly beg to shave bald as well (D01, D14). Alas, but for soap, scissors, and a razor, none of these begs are fulfilled. However,

The Shaving Kit makes its first appearance during *The Runup*, center Stage at the Nugget, when Penny and Coco produce it to assist Tiffany in shaving Steph bare and bald, climaxing her for a second time that evening, and leaving her naked (D23). Thus Steph becomes the first bare-bald-naked Cosmos. Still at the Nugget she lucks into the Duel Option, after Tiffany fails to take what is intended for her. Robyn carries the Shaving Kit, holding it in two hands, back to the Cosmos House on behalf of Steph, and orders it into Kimju's "kunny and kornhole." Kimju had silently accommodated Robyn's offerings, her mouth remaining gagged with the Dong. A long overnight (concluding D23).

On the morning of Day 24, Robyn moves the Shaving Kit from Kimju to Beka, who will flash her silvery Soap Sphere to hungry eyes during the Mermaid Parade (D25).

Beka transfers the Shaving Kit to Steph on the morning of D26; Steph will retain it but never gets an opportunity to shave Days of stubble. Steph will carry it to the Mansion Open House (Day 27), where Penny and Coco extract it (a final

humiliation for Steph), to shave an already-naked Elle bare and bald, let Elle ride the Glass Bull to a piss climax, and then secrets the Kit inside Elle to take with her as she streaks bare-bald-naked back to the Doghouse (D27).

This slight-of-hand confuses Steph, who believes that Penny and Coco absconded with it.

Elle still carries the Shaving Kit ensconced within her nook and nadir at the start of *The Beach Day,* including the walk down the beach (Beach Hike AM D28). Steph and others think it still resides with Penny and Coco, especially after they see the glint of the Double Penetrators in Penny and Coco's private parts later during *The Beach Day.*

During The Beach Day, Elle extracted The Shaving Kit from herself in full public view during *The Beach Day*; Elle then uses it to shave Beka as bare and bald and she is, also in full public view (D28). Elle then bequeaths the Shaving Kit to Tiffany, who uses it to depilate Molly, and who in turn depilates Tiffany, reducing the both of them to bare and bald except for their topknots (Beach Lineup D28). Now only Babs, Robyn, and Kimju have hair, Steph having been shaven top and bottom Days ago.

Penny and Coco manage to appropriate the Shaving Kit from Molly at the end of *The Beach Day,* adding it to the Double Penetrator's Ben-Wa Balls and Procto, already inserted. Thus with both pussies and rectums are occupied, and when their Clock strikes Midnight, the two newly-minted pair of Dong Whores can legitimately claim to be "Double-Double Penetrated." Thus they end *The Beach Day.*

Penny and Coco are taken orally while they still lie in the sand awaiting transport to Flesh Ranch; after that the Soap Sphere and the Cylinder of the Shaving Kit are moved vagina to mouth and rectum to mouth; likewise the Ben-Wa Balls and the Procto are moved, so that Penny and Coco may be taken orally, vaginally, and anally. They are Dong and Dirty Whores.

Ex-Pledge now Lockdown Lobelia Tiffany and Molly lose their topknots when they are cut apart in the Mudpit on the morning of *The Runout.*

It is not until during *The Runout* when now Goo Whores Penny and Coco visit the Seven Naked Cosmos Lobelia affixed to the Post Henge, that the Shaving Kit reappears (Post Henge LD2). The Goo Whores first reduce Kimju to as bare-bald-naked as the other Six former Cosmos Pledge. Next they render Babs equally bare-bald-naked except for a topknot, which will eventually need to be cut off to free Babs from her Henge Post. The Whores lather Babs' bush with goo, shave it off, and feed her the goo clippings. They shave her eyebrows off, trim her eyelashes, and clip off any ear or nose hairs.

The Goo Whores then inserted the Shaving Kit into the now stubbly Steph, bypassing an opportunity to tidy her up and frustrating her because of her own armbound inability to use it to shave her itchy self.

With the Double Penetrator passed to Molly, both Molly and Steph are protected from vaginal and anal penetrations. Following the divesture of these two Props, Penny and Coco no longer have to offer only one hole at a time, they are ready for double, even triple penetration.

Steph carries the Shaving Kit to *The Play Party*. If she has not already discovered that the Soap Sphere and Tool Cylinder are lively, she becomes super aware during the Party, losing all control of her vaginal secretions. On a more positive note, Steph does credit the Shaving Kit as providing a barrier to penetration

Steph thinks that come Midnight she will Opt Monitor, and absent the armbinder, extract the Shaving Kit, tidy herself, and beautify her Pledge. Fate provides an alternative, when China Doll removes the Shaving Kit from Steph after the first *Steph and William Sex Video I,* and takes possession of it within her own body. It is the last we see of it during the Term reported on.

Steph wisely begs to Whore after her *Sex Video I,* and begs Dong and Dirty Whore after her *Sex Video II.* Maybe Pimp Cowboy can butch the stubble so that it never stops itching, and so it scratches up every shaven male fucking Steph's socket.

§ Double Penetrator

The Double Penetrator is a Prop consisting of Ben-Wa Balls and a Procto, is treated as a singular item, even though it consists of two main elements: the Ben-Wa Balls residing inside the vagina, and the Procto which is lodged in the rectum. The Ben-Wa Balls contain highly advanced thermal, electrical, vibrational, and shape shifting forms with a local AI, one that is also connected to one of Automatron's Running Agents. The Procto can move up and down the colon and is equally intelligent/shape shifting.

The Procto is certainly able to train gape, and the Ben-Wa Balls train secretions.

Note that it is not necessary for both components of the Double Penetrator be carried by the same Player.

Also, observe that in the Index, that the term "Double Penetrators" is also indexed and includes references to all Props which can so function,

including the Double Penetrator but also the Shaving Kit (also a singular item).

The Double Penetrator is not seen during *The Arrivals.* During *The Runup* we discover that Penny and Coco share the Ben-Wa Balls and the Procto in different configurations: at various times each has retained both; at other times they have each carried either the Ben-Wa Balls or the Procto (D23, D27).

On *The Beach Day,* Penny and Coco are discovered to be carrying the Double Penetrator. Although it is mistaken by some to be the Shaving Kit (actually residing in Elle). The four different ways the two of them can share these two objects is detailed. Toward the end of *The Beach Day,* Penny and Coco will also acquire the Shaving Kit, making them double-double penetrated.

During their recovery and journey to Flesh Ranch both will be sexed first orally, then both Props are moved around so that each is sexed coitally and then anally as well (D28-ND1). Both get to A2M and to A2OPM off the Props.

During *The Runout* the now Goo Whores Penny & Coco visit the Cosmos Lobelia at the Post Henge (ND2), extract and use the Shaving Kit (detailed above), and bestow the Double Penetrator into Molly. Penny and Coco exit begging double cock penetration, triple cock penetration, and gangbangs.

The Double Penetrator prevents vaginal and anal cock penetration of Molly as Lockdown continues into *The Play Party.* Molly is the first Cosmos Lobelia to exit *The Play Party* (LD6), and expects to arrive at the Nugget mouth-ready. She will of course have to share if not give away the Double Penetrator after she arrives, and although Strippers can argue that "blowjobs aren't sex," no such argument can be made for coitus. Likewise, Strippers are forbidden anal intercourse, so that Molly can rest assured that her vagina and rectum remain virginal.

§ The Pogo

The Pogo is a device with a dildo on the end of a stick. In practice the Pogo may be handheld, but is more commonly rested with one end on the floor and the other deeply inserted into the Player standing above, secured to spreader bar so that self-extraction is impossible, or even deployed during a hogtie and insult the bottom with an anal intrusion the bottom is unable to eject.

Needless to say, the head of the Pogo incorporates many biometric sensors to measure everything inside its home, provide vibration, electrical, and temperature stimulation to its resident cavity, and share data with Running Agents. It also has the ability to shape-shift; obviously it effect on the body combines its acute awareness

The Pogo is first seen during *The Runout.*

The Pogo is deployed by Superiors after the Cosmos have been runout and are secured on the Post Henge (LD2/ND2). The Pogo is first used to arouse Beka. It is transferred to Steph, used to arouse her watching various Cosmos get pierced, and finally to Kimju, where it joints the long Centipede crawling her rectum, and the Cath, managing her urinary functions.

Kimju is emptied of props on her way to *The Play Party.* The Pogo reappears where it is inserted into a helpless and much reduced Babs to zone her in preparation of ravishing It (LD9).

§ The Cath

The Cath, sometimes lowercase, is a tube inside the urethra between the bladder and the outside of the body; it manages the excretion of urine, the pressure inside the bladder, and can irrigate as well as drain.

If indeed a normal catheter suspends ones control of ones pee, the Caths found in the Game contains not just valves and controls, but also monitors and learning capabilities. At its basics it monitors bladder pressure and determines urine release.

The Cath can certainly be worn alone, but it is frequently combined with Props which possess the vagina, rectum, and/or mouth.

"Once a Cath, anytime a Cath" is one of the Rules.

During this Term the Cath has been worn for extended periods by Kimju, especially by Babs and now for an indefinite duration, Robyn.

Babs knows about the Cath from experience: the Cath can grow bigger, electrify, vibrate, change temperature, and, most importantly, coordinate with other Props such as Pear and Snake. The Cath managed all of BB's urinary function from the time she was interrogated in the Basement at the beginning of *The Runout* until it was removed in transit to *The Play Party.*

But Babs knows the Rule. *I'm a Pee-Camer and Piss Mouth and I will be dancing naked, center Stage at the Nugget, with a catheter showing out and urine bag strapped to my leg.*

Kimju was also cathed during *The Runout*, If indeed Babs got to share the Cath with the Pear and Snake, Kimju shared the Cath with the Pogo and Centipede. It had been a briefer experience, the equipment had been removed prior to the

Amphitheater display, but the total violation had subdued Kimju into realizing she had absolutely no control over urine, bowels, or sex hole.

Kimju chooses to limit her imagination to *pinking center Stage and pouring shots.*

Babs and Kimju each know that the Cath can build up pressure in the bladder so it pushes against the sexual insides and drives their constrictions, torque, and secretions. Each knows she will be driven to sexual surrender when and where it pleases Gamers, and she will pee when and where this decision is made for her.

And so both appreciate the effects of the Cath inside the Plaster Mummy, with the Monkey Fist and Anal Intruder violating Robyn's vagina. And a Speculum that drains Robyn's runnel. Babs and Kimju both assume, if only from their own experience, that one of Robyn's functions is a runnel machine. Cybernetician the Running Agents may seek to maximize production. Or just schedule total isolation. So that when sound, pictures, and sensation might appear, Robyn will embrace them, and crave being surfed into the Zone.

Glossary

Alabaster Flask—A **Prop**. Kept in Bedroom desk drawer. Can contain **diuretic, aphrodisiac**.

Alumni Reprise—An **Event**, last **Term** with Tiffany & Janet, this **Term** with Kimju & Molly.

anal—An **Obeisance**, penetration of the **anus** and **rectum** by a **penis**, also by **strapon, dildo, dong**.

anus—The rear entrance to the **rectum**, a.k.a. asshole.

aphrodisiac—A substance which stimulates sexual desire.

areola, areolage—An **Exposure** or partial exposure of the areola of the **breast**.

ass-to-mouth (A2M)—The relocation of a **penis** from one's **rectum** into one's **mouth**.

ass-to-other-persons-mouth (A2OPM)—Moving a **penis** from a different **rectum** into the **mouth**.

Auditions—**Events, Pledge** including **Cosmos** beg to **dance at** the **Nugget & Opt Strip** next **Term**.

Automatron—A giant Artificial Intelligence (AI) data storage and analysis system somewhere.

bandeau—**Species** of **soutien-gorge**, which covers the **breasts** but lacks straps. Has two edges.

Backyard—A **Location**. Adjacent to the **Cosmos** House, contains Bell, Mudpit, Post Henge.

Baseboard Strippers—Two of the **Dining Room Pictures**, of Penny and Coco, both **naked & pink**.

begs, begging—Usually lower Caste Gamer requesting privileges or punishments from higher Caste.

bellage—An **Exposure** of the belly, not necessarily including the **navel**.

belly-up belly-down—**Bellage** above and below the **navel**, and certainly exposing it.

ben-wa balls—Spherical balls worn inside **vagina**; may be hollow or heavy, with hot/cold, vibration, electricity; AI, wireless to **Running Agent**. Combined w/**procto** to define the **Double Penetrator**.

bikini—A two-piece **Garment** consisting of a **soutien-gorge** and a **culotte**, maximally a **nombril**.

bra, brassiere –A **Garment** and **species** of **soutien-gorge** that covers the **breasts** and has two shoulder straps. A brassiere has four edges.

blowjob—An **Obeisance**. The gratification of a **penis** using the **mouth** and tongue.

body & exposures, an Exposure—A part of the body that is uncovered (e.g., breast, leg), also teases (e.g., titter, vagflash). A full list of **body & exposures** is found in the Index: body & exposures. Almost all are lower case words and indexed as: *GamerName:* body & exposures: *bodyPart*.

bodyparts—see **body & exposures**, also for index guidance.

boobage—An **Exposure** of one or both entire **breasts**, yet wearing a Garment above the waist, so *not* **topless**. Boobage may involve a single-bare-breasted maillot, an evening gown uplifting bare **breasts**, a bib, a cutout bra, etc. *See* **cleavage, areolage, nippage, titter**.

bottomless—A "**Garment**" which is the absent case of itself. The baring of the body below the waist. **Count** = zero. Presumes **pubage, buttage, leggage**. A topless + bottomless = nude.

breast(s)—Female anatomy **Exposure**, crowned by **areola & nipples**. *See* **boobage, breastplay**.

breastplay—An **Obeisance**. Arousal of **breasts** and **nipples**, either by one's self or another.

bukkake—An **Obeisance**. Discharges of multiple male ejaculate onto a subject's face and body.

butt, buttage—An **Exposure** of all or most of the buttocks. A **g-string** or **thong** is always buttage. Compare to **cheekage**. A buttage is not a **bottomless**, but a bottomless features buttage.

buttplug—A **Prop**, including the **Procto**, which is inserted into the **rectum** via the **anus**. *See* procto

Cam—A still or video camera, part of a hovering **Drone**; or a stationary **Location**.

Caste—One of eight ranks in the **Game**. The Castes are: **Game Mistresses or Masters (GMs)**, who manage **Slavesex; Madams** or **Pimps**, who manage **Whores; House Mom (**or **Dad) el Capitans (MomCaps** or **DadCaps)**, who manage **Monitors & Strippers; Monitors** who manage **Pledge**, and **Pledge, Strippers**, and **Slavesex**, who manage nobody and are managed instead.

Chant—A series of words, sometimes with an accompanying action, designed to train endurance, inculcate ideas, or produce arousal.

Charm—Possibly a magical property, which some Gamers think protects them and provides good fortune, and which some Gamers don't believe exists.

cheekage, cheeky line—An **Exposure** of the bottom, or cheek, of the **buttocks** out the bottom of briefs or shorts; the line where the **buttocks** meet the **leg** in a crease. The opposite of **rugage**.

clit—An **Exposure**, the sensitive ball of erectile tissue in a female above the **vagina**, inside a hood.

cleavage—Partial **Exposure** of breasts. *See* **décolletage, downblouse, leanover, lift-up, neathage**.

climax—An **Obeisance**. A male or female sexual release, possibly accompanied by fluids.

Clock—A timepiece that keeps track of **Days**. Index references Days (Dnn), nn range 01 > 28.

coitus—An **Obeisance**. The sexual joining of the **penis** into the **vagina**.

commitments—Exposures, Garments, Events, really anything a **Gamer** maintains on-going.

concerns—Anxieties and fears of **Pledge**, be they irrational or the result of careful evaluation.

conflicts—Situations between two **Gamers** that involve clashes of personality, style, and contests.

Corvette—One of eight **Houses** at the **School**, as well as a resident thereof.

Cosmos—One of eight **Houses** at the **School**, as well as a resident thereof (singular and plural).

costume—*See* **Garment**.

Count—*See* **Garment Count**.

Cravat—A **Prop**; a bondage frame for holding a **Gamer** in a fixed position for a prolonged time.

cream—**Valiva**, female **vaginal** secretions produced during arousal. The transuding of secretions.

culotte—A **Garment**; the generic term for a **bikini** or underwear bottom regardless of its **species**. Examples include **g-string**, panties, **tanga**, shorts, and a *bikini* **nombril**.

cum—Verb, meaning to **climax**, both for a male and a female. Noun, **semen**, produced at climax.

cum drinking—*See* **gokkun**.

cum sharing—*See* **snowballing**.

cunnilingus—Oral pleasure to the sex organs of a woman, by either a man or a woman.

dance, dancing—Movement of the body in a rhythm, often with music; may be sexually suggestive.

Day—One Day of the **Term**. Spans: *Arrivals* (D01>D14). *Runup*, (D15>D27). *Beach Day*, (D28). During *The Runout* the **Clock** is stopped for some **Players**, and a new **Term** has begun for others.

décolletage (décolleté, adj.) —An **Exposure**. Cleavage of the **breasts**, e.g., from wearing a low-cut neckline. Also a low-cut neckline that exposes the neck, shoulders, and parts of the **breasts**.

Dice—A **Prop** stored below the Desktop, in Bedroom; No Dice games are played during **Runout**.

dildo—A **Prop** designed to be inserted into the **vagina**. A **Dong** presents two simultaneous dildos.

Dining Room Pictures—Four Pledge last Term: Babs, Janet, **Baseboard Strippers** Penny & Coco.

dishabille—A state of partial, careless undress, often intentionally careless.

diuretic –Substance that induce the bladder in one's body to void urine.

double cock penetration—An **Obeisance**. Penetration of any two of the **mouth, vagina, anus** by two penises; three combinations, and three possible double insertions into the same orifice.

Double Dong, Dong—A **Prop** with special Rules and powers, seen at the Nugget as well as the Cosmos House. For those who are permitted the experience, the Double Dong enables two **Pledge** to share the Dong in their **vaginas, rectums,** and **mouths**, or any combination thereof. **Pledge** and **Whores** are allowed to Double Dong; **Strippers** may not, but may solo one-half as if a long **dildo**.

double penetration, DP—An **Obeisance**. The insertion of living or inanimate objects into more than one of these three orifices: **mouth, vagina, anus,** *See* **double cock penetration** for penises; *see* **Double Penetrator** also **Shaving Kit** for **Props**. Hybrids also exist.

Double Penetrator—One of several **Double Penetrators**, includes the **ben-wa balls** and the **procto**.

Double Penetrators—A pair of **Props**; that together, e.g., penetrate both the **vagina** and **anus**. Rules dictate that single **Gamer** may simultaneously enjoy both toys, or Roommates may share and each carry a toy. DPs include the **ben-wa balls** and the **procto**, and the **Shaving Kit**.

downblouse—An exposure of the **breasts** and/or **nipples** created by leaning forward.

DP—*See* **double cock penetration** for real penises; *see* **Double Penetrators** for **Props**.

Duel—An opportunity to pick any **Game** and play it with any Cosmos Pledge. A sure win.

Earpods – A cybernetic **Prop** worn in the ear which can silence sound as well as transmit sound.

ears— One **body & exposures**, and a part of the **head**. Sometimes managed by **Earpods**.

el Capitan—*See* **Caste**.

enema—An **Obeisance**, insertion of fluids into the **rectum** via the **anus**, often by a syringe or tube.

entailment—action synchronized at a distance, for example a Pledge **Game Rule** violation entails the Monitor to the same Rule violation, and to similar or more demanding consequences.

Eraser Heads—Running Agent controlled implants in nipples, able to stimulate nipple & surround.

Exposure—*See* **body & exposures**.

Event—A performance or contest, e.g., the **Mudwrestling Contest**, the **Alumni Reprise**.

eyes— An **Exposure**, and a part of the **head**. Sometimes managed by **Eyepods**. Often **face and eyes**.

Eyepods – A cybernetic **Prop** which can block vision as well as augment vision.

face and eyes—An **Exposure**, front part of **head** below hairline, including **nose**, extending to **ears**.

facial—An **Obeisance**. Semen ejaculated onto partner's face, often into the **mouth** for a **swallow**.

Fate—Each **Cosmos'** outcome at the end of the **Term** (at **Midnight**).

feet and toes—An **Exposure**, the extremity of the **leg** and connected to it at the ankle.

fellatee—The recipient of a **blowjob**.

fellator, fellatrice, fellatrix (pl) —The provider of a **blowjob**.

figure—An **Exposure**, and repository of details, indexed *GamerName:* body & exposures: figure.

finger-fucking—An **Obeisance**. The insertion of one or more fingers into the **vagina**, either by oneself or another individual(s). This behavior can also be applied to the **rectum**. *See also* **fisting**.

Fisting—An **Exposure**. The insertion of a fist into the **vagina**. Compare to **finger-fucking**.

force-cumming—The providing of a **climax** to a recipient.

Free-Fuck—Sex acts that violate Rules prohibiting sex, as for all Pledge & Strippers.

fresh, freshen—The exudation of **valiva**, a.k.a. **cream**, by a female.

fricatrice—he or she who provides a **handjob**. A handjober.

full-frontal—An **Exposure**. The baring of the **breasts** and the **pubis** (hairy or shaven). Not all **nudes** are full-frontal, and not all full-frontal exposures involve total nudity (e.g., hose and heels).

g-string—A **Garment**; a **culotte** that covers the **pubis** but not the **buttocks**, and ties with strings.

gangbang—An **Obeisance**. Sex by many individuals upon a single one; presume all holes taken.

Game—The metaverse reality practice at **School**. Also, a prize, possibly a **Garment** or **Obeisance**.

Game Mistress or Master (GM)—the highest Caste in the **Game**; *see* **Caste**.

Game Rules—The Rules of the **Game**. *See* the Index, Game Rules, for details.

Gamer—One who plays the **Game**, including the **Cosmos Players**, and **voyeurs** who join in.

Garment—A single costume piece that a **Cosmos** might wear. *See* **Garment Count**.

Garment Count—The number of **Garments** that a **Gamer** wears; determines Opt Up, Opt Down.

GM—*See* **Game Mistress or Master**. Not considered disrespectful.

gokkun—An **Obeisance**. Drinking semen, often from a glass, off a dish, out of a pan. **Swallowing.**

gokuraku-ojo—Sexual orgasm resulting in death, caused by hyper-stimulation.

goal—Something a **Cosmos** seeks to achieve. Indexed by *GamerName:* goals

Goo Gobbler—A **Player** who gulps **semen**. *See also* **gokkun, bukkake, swallowing.**

gugusse — An effeminate youth who frequents the private company of priests (Paris, 1880).

hair—An **Exposure**; used here only for hair on the **head** and sometimes the body, but to be distinguished from **pubic hair** and the partial exposure of pubic hair, a.k.a. **hairage**.

hairage—An **Exposure**. The partial exposure of **pubic hair**; including **pubic hair** that leaks out, be it above the top or to the sides of a **culotte**, be it an accidental or a deliberate **pullaside**, or, in relaxed usage, pubic hair viewed **upskirt** (via a **vagflash** or an extended spread).

halter—A **Garment** and **species** of **soutien-gorge** that covers the **breasts** and has a neck strap and a back strap. A halter has three edges and three standard fastening opportunities (neck, front, back).

handbra—Hands covering **breasts**. Included in "**Garments;**" species of **soutien-gorge**; **Count** = 0.

handjob—An **Obeisance**. The **masturbation** of the penis or vagina by the hand of a partner. May lead to **climax**. Does not include oral-genital contact (a **blowjob**), or self-arousal (**masturbation**).

Hand Signs—Commands made with hands and fingers to indicate body **positions** and **Obeisance**.

hands and fingers—An **Exposure**, the extremity of the arm and connected to it at the wrist.

headlights—An **Exposure**. Aroused nipples that form shapes through (typically opaque) clothing.

head—An **Exposure**, connects by neck to body, includes **face and eyes, mouth, nose, ears, hair**.

House—One of eight **Locations** where students who attend **School** reside. *See* the 2-story Plans.

House Dad el Capitan (DadCap)—Masculine. The third highest Caste in the **Game**; *see* **Caste**.

House Mom el Capitan (MomCap)—Feminine. The third highest Caste in the **Game**; *see* **Caste**.

Hover—Situation where a **Gamer** doesn't change **Caste** at end of the **Term**. Only available to certain Castes, including but not limited to **Monitors, MomCaps, GMs, and Slavesex**. Hover is not available for **Pledge** or **Strippers**, who must either **Opt Up** or **Opt Down**.

inguinal, inguinal line, inguinalage—An **Exposure**, this body landmark delineates **pubis** from **leg**.

Jail—See **Lockdown**. One quick way to **Jail** is to be apprehended while **streaking**.

Karma—Good and bad will disbursed into the **Game**, accumulated and traded by **Gamers**.

kissing—An **Obeisance**. Mouth upon the body of another individual; sometimes mouth-to-mouth and augmented with the tongue, a variation called French kissing. Same or opposite sex.

Kundalini—The sex force in the Universe, present in the **Game, Cosmos, Locations,** everywhere.

Lady-Part Words—Words tactical to individual **Cosmos' body** parts. These are not included in this Glossary nor the Index; there exists many Lady-Part Words, e.g., for the **breasts, areolas, nipples, pubic hair, vagina, valiva, buttocks, anus,** and many sex acts and characterizations.

lapdancing—An **Obeisance**; a **dance** by a **Stripper** performed in the lap of a Patron.

laxatives—Substances that induce a body to void bowels.

leanover—A body movement that permits a voyeur to look **downblouse**. The resultant **Exposure**.

legs, leggage—An **Exposure**, a **body part** which joins to the torso and **butt** at the **inguinal** and **cheeky line**, and which includes the thighs, knees, calves, ankles, and **feet and toes**.

lift-up—An action that rides a shirt upward, enabling **neathage** if not **titter**, **boobage**.

Lineup—The assembly of the **Cosmos Pledge** into a side-by-side line, often for morning **Reveille**.

Lingerie Kit—Two bags originally retained by Caroline & Wendy. Each contain(ed) five **Garments**; each **Pledge** wore any two at one time. The Garments are a bra, panties or thong, slip, hose, heels. At Midnight Caroline & Wendy, wearing hose and heels, discarded the Kit and its remaining Garments, and become **Monitor Caste**.

lipage—An **Exposure**. The exposure of the labial lips to the sides of the **vagina**. If opened, *see* **pink**.

Lobelia—Cosmos Pledge (& others) in **Lockdown**; timeless, rule-less, helpless (singular & plural).

Location—A place where **Events** take place, e.g., the **Cosmos House**, the **Nugget**, the **Backyard**.

Lockdown—A destination for select **Players** where space & time don't exist & **Rules** needn't apply.

lollydor—An **Obeisance**. One who licks up **semen** or **valiva**. Verb is "to lolly, lollying."

Madam—The second highest **Caste** in the **Game**, equivalent to a **Pimp**; detailed at **Caste**.

Makeup Case—A **Prop**, controlled by the **Monitor**. Contains makeup and beautification products and tools. As an upper case **Prop**, sometimes a primary Index, e.g., Makeup Case: *GamerName*.

masturbation—An **Obeisance**. Sexually arousing oneself, often by touching one's sex organs, or rubbing them on an external object. Sometimes helped by a partner, e.g., a **handjob**, hetro or not.

Measurement Nude—A **Media**. Full-frontal pictures provided by newbies showing naked body.

media—Records of Events, saved and served by **Automatron**, detailed in Index.

messy—An **Obeisance**. Coverage of the body by substances such as cum, food, paint, mud.

Midnight—The end of the last **Day** of the **Term** (D28). Comes to pass for some **Players**, Cosmos have their **Clock** stopped and await **Midnight**.

Mirror—A.k.a. the **Minxy Mirror**. A special mirror, located in the Bunkroom, which can simply reflect, serve as a **Screen**, and interactively manipulate who and what reflects on its surface.

Monitor—The fourth highest **Caste** in the **Game**; responsible for a **House** & Seven **Pledge**.

momentum—Forces set into motion that tend to maintain velocity and direction. Crafted into **Strip**.

montante—A **Garment**, a high-waisted **species** of **culotte**, with a waistline above the **navel**.

mouth—A **body part**. The oral entrance to the body; surrounded by the lips, includes the tongue, and exits to the throat. Used for **kissing, cunnilingus, blowjobs,** and **throating,** and **swallowing**.

Mudwrestling Contest—**Event** last **Term**; determined Opts this **Term** for Babs, Janet; Penny, Coco.

Mudpit—A **Location** in the **Backyard**, a pit of dry earth or wet mud; **Cosmos** may grovel here.

navel—A body landmark. A scar resulting from the detachment of the umbilical cord during birth.

navelage—The **Exposure** of the **navel**. **Cosmos** must be navelage 24x7.

neathage—A **cleavage** of the under-**breasts**, possibly produced by a **lift-up**.

nepenthe –An ancient drug to induce forgetfulness. Possibly employed for **redaction**.

Neroli Oil –A fragrance, a scent of nymphs beckoning out into night to celebrate beauty, love & life.

newbie—A **Pledge** attending their first **Term** in **School**; their first **Term** in the **Game**.

nombril—A **Garment**, a **species** of **culotte** with a waistline below the **navel** and wide sides.

nipples, nippage—An **Exposure** of the nipple. This infrequent term is dominated by **titter**. Do not confuse nippage (or **titter**) with **boobage**, the exposure of the entire bare **breast**, or **topless**, which is a "**Garment**" (not an Exposure), and the complete absence of a **Garment** above the waist.

nose—a part of the **face**.

Nude, naked—A "**Garment**" and absence of clothes. **Topless** + **bottomless** = nude. **Count** = zero.

Nugget –A **Strip** club near the **Village**. Some current **Pledge danced** at the **Nugget** last **Term**; some last-**Term Cosmos dance** there now; some current-**Term Cosmos** will **dance** there next **Term**.

Obeisance—A merit gained, or a forfeit made; examples include **shaving, pinking,** and **Pee-Camming, coitus**. Most Obeisance are found in this Glossary; *see* a full list at Index, Obeisance.

Opt Up, Opt Down –Change of **Caste** for next **Term,** and responsibilities thereof. *See also* **Hover**.

orders—Commands issued, usually by a **Gamer** of a higher **Caste** to a lower, to be obeyed.

paparazzi –Unauthorized gatherers of images and videos outside official **Game** channels.

pasties—plural, sing. **pasty. Garment**, species of **soutien-gorge**, glued over **areolas** & **nipples**.

pee—An **Exposure**. The discharge of liquid body waste via the urethra. *See also* **Pee-Cam**.

Pee hole—An **Exposure**. The sphincter in the vestibule where the urethra exits the body. *See* **pee**.

Pee-Cam—An **Obeisance**. A Pee-Camer urinates on camera and in public, in front of anybody.

penis—An **Exposure**, a body part of the male what can become erect, discharge **semen, pee**.

phlegm—Liquids produced in the back of the mouth, nasal passages, and throat. *See* **throating**.

pink, pinking—An **Obeisance**. The display of the inside of the sex lips, including the **vestibule**, **pee hole**, **clit** and **vagina**; also the action thereof, regardless of the actual color of the inside. Pinking presents invitation to **cunnilingus** and **coitus**; an element of **masturbation**, **finger-fucking**, and **dildo** penetration. Indexed as *GamerName:* pinking.

Pink Pages— Data sheet prepared for a **Stripper**, includes stats, naked **pink**, **dildo**, **pee** images.

Pimp—The second highest **Caste** in the **Game**, equivalent to a **Madam**; *see* **Caste**.

Piss Mouth—An **Obeisance** that involves getting pissed on, certainly all over and in the mouth.

Player—A **Gamer** playing this **Term**, for example one of the **Cosmos**, Game Mistress, Pacmo Pinky.

Pledge—The fourth lowest **Caste** in the **Game**; *see* **Caste**. Pledge are both singular and plural. Is not capitalized when used as a verb.

position—An **Obeisance**. A formal body stance, often in three parts stating stance-leg-arm positions, e.g., stand-spread-surrender (also a verb). *See* Appendix, List Of Positions & **Hand Signs**.

Post Henge—A **Location** in the Backyard containing seven Posts, two rows of three, plus end Post.

posterior rugage—An **Exposure**. *See* **rugage**.

Prefecture—The **Gamers** who view the **Events** of the **Cosmos** through **Screens** or read this book.

Procto—A specialized **buttplug** with hot/cold, vibration, electricity; has AI, wireless to **Automatron**. Combined with **ben-wa balls** for **Double Penetrator**.

Props—An object that may migrate among **Gamers**, especially **Cosmos**. Not to be confused with an **Obeisance**, which each individual **Cosmos** may take on, or a **Garment**, which has a **Count** value.

pubic hair—A **Exposure**, the growth of hair on the **pubis** or **penis**. Often trimmed or **shaven bare**.

pubis, pubage—An **Exposure** of the **vulva**, with or without **pubic hair**. Achieved with a **pullaside**, **upskirt**, **bottomless**. Indexed, for example, as *GamerName*: body & exposures: pubage.

puke—An **Obeisance**. The offering of stomach contents. Produced by throating, gagging, drugs.

pullaside—An **Obeisance**. The drawing of fabric in the crotch to the side so that the sex organs and/or **anus** may be displayed. One way to **vagflash**.

rectum—The excretory tube terminating the intestines and GI tract at the **anus**. *See* **anal**.

redaction—Various processes of removing memories and records of the past. See **nepenthe**.

Reveille—The morning **Lineup** of **Pledge** for inspection by their **Monitor** Boss.

rolliosis—an abundance of fat rolls, e.g., Janet, Molly, The Fat Lady.

Roommates—Pairs of **Cosmos**, defined by who shares over and under bunks in the Bunkroom and Bedroom. There are four pairs of Roommates in the **Cosmos House**. Also a practice for **Nuggets**.

Roommate Game –A **Game** played between **Roommates**; often the first Game of the **Term**.

rugage—A.k.a. posterior rugage. An **Exposure**, the top of the **butt** crack, sometimes also the butt crack itself. Opposite of **cheekage**.

Rules—*See* **Game Rules**.

Running Agent—A high level AI, coordinates tactical AIs, other Running Agents, Automatron.

sanpan—Without panties, possibly **bottomless**, or a discovery upon **upskirt**.

School—The place where the **Cosmos** study and the **Game** is played.

Screen—An area where images are displayed, may be stationary, floating, part of a Drone.

semen—Male discharge, ejaculate. Slang cum, goo, jizz, splooge, spunk. *See also* **swallowing**.

shave bald—An **Obeisance**. Removing all the hair from the **head**, including the eyebrows.

shave bare—An **Obeisance**. Removing all the **pubic hair** from the **pubis** or around the **penis**.

Shaving Kit—A **Prop**, consisting of a hollow stainless-steel ball and cylinder, intended to be carried inside the **vagina** and **rectum**, containing soap, and scissors and a razor. *See* **double penetration**.

sixty-nining—An **Obeisance**. Simultaneous oral sex by two partners. *See* **blowjob**, **cunnilingus**.

Skeleton Keys—A **Prop**; two keys. The 1st locks a door between the Kitchen & Parlor, the 2ed between the Dining & Living Rooms. Both together open the door between the Kitchen & Porch.

Slavesex—The most subservient (lowest) Caste in the **Game**; *see* **Caste**.

slitage—An **Exposure** descending from the top of the (often shaven) **vulva**; *see* **lipage**.

snowballing—An **Obeisance** practiced by **Whores** & **Slavesex** trading cum between mouths.

soutien-gorge—A **Garment** worn to cover the **breasts** but which may leave the arms and midriff bare. *See* **bandeau**, **brassiere**, **halter**, also **pasties**, which are also **species** of **soutien-gorge**.

species—of a **Garment**, a variation of a **soutien-gorge**, **culotte**, etc.; a **Garment** style.

spit, spits—An **Obeisance**, rather than an **Exposure**, connoting action, rather than body fluid.

strapon—A **Prop** permitted for **Strippers**, **Whores**, & **Slavesex**, which permits **dildo** insertion.

streaking—An **Obeisance**. The transport of oneself while naked from one **Location** to another. May be volunteered, required, punitive. Capture may involve **Jail**, **Lockdown**.

Strip, Strip Club—A **Location** where **Strippers** work. The **Nugget** is our most familiar Strip Club.

Stripper—The third lowest Caste in the **Game**; *see* **Caste**. Repertoire includes undressing, **nudity, shaving, pinking, cream, dildos, buttplugs, Double Penetrator, climax,** and **pee**.

swallowing—An **Obeisance**. Swallowing **semen**. Either following **facial, snowballing, gokkun**.

Switch– A **Gamer** who vacillates between dominance and submission, wittingly changing **Castes**.

tan lines—A.k.a. **edge lines**. The edges of a **Garment** such that if exposed to sunlight or ultraviolet the part of the skin not darkened will tan.

tanga—A.k.a., a **thong**. A **Garment, species** of **culotte** that covers the **pubis** but not the **buttocks**. It must have fabric sides, and fabric above **rugage**. Not to be confused with a **g-string**. See **tanga**.

tangá—A modifier on a **Garment**, primarily a maillot or **culotte**, describing fabric which that otherwise cover the **butt** that has been gathered into **rugage**, equaling **tanga** exposure.

Term—A collection of **Days** that entails a passage of learning at **School**. Projected 28 **Days**.

thermoprobe—A **Prop** and variety of **buttplug**; a long rectal probe that collects temperature and vital statistics. Can vibrate, electrically stimulate; communicates wirelessly with **Running Agent**.

thong—*See* **tanga**.

throating—An **Obeisance**. The insertion of a **penis** into a throat. Presumes a **blowjob**; the superior throater knows how to relax the gag reflex and allow the **penis** to pass down into the throat. Maybe used to produce **phlegm** and **puke**.

Tiffany Porn Star Calendar—A **Prop** in the Kitchen featuring Tiffany photographed when she was a Porn Star and **Whore**, containing twelve explicit images/virtual reality spaces.

titter—An **Exposure**. The flashing of the **breasts** and **nipples**. Often accomplished by a **leanover, downblouse,** sideboob, or **lift-up**. The transitory titter differs from consistent **boobage** or **topless**.

topless— A "**Garment**" which doesn't exist; the absent of a top, the baring of the body above the waist. Whereas **boobage** may still involve a **Garment** above the waist, **topless** may not. Not to be confused with a **titter**. A **topless** plus a **bottomless** equals a **nude**. **Garment Count** = 0.

transude—Verb; the process of excreting **valiva**.

triple cock penetration—An **Obeisance**. Penetration of **mouth, vagina, anus**; many combinations.

upskirt—An **Obeisance**. View of the crotch up a skirted **Garment**. Upskirt may reveal undergarments; if **sanpan**, possibly **pubage, slitage, lipage**, also **anus**, *see also* **vagflash**.

vagflash—A fleeting **Exposure** of the **vulva** (with or without **pubic hair**), and a special case of **pubage**. Achieved by **upskirt** or **pullaside**. A vagflash does not entail the opening of the sex lips to expose the interior of the **vagina**, (an Obeisance called **pinking**), or extended **pubage**.

vagina—The interior of the female sex organ when a **pinking** exposes the **vestibule** & **vaginal pipe**.

valiva—Female lubrication transuded from **vagina**; Index *GamerName*: body & exposures: **cream**.

vestibule—the flat valley inside the inner lips with the **clit** at one end, the **vagina** at the other, and the **pee hole** in the middle

Village—The town where the **School** is located and the **Game** is played.

voyeue—The individual watched or looked at, possibly surreptitiously, possibly knowingly.

voyeur—The individual looking at another individual, possibly surreptitiously, possibly knowingly.

vulva—The external parts of the female sex organ. *See* **pubage, vagflash**.

Watering Can—A **Prop**. Filled with water or other fluid, can help moisten **Mudpit**, or a **Cosmos**.

Whore—The second lowest **Caste** in the **Game**; *see* **Caste**. Porn Stars are of this **Caste**.

Zone, the; also zone (verb)— Sexual ecstasy by a Player climaxing for a sustained period of time; involves steady rapid heartbeat and breathing rate, self or assisted stimulation, penetration or not.

Index Introduction

Tips on Using the Index

§ Overall Comments and Guidance

The major topics in this Index, that is, topics that are listed at the **topmost level**, meaning main alphabetical order, include:

Gamers and Players
Locations
For Each *GamerName*
    Garments
    Body & Exposures
    Obeisance (including Positions)
    Other keywords (including media)
Props
Events

We will briefly explain each; followed by a short section on each:

The first and foremost **Players** are the Cosmos themselves. Indeed, all the Players who appear during *The Runup* get topmost level Index entries. Players are indeed Gamers, and all who appear during *The Runup* are also each detailed in the Manifests. This list of *GamerNames* includes the Eight Cosmos (Babs, Tiffany, Kimju, Robyn, Molly, Steph, Beka, Elle), survivors of the Eight Corvettes (including Janet and Darleen), ex-Strippers now Whores Penny and Coco, Madam Nurse Beautician, Game Mistress, and others.

Each *GamerName* in the Index is cross-referenced by their interactions with each other *GamerName*, with some exceptions detailed herein.

Locations ground all interactions. Solo actions, as well as interactions between two Cosmos, occurs at a Location. Also, many Locations carry latent agenda; they may be public or private, cammed or not, crowded or sparse.

Several major sections are found in the index beneath each *GamerName*, especially for each Cosmos, since they are the main

Players we observe. For the Corvettes and other Players the following may be indexed more sparsely.

Garments and **Body & Exposures** are "duels" in our Game because they complement each other; what the Garment covers determines what parts of the body are exposed. Garment Counts and Exposures determine are critical components of each Cosmos' Fate. If in previous Volumes (e.g. *The Runup),* there had been Garments to index, during the Play Party all Cosmos are indexed nude, with a Garment Count of zero.

Obeisances are attached to individual Cosmos. Obeisances may or may not be invisible; they usually involve sexual teases, sexual acts, and actions involving body fluid, although many of the latter are entailed in the just mentioned "Body & Exposures." Obeisance can include solo aspirations and activities, as well as interactions with other Cosmos/Gamers. Solo Obeisances include upskirt, pinking, masturbation; partnered Obeisances range from kissing, fondling, fingering, to oral activities and sexual penetrations. Many Obeisances are forbidden to Pledge Caste. The section below addresses their indexing issues.

Props tend to be physical objects; Props are not attached to individual Cosmos or to Players in general, more correctly, Players are attached to Props, sometimes possessed by them. More on this in the section below.

Events fall into roughly two categories: there are a series of specific events that have occurred during *The Arrivals* and *The Runup* (e.g., the Yacht Party, the Alumni Reprise at the Nugget, The Greatest House Roar, the Mermaid Parade, and the Mansion Open House). Events during *The Beach Day, The Runout, and The Play Party* are more individualized. There also exists a series of temporally-related words. These are listed in the Appendix and include Clock, Day, Term, and especially Midnight, which marks the end of the Term.

In conclusion, if we use the old Who-What-When-Where-Why model, then The Cosmos are the Players and the who. The Garments complement Body Parts & Exposures and are a what. The passing Days and time markers (for those whose Clock is stopped) are when, Locations are where, and the Obeisance and Props mold the why and provide momentum – the action dynamics.

§ Indexing Players, Locations, and Interactions

Players (a.k.a. Gamers) include all the **Cosmos**, as well as Players who reside at the Corvette and Peacock Houses, Strippers at the Nugget, other Players in other Castes, as well as you, since you are part of the Game, and a Gamer yourself.

Any Player detailed in the Manifests also appears in the Index at the topmost level.

The general index format for a Player is:

GamerName: *selectWord:* Description (Location Day)

where *selectWord* might be another GamerName, a Location, Prop, Event, Obeisance, Garment, or "body & exposure", e.g.

Tiffany: climax: always climaxes for real on Cam (Beach D28)

If the *selectWord* is a Player then there are most likely two index entries so that each Cosmos is indexed by the other Cosmos:

GamerName1: GamerName2: Description (Location Day)
GamerName2: GamerName1: Description (Location Day)

e.g.

Babs: Molly: Description (Location Day)
Molly: Babs: Description (Location Day)

If the *selectWord* is a position or a "body & exposure" then the indexing may proceed down one more level

Beka: positions: sitting-spread-secured: Details (Location Day)
Steph: Garments: nude: Details (Location Day)

Reciprocal index references are included for all Players of equal Caste. In previous Books, Monitors and Pledge are indexed reciprocally with themselves and all lower Castes, including Strippers, Whores and Slavesex. *In Book V* this remains true; and further attempts to make all Player interactions reciprocal, no matter what the Caste equality or difference.

That said, occasionally *GamerName2* is eluded and the index compressed, so bi-directionality is not always present. Threesomes and more complex relationships may also have incomplete networks, both in previous *Volumes* and in this one.

However, there exists a number of Player-Player relationships that, for space and other reasons, are not bi-laterally indexed in previous *Volumes*. In these cases a single pointer to the primary reference is provided.

More specifically, Players of higher Caste, especially Mistresses, Madams, and MomCaps (and their male equivalents, Masters, Pimps, DadCaps) do not necessarily index bi-laterally with lower Castes, so indexing is consolidated with them, and not subordinates. This has been the rule in the past volumes, for example (always Game Mistress: *GamerName*, never *GamerName*: Game Mistress). However in this Volume, most of these previous unilateral indices are now bi-directional; those that are not still include an appropriate pointer. The past practice, based on the power relationships of the two Players, has been relaxed in the interest of the reader.

In a situation where a number of Cosmos are in the same Location but one or two are relevant, the Index may or may not identify all Cosmos present, and tries to only cross-reference relevant interactions.

In addition to being indexed with each other, in situations where Cosmos which sub-index Locations, Garments, Body & Exposures, Props, Obeisance, and Events, frequently the inverse cross-reference index is included as well, especially when the item plays across many Players.

Locations. Each Location identified in the Location List in the Appendix that starts with a capital letter is included in this Index. All such Locations are indexed at the topmost level, as well as relative to a Gamer, so that each Cosmos is indexed by Location, and visa-versa, in other words, bidirectionally in the following manner:

Location: GamerName: Description (Day)
GamerName: *Location*: Description (Day)
e.g.
Backyard Lineup: Babs: Description (Day)
Babs: Backyard Lineup: Description (Day)

Sometimes the *Location* is transposed adjacent to the Day:

GamerName: Description (*Location* Day)

Babs: Description (Backyard Day)

Note that the Location may be the present time reference to an event that occurred somewhere else in the past.

Because the bulk of evets events during The Play Party occur in the Meatpacking Plant, there is no additional index.

Interactions involve two Gamers at a Location. A solo scene involves a Gamers at a Location, but an interaction requires two (or more) Gamers at a Location. All Scenes that involve two or more Cosmos are indexed by the two players and a single location.

Subsets of this have been presented above, the full basic format is:

GamerName1: GamerName2: Location: Description (Day)
GamerName1: Location: Description (Day)
Location: GamerName1: Description (Day)
GamerName2: GamerName1: Location: Description (Day)
GamerName2: Location: Description (Day)
Location: GamerName2: Description (Day)

e.g.

Babs: Molly: Backyard: Description (Day)
Babs: Backyard: Description (Day)
Backyard: Babs: Description (Day)
Molly: Babs: Backyard: Description (Day)
Molly: Backyard: Description (Day)
Backyard: Molly: Description (Day)

Within the Index some of these references may be abbreviated, condensed, and transposed. For example, removing one level from some of the entries and placing it next to the day:

GamerName1: GamerName2: Description (*Location* Day)
GamerName: Description (*Location* Day)
Location: GamerName1: Description (Day) --unchanged
GamerName2: GamerName1: Description (*Location* Day)
GamerName2: Description (*Location* Day)
Location: GamerName2: Description (Day) --unchanged

e.g.

"Babs: Molly: Description (Backyard Day)"

"Babs: Description (Backyard Day)"
"Backyard: Babs: Description (Day)" —no change
"Molly: Babs: Description (Backyard Day)"
"Molly: Description (Backyard Day)"
"Backyard: Molly: Description (Day)" —no change

Sometimes a cross-reference is deleted because it is already cross-referenced generically.

In the event a Location begins with a capital letter, it is indexed at the top Index level, same as the environment that physically contains them.

Locations in the Cosmos House, including the Kitchen, Dining Room, Bunkroom, the Minxy Mirror, Bedroom, Bathroom and other locations inside the House are treated as top level indexes, and indexed bi-directionally, as described above. Likewise the Front Door, Back Door, Front Porch, and Back Landing are treated as top-level locations. The Doors provide an index of passage. The Cosmos House is not visited during *The Play Party*.

Locations in the Backyard, including the Back Landing, Doghouse, Bell, Mudpit, Post Henge, and Garage, are all topmost level index items, and are indexed bi-directionally with individual Players. The Backyard is not visited during The Play Party.

The **Amphitheater**, within the School perimeter, in the past has been frequently indexed bidirectionally. The Play Party commences with the Cosmos Lockdown Lobelia secured in the Amphitheater, and from here they are transported to *The Play Party*. Herein the Amphitheater only marks the segments it reveals, and is entirely generic, since much involves recollections.

Locations in the Nugget. The Nugget is another destination never visited during *The Play Party*, although it is true that past Events that occurred on various Days at the Nugget still retain Karma into *The Play Party*. Certainly multiple Cosmos are headed to the Nugget and must pass through the Stage Door; whose guardian, the Back Door Man, may need coaxed with sex acts to gain entrance. And likely cammed, screened inside later while strip-dancing, and evidentiary as Whoring capabilities.

Locations inside the Nugget (including the Stage, Camera Lounge, Dressing Room, Champagne Room, Inner Sanctuary, and Stage

Door) are indexed subservient to the Nugget. The Stage, Camera Lounge, Dressing Room, and Champagne Room within the Nugget are open to Strippers; the Inner Sanctuary is only open to Whores.

Staff who inhabit the Nugget do not appear during *The Play Party* are not indexed in this volume. They include the Hat Check Girl, the Master of Ceremonies (M/C), the Maître d', the Nugget Shooter, and the Back Door Man.

§ Indexing Garments & Who Wears What

Garments, the official term for all costumes and articles of clothing, are listed in a roll call beneath topmost level "Garments". In past Volumes this has provided an overview of the costume landscape as well as clues about actions, trades, and forfeits and acquisitions. In *Book V* such actions are moot because all Cosmos are nude all the time. Garments are worn by Game Mistress, and ironically by Penny and Coco are indexed bi-directionally.

During *The Runup*, except for those Players of superior Caste, the diversity of Garments is less than in the past, if only because all Cosmos quickly resort to nudity.

Garment Count matters and determines Opting Up and Down in the Game. By definition topless and bottomless and nude are also indexed in the Garment department, although unlike all other Garments, they count for zero. Pairs of Garments count as singletons, e.g., pasties count as one, although a bikini counts as two Garments. Garment counts matter in the Game, although not all Cosmos with two Garments are equally exposed, or in control of their own exposures.

Garments are primarily indexed by who wears what, in the format (e.g., *GamerName:* Garments: *garmentName)*. Note that plural is style.

§ Indexing Body and Exposures

Body and Exposures. The compliment of Garments are the Exposures, or what mathematicians call a "dual," basically it is the skin exposed, what the costume doesn't cover. This can include body parts that are permissive in public venues as well as body parts more forbidden, or teasy.

The dual between the Costume and Exposure lies not only in rest states (e.g., standing up straight arms at the sides), but also in motion. A shirt can have long or short sleeves, or be sleeveless with big armholes that enable/ensure its wearer flashes her bra, might she be wearing one, or her breasts and nipples might she be smaller chested and braless. There are various tags and keywords in the "bodyart & exposures" section of each Player, e.g. downblouse, sideboob, liftup, spill, and among the Cosmos chroniclers, the granularity lies somewhere between topless and titter or nippage as Gamers call it.

Each Cosmos is indexed by their "body & exposures". A full list of body parts and their corresponding exposures is found in the index entry "body & exposures" at the topmost level of the index. This list includes parts of the body (e.g., face, breasts, belly, legs), body marginals which can detach from the body (e.g., hair, eyebrows, fingernails, cream, pee, spit), and exposures which are fleeting or perhaps lingering and suggestive or fleeting (e.g., upskirt, cameltoe, titter, vagflash).

The index entry for a body part / exposure for an individual Gamer takes the format:

GamerName: body & exposures: *bodyPart:* Descr. (Loc. Day)
e.g.,
Steph: body & exposures: nose: Nurse picks (Post Henge LD2)

Note that "body & exposures" and "Garments" together comprise many lines of each Cosmos' index world; together they occupy about ¼ to 1/3 of each Cosmos index. The distinction between a "body & exposures" and an "Obeisance," both of which are local to each Cosmos, may sometimes be blurry, and is discussed more at the end of the Obeisance description.

§ Indexing Obeisances including Positions

Besides Garments, Cosmos gain and trade Obeisance, be it a titflash in the backyard or a vagflash at a racetrack. Unlike Strippers and Whores and Slavesex there are a great many Obeisance forbidden to Pledge. But the forbidden list for Pledge does not include shaving bare-bald-and-naked, public nudity, pinking, masturbating, kissing, sharing the Double Dong, Pee-Camming, and the dreaded Piss Mouth.

Obeisance. Each individual Cosmos index may carry one or more Obeisances; an Obeisance implies some kind of action or commitment on behalf of the Player. Sometimes a Pledge begs for a particular Obeisance, sometimes an Obeisance is gifted upon her. Sometimes Cosmos seek to balance Obeisance with the acquisition or divesture of Garments they want to gain or lose. Unlike Props, which are often limited in number, there is no limit to the number of Player who can share an Obeisance.

A full list of around 50 items is found at "Obeisance" in the top level of the Index. Obeisances include solo teases as well as partnered sexual actions.

Solo Obeisances include breastplay, pinking, masturbation, climax, streaking, positions, and others. Partnered Obeisances include handjobs, blowjobs, vaginal sex, anal sex, creampies, facials, etc.

Again, as with Garments, note that an Obeisance is always subservient to a Gamer; they are never indexed directly; they are always **a** secondary index to GamerName (e.g., *GamerName*: pinking).

There exists structural difference between "body & exposures" and "Obeisance" as well as conceptual ones. Bodyparts are three levels down (e.g., *GamerName:* body & exposures*: bodyPart*) whereas Obeisances are two levels down (e.g., *GamerName: Obeisance*). A "body & exposure" typically identifies which part of a Pledge's body is exposed (including fleeting moments) whereas an Obeisance entails a Pledge behavior to an ongoing commitment that is an individual (solo) action, or an interaction with another Gamer.

Sometimes a sharp and obvious distinction exists between a Body & Exposure and an Obeisance within the Index. Sometimes the language is subtle but the distinctions are clear: the "anus" is a Body Part, whereas "anal" is an Obeisance, the act of inserting a penis into the rectum. It is less clear if "spit" is a body part or an Obeisance; perhaps it is both, as it is both a noun and a verb.

Many of the Obeisance listed in the Index are behaviors that are forbidden for the Cosmos Pledge as well as to Strippers. One rare exception concerns lesbian sixty-nine behavior, which is forbidden to

Strippers but permitted by Pledge. Likewise sharing the Double Dong is forbidden to Strippers but encouraged for Pledge. In practice Double Donging behaves like an Obeisance, however it is indexed as a Prop with its own Rules.

All "Body & Exposures" are lower case; all Obeisances are lower case also, except for Pee-Cam and Piss Mouth.

Positions are an Obeisance that has particular indexing peculiarities.

Pledge are required to respond to positions triads describing a body posture, e.g., "stand spread surrender" or "sit spread hands-behind-back."

The first element of the position denotes the orientation of the body (e.g., stand, sit, kneel, back, prostrate), the middle term the position of the legs (e.g., crossed, touching, ajar, open, spread), and the third element the deployment of the arms and hands (e.g., at sides, handbra, hands-behind-back, surrender (hands behind head), pinking. See the Appendix for more details.

Unlike most Obeisance, positions in past volumes have been indexed two ways. The richest is beneath the Gamer (e.g., *GamerName*: positions: *positionName*), and this practice continues in *The Play Party*. In Volume I-III, positions were also indexed generically (e.g., positions: *positionName, GamerName*), however this modus is not included in Volumes IV-V.

The value in following a Player's position is that this provides snapshots of when change occurs in a Player's Game, and detailed their different Locations and Days.

§ Indexing Cams, Media, Conflicts, Begs, Chants

The index for each Cosmos Lobelia (and for many other Players) is cross-referenced by Locations, by Garments, Obeisance, and in past Volumes occasionally by body part.

The index entries for each Player also include a set of generic themes. These include **Obeisance** they acquire; the Cams each Cosmos appears upon, media they appear in, their begs and Chants, and an assortment of themes including "assumptions, begs, commitments, compromises, concerns, conflicts & cooperations, consequences, goals, media, memories, momentum, motivation, names, and orders."

These gathered "buckets" hope this reveal character, motivations, commitments, fears, and often compromises. Some of these ideas have binary outcomes, for example one Cosmos goal is their Caste next Term, some Pledge desire to Opt Monitor, and some desire to Opt Strip. Some desires will be met, some won't. Other goals can be more subtle and have continuous possibilities, e.g., cleavage, piercing gauges, likewise Two Garments worn by a Monitor could range from a shirt and slacks, to heels and hose.

Cams are all housed in Drones, and can hover and move freely.

Cams are indexed, however, by who is captured by the Drone's eye, and not who might be guiding the Drone or collecting its feed, followed by the word "Cams" and a CameraName which usually belies its location, e.g., *Front Door Cam, Backdoor/Backyard Cam, Bathroom Cam.* Index style is:

GamerName: Cams: *CameraName*: Description (Day).

Note: Cams are not indexed as media (e.g., never *GamerName*: media: Cams) despite the duality between the Camera and media it produces, addressed next. Cams are also found at other locations, for example, at the Corvette and Peacock Houses, the Nugget, and the Meatpacking Plant. The Drones can be controlled locally, or remotely, by some guiding hand of the Prefecture via Automatron and a Running Agent.

Media includes live as well as recorded documentation, movies, pictures, stories. A list of media is found in the Index at media: *MediaName* (e.g., media: *Glass Bull Piss Climax Video),* however this is a list only; media are detailed thus, *GamerName:* media: *MediaName* (e.g., Elle: media: *Glass Bull Piss Climax Video:*). Note that titles are not indexed individually by title! And that some of the media listed in the Index at "media" may not be seen during *The Play Party*, although they may have Karmic effects.

Indexing media is complicated because it always exists in two (possibly more) times: the time of its creation and the time of its viewing. This difference, between the who-what-where-where-why at the time of the media's creation, and the who-what-when-where-why when the media is displayed can be evidentiary, Karma-charged, influential, and stimulate Kundalini. Media thus plays a role of time-warp, verification, resonance, and love.

Screens are contained in all Drones, and are usually referred by a name that belies the Drone's location. There also exist relatively fixed screens in the Dining Room and Kitchen of the Cosmos House, throughout the Nugget and the Meatpacking Plant. The Minxy Mirror, which runs the length of the Bunkroom, is also capable of Screening in a wide variety of functions, including interactively. The Desktop in Monitor Babs' Bedroom is itself a touch sensitive screen.

In earlier Books, Screens are indexed by a Location, and secondly by *GamerName*, (e.g., Screens: Nugget Lobby: Elle begs play her *Gonzo Video*...). Note that a screen and the media it displays are separate entities.

In this *Volume*, Screens are presumed to be fully visible inside the Meatpacking Plant, more fundamentally, once the Cosmo Lockdown Lobelia are prescribed Eyepods and Earpods, visualization and hearing may be specific to individual, or group of, Lobelia. The index attempts to track all changes in Eyepod and Earpod status for all Eight Cosmos Lobelia, and occasionally for others. When they stand, "blind-deaf-mute", the mute means a Gag.

Conflicts and Cooperations: In Cosmos interactions, "conflicts & cooperations" are where tactical interactions between pairs of Players are indexed. These interactions may include power struggles, power alliances, and situations where Fate casts the pair in a conflict or cooperation.

The indexing of these conflicts & cooperations tends to be indexed bidirectionally. Relationships which are of equal or adjacent Castes are indexed bidirectionally; relationships between wider-spaced Caste differences have, in the past, tended to be indexed by the superior Caste, however in this Volume these have been expanded to be bi-directional too. Convenience sometimes drives exception to these guidelines.

When the interactions between Players are few or the Players are not Cosmos, the "conflicts" part of the hierarchy frequently eluded, and the index entries slide up a level.

There does exist a correlation between Scene names in the Index and the Scene Titles (§) in The Chapters, but the match is not a lock step. Scenes typically change when one or more Gamer(s) enters or exits, or when the Location changes.

Begs and Chants are two different actions, albeit that a Chant often involves a beg. Generally speaking, a beg is a spoken statement, customized to the needs and desires of the beggar. It is required to be predicated with the title of the one being addressed, for example, "Ma'am, please may I." and ending with "Ma'am" (or whatever the appropriate title). The request may be stoic ("Ma'am, please let me sleep naked in the Mudpit tonight, Ma'am."), to the plaintive ("Ma'am, may it please you to shower me so I may never be dirty your presence, Ma'am."), to even the self-indulgent ("Ma'am, please may I strip naked and masturbate my Post while the neighbors watch, Ma'am.").

A Chant often also involves spoken language, it may incorporate a beg, but by contrast, a Chant is formalized, institutionalized and impersonal. A Lineup of Pledge frequently practice chanting in unison. A Chant may only involve recitation (e.g., "Hot hot hot. Titters and twat. 98.6 up my anus."), but a Chant frequently also involves body movement (e.g., "Please let me Pledge naked & cum be a Stripper next Term. Titty titty. Clitty clitty. Hole mouth."), a chant which incorporates hand movements with breast play, masturbation, tasting valiva, and surrender position.

In general both begs and Chants should be in quotes in the Index, since they are spoken dialog, but they are indexed differently.

Begs are only indexed under each Gamer (e.g., *GamerName*: begs: 'Beg text here' (Day).

Chants are primarily indexed by the Chant (e.g., Chants: *Caste*: 'Chant text here'), and they are also more sparsely indexed under each Gamer (e.g., *GamerName*: Chants: 'Chant text here' (Day). "Sparsely indexed" means that not all instances are indexed, the reason being that Chants are frequently recited by multiple Cosmos, but that tactical changes (who joins or leaves the group) can matter.

§ Indexing Props and Events

Props are objects separate from Garments that might be congruent with, but not belong to a Cosmos; Props move around between Players and for this reason are sometimes the primary index entry, with the Player a secondary, sometimes the secondary index entry (with the Player first), and sometimes bidirectional. Upper Case Props are frequently bidirectional, whereas props beginning with lower case letters tend to be indexed subordinate to a GamerName (e.g., Tiffany: buttplug). Note that neither of these guidelines are strictly followed; although in all cases every attempt is made to direct the searcher toward where that index item is resolved.

Props never contribute to Garment counts.

A list in the Index at "Props" includes all the Props that use Capital Letters; these also comprise the "Prop Words List" in the Appendix. See especially the prolonged introduction in the Prop Histories elsewhere in these Appendices, especially the Three Props that can possess more than one player, e.g. the Double Dong, Shaving Kit, and Double Penetrator. These three Props are always double indexed.

Events include roughly two categories: a) specific events such as The Greatest House Roar or the Mansion Open House (both of which occur during *The Runup*), and b) time-related words and moments, including descriptions such as Clock, Day, Term, and Midnight.

See the "Events and Time List" in the Appendix for a list of Events, and see "Events" in the Index.

Some Events in the Index occurred in the past Term (e.g.,; the e.g. the Mudwrestling Contest). Some Events occurred in present Term during *The Arrivals* (e.g., the Figure Drawing Class (D08), Medical Exam (D08), and Bachelor Party (D09). Some Events occurred during *The Runup* (e.g., the Yacht Outing (D17), an Alumni Reprise and Audition at the Nugget (D20), the Greatest House Roar (D21), Steph's Nugget Reduction (D23), the Mermaid Parade (D25), and the Mansion Open House (D27). In some events only one Cosmos prevails, in other contests determine outcomes. *The Beach Day* is itself an Event (D28). Clocks stop during *The Runout* (LD1-LD3) and *The Play Party* (LD4-LD9), for the ex-Cosmos, but not for other Players. Time for the Cosmos is frozen; their Clock is stopped, so technically it is still Day 28 for them. For the Corvettes, including Janet, Midnight has come and gone and they are on the new Days of the new Term. This is also the case for former Strippers and emergent Whores Penny and Coco, for Madam Nurse and Pimp Cowboy, for Madam and Pimp Eye, and for Game Mistress.

Temporally-related words can provide useful searches might one need to look by "Day" or "1 Term before Term ending Midnight" which is a long version of "1 Term ago" and used because this has different meanings for different Players, for many players Midnight has past, for the ex-Cosmos and now Lockdown Lobelia, Midnight lies in the future.

For convenience the Events that occur during *The Runup* are grouped into three time frames. For those Players whose Clock is stopped they are, LD1, LD2, LD3; for Players past Midnight and in the new Term the three time frames are ND1, ND2, ND3. Nothing prevents Players in these two time frames from communicating.

Roughly speaking LD1/ND1 correspond to the events involving the discovery of Robyn's absence and the questioning of the Cosmos; LD2/ND2 corresponds to time spent on the Post Henge and visits by Nurse, Cowboy, Janet, and Penny and Coco; LD3/ND3 corresponds to events in the Amphitheater.

The Play Party begins LD4/ND4 in the Amphitheater and the transportation to the Party at the Meatpacking Plant. The Cosmos Lobelia are visited by Penny and Coco (LD5/ND5). LD6/ND6 corresponds to Robyn's visit. LD7/ND7 details Beka & Elle and Gimbled It. LD8/ND8 resolves Tiffany and Kimju's Fates. LD9/ND9 resolves Babs & Steph & William & Rodney Fates.

Events and time-related words are indexed because Events often involve multiple Players, so they form the primary index (e.g., Bachelor Party: Molly); once again, the reciprocal index is *not* supported in previous Books.

Lineups, where three or more Players form a line, are indexed as Lineups: *HouseName: Description (Location Day NN)*.

The index is created when a Lineup is formed or an existing Lineup is reduced or augmented. Lineups during *The Play Party* include fixed positions group presentations, as on the Risen Cocks. Frequently the position practiced during a Lineup is indexed in the positions section.

§ Style Decisions & Unilateral vs. Bilateral Indexing

Alphabetical vs. Cosmos Lineup Sequence: Gamers are reminded that the Index follow alphabetical and *not* temporal sequence. Use the Day numbers (e.g., D28) and page numbers to help sequence. Also, the alphabetical order of the Cosmos is not their Lineup order, nor reflective of the Roommate pairings.

In the text the order of the Cosmos' names always follow their "position in the Lineup" and not their alphabetical sequence. In the Cosmos House, the "position in the Lineup" sequence is: Babs, Tiffany, Robyn, Kimju, Molly, Steph, Beka, and Elle. Initial Roommates were Babs and Tiffany, Robyn and Kimju, Molly and Steph, and Beka and Elle, but during *The Runup* this changed so that at the beginning of *The Beach Day* the Roommates are Babs and Robyn, Tiffany and Kimju, still Molly and Steph, and still Beka and Elle. In other words, a scene with Robyn and Kimju and Elle is always indexed with these three Cosmos listed in this order. And to repeat what one might expect to find in the Index, each of these three Cosmos plus the Location should all be indexed to each other.

Janet shares rank with Babs but since the Cosmos is Babs' House, Janet extends Babs the courtesy of going first, so always Babs and Janet. However, Game Mistress, Madam Nurse Beautician, and MomCap always precede Babs in a sequenced list.

§ The Lady-Part Words

Neither the Glossary nor the Index records Lady-Part Words.

Lady-Part Words are terms used by Cosmos to refer to their own, as well as each other's intimate body parts, including the breasts, areola and nipples, pubic hair, vulva, clitoris, vagina, anus, rectum, and valiva (a.k.a. cream). They are also used to refer to sex acts including fellatio, coitus, anal, facials, ectaras.

Lady-Part Words are unique to each Cosmos (and other Players); they range from the benign and fanciful to the vulgar and gross.

In general Lady-Part Words share the same initial letter or sound as the name of the Cosmos Pledge, except for Elle, whose Words begins with "n," for reasons scholars debate. Astute Gamers recognize that although both Babs and Beka share a "B" that they have mutually exclusively Lady-Part Words: Babs begin with "ba, bd, bg, bl, bu," and Beka begins with "be, bi, bo, br".

Gamers recognize that Lady-Part Words are not always equal. Space and time are elastic. Sometimes it matters from whose mouth the terms emit, sometimes not. Some Lady-Part Words are self-referential, some are generic and professional, some flatter, and some intend to debase and vulgarize the referent. Robyn especially favors insulting talk.

Index Items

Robyn
  Madam Nurse climaxed Robyn while 2x piercing Kimju's tongue (Amphitheater ND3), 36
  visits the Party, details, Lobelia never see (Play Party ND7), 179
Madams & Pimps
  Game Rules. *See* Game Rules: Madams & Pimps
  histories, *See* Other Players, Caste Changes & Pleadings (to Play Party LD4), 73
  Inquisitor. Madam Inquisitor, a.k.a. Madam Eye. *See* Eyes
  Interrogator. Pimp Interrogator, a.k.a. Pimp Eye. *See* Eyes
  Madam Nurse Beautician. *See* Madam Nurse Beautician
  Pimp Cowboy. *See* Pimp Cowboy
  The Eyes, Madam Eye, Pimp Eye. *See* Eyes
maillot cutout. *See* **Robyn: Garments: strapless maillot cutout**
Maître d'. The Nugget Maître d' welcomes Strippers & Patrons but is not seen during *The Play Party*
Makeup Case. Babs gives to Madam Nurse Beautician who gives to Caroline
Manifests
  located here (Manifest *The Runout*), 331
  overview found here (Appendix), 331
Master of Ceremonies (a.k.a. M/C). Nugget M/C welcomes attention, gives attention. Not seen during *Play Party*
masturbation. *See* **GamerName: masturbation**
Measurement Nudes. *See* **GamerName: media: *Measurement Nudes***
Meatpacking Plant
  Babs observers details, Players (Play Party LD5), 111
  details of William & Rodney's panoramic view (Play Party LD9), 268
  physical description, transport system, cages, fire, Lineups (Play Party LD4), 80
media
  media: *A2OPM Suck Anal Climax w/Gimbled It*
    documents Beka's Play Party performance & her firsts (Play Party LD7), 218, 220
  media: *Alumni Reprise Video* (1 Term before Term ending Midnight). then Pledge Janet was climaxed by then Whore Tiffany
  media: *Alumni Reprise Video* (D20). Made at Nugget when Strippers, now Cosmos Kimju & Molly
  media: *Automatron.* *See* Automatron
  media: *Beka & Elle Cock Prep Train Fuck Cleanup Video* (Stage Door LD7)
    train fuck, Beka preps cocks & Elle pops them, 229
  media: *Beka & Rodney Fuck Video* (Peacock Garage D26). Made secretly, revealed during *The Runout, See* Beka: media: *ibid, see* Rodney: media: *ibid*
    Beka conflicted, wants Gamers to watch vs. implications (Play Party LD7), 199
    Beka has Immunity because of confession, Rodney does not (to Play Party LD4), 105
    Beka recounts Cowboy screening to her Eyepods LD2, details (Play Party LD7), 197
    discovered, shown to Beka, Peacocks, no other Cosmos (Post Henge LD2), 42, 46
    Game Mistress 'you have been shown, you're a Free-Fucker now' (Play Party LD7), 194
    Game Mistress orders screened to all but Robyn & Molly (Play Party LD7), 200
    Peacock Pledge have screened, Janet aware, told Babs (to Play Party LD4), 57
    revelation of *Video* makes Beka wonder *did Rodney cam Steph?* (Play Party LD7), 228
    revelation of *Video* makes Steph wonder *did Rodney cam me?* (Play Party LD7), 231
    Rodney has Whored, ergo William shall Opt Whore also (Wheel LD4), 105
    Screened, Rodney eats, two fuck positions, vaginal creampie (Play Party LD7), 201
    Steph *how did Gamers find out? Rodney will Whore* (Play Party LD7), 232
    Steph unaware of existence, Beka's role, Rodney's Fate (to Play Party LD4), 105
    Steph wonders *did Rodney shoot or was William involved?* (Play Party LD7), 232
  media: *Birthday Cake Pee Video* (D07-D20). Penny & Coco put out candles at bachelor party
  media: *Camera Lounge Video* (D20). Beka & Elle dance naked, pink upon first arrival at Nugget
  media: *Cams.* *See* GamerName: Cams
  media: *Corvette Baseboard Worship Video* (D11). Beka & Elle get anal training at Corvette House
  media: *Corvette Mermaid Parade Video* (D25). Robyn gets humiliated as do other Cosmos present
  media: *Cosmos Baseboard Worship Video* (*Arrivals* D14). Steph and Beka enjoy rectal training

The Cosmos *The Play Party* Backstory

More than twenty eight Days have passed since the first Cosmos Pledge arrived at the Cosmos House, that somewhat magical virtual reality metaverse with its School and small Town.

Since *The Arrivals*, our Seven Pledge and their Monitor Babs have been hazed, humiliated, rendered filthy, tittered, pinked, climaxed for the Prefecture, and memorialized in the giant Automatron, custodian of all Pledge media streams and downloads.

Midnight has come and gone for many Players, but not our Cosmos. Their Clock is suspended; their bodies stripped, spread, shaven, secured: Robyn Runaway has been recovered, and the Cosmos are invited to a Play Party where they might enjoy her Fate.

Beka and Elle surrender the Double Dong to Penny and Coco, then both make a public display of their sexual misbehaviors in conjunction with Slavesex Gimbled It's huge purple-stained penis.

Tiffany, begging to Opt-Strip, and the unfortunate Kimju, scheduled to Opt-Whore, get proposed to trade Castes.

The final showdown between ex-Monitor Babs and ex-Pledge Steph occurs when William and Rodney are rolled into the Party on a giant Wheel. Gamers appreciate the dynamics of Steph's misdeeds and lies, and know that Media are bursting to play out. But giving away the dynamics of how these final four Players are engaged (if not crushed), would be to miss the fine grind.

Kundalini, the sex force of Nature, assists in making all Eight Cosmos Lobelia craven for sexual release. They shall leave the Play Party begging to display their affection, their sexual submission, and their sharp fingernails.

Game Mistress dominates at The Play Party; her able assistant, Slavesex China Doll, assists with turning the Cosmos Lobelia into craven sex animals. The Play Party ends when the Clock restarts, strikes Midnight, and the Term and the Cosmos Saga ends.

Yes, the Cosmos is a work of fiction, but it has an Index and Appendices because the Eight Cosmos really are playing a Game, a grand Game with winners and losers, gains and losses, tradeoffs, cheats, victims, and exploiters. And where the currency of the game is Castes, Garments, Props, Body Exposures, Locations, Media, and a calibrated Obeisance of sexual provocations and acts.

www.ingramcontent.com/pod-product-compliance
Lightning Source LLC
Chambersburg PA
CBHW071628260626
47170CB00001B/16